MARK ARSENAULT

SPIKED

SPIKED

MARK ARSENAULT

ibooks
new york
www.ibooks.net

DISTRIBUTED BY SIMON & SCHUSTER, INC.

A Publication of ibooks, inc.

An ibooks, inc. Book

Distributed by Simon & Schuster, Inc.
1230 Avenue of the Americas, New York, NY 10020

ibooks, inc.
24 West 25th Street
New York, NY 10010

The ibooks World Wide Web Site Address is:
http://www.ibooks.net

The Poisoned Pen Press World Wide Web Site Address is:
http://www.poisonedpenpress.com

ISBN 0-7434-8706-0
First ibooks, inc. printing August 2004
10 9 8 7 6 5 4 3 2 1

Printed in the U.S.A.

This book is dedicated to Julia McCarthy,
who possessed nothing but an exceptional soul.

Chapter 1

Lowell, Massachusetts
Monday, October 19
7:50 a.m.

Eddie Bourque gulped the last of his bitter Arabica, then lifted the empty mug over his head and wagged it at the waitress. He put it down, exhaled noisily and looked out the window at the hard sleet slanting to the street. His flip-top reporter's notebook, on the table, was still empty.

"Just amazing," continued Councilman Eccleston. "In the front of the spoon I see myself upside down. But when I look in the back," he flipped the spoon, "I'm upside up." He grinned, delighted, then pumped his eyebrows up and down.

"Councilman, you started to say—"

"In a minute, Eddie," Eccleston said, turning the spoon.

The waitress filled Eddie's mug with black java that looked an hour past its prime. She left four shots of non-dairy creamer on the table and went away. Eddie added two creams and stirred the drink with his ballpoint.

Eddie's partner on the newspaper's political beat, Danny Nowlin, had assured him that the councilman had a tip—a tip so hot that Danny would have followed it himself if he weren't too busy on a long-term news feature. But two coffees into the interview, Eccleston had offered no sizzle, not even a news brief.

If Danny's going to dump Eccleston on me, I hope he's chasing a Pulitzer.

Five-term City Councilman Manuel Eccleston was sixtyish. He had greased-down ginger hair, a flushed, overscrubbed complexion, and an enduring dazed look about him—one part curiosity, two parts brain concussion. A former Lottery Commission hack, Eccleston had retired on a disability. Bum leg, blood clots, sciatica—he had claimed them all, which meant he could only golf where nobody knew him.

Eccleston flipped the spoon again. "You ever seen this trick?" he asked.

"No," Eddie said. "It doesn't work for me." Eccleston looked up, and Eddie pounced. "It must be tense times for you incumbents, three weeks before the election. The opinion polls have it close."

It was an educated guess. Eddie had seen no polls—no news agency had commissioned one, and the politicians guarded their own poll results like missile codes. But whenever eighteen candidates compete for nine open seats, there has to be a close race *somewhere.*

Eccleston struck at the bait. "It's a crazy season, like they say—all politics is *loco.*"

Eddie bit his bottom lip until it hurt. In political circles, Eccleston was known as Manny the Mangler for his regular assassination of the King's English. If the King were still around, Manny would hang.

Eccleston went through the election ticket, top to bottom, rating each incumbent's chance for reelection. He offered a rosy, but plausible, analysis: that Manny and four of his political allies would survive.

"So you think your block will keep its majority."

Eccleston shook the spoon at Eddie. "We better. This city is at a critical conjunction."

Manny was swimming near the hook, and Eddie didn't want to spook him. He shrugged, resisted the urge to reach for his pad, and inwardly begged for more.

The councilman leaned over the table. He said, "Government needs to take a lesson from business." His breath smelled mysteriously like baking soda. "What does business do with employees who don't pull their own freight?"

Eddie bit his lip again.

Eccleston rapped the spoon on the Formica. "They fire 'em." He leaned back. "And a certain neighborhood of this city ain't working out."

That didn't make any sense. Eddie drained his mug. He said, "You can't fire a neighborhood."

Eccleston's index fingers came together at eye level. "We have to think outside the box," he said, as his fingers traced a triangle in the air.

Eddie reached for his pad, a narrow spiral notebook with a red "E" emblazoned on the cover. The councilman's eyes got big. "You're not writing this down, are you?"

"Got to," Eddie said. "Forgot to wear a wire this morning."

Eccleston gave a nervous laugh. He scratched his scalp with the spoon, and kept his voice low. "This ain't for the paper."

"Councilman," Eddie said, sounding like a disappointed father, "you didn't arrange this meeting to send me home empty-handed."

Eccleston looked outside. He tapped the spoon in his palm. "The situation isn't ripe yet."

Eddie got it—Eccleston was playing defense. He wanted to tip Eddie to something juicy, off-the-record, with a conditional release date. Then, even if Eddie heard the news someplace else, he would be bound by the embargo, and the councilman could be sure the story wouldn't run before it was ripe.

Of course Eddie could refuse the deal and pursue the story on his own. But then there would be no guarantee he'd get it. Later, when he was ready, Eccleston would leak it to the TV stations.

Eddie looked in his coffee mug. He shook a last drop into his mouth. "You have me curious, councilman," he admitted. "What's your timetable?"

"After the election."

"Christ Almighty, this *is* big," Eddie muttered.

Too big, he decided, to pass up. He tucked his pad and pen into his overcoat. "Okay, deal. Now empty your pockets, and make it good."

It was an urban renewal project, Eccleston explained. A big one. Some of Lowell's powerbrokers were scheming a total makeover of the immigrant neighborhood known as the Acre—out with the low-income tenements, in with the luxury condos. Tearing down a neighborhood? That would be six months of screaming headlines, once the story broke.

Eddie drummed his fingers on the mug. He found himself looking forward to a controversy that would break a long string of ordinary days. "The neighborhood groups will hate this," he predicted. "I can't imagine how much political heat this might bring."

"If you can't take the heat," Eccleston said, "then get out of the frying pan."

Eddie bit his lip a third time. "Is Congressman Vaughn on board?"

Manny frowned. "Vaughn's a pain in the ass. But people are working on him."

"The real question," Eddie said, "is *why* is this happening?"

The councilman sat back. A smile spread across his face. He rubbed his finger and thumb together in the pantomime that means money.

"How much?" Eddie asked. "Who's getting it?"

Eccleston pulled an imaginary zipper over his lips.

"Come on, Manny," Eddie pleaded, "that's the key to the goddam deal."

Eccleston grimaced. "If anyone figured out I took a leak to the press, my butt would be in a sling." He rubbed his chin. "But I might have something else you can write about later this week. I'll let you know."

They finished their coffee over small talk. Eddie paid the tab and pocketed the receipt for his expense report.

As they stepped outside, Eccleston turned up his collar. "Remember," he said, "you and I did not have this conversation."

"What conversation?"

"Good man." He leaned into the sleet and walked off.

Eddie strolled toward downtown with the sleet at his back. The Lowell Daily Empire Building rose behind a row of low brick offices.

The newspaper's ten-story tower is among the tallest buildings in downtown Lowell. But it stands out more for unique style than for height. The men who owned the textile factories of the Industrial Revolution built nineteenth-century Lowell mostly of red clay. Main Street is an alley between rows of interconnected brick buildings, three or four stories high. Most look like banks, handsome and serious, trimmed with granite arches and marble sash. But the theater magnate who founded The Empire in 1920 built his newspaper a limestone tower, ringed by black marble ledges at each floor.

A later publisher lit the tower's roof with fat tubes of neon gas bent into a letter "E" two stories tall. The Empire E flickered red like fire in a bottle.

Eddie took a shortcut through a cobblestone alley. Manny had dished a good tip after all, even if it wasn't on the record yet. *How hot is Danny's story if he took a pass on this one?*

Eddie hadn't gone twenty paces when his pager buzzed. He checked the telephone number displayed on its screen, and then called the city desk on his cellular phone.

City Editor Gordon Phife answered. "Start hustling toward the cop shop," he ordered. Phife's voice was all business. No silly impressions, no movie quotes, which were Gordon's trademarks. His serious voice was rare; it could make a routine assignment feel like the biggest story on the planet.

Eddie broke into a trot toward police headquarters. "I'm on it," he said.

"Crack dealer shot up the basketball courts on Lila Street early this morning. A teenager got hit, not fatal—we think.

My police reporters aren't in yet and I goddam can't find Nowlin, so I need you to jam this one on deadline. The cops have a press conference scheduled for right now. If you get me a story by ten, we'll make the late editions and be on the street before the noon news."

Eddie sped up. Sleet stung his eyes. "How much space do I have?"

"I'll hold a five-inch hole on page one, and maybe another six inches inside. I could yank an in-house ad if you need more, but I doubt you'll have the time for it."

The police station was in view. Three television vans from Boston news stations were parked outside, their silver satellite antennas reaching thirty feet high. "Looks like everybody's here," Eddie said. "Channels Four and Five, and that blow-dried asshole from Channel Eight."

"Chuck Boden? The Empire's most famous former reporter?"

"Yeah, I've seen him on assignment, but haven't spoken to him since I've been back in Lowell."

"You *know* that TV tabloid hack?"

Eddie felt the sweat from his short jog, hot on his back. "Before you came, I *interned* here with Chuck Boden—"

"You shittin' me?"

"—And I can tell you, he was all hair and ego back then, too."

"Well, pop that guy in the head for me," Phife said. "Then get back here with my story."

Eddie laughed and hung up. Police headquarters was a two-story cement building with a few skinny windows, tinted black. He bounded up four stairs and slipped into the main foyer as the police chief stepped to a podium cluttered with microphones. There was a stack of press releases on a table. Eddie grabbed one and skimmed it. It was a simple story, and a good one: At three-thirty in the morning, a street dealer peddling cocaine mixed with crushed aspirin had an argument with an unsatisfied customer swinging an ice axe. The dealer insisted all sales were final, and whipped out a pistol. A stray bullet hit a teenaged runaway, and everybody ran like Prefontaine when the cops showed up.

The chief's remarks were vague and unhelpful. Eddie jotted down a few throwaway quotes about how hard the police were working to solve the case. During the Q&A, Eddie asked about the caliber of the gun and the number of shots fired. The chief ummed and ahhed, asked himself another question and answered that one. Eddie pressed, and the chief gave it up. It was a .40 caliber gun. And there were two shots. He refused to say if the police had found the pistol.

Eddie started to press him again, but Chuck Boden from Channel Eight cut him off.

"Chief," Boden began, his voice a rich baritone. He looked away and paused a moment for drama. "If you could speak directly to the people who committed this terrifying act near the heart of this great city, what would you say? And what *can* you say to the residents afraid to come out of their homes while this shooter is still at large—perhaps ready to strike again?"

The chief frowned and looked Boden over. The TV man had coiffed sandy hair, a square jaw and a deep tan, even in late October. His olive-colored suit tapered from his broad shoulders to his tiny waist. The chief said, "First, let me assure the residents that this violent act will not go unpunished. The detective squad is pursuing leads, and we're confident an arrest will be forthcoming. To the perpetrator, I'll say this. Turn yourself in, because we're going to get you."

Boden smiled, all shiny white teeth. He had his sound bite.

The press conference broke up and Eddie went for the chief with more questions. Boden got to him first, and put a microphone in the chief's face. The Channel Eight cameraman filmed over Boden's shoulder, as Boden lobbed a few more softballs. When he was done, the cameraman walked around to film over the chief's shoulder. Boden pulled a comb from his pocket and dragged it once through his hair. Then he nodded in silence for the camera for ten seconds. That footage would be spliced over the chief's comments to give the illusion that their conversation was filmed simultaneously from two angles.

Eddie edged past the cameraman, keeping his back to Boden. But the TV man's voice boomed in his ear.

"Eddie Bourque?" Boden said. "I was so happy when I saw my old pal's byline back in The Empire." His sarcasm was as subtle as his breathless news reports. "It's been what, seven or eight years? And look at you, right back where you started." Even his *grin* was sarcastic.

Eddie responded to Boden's uppercut with his jab. "Kicking your ass on stories around here is a habit of mine. You'll find I guard my news tips more carefully than I used to."

Boden's grin fell. "Those were *my* tips," he said, the words grinding in his throat. "You still can't accept that anyone could have beaten you to a story." He caught himself, shook his head, and broke out a new grin, this one patronizing. "Anyway, it's great to have you back in the market. I'm sure they miss your reporting in Maine."

"It was Vermont," Eddie corrected, immediately regretting that he had acknowledged the slight. "Check my clips since I've been back. I'm a couple scoops ahead of you."

Boden chuckled. "You scooped me where? In The Empire? You mice can roar all you want—around here, nothing is news until *I* say it's news."

"You mean the daily hype you do?" Eddie said.

"I got a million viewers every night at six and eleven. What's your circulation? Forty thousand?"

That punch stunned Eddie. Then Boden swung the hay-maker. "Speaking of Vermont, I hear there's going to be a wedding up there in the spring, for another former colleague of ours."

Eddie felt battered. He tried for nonchalance. "Pam and I are still friends," he said, "and I couldn't be happier for her."

Boden moved in to finish him off. "I never thought it was in her best interest to follow you from Lowell to Vermont," he said. "But I guess I was wrong—she found the man of her dreams. He's a teacher or something?"

"A college professor, in journalism," Eddie corrected.

Boden looked delighted. He waved, flashing his white caps. "See you around, Ed. When you come to Boston, let me know. I'll arrange a tour of a big-city newsroom for you."

Eddie for an instant savored the mental image of his fist shattering ten grand in dental work. But that was not his style, especially not while at the police station. He was livid he had let Boden get to him. *This job is just temporary,* Eddie reminded himself.

The police chief was finishing another TV interview. Eddie shook Boden out of his head. He was here for a story, and nothing was more sacred than the news. He put his fingertips on the chief's shoulder to turn him away from other lingering scribes, and kept his voice low. "Did you recover any bullets or shell casings?"

"Not yet. The shooter may have grabbed the casings. We'll be looking to dig a slug out of a wall or a fence."

Eddie said, "If you know the caliber of the gun, and you don't have a slug, I'm assuming you have the weapon, right?"

The chief looked at his shoes to see if his pants were down. Trapped, he gave up the info. "We believe our officers have found the weapon, which could have been dropped when the shooter jumped the fence around the basketball court."

That was all Eddie could get; the chief was back on guard. He thanked him and ran out of there. Cars honked in protest as Eddie ignored the signal lights and dashed across the intersection toward the Empire Building.

Phife called out the moment Eddie burst off the elevator. "Twenty minutes, Eddie. I need time to read it."

Eddie nodded and slammed into his chair. A paper cup on his desk held two inches of tepid coffee the color of potting soil. It had been terrible on Friday when it was fresh from the vending machine. Eddie downed it in one gulp and pounded the keyboard with his middle fingers:

> LOWELL—*An argument over impure cocaine burst into violence early this morning when a man fired two gunshots into a crowd on Lila Street, wounding a teenaged runaway who was not involved in any drug transaction, police said.*

He probably could write a better opening with more time, but it would do. He phoned the hospital and asked about the victim; she was listed in good condition with a wound in the shoulder. In a second paragraph, Eddie typed her name and her prognosis. In a perfect world, he'd call her family for comment, but deadline is imperfect.

The third graph stated plainly that the shooter fled and got away. The fourth, that police had recovered a gun. It was the one detail nobody else got at the press conference, and Eddie wanted it high in the story. Let Chuck Boden choke on it.

Then, some description:

> *Lila Street is in the heart of the Acre, the neighborhood home to most of the city's low-income and working-class immigrants. The street is tightly crammed with triple-decker apartment houses that were once home to mill workers in the city's days as a nineteenth-century textile power.*

> *Now, many of the buildings are decrepit, with peeling paint and sagging porches. Yet, most are overfilling with families, many of which came to Lowell from Cambodia in the 1980s in flight after the genocide of the Khmer Rouge regime.*

The language was bumpy, but Eddie had no time to smooth it. In the five minutes he had left, he added the details about the gun, the number of shots fired and the chief's promise to solve the case.

Bang. He smashed the send key to file the story.

"You got it, Gordie," he yelled across the newsroom.

Phife flashed thumbs-up and called up the story on his own screen to edit it.

Eddie leaned back and looked around the newsroom for the first time that day. It was a long, narrow space containing twenty-five beaten metal desks, layered with strata of newsprint, overstuffed manila folders, reams of government documents and empty Chinese food boxes. Eddie's desk was messier than most. He filed paperwork by the geological method—oldest stuff on the bottom. Nowlin's desk, the next one over, was neater than most. It held only his computer, a desk blotter with his appointments printed neatly in ink, a foam wrist pad to ease his carpal tunnel syndrome, and a framed picture of his wife, Jesse.

With the writing deadline for the last edition gone by, the room was quiet. Most of the reporters on the day shift were out meeting sources. A few worked the phones.

Look at you, right back where you started.

Eddie picked up his telephone, changed his mind, and slapped it down.

What are you afraid of? He snatched back the receiver and dialed a Boston number with the eraser end of a pencil.

A man answered. "Boston Globe, where may I direct your call?"

"Human resources, Patricia Dannon, please."

The phone rang seven times.

A woman answered, pleasant but rushed. "Ms. Dannon's office, may I help you?"

"Yes, yes," Eddie said, keeping his voice low, yet trying to sound breezy. "Edward Bourque from The Daily Empire in Lowell. Is Ms. Dannon available?"

She wasn't. Eddie took a deep breath and plunged on anyway. "I sent Ms. Dannon my resumé and some story clips some time ago, and I haven't heard from her. I wanted to make sure my material arrived. Perhaps I could make an appointment—"

The secretary cut him off, icy and efficient. "That won't be necessary. I'm sure your material is here, Mr. Bourque." The woman's voice sweetened. "Please be patient with Ms. Dannon. She's four weeks behind on her rejection letters."

A million hot ants tangoed over Eddie's face. He thanked her—out of habit, nothing more—and hung up, muttering. "Save the stamp."

Across the newsroom, more potential bad news. Franklin Keyes, the paper's executive editor, was reading Eddie's story over Phife's shoulder. Eddie trusted Phife, but Keyes outranked him as second-in-command to the publisher. It was too bad; he wasn't half the editor Phife was. A good editor is more than a magician with rough news copy, a good editor is a bullshit-stopper who protects reporters from dumb assignments or silly decrees rolling downhill from upper management. Franklin Keyes was a bullshit superconductor. When it hit him, it accelerated.

Eddie's phone rang. It was Bruno, his barber, whose shop faced Fire Department headquarters.

"I just-a saw the dive team scrambling," he said, the words running together in a thick Italian accent that was a put-on. Bruno was third generation American. He thought an accent was good for business in an immigrant town.

"You gotta have-a somebody in the shop with you," Eddie said, mimicking the barber. "Because I know you were-a born in Worcester, and not even the Italian section."

Bruno laughed. "You keep the secret, Eddie, or your next flat-top not be so flat."

Eddie chuckled and hung up. The dive team rolling usually meant somebody had spotted a floater in the canals. He called the Fire Department. The dispatcher was abrupt, but Eddie got an address out of her. It was just a few blocks from the paper.

Phife was still tied up with Keyes. Eddie typed him a one-line message about the body in the canal and sent it to him electronically.

Outside, Eddie walked three blocks to Dunkin' Donuts. The sidewalk was deserted. There were few footprints in the fresh snow. In summer, Merrimack Street was crowded with businesspeople in suits and shoppers hustling between the boutiques, old men leaning their crooked backs against brick walls and talking conservative politics, and packs of teenaged girls comparing their glitter lipsticks and their babies.

Eddie bought a large dark roast with cream, and then trudged into the wet sleet toward the Worthen Canal.

Nineteenth-century Irish immigrants had dug Lowell's canals to channel the muscle of the Merrimack River to the city's textile mills. The mill companies had long gone south in search of cheaper labor, but the canals—six miles' worth—still churned out bodies. Most were heroin addicts with blue skin and sticky white lips puckered in an overdose kiss. Other addicts, stoned stupid and too scared to call 911, dumped the bodies into the canals. They floated with the trash, the brown bubbles and little oil slicks, passing over stolen shopping carts and discarded tires. There was barely a ripple as the canals dragged their dirty cargo around the city like tired blood.

The Worthen Canal, which passes through some of the city's roughest neighborhoods, was known to produce a murder victim on occasion. Since it flowed from the outskirts of the city to downtown, it was usually impossible for police to pinpoint where a body had been dumped.

Diesel exhaust was heavy at the scene. Three cruisers with blues spinning, a fire engine, and an ambulance idled in a semicircle near the edge of the canal. A swelling crowd of scanner junkies had gathered, kept back from the interesting stuff by yellow police tape.

It seemed a big production for a dead drug addict. *Better put Danny on alert. I might need a hand with this one.* Eddie paged Nowlin to his cell phone number.

Eddie didn't know the uniformed cop working crowd control along the police tape, but that wasn't usually a problem. The trick was to hold the notebook in plain sight and act like you were invited.

"Captain McCabe here yet?" Eddie asked the cop as he ducked under the tape.

The officer's whole face squinted, like a guy waking up to a bright light. "He's back there. Who are you?"

Eddie walked on. "Edward Bourque, from The Empire. If McCabe comes this way, tell him I got here as fast as I could. Thanks."

He didn't look back.

Gerald McCabe was a source of Eddie's. Both used to work the graveyard shift. Eddie would tip off McCabe whenever the patrolmen's union planted a story in the paper whacking police management. And anytime Eddie missed a late-night car wreck or bar stabbing, McCabe would ring Eddie's cell phone.

The captain's thick frame—an oil drum on cannon legs— stood out among the handful of uniformed officers breathing steam in the winter air and peering into the water. A police photographer clicked photos. A diver in a skin-tight blue suit dropped a rope ladder over the canal's edge. Another diver crouched ready with a large vinyl sack.

The stone and concrete canal was about as wide as a city street. It smelled like a wet basement. Water ran through it about five feet below street level. Two weeks of relentless cold had iced the canal at its edges, narrowing the flow of water to a channel down the middle.

A body lay face down, partially trapped in the ice. It was a man, judging by the gray trench coat. He was maybe five-foot-nine, dressed in dark slacks with black-stocking feet. The left sleeve of his raincoat was torn off at the shoulder, exposing a bare arm, ugly white and bent back the wrong way at the elbow.

Eddie had seen bodies before—real bodies, like this one, so unlike the illusions in caskets made up by an undertaker. He asked McCabe, "Suicide or overdose?"

"Neither. The chief's on his way."

The chief didn't go out in the snow for accidents or for addicts. Eddie gulped the rest of his coffee, wished he had another, and then got to work. He sketched the scene and the position of the body in his notebook, and listed the cops he recognized.

He scanned for details that would illustrate the story. The closest building was a three-story brick cube, the backside of a hardware store. There were two faces in a second-floor window, probably store employees on a gawk break. In the other window, somebody had taped a red and blue political sign. It read "Re-elect Hippo Vaughn to Congress." The sign was either a year old, or a year premature. Vaughn had been reelected in a landslide last year, but it reminded Eddie he had promised Phife a campaign analysis on the upcoming city election.

Above, on the building's roof, something drew his eye. A silhouette against white sky. He shielded his eyes with the notebook. A woman's face teased from behind long black hair. She swept the hair back with a red mitten, revealing skin the shade of clear tea. She was young, maybe late twenties, and striking—Cambodian, most likely. Eddie's eyes lingered on her.

A yelp echoed off the canal walls.

"Shit! This is cold," a diver yelled from the water. "My balls are shrinking to BBs."

McCabe bellowed at him. "You don't need 'em. I wear out your old lady whenever you work a double shift."

All the cops chuckled. The diver yelled back, "Small price to pay for overtime."

The divers slipped the bag under the body and fed straps up to the cops on the ledge. The uniformed guys pulled up the corpse and set it face-up on the ground. McCabe wrestled his huge hands inside rubber gloves and squatted next to the body in silence for a minute, touching nothing.

He deadpanned, "Boys, I don't think this guy's gonna make it." Eddie made a note that the body still had a wristwatch, a black sports model, on the left wrist.

"White male," McCabe said. "Severe trauma, face and head."

That was police understatement. Something had smashed this guy's nose to pulp. The lower lip was split. The cheeks were beaten to the bone. Maybe he jumped off a building, or stumbled drunk into a passing truck—or maybe this was a homicide.

Eddie's little canal story had become page-one news.

Where the hell are you, Danny?

He paged Nowlin again.

McCabe stepped aside to let the police photographer take some more shots. Eddie looked again to the woman on the roof. There was only the sky.

The photographer finished his work. McCabe stepped back to the body. He ran his hands inside the coat and checked the breast pockets. "No wallet," he said. He patted the front trouser pockets. Nothing. Suddenly his arm recoiled. "Christ!" he yelled.

Eddie jumped back on reflex.

McCabe reached in the coat and yanked out a small black box. "I felt something moving," he said. "His goddam pager is going off."

A breath of Fear chilled Eddie's neck. He had met Fear—or, more accurately, invented her—when he was ten years old, and his curiosity had gotten him trapped in an abandoned well rumored to have been filled with bones. He had never been more terrified. During that night, his fear took on a personality. It became Fear, a leggy redhead with flaming red nails and lips—part biker-chick, part vampire. At the same time sexy and frightening.

McCabe wiped a thumb over the pager's tiny digital screen and frowned. He looked at Eddie. Fear nuzzled up from behind and pressed her icicle tits to Eddie's back.

"Hey Ed," McCabe said. "On this guy's beeper, ain't this your number?" He double-checked the digits recorded on the pager. "You want this stiff to call your cell phone?"

Chapter 2

There were no tears for Danny Nowlin in the newsroom.

It's not that reporters are cold to tragedy, just detached, too consumed with trying to get the story right. Readers are easy to educate, but how do you make them feel? The best tragic stories bring a stranger to life, and then take that life away. Reporters see the production from backstage; they recognize the details that are moving, but can't afford to be moved by them.

The newsroom's stunned silence quickly evolved into action. Everyone on the staff had written tragedies before. They decided that for Nowlin, they would write the best one ever published in The Empire. Several volunteered to cull through Danny's old stories for excerpts of his work. Copy editors stayed late on their own time to perfect the layout. Everyone on the news staff composed a quote about Danny, to run under a head shot of the author. For his quote, Eddie typed, "He would have won a Pulitzer before his career was over, by creating the kind of journalism that changes our lives. We will never know how great is our loss."

The medical examiner confirmed the identification with dental records later that evening, and announced an autopsy for the next day. The cops released precious little news. No official cause of death, no estimated time. Accident? Suicide? Homicide? They wouldn't speculate for the record.

Nowlin's wife was away, visiting her parents in Rhode Island over the weekend. The police said she wasn't coming back until morning. She told a detective by phone that she had talked to Danny on Friday. She had tried to ring him over the weekend. No answer.

A dozen reporters stayed late to write the stories and sidebars for the next day's edition. They wove in Eddie's details from the scene. Their writing styles, all their voices, blended like a choir.

Somebody had to do the grunt work—to write the obituary. Eddie volunteered. He had written hundreds of obits in his career, but never for a person he had known.

The first draft was clumsy. It read forced and too tight. Phife edited out the tension, while keeping the formal obituary format:

> LOWELL—*Daniel P. Nowlin, 28, of North Road in Chelmsford, a political reporter for The Daily Empire, died suddenly over the weekend of an undetermined cause. (See story, Page 1.)*
>
> *Mr. Nowlin leaves his wife, Jesse; his father, Sean T. Nowlin, of Pelham, N.H.; a sister, Daisy O'Leary, of Lancaster; a stepsister, Mary Reston, of New York City; and numerous aunts, uncles and cousins. He was the son of the late Deborah Ann Nowlin, who died nineteen years ago.*
>
> *Mr. Nowlin also leaves a newspaper staff weakened by his loss, and already missing his counsel.*
>
> *He was born in Brandon Village, Ireland, and moved to the United States with his family as an infant. He grew up in Malden, Mass., graduated from Salem State College with a degree in psychology, and then completed graduate studies in print journalism at Boston University.*

After a summer in Phnom Penh, Cambodia, as a copy editor on an English language weekly newspaper, Mr. Nowlin became a reporter at the Clinton Voice, and then worked at the Gloucester Guardian-Leader, before accepting a job at The Empire two years ago.

Mr. Nowlin was a tenacious reporter, who had a reputation for working long hours, sometimes straight through the night, despite his chronic carpal tunnel syndrome.

Last year, he completed the Boston Marathon in 3:21.55.

What his loss means to this newspaper, in his production as a reporter, in his attitude and in his dedication, is incalculable.

The obituary ended with wake and funeral details.

Gordon Phife was pleased with it. "Reads fine," he said.

Eddie didn't know why he disagreed. "Seems somehow insufficient."

"It's not. It's what Danny deserves," he said. "This is not a competition, Ed. Go home, call your aunts, tell them you love them, and go to bed."

Phife was right; it was time to go home.

Eddie steered his sputtering Chevette through the quiet streets of Lowell's working-class Pawtucketville neighborhood. The car moaned on the uphills but otherwise didn't mind the work. The Mighty Chevette was twelve years old, and long ago paid for. Pale yellow and spotted with rust, it looked like a giant sneaker made of butter and covered with toast crumbs.

Had Danny been mugged? Or had he been careless on some icy bridge? Eddie thought about the way Danny used to push him to work harder, and about their unspoken competition for jobs at bigger newspapers. The competition was over. Eddie shivered and turned up the heat.

He pulled down a street crammed with single-family homes shaped like the houses in the Monopoly game. He parked in front of a gray one with asphalt shingles. Three cement steps led to a bright red door—unlocked, as usual. The people of his mostly Catholic neighborhood worked too hard to squander their souls for the contents of Eddie's junk drawer, his mismatched silverware, and the handful of medals he had won in high school track and field.

The place was chilly. The thermometer read sixty degrees, though he had set the thermostat to seventy. The old furnace always struggled to keep up with the weather.

The answering machine had no messages, which meant his aunts hadn't heard about an Empire reporter turning up dead in a canal. Eddie wouldn't be the one to tell them, he decided. Let them have one more good night of sleep before they started worrying.

He tossed the day's Empire, still unread, onto the arm of a black leather recliner. A chessboard on his coffee table needed a minute of attention. The pieces were deep into battle; the vanquished soldiers were on the sidelines. *Ah-ha!* He captured a white bishop with a black knight, and then spun the board around for tomorrow's move.

A skinny shorthaired cat trotted out from the bedroom. Its charcoal coat was shiny at certain angles, like the ocean in moonlight. Its eyes, the color of lily pads, were half shut; Eddie had disturbed a nap.

"Hello, General VonKatz," Eddie said. "Sorry I'm late. Bad day. I suppose you wanna eat?"

Eddie scooped up his cat, stepped over a pizza box on the floor and collapsed on the recliner, the one soft item in a room furnished with a maple coffee table, a straight-back pine chair, and the mysterious upright piano that had come with the rental house. A forgotten tenant had long ago abandoned the piano. Eddie had tried to sell it, or to give it away. It played just fine, and there were takers. But nobody could move the thing. No amount of human muscle power could lift that goddam piano. Either it was cast from lead, or fixed somehow to the floor. Eddie once tried to lighten it for a trip to the landfill by ripping out wires and washers and whatever else he could detach from the belly of the thing. Made no difference. So Eddie made peace with the piano; it was a fine TV stand.

The General squirted out of Eddie's arms and headed for his food dish. "All right, I'll open a can of something," Eddie said.

As he stood, a headline in the paper, low on page one, caught his eye:

"Shots Fired No Threat to Downtown Lowell."

Eddie's byline was beneath the head, but he didn't recognize the story.

> LOWELL—*Two small-caliber gunshots fired during a neighborhood disturbance in the Acre early this morning posed no danger to revitalized downtown Lowell, nearly one mile away.*
>
> *An argument, most likely between people who live in that neighborhood, escalated when one participant fired shots into the air. A teenager was grazed.*

What the hell's with this? Fired shots into the air? A bullet grazed a teenager? His work on the shooting had been rewritten. The information about the cocaine—the heart of the dispute—was gone from the first paragraph. He read on. More of the same—twisted facts and half-truths, arranged to minimize the incident. Nothing was an outright lie, and the information about the cocaine was still there, but buried at the bottom where nobody would ever see it because the piece was now so goddam boring. His one exclusive fact that police had found the gun had been lost in rewrite.

He read it again, seething and scalding red with embarrassment. *This is under my name, as if I had wanted it this way.* As if Edward Bourque did not give a damn about his readers, or about the truth.

He jumped up and paced the room. *I'm being edited like an intern.* He wanted to break something. Smash it to atoms. He settled for kicking the pizza box. It skipped across the room and dumped a leftover slice of extra cheese, greasy-side down, on the carpet.

Eddie twisted the newspaper into rope.

Chapter 3

Eddie woke in the recliner, slouched and sore. The morning had dawned filthy gray, like Eddie's mood. Wind rattled the storm windows. General VonKatz dozed on Eddie, bent around his neck like a fur collar. As his human stirred, the cat hopped up, stretched out thoroughly and ambled to a window to curse at the chickadees mooching from the birdfeeder.

Coffee. Eddie needed his strongest blend.

He found a bag of Sumatra beans in the freezer. He ground them fine, let the brew drip chocolate brown and gulped it black. It was bitter and nourishing. He pictured a tiny Indonesian boy on a decrepit family farm, his little back bending beneath the sack of raw coffee beans he would lug a mile to market to make a dime. With his mug raised in salute, Eddie spoke aloud, "Keep it coming, kid."

Yeah, he was going to be a bastard today.

Eddie moved mechanically through the morning, barely paying attention to the road along the eight-minute drive to the office. He had to find out what had happened to his shooting story, what the police had learned about Danny's death, and he had to steel himself for a difficult interview. Today he would call Nowlin's widow, Jesse, for a follow-up story.

The elevator doors opened as the morning news meeting was breaking up. The meeting was a ritual at just about every daily newspaper. At The Empire, the city and suburban desk editors, and representatives from the sports, business and lifestyle pages, met in Keyes' office early each morning to hash out the story budget for the afternoon's edition. The editors pitched their favorite stories for page one. Keyes had the final say.

Gordon Phife was last out of the meeting, his face buried in his notes. Phife wore a monochromatic gray outfit, a shiny gray tie and white high-top sneakers. Eddie stopped him. "We have to talk, Gordon. That story—"

"Not here," Phife said in a low voice. "Later."

"We should run a correction in today's paper—"

"Just calm down, Ed."

"—Saying that I had nothing to do with that piece of shit."

Phife glanced around. "We'll talk tonight. On the driving range." He started to walk away.

"Gordon!"

"I'm dealing with a dead reporter and a bunch of live ones trying to put out a newspaper," Phife said. "And you want answers *now*? Tonight, Ed. You know what I drink."

Eddie sighed, exasperated. "Call me," he said, "when you're ready."

Keyes was alone in his office. Eddie knocked. The editor waved him in.

Franklin Keyes was half the reason his reporters liked to say that The Empire was two funerals from being a great newspaper. He was stumpy and pot-bellied, with thick wavy hair, dyed an impossibly perfect black. His hands were plump and soft, like pudding in rubber gloves, his tongue often stained a color of the artificial rainbow from the lollipops he ate throughout the day. Keyes had never done a hard day's work in his life. He had married well, latching onto the daughter of The Empire's venerable publisher, Alfred Templeton. Keyes had become the editor without ever having been a reporter, which was like teaching flight school without having piloted an airplane.

His office was as insubstantial as the man. The bookshelves held none of the great books on the craft of journalism. Instead, Keyes had cluttered the place with photographs of himself with the famous people his position had enabled him to meet, many of them on the golf course. His gold letter opener was shaped like a putter. The ball from his alleged hole-in-one, ten years ago, was mounted on a plaque.

Eddie sat down and waited. Keyes flipped through a book of wallpaper samples. He held a maroon paisley print to the wall and said, "I think you'll do fine."

"Are you talking to me?" Eddie asked.

"I'm a little occupied right now, Bourque," he said. "What do you want?" His tongue was green.

"What's the plan for the Nowlin follow-up stories?" Eddie asked. "I figured I'd interview Jesse today. Maybe Spaulding can work up a sidebar on the investigation?"

Keyes dismissed Eddie's ideas with a sour face. "I want you concentrating on the political beat. We have an election in a couple weeks, and I don't think we're ready for it."

I'm off the story? Disappointment pooled in Eddie's gut. He couldn't imagine whom Keyes would assign to write the follow-up. He probed for the answer. "I suppose Melissa will do better with Jesse, anyway."

"Melissa's too busy to talk to Jesse Nowlin."

Not Melissa, either? "Don't you think a straight police follow-up is a little weak to lead second-day coverage?"

Keyes sighed, annoyed. "Did Alfred make you editor while I was in the can? You cover politics. Go get me some, and leave the Nowlin matter alone. We're all sad about Danny, but this institution is going to move on."

"But the story—"

"The matter is being handled, Bourque," Keyes said, cutting Eddie off. He pointed a chubby finger toward his office door. Eddie threw up his hands, and followed the finger out of there.

The story's being handled? Who's handling it?

In the newsroom, Eddie found a heavy-set woman with thick wrists sitting at his desk. She looked around forty, very muscular in the shoulders—maybe too muscular. Her hair was pulled back in a bun so tight it stretched her skin like a bargain face-lift. Another woman, thin, late fifties and graying gracefully, was at Nowlin's desk. Eddie didn't know either of them.

"Who are you two?" he demanded.

They paid his rudeness no attention. The one at Eddie's desk answered. "Mr. Bourque? I'm Detective Orr from Lowell Police. This is Dr. Mary Chi, a computer science professor at the university whom the department consults from time to time. I'm investigating Daniel Nowlin's death. Your editor, Mr. Phife, says you might know Daniel's computer password?"

"Sorry," Eddie mumbled. "I don't recognize you from when I covered the cops."

"I just made detective," Orr said. She looked Eddie up and down, and then stared at his face, like she was memorizing every ridge, mole and crease.

Eddie leaned over Dr. Chi and tapped in *rottenbastards*. Nowlin had meant his password to refer to the politicians he covered.

Chi's slim fingers rapped on the keyboard. She culled through directory trees, isolating text files. She said, "Mr. Nowlin kept copious notes. He left an electronic address book." She smiled. "And he liked to play Doom."

"Copy the notes on one disk, the address book on another," Detective Orr ordered.

Chi popped a floppy into the drive, and then played the keyboard like Rachmaninov.

"What's this all for?" Eddie asked.

Detective Orr responded with a non-answer. "This is an investigation into an unexplained death. I'm looking for an explanation everywhere I can."

"Do you know how he died?"

"That's being determined."

"You think it's related to a story?"

"I did not say that," Orr answered, sharply. She smiled. "And as I'm sure you realize, I can't talk about the details of an ongoing investigation."

She was professional, polite, and infuriating. And obviously hiding something. Eddie opened his mouth to argue, when Dr. Chi spoke out, her thin voice at a high pitch.

"What's happening here?" she said, fingers clicking still faster over the keys.

The screen went blue. Strings of error messages appeared. A page of text opened on the screen, flashed into garble and then vanished. Another one appeared, and then also changed to garble. The computer's hard disk spun and crackled.

"This is an error. A big one," Chi said. She held down the reboot keys: Ctrl, Alt and Delete. No effect. More text flashed into view, and then flashed out as garble. Chi reached below the desk and pressed the computer's power button. The machine ignored her. The hard disk continued to spin and whir. Text files flashed on and off the screen too fast for Eddie to recognize the words.

"It's destroying the files," Chi shrieked. "Cut the power! Get the plug!"

The three of them dove beneath the desk, knocking skulls. Eddie muscled past Chi and reached behind the computer. He felt wires and yanked at them. Wrong ones. The disk kept spinning.

"The fat black wire," Chi shouted in his ear.

The machine suddenly throttled down and stopped. Eddie got up. Detective Orr held the plug in her hand. "Can't tell a power cord from speaker wire, Mr. Bourque?" she said.

"I grabbed whatever I could," he said, embarrassed.

"Uh-huh." To Dr. Chi, Orr said, "Take this machine to your office and see what you can salvage from it." And then to Eddie, "Let's hope this Keystone Kops episode didn't ruin anything that could be evidence."

Chapter 4

The telephone woke Eddie at three-fifteen in the morning. He didn't bother to answer. Still dressed in work clothes, he got up, creaky, and stepped into his shoes. He pulled on a sweatshirt, popped a Red Sox cap on his head, and wrestled into a wool overcoat. He shuffled to the refrigerator for the beer he had bought on his way home.

General VonKatz was up. He whined around Eddie's feet. Eddie bent over—cartilage cracking in his back—and showed the General what was in the bag. The six bottles inspected and sniffed for his records, the cat trotted off in search of new adventure. He spied a moth on the ceiling. Not much meat on it, but the General settled for whatever prey wandered in. He coiled, tail flicking, on the mysteriously heavy piano, ready to strike should the moth come a little lower.

"Don't eat him," Eddie advised as he went out the door. "He'll give you moth breath."

Eight minutes later, Eddie was downtown. He left the Chevette around the corner from the Empire Building and walked to the office. The elevator took him to the tenth floor. He passed a glass door stenciled with "Alfred T. Templeton, publisher," and let himself into a closet where the cleaning crew kept the mops. There was a ladder there.

Eddie shoved open the trap door at the top of the ladder. Red light poured in. The Empire's giant neon E hummed overhead. It crackled and popped as it flickered. The roof was as big as a baseball diamond, and ringed by a knee-high safety wall. A roofing of tar and loose pebbles crunched under his Doc Martens. The air was thirty degrees but completely still; it felt much warmer.

Phife was behind the E, reclining in the giant white satellite dish that captured the Associated Press news feeds from around the world. Gordon Phife was forty, a bachelor and a lifelong newsman, who had bounced around the Atlantic seaboard his whole career, slowly climbing the ranks of news editors. His skinny face, narrow shoulders and slight beer belly gave him the look of a former fat man nearing the end of a long diet.

Phife always had a sly, sleepy-eyed look. The red neon tinted his freckled face and close-cropped blond hair. He looked drawn; the dark spots beneath his eyes stood out like purple thumbprints. He wore jeans, a puffy ski jacket and the leather driving gloves Eddie had given him last Christmas. There was a golf club leaning against the dish.

"I figured we'd practice a fairway iron tonight," Phife said. "Once I fix your slice, I'll let you swing the driver again."

Eddie handed him a lager from the bag, and then took one for himself. "I knocked over a TV antenna last time with the driver," he said.

Phife answered as Yoda, from *Star Wars*. The impression was dead-on. "You hit ball a long way, do you now Eddie? But you must learn to use your power for good, not for evil." He smiled.

They clinked bottles. "To Danny," Phife said. He drank, and then asked, "Did you see Boden at the press conference?"

"He let me have it for coming back to where my career started."

"Aw, fuck that guy," Phife said. "You've been eating his lunch since you got here."

"You and I know that," Eddie said. "But I can't get noticed in Boston. Coming back to The Empire was a tactical move, to get back in the market every day, and to build the resumé for the big metro dailies."

"Give it time. You're only starting your second year."

"There wasn't supposed to *be* a second year," Eddie said. "I gotta move up. Since the mills died off this town has been Second Bananaville."

"You're dissing the birthplace of Jack Kerouac and Bette Davis?"

"Yeah, I've read the tourist brochures. Ed McMahon from the old Tonight Show grew up here, too. For Christ's sake, he's the biggest second banana in television history. And Charles Sweeney was born here."

"Who?"

"Bomber pilot. Dropped the *second* most famous bomb in history, on Nagasaki."

Phife sighed and shook his head. From his jacket he produced a cloth sack and dumped twenty golf balls onto the roof. "People will do all kinds of insane things for what they love," he said. "You're doing what you love. That sucks if it doesn't make you happy."

Eddie shot back, "And you're satisfied here? Working your seventy hours a week? When was the last time you went out of your house, except to come to The Empire?"

Phife let out a long, exaggerated sigh. He said, "I've been staying at home a lot. It's a great thing to have a lady aboard with clean habits."

That had to be a movie quote. Phife was a former movie reviewer. He lost the job because he never hated a picture; he saw hidden brilliance in *Howard the Duck*. Eddie had no idea from which film Phife had lifted the line. Gordon wouldn't tell him unless he guessed, at least once.

"*Kramer vs. Kramer?*" Eddie said.

"Nope. *The African Queen*." Phife stumped Eddie most of the time, and Eddie had never snuck a movie quote past Gordon.

Eddie saw Phife's satisfied grin, and then shouted, "You son-of-a-bitch, you got a new woman!"

The grin got bigger.

"Docked the Titanic yet?" Eddie asked.

"A gentleman doesn't tell."

"That means no."

Phife beamed. "But I ordered an armoire. Solid maple."

"For what? For your rathole pad?"

"For her stuff," Phife said, a little defensive. "A girl's gotta know that her guy cares. And a little style never hurt." He stretched on the satellite dish like a cat in the sun, a dreamy little smile on his lips. "I haven't closed the deal with her, but the decks are clear. You should feel the Earth moving pretty soon."

"Keep it under six on the Richter scale, okay?" Eddie said, dryly. "Or you could be crushed by a falling armoire." He bent—ouch! damn back was still creaky—and twisted his beer bottle into the pebble roof. Then he rolled a ball into position with the club and addressed it. The club was a four iron, the identical brand Eddie played, the weight of it familiar. He lined up the shot, eye on the ball.

"What the hell happened with the shooting story?" Eddie said.

Whack. Pebbles sprayed up in a cloud. The ball sailed over the safety wall and started down the street below, then sliced hard right and banged off a Dumpster in an alley, ten stories down. The blow echoed through deserted streets.

"You're not rolling your right hand over," Phife said. "The club face is too open at contact."

Eddie lined up another shot.

"I got pressure from Keyes to downplay the story. I did my best with it."

Whack. The ball tailed left and plopped into the Merrimack Canal, which paralleled the street. "Well, your best sucked. There's no excuse for what ran under my name. You should have pulled my byline."

Phife shouted back, "*You* try dealing with the pressure I get."

"Pressure to make me look like an idiot?"

Phife took a sip of beer, and then answered in a calm voice, "This ain't a fight worth losing. I'm telling you—a friend as always, and the only man in this sordid town that wants to save you from yourself."

Eddie was in no mood for movie quotes. "*Casablanca*?"

"*Clockwork Orange*."

"What are you saying? That I'll get fired if I complain?"

Phife guzzled beer. When the bottle came down, he seemed glum. "There's something going on, man. Something I've never seen before."

"Is that another goddam quote? I've had enough tonight."

Phife whispered, "Not a quote." He glanced around the roof. "This isn't the first time I've felt the pressure to rewrite basic crime stories, only now it's getting worse. Keyes didn't say it straight out, but he made it clear that the rewrite order came from the publisher's office."

"From Templeton?"

"Yup." Phife shivered. "That guy creeps me out. It's always pitch black in his office. And his voice—like Satan's little brother." He tried to drink and dribbled beer down his coat.

"Why would Templeton care about a shooting in the Acre?"

"Who knows? But I'm starting to wonder if we've gone from reporting the news to managing it."

Eddie lined up another ball. "Like with Danny's death?"

Phife nodded. "Keyes pissed on any discussion about Danny at the morning news meeting. He pulled Spaulding off a sexy budget story. He put our rabid attack dog—and you've seen Spaulding, the way he foams around the mouth— he put him on a feature about kids painting flower planters."

Eddie's hot anger cooled to something hard and heavy in his chest. Now he was curious. What was going on at The Empire? He swung the club and shot the ball into the safety wall. It ricocheted back, clanged off the satellite dish and sent Phife sprawling. Eddie shrugged. "Fore."

Phife smiled and shook a fist in the air. "You did that on purpose!"

"I wish," Eddie said.

"I screwed up, Ed." He paused, frowning. "I'm sorry."

"That new girl must be something."

Phife grinned again. "I've had some late nights."

Eddie grunted and lined up another ball. Even a pro can take a bad swing. A motorcycle screamed up the street below. "Do you know what Danny was working on when he died?" Eddie asked.

"No. He didn't publish much the last month. I assumed he was on a project for some other editor. Why?"

Eddie took a practice swing. Gordon was his best friend in Lowell. "I met that new detective today." He told Phife about his conversation with Detective Orr, and about the computer crash.

Phife rubbed a day's worth of whiskers on his chin. "I'd love to know what the cops think they have, but Spaulding tells me the investigation is airtight—absolutely no leaks."

"Let me take a run at it tomorrow," Eddie said. "I know a back door."

"Okay. If questioned, we are sewage workers on our way to a conference."

Eddie knew that quote. "*The Life of Brian.*"

"Very good. Of course, if Keyes finds out you're poking around on this against his orders, you'll be covering the Landfill Committee."

"I can handle Keyes," Eddie said, sounding more confident than he was. "I want to know how Danny died. The cops know *something*, and I'm going to find out what."

Eddie lined up another shot and took a slow, measured swing. The ball sailed true, bounced in the middle of the street and rolled out of sight.

Phife clapped his hands once. "There's hope for you yet, Bourque."

Chapter 5

"Eeaaaaa!"

"Eeaaaaa!"

The General's whine woke Eddie from a dream involving two female golf pros and a bubble bath in a satellite dish. He understood the interruption to mean it was precisely six o'clock. Breakfast time.

Sleep. Need more sleep. He ignored the cries.

But General VonKatz had no snooze button. He stood on Eddie's chest and pawed his chin. Eddie lay still. The General flicked a claw on his bottom lip.

"Ow! I'm up," Eddie yelled. The clock read ten past six. Hmmm, maybe he did have a snooze button.

The refrigerator that morning held two bottles of Sam Adams beer, a can of Guinness stout, a bottle of spicy mustard, two slices of smoked turkey cold cuts, a chunk of provolone and whipped cream in a spray can. Eddie split the turkey with General VonKatz and ate the cheese himself. For dessert, he had two shots of whipped cream in the mouth. That day, the morning of Nowlin's wake, Eddie chose a coffee roast from Costa Rica, a light bean with a nutty flavor. The caffeine numbed a mild headache left over by the three Rolling Rocks he had drunk with Phife.

Eddie grabbed his business suit from the closet and laid it on the bed. He had last worn the gray two-piece to his job interview at The Empire. Size forty-two long. The jacket was snug in the shoulders. The wool trousers, thirty-two inches in the waist, still fit well, which nobody would see under the poorly fitting jacket.

It felt funny to wear a suit to work. Eddie's usual style could be called business rumpled—a cotton dress shirt apparently laundered on the "wrinkle" cycle, faded khakis and a Jerry Garcia tie. But the whole Empire staff had dressed up today. Some were going to the ten o'clock calling hours for Nowlin. Eddie had promised Melissa he'd walk her to the funeral home for the afternoon session.

At the office, Eddie's voice mail held two messages, both from City Councilman Eccleston. No details, though. Eddie made a mental note to call Eccleston, which he promptly forgot in his haste to persuade an old friend to penetrate the secrecy around the Nowlin investigation. He dialed the Lowell District Office of U.S. Representative Hippo Vaughn.

"It's Bourque," he told the receptionist. "Is he here today, or in D.C.?"

"The congressman is down there, Eddie. I'll patch you through on our office line."

Sure, let the taxpayers pay for this long-distance call to Washington.

Eddie spoke to the press guy in D.C., and then waited on hold. Vaughn's hold music was a loop tape of Boston Red Sox play-by-play calls by announcer Dick Stockton. Eddie waited on hold a long time, thinking about the first time he met Hippo Vaughn.

It was late August, during his internship at The Empire. The Red Sox were on cable, so Eddie had settled into a downtown pub decorated with sports memorabilia, three dartboards, and two TVs. He watched the game with a working-class crowd of Red Sox fans. At one Guinness stout per hour, this was a four-beer game. When the Sox blew a ninth-inning lead, plumbers, carpenters and truck drivers— thick-armed men with curled lips and bad beer buzzes—

stormed from the bar and onto the cobblestones of Middle Street, in search of human skulls to crack in frustration—each other's, perhaps. The loss had ended Boston's playoff chances. There would be another year without a championship.

Eddie liked his skull the way it was; he had waited at the bar and ordered coffee. As the crowd cleared, he had noticed an old man alone at a table across the room. His white hair was nearly transparent, like fine fishing line. He was impossibly skinny, like the Mister Salty pretzel guy, come to life and aged into his eighties.

The man had pushed himself up on a bone-colored cane with a sliver knob. His spryness made the cane seem like a prop. "All hail the goddam Red Sox," he yelled bitterly to nobody in particular.

The old man had pushed through a wreckage of chairs to the back of the bar. There, he peeled from the wall a giant foam finger—a ballpark souvenir. He stuck his hand in the mitt and waved it around, shouting: "All hail the mighty Red Sox."

He spotted Eddie watching him.

"Dr. Baseball will be right with you, young man," he had hollered to Eddie. "Just bend over for your annual Red Sox prostate exam." He jabbed the giant finger in Eddie's direction.

Eddie leaned to the bartender. "Time to shut that guy off."

The barkeep shook his head. "He only drinks tea."

Was this guy for real? Eddie ordered the man a tea and waved him over. His name was Hippo Vaughn Pulaski. He went by Hippo Vaughn. And he believed he was cursed.

Momma Pulaski had delivered him eleven minutes after the Red Sox forced the final out to win the 1918 World Series, four games to two. His parents, both fans and delirious with joy that day, could not have imagined that Boston's win marked the start of a championship drought that would stretch to the next millennium.

Poppa Pulaski wanted to name his son after Carl Mays, the winning pitcher in the deciding game. But his mother's heart had melted for a hard-luck loser on the Cubs, who had allowed just three runs in twenty-seven innings but still lost two games in the '18 Series. His name was Hippo Vaughn.

And with that moniker she had cursed her infant son to a life of obsessive overachieving. Hippo Vaughn Pulaski drove himself to overcome the bad karma of the name. He didn't fear obstacles, he steered for them: bombing runs over Germany, medical school, and then law school. He passed the Mensa test, then refused to join. In his spare hours, he invented doodads for the electronics industry, and made enough dough to buy the Broadway theater at which he met his ballerina wife. He retired as a Superior Court judge with sixteen unblemished years on the bench.

But as Vaughn neared the end of a long life, he realized he was probably the oldest person drawing breath never to have experienced a Red Sox championship.

Missed it by eleven minutes—that epitaph horrified him.

At the bar that night, Eddie and Hippo talked about Fisk's home run in Game Six in '75, and Joe Morgan's appalling single in Game Seven. They commiserated about the "Boston Massacre" in '78, about Mike Torrez and Bucky Dent, Stanley's wild pitch, and about Mookie and Buckner. Vaughn told Eddie about the "William's shift" in '46, and Bob Gibson's domination in '67.

And they talked about life: how Hippo had persevered when his only son vanished in Vietnam; how Eddie's big brother had destroyed the family when he went to prison.

The day after they had met, Vaughn had declared himself a candidate for Congress as a Democrat. He never explained why he ran. Possibly he did so because some fool told him he could never win. Few voters knew him, but four million of your own bucks will buy a lot of name recognition.

Senior citizens liked the candidate's wrinkles. Younger voters liked his resumé, his harmless eccentricity and the way he talked. Sure, he was rich now, but he had grown up blue-collar and never forgot the language. Cuss words slipped from his lips, and he worked the Red Sox into every speech. It became his trademark.

His Republican opponent, a purebred from Concord, was ahead in the polls when he tried his own off-the-cuff Red Sox reference. He referred to Carl Yazstremski as a *center* fielder, and the polls flip-flopped overnight.

A click cut off the recording and Vaughn picked up the line. "So sorry about Danny," the congressman said.

They talked about Nowlin for a while, what a nice kid he was. That led Eddie to the point of the call. "I need Danny's autopsy report," he said. "It's sealed up. Spaulding can't get it from the cops, and neither can I."

Vaughn was silent a moment. Then he growled, "Living Christ almighty, Bourque. You want me to undo the Babe Ruth trade too?"

"The Sox could use another RBI guy. But of the two, I'll take the report. Unless you don't think you can get it."

Eddie set the telephone receiver on the desk and listened to the congressman's tirade of profanities. Even when Vaughn knew you were playing him for a favor, the man could not stand to be doubted.

Chapter 6

Reporter Russell Spaulding threw his own work on his desk. His hands tensed into claws, which he dragged over his bald scalp, scratching little channels through the sheen of sweat on his head.

"My flower planter story—on page one," he said to Eddie. He picked the paper back up and smacked it on the desk like he was killing a fly. "This is why I couldn't do my budget story. This crap." He sighed and slumped in his chair. "This place is going all to hell."

Spaulding was a chunky cop reporter with a shaved bullet head, gray eyes, and an in-your-face intensity. He was known around the newsroom as "A.K. Forty-seven," after the Russian assault rifle, because someday Spaulding was going to snap and climb a clock tower with one. Spaulding's best feature was his healthy contempt for the people he covered. There was no danger he'd go native and start referring to city officials as "we" and "us." As in, "So chief, did we get that grant to overhaul the radio room?" Once a reporter jumps that fence, so goes objectivity.

Eddie stood on his tiptoes and spoke to a sprinkler head in the ceiling. "For the benefit of the stenographer secretly recording this conversation through a hidden microphone, let me say for the record that it was Russell Spaulding who said this place is going to hell. And Eddie Bourque certainly does not agree with his lies."

Spaulding chuckled, and then suddenly sobered. "Keyes is coming," he said.

The boss had a lollipop in his mouth and a one-page fax in his hand. "Nice job on the planter story," he said.

Spaulding frowned. He seemed unsure if the compliment was meant to be sarcastic. "Now you can turn me loose on my budget story."

Keyes wrinkled his nose and shook his head slightly, as if sending back some caviar not to his liking. "Not ready for that one yet," he said. "The publisher has something more immediate for you." He glanced at the fax. "McGruff the Crime Dog is visiting classrooms at Varnum School tomorrow, and we want you there. Looks like a cute feature, right up your alley." Keyes cocked his thumb and aimed his index finger at Spaulding like a gun. Pooh! He shot him.

The reporter known as A.K. Forty-seven took a deep breath. Eddie glanced around to make sure the exits were clear. A.K. repeated his instructions, slowly. "McGruff the Crime Dog? At an elementary school?" A red wave washed over his scalp. He trembled and squirmed, like a guy trying to get comfortable in the electric chair. His voice was calm. Too calm. Eerie. "Let's make sure I understand, all right? I'm trained as an investigative journalist—hell, that's why you hired me. And I have a lead on a story about an alleged misappropriation of taxpayer money."

Spaulding swallowed a few times, and then got much louder. "But I can't do that investigative story because I gotta write an important feature about McGruff." He shouted this next part. "McGruff—the crotch-sniffing, ball-licking, leg-humping Crime Dog!" He threw up his hands. "Dammit, Frank. If you won't let your pit bull start any fights, why keep me around?" He snatched the press release from Keyes and spun around in his chair.

Keyes twirled the lollipop and pretended to just notice Eddie. "Oh Bourque, haven't seen your byline too often lately. Do you still work here?"

"Hard to tell after what happened to my last story."

Keyes got angry and more direct. "Then maybe you should write more often. We have other reporters who produce three stories a day."

Eddie shrugged. "Would you rather I explored the depths of one good story, or the surface of three? If we only report what's obvious at first glance, we're no better than TV news."

Keyes took the lollipop from his mouth, a red one, and shook it at Eddie. The gesture was meant to be menacing, but there is simply no way for a grown man to intimidate another man with a lollipop. "Television is taking our readers," he barked. "According to our marketing polls, people think TV is more trustworthy than us. And that TV news is more pertinent. So take a lesson."

He marched off.

Eddie muttered, "He's dumbed-down our coverage and we've lost readers. So his answer is to give them more of what they don't want."

"For the record, that was Eddie Bourque speaking," Spaulding said, with a glance to the sprinkler head.

Eddie deadpanned, "As a reader, Russ, I'm interested to know how McGruff drives the squad car with his snout out the window."

A.K. Forty-seven gave Eddie the finger over his shoulder without turning around.

Eddie spent an hour on the phone with City Council candidates, prepping for his election analysis. The candidates essentially were divided into two camps, the incumbents, and the reform slate. The incumbents supported spending public money on major revitalization projects. The reformers wanted to shore up public services and spend more on schools. They said the private sector should pay for brick-and-mortar development. Eddie could see why Manny Eccleston had been so cautious with his tip—nobody on the reform slate would ever support the destruction of the Acre.

Around three o'clock, Eddie pulled on his overcoat and walked to City Hall to make his rounds. City Hall is a grand stone building with a high clock tower and a tin roof, tarnished green. Inside, worn white marble stairs wind to the upper floors.

At the City Clerk's office, he checked campaign finance reports filed by the candidates. The incumbents had raised more money than the challengers. That was no surprise. But one detail interested him. Six incumbents fighting for reelection had recorded contributions from the "GLCI Political Action Committee." It was a Lowell-based PAC, according to the contribution disclosure forms, but Eddie had never heard of it. Each contribution was for the maximum allowed by campaign finance law. It all went into the notebook for a possible story.

Eddie headed back to the office just before four. Melissa was waiting in the lobby. They hugged. There was nothing special in her touch. She wore a black skirt and tights, a thick knit sweater, gray like Eddie's suit, and a beige beret. Her jacket was tan suede with fake fur around the wrists. They headed up Market Street toward The Dead Zone.

Melissa Moreau was The Empire's top general assignment reporter. She was nearly six feet tall and spindly, lacking deep curves. But her eyes! Melissa's brown eyes were huge, round and dark as French-roast coffee beans. They were always moist, like they were holding little tears about to spill out. Lots of men looked into Melissa's eyes and yearned to protect her. Men couldn't shut their mouths around her, even when she was taking notes. Some men never learned. Some like Eddie. He'd thrown a dozen passes her way, all incomplete.

Melissa talked like she wrote, a little too dramatic. They had gone only a few steps when she said, "I don't know what

I'm ever going to say when we see Jesse, that poor woman, all alone in the world."

"Maybe the answer's in here," Eddie said, pulling her furry sleeve toward The Umbrage, a gourmet coffee spot.

She sighed. "You're so addicted."

The one-room restaurant had its usual gathering of pale, skinny people dressed in the all-black uniform of the tortured individual, brooding over their lattes. "I'm just here looking for something to say at the wake," Eddie whispered to Melissa. "Who knows more about death than this crew? This looks like a casting call for a vampire movie." In a loud Dracula voice he said, "If you stay up late feasting on human flesh, you'll need that caffeine kick in the morning."

Melissa scolded him, "Edward!"

He ordered an Italian roast, black. Melissa didn't want anything. She picked at her cuticles while Eddie's order was filled.

The cold front that had dawdled over New England for two weeks hadn't budged. Gusts of icy wind passed like X-rays through Eddie's overcoat. They walked toward the funeral home, zigzagging through the Acre neighborhood, past Asian restaurants emitting odd and wonderful smells, and Khmer markets with bottles of strange brown spices in the windows, which, when added in the right proportions to stirred vegetables, created those odd and wonderful smells.

People sat on their front steps, watching what went by. Children giggled and chased after each other, unaware they were underdressed for the cold. Graffiti, peeling paint and plywood windows became common. Trash blew against rusty chain fences. Parked cars with two wheels on the curb shared the cracked sidewalks with pedestrians.

But there were also patches of pride amidst the decay. Immaculate little yards. Bushes trimmed into spheres and cubes. Victorian architecture lovingly restored, from the fieldstone foundations to copper cupolas. And washing over the neighborhood as dinnertime drew near, came the voices of mothers and fathers calling for their children in Spanish, in English, and in words of Southeast Asia, which Eddie could only guess were from Vietnam, Thailand, and Cambodia.

Eddie and Melissa walked in step, her stride as long as his. For the first half mile, neither of them spoke. Eddie fought the cold by gulping coffee that nearly scalded his insides. Melissa broke their silence. "You haven't said much about Danny since he died. You two were friends, weren't you?"

Eddie finished his coffee and pushed the cup into an overflowing can somebody had dragged to the curb for trash day. "We were beat partners," he said.

Melissa wouldn't take his politician's answer. "But not friends?"

Eddie bristled. "Danny and Jesse had me over a couple times. I spent Christmas afternoon with them last year."

She said nothing. Her heels fell harder on the asphalt sidewalk.

Eddie sighed and gave her what she wanted. "There was a distance between Danny and me, a professional distance."

"Professional?"

"It was unspoken, but we both wanted out of The Empire. There are only so many journalism jobs in New England, and only so many of those go to political reporters. Danny and I were teammates in Lowell, but competitors for jobs everywhere else." Eddie hoped to end it there, but she elbowed him. "Danny was the best reporter I've ever seen, but not the best writer. His raw copy was sloppy and too wordy."

"Always read fine to me," she said.

"Danny got good editing."

"Gordon?"

Eddie nodded. "Phife rewrote Danny's stuff. But Danny was making progress. As soon as his writing caught up with the rest of his skills, he was out of here."

"And you were afraid he'd take a job from you?" The truth sounded pathetic coming from her mouth.

Eddie confirmed her conclusion with silence.

She waited a moment, and then said, "Your competitor is dead. But at least you didn't lose a friend."

Her words hammered him. The blow cracked something open inside Eddie and spilled his own foolishness all over him. An acid tear burned his eye. He blinked it away, gave her a little smile and said, "You must have been a reporter from birth—you're a natural."

"Actually, interior design class was full," she said, "I needed three credits, and journalism fit my schedule." She laughed. "True story. And you?"

Eddie felt closer to Melissa than he ever had before. "There was this perfect little forest of white pine near my neighborhood growing up, with deer tracks and windy trails running through it."

"It's probably a subdivision now," she said.

"Goddam condos. Anyway, none of the kids dared to play around there because the forest had an abandoned well in the middle of it. It was dry and capped, perfectly safe, but the story had gotten around that the well was where the town fathers used to dump crazy people from the state hospital, and that the bottom was full of bones."

Melissa clapped her hands. "I *adore* urban legends."

"I didn't," Eddie said. "I was ten years old and wanted to play in that forest. So I took my aunt's Polaroid and some rope from her clothesline."

"You didn't!"

"Yup. Left some wet sheets on the lawn. The cap over the well had a trap door. I smashed the lock with a rock, tied off the rope, and lowered myself down. Problem was, I was heading down a forty-foot hole with about thirty-three feet of rope."

She laughed.

"When I ran outta rope, I jumped."

"Did you find bones?"

"Naw, just the carriage of an old wheelbarrow. It might have looked like bones from above, which was probably how the legend got started. I snapped a picture, and then realized I couldn't reach the rope. I scraped my hands red trying to climb the wall."

"You must have screamed bloody murder."

Eddie admitted, "Never been so hoarse. When darkness fell I started to believe that I hadn't debunked the legend at all—I was going to prove it true with my own bones. A search party of neighbors heard me pounding stones the next morning, digging in the bottom of the well, and got me out of there."

"Why were you digging?"

"Not important," Eddie said. He blew into his hands. He had never told anyone about his sleepless night at the bottom of the well, where Fear had first visited him, perfumed in mold and mud, and had persuaded ten-year-old Eddie Bourque to dig himself a proper grave. "Anyway, it didn't go the way I planned, but my investigation worked out. A writer at the Weekly Chieftain wrote a few inches about me at the bottom of his column, and ran my Polaroid from inside the well."

"You must have been the hero of the adolescent world."

"Sure felt like it. Nobody was ever afraid to play in that forest again, and I realized how powerful the press could be. I was a reporter from that day."

They turned onto Pawtucket Street and walked into The Dead Zone, a stretch of six funeral homes along just a few blocks. They were fat Victorian-style buildings with plenty of parking and canvas canopies between the sidewalk and the front doors.

A line of dark suits and overcoats snaked from under one white canopy. Danny Nowlin was an impressive draw. Some local pols were there, including Councilman Manny Eccleston.

Eccleston spotted Eddie and waved him over. Eddie walked Melissa slowly up the line, warning under his breath, "It's Manny the Mangler."

"Huh?"

"Just don't laugh."

Eddie introduced Melissa to the councilman. They shook hands, and then Eccleston said gravely, "Danny was a pillow of the community."

Eddie felt Melissa's gaze, but kept a solemn face pointed to Eccleston and apologized for not returning his call immediately that morning. The councilman leaned close to talk business. The only wake that slowed down a Lowell politician was the very last one he attended.

"I want to feed you a story about the old church," Eccleston whispered. His breath smelled of boiled eggs and Listerine.

Eccleston was referring to St. Francis de Sales. The diocese had closed it nearly twenty years ago. Eccleston had been floating a plan to take the land by eminent domain, and tear down the old church to make space for public projects. Eddie had heard rumblings of opposition from a neighborhood group.

Eddie cupped a hand to his ear. "I'm listening."

"That old building is a real sore eye," said Eccleston. "It's been an Alcatraz around the city's neck for years. I'll leak you a report that demonstrates absolutely no integrity."

"Huh?"

"The building—no integrity."

"You mean the building lacks structural integrity?"

"Right. I'll have it on your desk by the end of the week."

Eddie nodded. There were more handshakes, and then Eddie walked Melissa back to the end of the line. She whispered to him, "I nearly bit my poor tongue clean through."

They shuffled along with the crowd, winding down stairs and through three pine-paneled rooms in the basement of the funeral home. The hushed mourners seemed like zombies in a catatonic line dance, plodding across the undertaker's rose-colored carpet. Eddie left his overcoat and Melissa's jacket with the coat checker, and then hunched his shoulders to hide the ill fit of his suit. His cell phone vibrated. Caller I.D. showed that Phife was on the line, but there was no place to talk. Gordon would have to call back.

Near the end of the line, a small table draped in shimmering pink fabric displayed Nowlin's photo in a stand-up frame and a few relics from his life, including a twelve-inch lock of reddish hair, braided into a ponytail. Nowlin had worn long hair until his wedding. He let Jesse snip it at their reception with hedge shears. There was a reporter's flip-top notebook on the table, opened to a page of scribbles done in black ink, and Nowlin's laminated press identification card from the state police.

The line finally brought them to the closed casket—a deep brown poplar model with silver hardware—and to Jesse. A golden shaft of sunlight streamed into the basement chamber through a window high on the wall above the coffin. The light illuminated bits of dust spinning above Jesse's head.

Danny's widow was twenty-nine, the director of a small art gallery in upscale Concord, a half-hour south of Lowell. She was barely five feet tall, nicely proportioned, with sweet blue eyes, like a newborn's. For her husband's wake, she wore an unflattering black dress that hung straight from her shoulders and hid the heart-shaped tattoo on her ankle. Her short blonde hair, usually worn spiked, was jelled back flat against her scalp.

There were no children with her. Jesse could not conceive, and the Nowlins had planned to adopt. Last year, Danny had written a first-person commentary about the red tape hassles of adopting from overseas. Today it seemed a blessing. Jesse embraced Melissa lightly, and then Eddie. Her touch was distant, the way a political opponent hugs to fake reconciliation after a nasty primary.

"You don't have to go through this alone," Eddie said.

"You get used to being alone," Jesse said. Her voice was flat. Her eyes looked past him.

Used to it? "Is there anything I can, ah, do for you?"

"Thank you, Danny's done quite enough." With that, she turned to the next person in line and the current swept Eddie along. He gave Melissa a raised eyebrow, but she showed no reaction.

They greeted Nowlin's father, his sister, stepsister, and assorted relations arranged in what seemed to be decreasing order of emotional distress. Nowlin's father could barely stand. The teenaged cousin from Oakland at the end of the line probably got more upset when the Raiders failed to cover the spread.

The line emptied through a wide archway into a reception room. It was crowded with mourners, many of them holding flaky pastries and collecting their crumbs into white cocktail napkins.

Pastries? Then there had to be coffee.

Eddie left Melissa and eased through the crowd as fast as courtesy allowed. He tried to make sense of what Jesse had said. She was used to being alone? Nowlin worked long hours when the news got hot, but all the reporters did that. And Danny had done quite enough? Enough what? He got himself killed somehow. Is that what she meant?

There was a two-gallon chrome coffee carafe on a long maple table in the back of the room. Eddie grabbed a Styrofoam cup and pulled the handle to let the mind-juice flow.

Damn. Empty.

He held the cup in place and tilted the dispenser forward. Watery brew dribbled out. Slowly, slowly. Just a little more—

A reflection in the chrome caught his eye. Red mittens. And a face he had seen before. Eddie glanced over his shoulder. In the window above the casket, a woman peered into the chamber. Her breath froze a small white patch on the glass. The wind pulled her hair and the ends of her white scarf.

She was the Cambodian woman who had watched from the rooftop when the police took Nowlin from the water.

She looked older than Eddie had guessed before, maybe mid-thirties. She was also more stunning that he remembered. High, sharp cheekbones, a strong jaw, and cords of muscle running down her neck, like an adolescent boy's warrior-princess fantasy girl, peeking into the wake of the man she had watched police take from the canal.

Eddie paid attention. There was no such thing as coincidence.

The woman stepped out of sight, only to appear a moment later across the reception room. She spoke to no one as she walked past people waiting in line, then stopped before the table with Nowlin's picture. She studied it briefly, then glanced about the room. Eddie turned around and pretended to get more coffee. He watched her in the chrome. She stepped toward the table for an instant, spun around and paced toward the exit.

Melissa was tied up, nodding politely as two school board candidates bent her ear. Leaving her behind, Eddie exited faster than courtesy permitted, covering bumps and gentle shoves with a string of apologies.

By the time he had reached the street, the woman was already a block away. With no time to collect his overcoat, Eddie turned up the collar of his suit jacket, jammed his hands in his pants pockets and walked after her. The winter air iced his sinuses and the wind shredded his coat as he followed her deeper, into the jumble of windy streets, misshapen city blocks and triple-deckers known as the Acre.

Chapter 7

He had lost her.

The three kids yelled Spanish over the pulse of American rap music beating from a radio so big it should have had wheels. They discussed Eddie's loud and haltingly spoken questions and wild gesticulations that were meant to ask: Have you seen a woman with red mittens?

Somewhere in this labyrinth of streets, originally laid out by Irish immigrants to resemble the labyrinth they had left back home, the woman from the funeral home had vanished. In his search for her, Eddie had twice walked past these kids playing music and kicking a beanbag to each other without letting it touch the street. A woman with centerfold looks wouldn't slip unnoticed past these three boys sprouting puberty's peach fuzz above their lips. It was just a matter of slogging through the language barrier. Eddie's command of Spanish was limited. He could count to eight. For words, he knew *muchas gracias*. That would be handy if the kids were able to help him.

The kids were patient. Eddie's pantomime of pulling mittens on his hands and combing long hair eventually got the question across, or seemed to. The kids covered their mouths and laughed and howled. Yeah, they saw some woman, all right.

They pointed down the street, toward a row of triple-decker tenement buildings. The kids nodded and chattered with excitement.

"Down here?" Eddie said, pointing where they were pointing.

Yes, yes. They were quite sure of it.

"This house?"

No not that one. The next.

"That one?"

Yes, yes. They all agreed.

Eddie tapped fists with each of them, and thanked them in Spanish. They said, "you're welcome" in English, and resumed the beanbag game.

The triple-decker was shedding its skin. Light blue paint curled off the building. A witty drug dealer had scrawled advertising on the house: *"Got crack?"*

The building had a covered porch supported by old wooden columns, gouged by dry rot. Three windows jutted out in a first-floor bay. They were covered by weathered plywood streaked with rust stains from the nails. Windows on the second floor were glass, though each was cracked in a spider-web pattern, a small hole in the middle, where the spider would sit.

There was no front door—just another tall sheet of plywood, attached crooked to the doorframe by two brass hinges. A V-shaped chunk was missing from the board about halfway up, opposite the hinges. The wood was brighter around the damaged section, not aged gray like the rest. Somebody had recently smashed off a padlock fixture.

Three great granite steps led to the porch. Eddie climbed them, and then pulled the makeshift door. The hinges groaned. Eddie gasped at the sound and clenched his free hand into a fist. It was a fight-or-flight instinct, in case he had to throw a punch before he could run. But nobody was there. There was a damp smoky smell inside, like from an old campfire.

Bizarre graffiti covered the walls of the narrow hallway behind the door, a dozen grotesque caricatures, each as tall as Eddie, drawn in black and red, as if Van Gogh had painted an acid trip on Easter Island. The bodies of the figures were stick frames, skinny and twisted. Their giant, elongated heads were warped and lumpy. They had gaping mouths full of jagged teeth, and their eyes were rotated half a turn, so that they watched Eddie vertically. Each head had a gushing red wound.

Eddie reached in and touched the painting closest to the door. Red paint, still tacky, came off onto his fingertip. The heat from his walk through the Acre drained away and he shivered. Fear kissed his cheek.

He saw a large room at the end of the hall. Dim yellow sunlight fought through dust on the windows. There was a dirty sofa down there. It might have been white once. A wool blanket was neatly folded and laid over the sofa back. There were soda bottles and brightly colored fast food wrappers on the floor, and a shopping cart on its side.

Eddie stuck his head in the door and listened. If there was anything to hear, the rap music blaring down the street swallowed up the sound. Eddie closed the plywood, turned away down the steps and blew hot breath into his cupped hands. The police would want to know about this place, and about the woman from the rooftop and the wake.

He stopped to think.

If the woman with the red mittens was there, and if she knew something about the case, the cops would sit on it for a week, and then call a press conference. Channel Eight would send Boden and he'd lead the six-o'clock broadcast from these granite steps. Eddie would have the story in the next day's paper, one news cycle later.

Eddie blew a long cone of frozen breath. He climbed the steps again and pulled open the door. *Let them all read about this place in The Empire.*

The house had no heat, but at least no wind. Eddie inched down the hallway, past the giant painted heads. The rotten floorboards had an unnerving, creaky spring to them.

The room at the end of the hall was once a parlor. There was a tile fireplace at one end, though the mantle had been pried away. Black ash was spread in a half-circle around the fire pit, like somebody had cleaned the pit by kicking ash into the room. At the other end of the parlor, grand wooden stairs curved up to the second floor. Spindle rods stuck up from a few of the steps, where once had rested a banister.

There were a dozen more giant graffiti heads here. Most resembled the ones in the hallway. But one was much larger, stretching from the floor to the ten-foot ceiling. Its eyes were black circles, the size of manholes. Its body was stubby and meatier than the rest. The head had a pair of horns curling up, like a ram's. Both arms ended in pistols in the place of hands. Squiggly hand-painted letters, like those on signs at Cambodian markets around the neighborhood, spelled things that Eddie could not understand.

If you measured art by its effect on the viewer, this decrepit house was a masterpiece. The painted figure stole Eddie's breath like hands around his throat. His eyes passed from the horns to the guns and settled on the big black saucers. They were more like holes than eyes, burned out by something they had witnessed.

He kicked through the trash. Nothing. And then through the fireplace ash. He discovered a stain on the floor. Blood?

There was a noise, a light bump above him. Eddie looked to the ceiling. Puffs of white dust dropped from a crack in the plaster. Somebody was walking across the room above.

Fear joined Eddie in the parlor.

He inspected the stairs. Fresh footsteps had swept a track through the dust, up the center of the staircase. Eddie held his breath and rested a foot upon the first stair. He let the breath out and eased his weight up. The stair moaned. Eddie grimaced and froze in place. To his ear, he might as well have stepped on bagpipes. He fought the urge to run.

Thirty seconds passed.

Nothing happened.

Eddie took another step. That stair didn't complain.

Up the stairs and out of sight, somebody—a man—spoke out loud. It sounded like chanting. Eddie couldn't make out the words, just the rhythm. The cadence seemed to repeat itself. It didn't come any closer so he waited, listening. It repeated over and over, as if the voice was stuck on the same line in a song or poem.

Fear brushed her chapped lips over the little hairs at the top of Eddie's spine.

Eddie decided on a plan. He would see what was up there, and run if anybody saw him, right to the cops. He tried to ignore Gordon Phife's voice in his head, quoting from the movie *Tremors*: "Running's not a plan. Running's what you do when a plan fails."

The voice covered any noise from the stairs, and Eddie hurried on his toes up twelve more steps to a darkened hallway with dirty white walls. He peeked around the corner. An open doorway at the end of the long hall glowed red. From the top of the stairs, the voice was clear. It was low and raspy, repeating a short chant, maybe a sentence or two, in a language Eddie did not understand; certainly not Spanish, probably something Southeast Asian. He tried to memorize the chant phonetically.

Too fast. I'll never remember this.

Eddie pulled out his cell phone and dialed The Empire. He punched in his own extension. It rang four times, and then transferred to voice mail. He waited for the beep, and then held the phone toward the red-lit room. He let the chant repeat twice, and then broke the connection.

The phone grew slick in his sweaty hand. He squeezed it and edged closer to the voice. Halfway down the hall, he could see a sliver of the room. There, on a knee-high pile of newspaper by the door, was a pair of red mittens.

Edging closer, he peered from darkness into the red light.

The Cambodian woman stood with her back to Eddie, in front of a round kitchen table draped in newspaper. The chanting continued from deeper in the room, out of Eddie's view. Above the table, strung on a wire, hung two small battery lanterns. They were wrapped in red plastic tape. To the right of the table stood an easel. It displayed a large black-and-white photograph Eddie had never seen before, but recognized in an instant.

It was a picture of Danny Nowlin.

The photo measured about fourteen inches diagonally, and was of poor quality. The pixels were too big, like it had been enlarged from a smaller print without the negative. Danny sat alone in the picture, a posed smile on his face.

The chanting stopped and the woman stepped aside. On a square of white handkerchief at the center of the table rested Nowlin's reddish ponytail. She had stolen it, stolen it from the wake in front of everyone. Stunned, Eddie fixated on the lock of hair.

When he glanced to the woman again, she was staring back at him.

That's when Fear nestled up behind him and raked her razor red nails over his Adam's apple. Eddie tried to swallow the lump in his throat. It went down like a fistful of bobby pins.

The woman was still. Her expression said nothing. They both waited, waited. *Good God, she's beautiful—*

Bzzzzzzz.

"Hey!" Eddie yelped. The telephone in his fist was ringing. *Not now Gordie!*

A man's voice called out.

Eddie spun and ran with abandon, thundering down the hall.

The man yelled again. The language was a mystery to Eddie, but he understood the angry tone. Heavy footsteps pounded after him. Running seemed like a fine plan after all. Nobody could catch him, not with the lead he had.

Shadows flickered on the wall above the stairs. He thought he smelled smoke.

Then he heard a piercing crack, and the squeal of old eight-penny nails tearing from place. The floor rushed up at him and Eddie fought for balance. His right foot plunged through a broken floorboard, straight through thin ceiling slats and plaster, and then into space. His chest crashed to the floor and there was another loud crack.

The blow knocked the wind out of him. Pain crackled up his spine like electricity along a ragged wire. A scream stuck fast inside the vacuum of his empty lungs. Eddie clawed wildly at the floorboards, and then fell through them. He thrashed in the air, grabbing for something solid in the debris, and then instinctively wrapped his arms around his head and waited for the parlor floor.

Chapter 8

Eddie woke to purring.

He listened a while and decided this was not a cat's purr, which goes in and out like a man sawing wood. This purr held steady. A motor, he thought. Powerful, and in perfect tune. He felt a swaying, like being below decks on the ferry to Nantucket, but not so predictable.

He thought to open his eyes. And then realized they were open and everything was black. He was on his right side. His knees were pulled up to his chin. Eddie's hip ached and his head felt magnetized to the floor. His cheek pressed into scratchy carpeting, and he tasted blood. His left hand was sticky and there was grit between the fingers. He reached up and felt the ceiling, very cold, just above his head.

His concussed brain correctly reasoned that this was the trunk of a car. But it could not decide if this was where he should be. And then the world phased back out.

A low grunt came next. It was a self-satisfied noise after a tough job done well.

Eddie was weightless, floating in space, arms stretched out like Superman.

It was so quiet out here.

The crash rattled back some of his senses. A low crack echoed once, and an icy shock bit into his flesh. Eddie lifted his head from water and silently gasped. He had landed face-down on milky ice. A section of ice had broken off under his weight and had dipped below the water. It bobbed back to the surface like a raft, with Eddie on board.

He recognized the walls of a mill canal on either side of him. A spiked wrought-iron fence ran along the top of the wall. Parts of the Worthen Canal had such a fence, he recalled. That canal flowed through low-income housing along the western edge of the Acre, into an industrial area, and then under the street where the police had found Danny.

On the ice, a few inches from Eddie's face, a rat was posed on the spot it had died. Its greasy gray hair looked brittle, like glass. Its pink tail snaked out under a coating of ice. The rat had stopped here long enough for its tail to become frozen in place. Why would it stop? Maybe for a last meal before a death struggle against its own tail. How long did it suffer?

Eddie was still.

A harsh whisper from above said, "If you tried all day, could you *be* any more stupid? It's floating away on the goddam ice."

"Must you use the name of our Lord that way?" said another voice.

"Shut up. Get a rock."

Eddie thought about General VonKatz. The cat could drink from the drip in the tub. And he could live hungry for a week, couldn't he? Longer, maybe. Somebody would check the house by then. Melissa would remember him. Eddie thought about the General's last ear infection. He wouldn't take his pills. Eddie had crushed them into some gravy and added catnip to hide the medicine smell. Would anybody think of that?

Something splashed beside his head.

Eddie hadn't the strength to swim. And even if he did, the water was too cold, the walls of the canal too sheer. To slip off the ice would be to drown. He tried to fuse himself to the ice with his will. Shivers shook blood from Eddie's head. The red droplets ran like bugs on the wet ice.

There was a bigger splash. The ice wobbled. An archway of rough stone appeared above him.

"You missed again, you idiot," said a voice. "Now it's floating under the bridge."

"Forget it," the other voice answered. "It'll sink before it comes out the other side."

Two car doors slammed and an engine purred off.

Eddie clung to the ice a while. It seemed a long time.

He thought about the Red Sox. If they could just add one decent starting pitcher this off-season, and one infielder who could run. He thought about Nowlin, floating face down in this canal with no ice under him. He thought about Bruno, his barber, dialing Eddie because the dive team was scrambling. Eddie's mind heard his phone ringing with the barber's tip. But nobody would answer it.

There was no more pain, not from his hip, nor the cold, not from the wounds that had bloodied his hands. Eddie was glad to be feeling better. His shivering went away. There was no sound beyond his own breath, so soft and calm, like a sleeping child without grown-up worries.

He studied the rat. Its eyelids were open and the eyes frozen white.

My eyes are brown. He was glad to be feeling better.

Chapter 9

"Hey Gab! Help me—this one is alive. Get him up."

"God, Leo, what a mess."

Hands pulled at Eddie. He saw two blurry faces.

"Put the shawl over him."

"Eew! Look at that rat."

The hands passed Eddie around. They stretched him into a cross—arms out to the side. His face flopped forward; the ground passed under his feet. Eddie's shoes scuffed on the asphalt. The heads under his armpits wheezed and coughed as they carried him. Eddie smelled foul breath; these heads were rotting from the inside out. His shoes knocked against railroad tracks. The rails were polished like silver and they reflected the moonlight. The head under Eddie's right arm yelled out, "Kent? Snake? Get over here."

"Kent's on the nod—he's long gone," called another voice. "Did you get the stuff?"

"Yes, and something else."

"Jesus—where'd he come from?"

The railroad tracks were gone. Now there was dry grass below his feet. Then Eddie's nose was in the grass and he smelled oil. The hands took him up a steep hill.

"Just lay him on his back and drag him along the ledge. Watch for the ice—do not lose him."

They rolled him, and suddenly the night stars appeared. Eddie recognized Orion the hunter. He tried to tell them that the Egyptians built the Great Pyramids in a line with Orion's belt. But it came out in a gurgle.

"Easy, man," a voice said.

Silhouettes passed over Eddie. They hid the starlight like black holes.

They moved him in small steps, grunting as they dragged him and panting when they rested. Soon Eddie was under rows of great steel beams, rusted orange and lit by flickering light. The place smelled like a campfire. A truck rumbled overhead. Above the beams, there was a concrete ceiling. They had taken him under a bridge.

"Take his clothes off." The woman's voice was low and throaty.

Hands pulled at Eddie's belt. The man undressing him had curly black hair like steel wool, and a gray stubble beard. Shadows filled his deep eye sockets and the hollows in his cheeks.

Eddie struggled to ask them, who are you?

"Can't understand a word you're saying," the woman said.

Eddie watched her in the campfire light. She spread out a blanket and sat on it. Her light hair hung limp to her shoulders. Dainty brown eyebrows seemed out of place on her ashen face, which was pockmarked by little scars. She pulled a faded pink sweatshirt over her head and exposed her breasts, which sagged into ovals. She undid her jeans and slid them off. Her legs were skinny, the color of buttermilk.

The man dragged Eddie to the blanket. Eddie's clothes were piled on the ground.

"Got to raise your core temperature or you'll die," the woman said.

She pressed her body against his and the man wrapped the blanket around them. He spread another blanket over the first one. It smelled like piss.

The fire heated Eddie's face. Another man, bald with a reptile skin tattoo around his neck, stoked the flames with hunks of a broken rocking chair. The bridge rattled under the traffic.

Soon Eddie began to shiver again, and pain seeped back into his hip and his head. His shakes grew violent. The woman slid an arm over his chest and squeezed. "Don't fight it," she whispered. "That's your life coming back."

A fire engine howled across the bridge. She waited for the siren to pass, and then said to the man with curly hair, "Leo, honey, fix the spike for me, would you? I'm starving for it."

He smiled, saying, "Already done the cooking." From inside his soiled wool overcoat, he produced a syringe. He pulled off the safety cap and inspected the needle in the fire's light. He flicked it twice with a finger. "It is ready, Luv."

Chapter 10

Eddie woke alone to the bustle of the morning commute clattering across the bridge overhead. His hip ached. A lump on the back of his skull throbbed when he rolled over on it. He was stiff from sleeping on cement. The cold air had tempered overnight to something more seasonable, maybe forty degrees. The sun blazed brightly outside the shadow of the bridge.

He lay wrapped in blankets on a cramped ledge, the size of an average living room, which jutted out from a concrete bridge abutment. Nine parallel steel I-beams, five feet overhead, carried the bridge to another abutment, maybe fifty feet away.

All sorts of trash was strewn around the ledge: empty soup cans, cat food boxes, fast food and cigarette wrappers. Old clothes, dirty sheets and blankets were in piles. A yellow plastic milk crate nearby held coffee mugs, cutlery, two long white candles, a bottle of lemon juice and a handful of new syringes wrapped in plastic.

Eddie crawled naked to the edge of the ledge. It dropped twenty-five feet straight down a wall of granite blocks to two sets of railroad tracks. To his left, the tracks gently curved out of sight between chain fences, to his right were numerous tracks and switch-offs, where trains would be stored. Eddie realized he was near the train station, just outside of downtown Lowell, and that Chelmsford Street, one of the city's busiest arteries, ran above his head.

A much narrower ledge, like a catwalk, led away from the main ledge and followed along a tall granite retaining wall for about a hundred feet, ending at a steep, grassy knoll. The two-foot-wide catwalk looked like a dangerous exit from this place. It was a trek over patches of ice—a sheer stone wall on one side and a drop of more than two stories on the other.

Did they really drag me down that walkway?

The campfire had aged to coals. Somebody had spread Eddie's suit near the fire. It was cold and wet and he shuddered at the thought of putting it back on. He crawled to a pile of clothes and picked through it. He found blue jeans with holes in the knees. They were short in the inseam and snug in the waist. He pulled on a rust-colored wool sweater with grease smears on the sleeves, and laced up red canvas sneakers, size eleven, one size too big. He tied them tight. He still needed a jacket. There was a large pile of clothes and blankets toward the back of the ledge, heaped against the abutment. He squatted in front of the pile and pulled out a black fleece pullover.

There was a human head beneath it.

Eddie's head smacked a steel girder. The pain started at the back of his skull, roared up over his brain and shot out his eyes in a flash of light that washed the world white for three seconds. He massaged his lump and then crawled back to the pile. The head was attached to a man, buried in dirty laundry; it was the bald guy with the snakeskin tattoo who had tended the fire. His eyes were closed, his breathing slow and noisy.

"You okay, man?" Eddie said, tapping the man's cheek. "I'm just looking for something to wear."

He turned his head and looked at Eddie. His pupils were specks. From his nostrils, drops of clear liquid streamed to his lips. He blinked a few times, and then turned away to sleep.

"I'm assuming you don't mind if I borrow a jacket."

The pullover smelled like sweat and campfire smoke. In the pocket Eddie found a wallet. It was an excellent tanned cowhide, or at least it used to be. There was an imprint of a polo player on it. Ralph Lauren? This was a pricey wallet.

A voice said, "Those shoes do not match with that jacket." Startled, Eddie dropped the wallet and spun around.

The curly-haired man had come along the walkway to the ledge. He was kneeling, watching Eddie under the girders. He had an armful of dry sticks. Behind him, the woman who had warmed Eddie in the blanket edged along the walkway. She stepped sideways, her back to the retaining wall.

"I needed clothes," Eddie said. His eyes flickered to the railroad tracks below. A long way to jump.

The man saw Eddie eye the tracks. His smile showed beige teeth. "We will trade clothes," he said. The accent was Middle-Eastern. His language was formal, like he had learned English in a classroom. He looked about forty-five years old. "Then I will have a suit to wear to my board meetings."

They both smiled. The man lobbed the wood at Eddie's feet and pointed to the fire. Eddie gathered the kindling and stirred the coals to revive them.

The woman reached the ledge. She looked late forties. Forty-seven, Eddie guessed. "You look better," she said to him. She had the voice of an elderly woman who had smoked all her life.

"I'm doing better than that guy." Eddie pointed to the man under the laundry.

"Who? Snake? He's as good as it gets. He's on the nod." She saw Eddie was puzzled. "He shot up this morning. Still on his wake-up hit."

"Heroin?" Eddie asked.

"A rose by any other name...." She stopped in midthought and pointed down the catwalk. "Leo, here comes Fat Boy."

A calico cat trotted along the ledge. He was fat, all right, maybe eighteen pounds. The man grabbed a box of cat food and shook it. The cat hustled on stumpy legs. "Fat Boy's a regular," the woman explained. "He loves Leo. They all love him. We don't eat sometimes but those cats always do." She rolled her eyes at the man, but she smiled, too.

The cat rubbed its bulk against the man's shin and lifted its chin so he could scratch its neck.

"Fat Boy trades his affection for food," the man said. "That is how he stays fat. Not all of his kind has learned this." He dumped a pyramid of dry food on the cement. The cat nosed into it.

Eddie had the fire crackling again. They sat and talked. The man and woman who had saved him from the canal held hands. Her name was Gabrielle, he went by Leo, and this ledge was their home. They were part of a community of heroin addicts, a dozen or so, who often stayed under this bridge, though rarely more than a handful at a time. They had found Eddie in the water by chance, they told him. Ice had narrowed the swath of running river in the canal, and Eddie's ice floe had become lodged.

"How long have you lived here?" Eddie asked.

Gabrielle answered, "Since we came from Montreal." To Leo, she said, "What? About eighteen months?"

"You don't have to stay here, do you?"

She shrugged. "Heroin is a full-time job. We can't pay rent."

"What about the homeless shelter?"

"They got big hearts down there, they do," she said. "They check on us here sometimes, bring us coffee and they'll give us clothes or a new blanket. But it's a dry shelter. You can't shoot up there, and they don't let you in if you're hooded."

"Hooded?"

"You know—if you've been using."

"So you'd rather stay here, under this bridge, so you can shoot up?"

They said nothing because the answer was obvious. Eddie pressed the point. "You don't have a home, you don't have heat or a phone. Christ—I don't see a toilet under here."

Gabrielle looked sweetly on the naive stranger in her home. "That's smack," she said. "It knows everything you don't have. And that's what it gives you. Every time."

Eddie looked to Leo for confirmation. He nodded. "My wife tells it correct."

"You two are married?" Eddie asked, surprised.

"In the eyes of everyone except the law," Leo said. He grinned and kissed her cheek.

By questioning them, Eddie got their biographies. Leo was born in Iran, moved to Paris at fifteen and studied philosophy as an undergraduate. His parents died young, and he moved to Montreal in his mid-twenties for graduate studies. There, blind drunk in the men's room at a German-style pub on St. Catherine Street, he snorted heroin off the book jacket of Friedrich Nietzsche's *The Birth of Tragedy*.

Leo shook his head at the irony. "I had a backpack full of text with me. Plato, Kant, Hume, Bertrand Russell. But I chose Nietzsche." He shrugged. "I did not even like Nietzsche."

Leo dropped out of school within a year of starting his habit, and took a job as a sausage cart vendor. His wages went to heroin.

Gabrielle first used heroin with an old boyfriend in Montreal, in her first year of nursing school. He dumped her after she was expelled for stealing needles. She met Leo at the sausage cart, after a Canadians hockey game.

"He was so shy," she said. "He couldn't look any of the girls in the eye, and such a gentleman. I knew right then, he was the one I was looking for." They shacked up within a month. "We made a home together before we made love."

They stayed in Montreal six years together, shooting up as many as six times a day, until an overdose nearly killed Leo. Gabrielle wiped a tear as she remembered. "We made a pact to get cleaned up together and start over in Lowell, because I got a cousin here someplace."

They rehabbed in Canada for two months, and then rode a bus here.

"We got this motel room," she said. "The guy in the next room was selling heroin. There's no excuse. It was there. We bought it."

Their money soon ran out. Other addicts had taken them here.

"What about your cousin?" Eddie asked.

She shrugged. "That's the part that didn't work out."

"What do you do for money?"

"Leo works at a garage sometimes, under the table," Gabrielle said. She looked to Leo and frowned. "I did some streetwalking, but when he found out it broke his heart so I stopped."

Leo pretended not to hear her. He let go of her hand and tossed a stick on the fire, which was burning just fine.

They were so blunt, so open with their story. Would they tell it to the paper? Eddie couldn't help himself—despite Danny's death and his own near miss, he was born to tell stories such as this. He trembled at the possibility. "Does the city know you're here?" he asked.

"Cops do," Gabrielle said. "They kick us out every few months when they're looking for somebody on a warrant. We find someplace to bed for the night, just for one night. Mostly they don't mind us. None of them want to come down here."

"What about rehab?"

Leo and Gabrielle glanced to each other, sharing past hardships with their eyes. He took her hand again. "Leo's been to rehab three times," she said. "I been twice." She patted Leo's knee with her other hand. "The last time he did real good. He got a Section-Eight apartment in Centralville for a couple months. But when he couldn't get me to stop, he started using again."

Eddie shook his head. "You guys are not what I would have expected in heroin addicts."

"What is that?" snapped Leo, suddenly annoyed. "You thought we would be gibbering like lunatics and lying in our own piss? Eh? That I could not talk to you like a person? Or love my wife like a man?"

Eddie said nothing. Leo was right. Eddie had not expected they'd be human.

Leo took a white candle and the lemon juice from the milk crate.

"Let me tell you about heroin," he said with no trace of annoyance. "It is the heart of this city's underground economy. Think of the heroin trade like the *shadow* of regular commerce. It lies just behind it, and touches only at the bottom. This economy works in a circle. I will explain."

He twisted the butt end of the candle into a hole in the cement. "Addicts, as you say, people like me, get money for heroin from petty theft—car radios sometimes, smash-and-grab. The pawn brokers and the glass shops get some spin-off business—this is our economics." He flashed that beige smile.

He pulled from his coat a tin snuffbox and a fat pinch of tan powder twisted in plastic wrap. He held it up. "The hero of the underworld," he said. He emptied the powder in the tin and shook his head. "It is crap. Mostly brown. Not the best. Not pure."

Eddie nodded.

Leo stroked Fat Boy as the cat wandered away. Then he continued, "Look at the other economic forces working here. To stop my petty crime, the city hires more policemen. But you cannot fit all of us in the jail, right? So you treat us." Leo lit the candle with a cigarette lighter. The wick was too long and the flame burned tall and smoky.

"To treat all of these people, the government starts new programs. And they hire more counselors to rehabilitate us. That is a net job creation. Economics—see?" He sprinkled a few drops of lemon juice in the tin. "Some of us make it and become clean. Some go back to the spike and die."

He swirled the tin in the candle flame. "To make new customers, maybe my paper boy cuts his price, maybe a little—"

Eddie interrupted. "Your paper boy? Is that what you call your heroin dealer?"

"Yes. This is funny to you?"

No, not funny, just ironic. Eddie didn't want to say yet that he worked for the paper. He cocked an ear toward the distant clack of a coming train. "Are we safe under here?"

"The train comes every hour at quarter past," Leo said. He smiled. "It is a most noisy wristwatch."

Eddie said, "So you were saying, the dealer cuts his prices?"

"Maybe a little, and he adjusts his strategy," Leo explained. "You can snort heroin too, he tells everyone. And you—mister nine-to-five job—you might say you would never touch the needle. But you will sniff the powder. Maybe you cut it with ecstasy the first time, that yuppie drug. This is just recreation, right?"

He blew out the candle and fanned the mixture in the tin with an open hand.

Leo stared Eddie in the eye. "I promise you would like it, you would. Just takes a week and then you have a habit." He grinned, and then whispered. "But the secret is this—snorting is never as good as the first time."

He took the needle from his coat and held it up. "Ah-ha!" he yelled in joy. "You hear that shooting in the vein is better than snorting—maybe it's more like the first time, you hope." He loaded the needle with the mixture in the tin. It was the color of root beer.

His smile fell and he said, "And then you are here, with us, under this bridge. And you steal for money, smash and grab. It is a circle."

Gabrielle clapped lightly. "I love to hear you talk," she told Leo. To Eddie, she said, "Couldn't he have been a professor?" She didn't wait for an answer. Instead, she wrapped a tourniquet of torn nylons around her left biceps and slid up her sleeve. Swollen needle marks ravaged her forearm like little purple leeches. Leo gave her the needle.

Eddie had seen enough. He crawled to his suit. His wallet was still in the jacket pocket. The crisp twenty-dollar bill he had was gone—probably on its way into Gabrielle's arm. Small price to pay for a lift from the canal, he decided. His cell phone and shoes were gone, but his keys had survived the trip down the canal in his pants pocket. He left the suit for Leo. It was too small anyway.

Gabrielle pulled out the needle and slipped the syringe behind her ear like a pencil. After just ten seconds, she tilted her head back and moaned, "Candy-coated."

Leo lit the candle again. Eddie's mind raced for the right way to ask if they'd sit for an interview. Sweet-talking was out—they had no vanity to flatter. A direct approach, he decided. He said, "Aren't you guys curious about what I was doing in the canal?"

Leo shook his head. "You made somebody mad, probably. You are not the first. I do not want to know any more."

"That's right," Eddie said. "I'm a writer at the paper. I got in trouble sticking my nose where I shouldn't. Look, I need a new story, and I think you two would be great."

Gabrielle said nothing. Did she even hear him?

Leo thought for a moment and then dismissed the idea. The approaching train grew louder. Under the bridge, the noise echoed chaotically. Leo spoke up over the rumbling, "Us? Nobody wants to read about what they wish did not exist."

Not exactly a yes, but short of a no. There was hope.

"People need to see their community, all of it," Eddie shouted. "If they don't like something, maybe that forces them to do something about it."

"Like run us out of here?"

That was still not a no. "Like getting you some housing and more treatment. Maybe by spending more money on the methadone clinic." Over Leo's shoulder, a chewed-up black cat spied on the humans from behind a pile of empty soup cans. It was missing half an ear. Eddie pointed to the cat, "And by getting that guy a warm home."

Leo looked. "That is Ghost Cat. He will not eat if we are watching." He poured more cat food onto the cement. "Pretend he is not here. Be busy for a minute."

A silver freight train barreled into view. Eddie crawled toward his suit to check the pockets again, but stopped at the stained Polo wallet he had found in the jacket. No money inside, no family photos. There was a Massachusetts driver's license in a credit card slot. Eddie knew the face.

The wallet belonged to Daniel P. Nowlin.

Leo was paying Eddie no attention. He knelt beside the candle, melting more heroin. He tilted the tin to collect the brew in a corner. The edge of the metal box split the fire into a forked tongue.

A guttural roar escaped Eddie's throat. He scrambled on all fours to Leo, grabbed his overcoat and slammed him to the cement. The cat hissed and dashed away. Adrenaline hardened Eddie's lazy muscles. He stuck the wallet in Leo's face and screamed over the roar of the approaching train, "Where did you get this?"

Leo whimpered. He struggled to wrench free. He was so weak. *How did he ever carry me up here?* Eddie gripped Leo's coat with both hands and shook him.

"Where did you get this?"

"Found it," he stammered.

"You found it where?"

"Let me go."

Eddie pulled him close and spoke slowly. "Tell me where you found this wallet or you're going over the ledge."

The train sped into the shadow of the bridge on a cyclone of wind. Paper hamburger wrappers around the ledge danced in glee.

Leo looked Eddie in the eye, and then glanced past him, over Eddie's shoulder.

Eddie turned to see. Too late. The snakeskin-tattooed man was planted behind him. He cocked a four-foot length of firewood like a baseball bat. Eddie shut his eyes.

"Snake!" Gabrielle's voice was loud over the train, but calm.

Eddie looked in time to see Snake check his swing. Nobody moved. The four of them waited as the train clattered under them. Their eyes blinked out swirling dust. Eddie coughed. The last car finally passed, sucking the energy from a furious cloud of paper trash under the bridge, which floated, exhausted, to the ground.

Gabrielle shouted at Eddie, "We buy from a guy in the Acre who works the projects near the canal. We were walking to meet him when we took the wallet off a guy, okay? He was in the water, just like you were. But he was dead, froze like ice, that guy, and beat to shit. He didn't need the money."

Eddie let Leo go. Both men panted. Eddie's hands trembled with unused adrenaline. Could he believe them? *If they killed Danny, why save me?*

"I'm sorry," Eddie said. He held up Nowlin's license. "I knew this man. I think somebody killed him. And I thought—you folks saved my life. I had no business—" His head ached behind his eyes.

Leo smiled beige. "You shocked me," he said. "Passion is rare among the numb." He glanced to the tracks. "Would you have thrown me off the ledge?"

Eddie shook his head. "A bluff."

Leo grinned at Gabrielle. "Do you think it is safe to sit for an interview with this man?" he asked her. "Maybe we pick someplace lower to the ground, eh?"

Chapter 11

Eddie planned the structure of the story while under a scalding shower at home. He'd open with Leo and Gabrielle under the bridge, recreating the first time they shot up together on the ledge. Then he'd flash back to earlier in their lives, and tell their story chronologically from there. The story would need a hundred and fifty inches of newsprint to be told right, he figured.

Reporters dreamt about this kind of material. Maybe this story could win the Associated Press editor's award Eddie had been chasing for years. That was a ticket to a big-city daily.

Eddie left a message at the police station for Detective Orr. He was battered and aching, joyful to be alive, and done nosing into Nowlin's death, but Orr needed to hear about the old triple-decker, and about the two guys who had dumped him in the canal.

The news deadline had long passed by the time Eddie dragged into work in mid-afternoon. Reporters slouched around their desks, working the phones without the pressure of deadline.

Boyce Billips, the paper's editorial intern, dashed to Eddie. He was a tiny, nervous kid of twenty-one, with a pinched face and a giant triangular slab of nose. You couldn't plug Boyce's nostrils with Spanish olives, though it might be funny to try. Boyce was the product of too much therapy; he was an over-analyzed hypochondriac addicted to his own ailments. Some people coddled Boyce and his neuroses; Eddie liked him too much for that, though he was annoyed with Boyce at the moment over the useless emails he perpetually forwarded to Eddie's account, usually health warnings for diseases nobody had ever heard of.

Boyce looked whiter than usual. "I think I'm dying," he moaned.

"Everybody's dying, Boyce," Eddie said. "Interns who spam my email account tend to die sooner, so knock it off."

"But my little finger just moved."

Eddie walked toward his desk. "If my hands weren't so sore, my middle finger would be moving with a message for you."

Boyce persisted, shadowing him. "No, I mean it moved by itself," he said. "That's a spasm. What if it's Parkinson's?"

"Have you been surfing on-line medical pages again? Last time you thought you had rabies."

Boyce was indignant. "There was a sparrow in my bedroom the last time."

"I know, I know—and it was acting all crazy."

"There's no cure once rabies sets in."

Eddie sighed and rubbed his temples. "Boyce, the sparrow went crazy because it got locked in your house. Wild animals don't appreciate indoor living."

"What about my finger?"

"Keep it off the panic button."

Boyce stopped and considered the advice. He called after Eddie, "Keyes is looking for you."

"Good. I'm looking for him."

Eddie left the intern in his wake and settled gingerly in at his desk. The overcoat he had left at the funeral home was over the chair. *God bless you, Melissa.*

The day's edition of The Empire was on his desk. Eddie scanned it—no mention of Danny Nowlin. He slapped it down. His hand throbbed. *There wasn't going to be any follow-up, was there?*

A receptionist had taped a pink while-you-were-out message to his computer: Congressman Hippo Vaughn had called the newsroom three times.

Eddie paged the congressman.

Vaughn called back in two minutes. "Where have you been?" he demanded.

"On ice."

"I found some things you'll want to know."

Eddie cleared his throat. He took a deep breath and pushed it out in a huff. Vaughn didn't like to be disappointed. "No hurry, Hippo," he said. "I'm not as hot for that info as I was."

"What!" The cry burrowed into Eddie's eardrum. "God-dammit," Vaughn raged. "Are you bagging this like Clemens did in the eighty-six World Series?"

"Something like that."

Hippo Vaughn did not give up easily—or ever, really. "There's a candlelight rally to save the old church tonight at six," he said. "I gotta wave the flag there before Manny Eccleston and his henchmen tear it down. See my press staff when it's over. They'll have something for you."

"Can it wait a day?" Eddie said. "I'm feeling a little beat up, Congressman."

"Don't get formal with me, you little shit," Vaughn shouted. "You'll be there." Click.

Franklin Keyes was in his office, behind the desk. The room smelled like drugstore aftershave, a brand a high school boy would wear on a date. Keyes checked his watch when Eddie came in. "Bourque, I was going to send for you in a few minutes."

"I have an idea to pitch," Eddie said. "Strong stuff, but it's going to take some off-staff time to do it right. Maybe two weeks. And I'll need a photog."

Keyes gestured for Eddie to sit down. "Wow—what happened to your hands, Ed?" he asked.

"It's nothing. This story—"

"Doesn't look like nothing," Keyes said, interrupting. "Looks like you got into something. I'm worried." He folded his hands on the desk and bunched his brow in a look of concern. He was baiting Eddie, but into what?

"I'm all right, Franklin," Eddie said, using the editor's full first name, which subordinates rarely did at the office. "Let's talk journalism, all right?"

Keyes nodded.

Eddie told him about the community of addicts under the bridge, about Leo and Gabrielle and the stray cats. "At heart, this is a love story," Eddie explained. "Leo and Gabrielle, like Romeo and Juliet with needle marks. It's fabulous material."

Keyes shrugged. "Doesn't Romeo die in the play?"

"They both die." He sighed. "Forget Shakespeare—that's not the best example."

The wrinkles in Keyes' brow spread to the corners of his mouth. "What is?"

"Just look at the danger they're in under that bridge."

"Like they're killing each other?"

"Like they have no home and they're addicted to heroin," Eddie said. "Any injection could be fatal. Yet they're still together, as a couple. Love triumphs over all."

Keyes grabbed a purple lollipop from his top drawer and unwrapped it with the rapt attention of a man defusing a bomb. With the pop in his mouth, he said, "Sounds like a bunch of dope addicts in love with dope."

"Addiction isn't love," Eddie offered. "But you could say heroin has muscled in on their relationship and made this a love triangle—all the better for the drama of the story. These people appear to be the dregs of the city, yet they have their own kind of honor and compassion." Eddie found himself writing the story out loud. "And they have love, Frank, a deep, soul-rattling love. Our readers in suburbia pay thousands to marriage counselors in search of the love that these addicts manage to have under a goddam railroad bridge."

Keyes shrugged. He jiggled in his chair. "Why should I care?"

Wasn't it obvious? Even to Keyes? "Because every good story is about people and their struggles," Eddie said.

"And?"

Eddie felt his face flush. This wasn't supposed to be so hard. "Most of Lowell travels that bridge every day. The citizens of this underworld are literally right under our noses."

Keyes paused a moment. He twirled the lollipop, and then his face creased like a raisin. He shook his head. "I'm not impressed," he said. "Why do we want to glorify a bunch of dope fiends?"

"Nobody is glorifying anything," Eddie answered, his voice rising. "These people are part of Lowell. We cover Lowell."

"So why don't they get jobs?"

"You got openings for heroin addicts?"

Keyes snickered. He sucked on the pop, and then pulled it out, waved it back and forth and said, "I don't know why some reporters are drawn to this stuff. Must be some kind of liberal bent."

He's going to torpedo the story. "These people are as much a part of Lowell—"

Keyes cut him off. "Aren't there some respectable people you can write about?"

"What do you mean by respectable?"

"People who take lunch pails to work every day. How about them?"

Eddie's mouth dried out. "Nobody wants to read about the plane that lands safely."

"And so who are these bridge people? The plane crashes?"

"In a manner of speaking."

Keyes leaned forward on his elbows. There was finality in his voice when he said, "If your dope-fiend friends go down in an airplane, you can write about them."

Eddie's chest tightened. He said weakly, "You're spiking this idea?"

"Consider it spiked."

Eddie sat quiet for a moment. He got an involuntary mental image of his resumé curling black in the flame of Leo's candle, under the bridge. Without thinking, he blurted, "What are you pulling here?"

Keyes looked at Eddie. He crushed the lollipop between his molars and chewed the candy down. Then he said, "I'm pulling your idea. And if I don't get some production out of my political reporter, I'll be pulling you off the beat."

Eddie ignored the answer. He tried to ignore his shaking hands, decided he couldn't, and tucked them under his armpits. "You forced Phife to rewrite my shooting story, you pulled the plug on the Nowlin follow-ups and now this. What's going on, Frank?" He studied Keyes' face for a reaction and saw nothing unusual, just heated arrogance.

"I should be asking you what's going on," Keyes said. "When this paper took you back after all these years, it expected a better return on its investment."

"Me? What are you talking about?"

"You sensationalized the shooting. This isn't a supermarket tab."

"That story was dead-on."

"And now you want to glorify a bunch of drug dealers."

"They're not dealers, they're addicts," Eddie said, sharply.

Keyes slapped his hands over his heart and rolled his eyes. "Forgive me," he roared. "Wouldn't want to slander their good name."

Eddie fought to get back to his point. "What about the Nowlin follow-up stories? You can't pretend that's not news."

Keyes shook a finger at Eddie. He lowered his voice. "That's not for you to say. This organization will act in the best interest of everyone involved, including Daniel and his family. There's no need to drag them through the mud."

"Not if it turns out to be accidental," Eddie said. Not likely, considering his own experience. "But what if it was murder? You gonna sweep a murder under the rug?"

"There you go, sensationalizing again," Keyes said. He glared at Eddie. "I have sources in this town, Bourque, people who wouldn't tell you the time if you had a subpoena, and going by what they tell *me*, you got it all wrong." Keyes paused, looked down at his desk and said, "There was no murder."

Keyes' position did give him contact with the city's power-brokers, including the police. But what could he have learned about Danny?

Somebody knocked three times on the glass door.

The editor waved that somebody into the office. Detective Orr. She was out of uniform, taking "plain clothes" too literally in a long tan dress that hung like a sack.

Eddie stood when she entered. Pain zapped him in the hip.

Orr slapped her silver metal briefcase on Keyes' desk and clicked the locks open.

Keyes watched her open the case. "Detective, you didn't have to come all the way here for this." To Eddie, he said, "Weren't you just leaving?"

"Mr. Bourque stays," Orr said, rooting around in her briefcase. "As I explained on the phone this morning, Mr. Keyes, we found something that belongs to this newspaper."

Orr took a plastic zipper bag from her briefcase and plunked it on the desk. There was a cellular telephone inside, or what was left of one. The device was melted and smeared with soot. Something worse than roaming charges had gotten to Eddie's phone in the old triple-decker.

Keyes frowned at the phone, and then said to Eddie, "Did you lose something at that fire last night?"

They stared at him. The weight of their eyes pushed Eddie back into the chair.

"I don't—what fire?" he said.

Annoyed, Keyes said, "Haven't you seen the paper today?" He held up a copy. A firefighter was silhouetted against yellow flames in a two-column photo on page one.

Eddie snatched the paper from him. "I saw it," he admitted, "but I didn't read the story."

The headline said:

FIRE CONSUMES VACANT HOUSE
Officials Suspect Arson in Acre Blaze

Eddie recognized the house; it was where he had fallen through the floor.

He read the story:

By Russell Spaulding
Empire Staff

LOWELL—*A three-alarm fire leveled a vacant triple-decker apartment house in the Acre neighborhood last night, forcing the temporary evacuation of a dozen nearby homes.*

Nobody was hurt by the fire in the boarded-up building, though one firefighter suffered an apparent heart attack on the scene and was transported by ambulance to Lowell Methodist Hospital. He was listed this morning in serious condition.

Fire officials have labeled the blaze "suspicious," and are searching the rubble for evidence of arson....

Detective Orr gave him time to read to the end, and then said, "The firefighter who was stricken on the scene has four kids, Mr. Bourque. In grade school."

Is she accusing me of arson?

"I don't know anything about this fire," he insisted.

Keyes suggested, "Maybe you lent your company cell phone to some arsonists, and they roughed you up when you asked for it back? Or are those burns on your hands?"

Detective Orr looked Eddie up and down. Eddie saw her eyes linger a moment on his hands.

"Mr. Bourque and I need a place to speak in private," she said to Keyes.

"Don't worry," Keyes said, clearly enjoying himself. "They can't hear us in the newsroom."

Detective Orr scrunched her brow. "I'd prefer if *nobody* could hear us."

"I had this office soundproofed," Keyes assured her. She frowned at him and he got it. "Oh." He looked at Eddie, who jerked a thumb toward the door. Keyes made a sour face, took a yellow lollipop from his desk, and then left, yanking the door shut.

Eddie held up his hands. "These aren't burns."

"Obviously," Orr said. "You should ice that bump on your head, it will keep the swelling down." She was calm and businesslike. Eddie didn't like that, though he couldn't decide why. She leaned against Keyes' desk, folded her arms and said, "This is the part where you tell me what happened to you last night."

He noticed how she had put the question. *What happened to you?* was less accusatory than *what did you do?* It was an old reporter's technique to avoid putting people on guard. This cop was good, Eddie decided. But he was already on guard, rattled by the news of the fire and by his conversation with Keyes.

Eddie said, "I want to know what happened to Danny."

"So do I."

He told her about the Cambodian woman at the wake, and of his fall through the floor and splashdown in the canal. "Some, ah—homeless people saved me," he said, glossing over his night with the addicts. No need to get Leo and Gabrielle busted on heroin charges, he told himself, though he also felt a twinge of instinct to protect his story, spiked or not.

"I don't know anything about the fire," Eddie insisted. "I'm as shocked as you are." His words sounded ridiculous to his own ear.

Detective Orr didn't seem shocked. She didn't seem *anything*.

"How did you know to follow this woman from the wake?" Orr asked.

"I saw her at the scene when your buddies found Danny's body, saw her just for a second. Seemed suspicious she'd be at the wake, too."

"And you remembered her? With all that was going on?"

"You don't forget this woman." He quickly added, "Or I wouldn't, being a man—though, I guess, some women might remember her, too. I didn't mean *you* when I said you don't forget this woman—um—she was sorta tall." *Oh please just shoot me.*

Orr opened her briefcase again, taking from it a yellow legal pad and a cheap plastic pen. She sat in Keyes' chair. "Do you have family in the area?" she asked.

The questioned jarred Eddie. He fidgeted. "My mother's two sisters, the women who raised me, still live in Dracut," he said.

Orr wrote that down.

"My mother lives outside of Boston. It's been a while since I checked where. My father lives in Arizona."

"Any siblings?"

How to answer that? "A brother. Henry Bourque," Eddie said. "He's not in the area. He lives in New York." Eddie thought about stopping there, but figured she'd hear the whole story eventually. He added, "He's in prison, for murder."

If Detective Orr was surprised, she didn't show it. She wrote the information down, and then said, "Let's go through yesterday's events again from the beginning, more formally this time."

She's testing me. He felt Nowlin's wallet in his back pocket, and for a moment considered showing it to Orr.

But then he thought about what Keyes had said. *Who had told Keyes that Danny's death wasn't a homicide?* Was that why the paper had been so quick to drop the Nowlin story without pushing the police to release the cause of death? It stunk like a cover-up, and Detective Orr could be in on it.

Eddie retold his story, omitting Danny's wallet. He would check it out later.

Orr recorded Eddie's tale in shorthand. When he had finished, she read over what she had written. "What are we missing?"

Eddie sat there, thinking about how often he was blinking, and whether it was too damn often or not often enough. "That's all I know."

Detective Orr lifted an eyebrow. She picked up the bag holding Eddie's melted cellular phone, held it to the light and inspected it, frowning. "I'll call you, Mr. Bourque, when I find your nameless ponytail-swiping Cambodian woman.

"And if this unforgettable woman tries to contact you," Orr said, "I would recommend that you not forget to call *me*."

She tossed him the bag.

Chapter 12

"Edward Bourque, you are such a rat."

The insult carried across the newsroom. Eddie tried to steer around Melissa, but she stepped into his path, hands on her hips, her right foot tapping.

"You abandoned me at that funeral home yesterday and all sorts of dreadful political types spent the afternoon slithering all over me," she said. "How do you deal with those people?" Her breath smelled of coffee, some sort of hearty dark roast.

Coffee. Eddie hadn't had any coffee. No wonder his head ached and his IQ had fallen by fifty points.

"I'm sorry," Eddie said. "I got problems."

"I could name a few," she offered.

He threw up his hands. "Keyes just spiked the best feature idea I've ever had, the cops are on my ass, two goons tried to maroon me on an iceberg, my hip is killing me, and if my caffeine withdrawal gets any worse, I'm driving to the train station to piss on the third rail."

He walked around her.

Melissa called after him, "Maroon you on a *what?*"

"Read about it in my obit."

The lunchroom coffee machine took Eddie's three quarters and filled a paper cup with a long squirt of steaming gray java. It burned away his brain fog like morning sun.

Back at his desk, Eddie locked Danny's wallet in a drawer, and then threw himself into his job to escape the problems of the morning. He rewrote two press releases into briefs for the political page, and then harassed a few candidates by phone for biographical information he needed for his election coverage. Then he drafted a top for his election analysis:

LOWELL—*The November City Council election will be about the philosophy of spending taxpayers' money.*

Not whether to spend it—all the candidates have plans for every penny of bounty from the city's property taxes. The question is what that money should buy.

A block of powerful incumbents, led by Councilman Manuel G. Eccleston Jr., favors spending public money on brick-and-mortar capital projects. Public development begets private investment, they argue.

Most of the challengers want to spend more on social service programs. Basic human needs, such as education and housing, must come before concrete and steel, they insist.

Okay, that was the premise. Now he had to back it up. For that, he needed a few more interviews, and the background clips on the candidates, which at this time of day were a pain to get. Twice a day, the library courier was paroled from the basement—Middle Earth, it was called at The Empire—to deliver any files reporters had requested. But the morning run had already come. He'd have to fetch the clips himself.

The elevator doors opened to the mildewed smell of eight decades of newspaper clippings decomposing inside scores of metal filing cabinets. The Empire library was a file cabinet graveyard. Every old four-drawer, too creaky, dented, or homely for life in the office world was condemned to eternity there, damned to hold generations of hackneyed clippings, from breathless reports about the crowds at the Lowell Folk Festival to every recorded nuance in the history of septic systems in Dunstable.

The cabinets ringed the four walls of the windowless basement, and three sides of the elevator shaft. More cabinets, stacked back-to-back, formed islands throughout the chamber. Slanting stacks of newsprint were piled everywhere upon the cabinets. Some piles reached to the flickering fluorescent tube lights in the ceiling. They cast shade on the floor.

Eddie called out over the maze, "Durkin?"

"Who's there?"

"Eddie Bourque. I need a file."

There was a clink-tap, clink-tap of metal crutches and one boot on the cement floor. Durkin, the records librarian, liked to come to you. Showed that he was not a cripple just because a North Vietnamese satchel charge had blown off his left leg when he was a teenager on patrol in the A Shue Valley. Above his crutches, Durkin's huge shoulders bulged and throbbed like he was smuggling pot-bellied pigs up his sleeves. His silver hair was slicked straight back and his goatee was stiff like wire. He kept a diamond stud in his left earlobe.

He looked Eddie over and grinned. "Who beat the shit outta ya?" His voice was deep and hoarse.

"I fell."

Durkin laughed. "Into a wood chipper, it looks like. What are you bench pressing these days?"

"Not as much as you."

"Obviously." He balled his right hand into a fist the size of a croquet ball, which he shook at Eddie. "Why, I could lick you with one arm."

"You'd have to catch me first on that one wheel, old man," Eddie said.

Durkin chuckled, like an idling bulldozer. Durkin thrived on conflict. Eddie had met his challenge, and now Durkin was ready to help him.

"What do you want?"

"The clip file for the current crop of City Council candidates."

"Oh yeah, bunch of Einsteins there, eh?" He tugged his beard, in thought. "Council candidates—right—right. That's filed under general heading O, in the temporary drawer of subcategory P. Over here, row five." He crutched through the alleys between the cabinets.

Durkin's filing system had for years confounded the newsroom staff. "Why wouldn't it just be under C?" Eddie asked.

Durkin roared, "C? That wouldn't work." He explained, "Would that be C for council, for city council or for candidate? Maybe C for city of Lowell?" He grimaced and shook his head. "Too many options. Gets confusing. In the old days, we'd file it under E for election, but there's so many E's in modern language. Most popular letter in the alphabet. Did you know that, son? Though I prefer S."

Eddie nodded.

"In a perfect world, we'd find the candidate file under V, for vote," he continued. "Except that the V cabinets are full. So we drop to the second letter of the word and look in O." He stopped at an unlabeled cabinet and drummed his fingertips on the top. "That's this year's election, so we go to subcategory P, for the present. That file stays twelve months in what we call the temporary drawer, and then we move it to subcategory L, for last year."

Eddie started to ask what would happen after next year, but thought better of it.

Durkin yanked open the top drawer, thumbed through manila files and handed Eddie a thick folder marked "City Council candidates." In it, Durkin had filed every story written about the council race this season.

Eddie nodded and thanked him.

Durkin tugged his goatee again. "Before you go, Bourque, I got something to ask you. Over here."

Eddie followed him to his desk, which was covered with file folders, cuts of newspaper, and back issues of *Soldier of Fortune*. Durkin looked through a ledger. "Near as I can tell, you have three outstanding files," he said. "These are the archives, son. Archeologists will uncover this place in a thousand years. With any luck, by then I'll be dead. But I want these records to be complete. You've got two files on political appointments and the housing sale statistics from last year."

"You gonna fine me three cents a day?"

"Nope. But I may twist your head backwards so you can watch me kick your ass."

Eddie laughed. "Fair enough. I'll send the files back."

Durkin glanced further down his list and frowned. "Another thing," he said in a low voice. "Nowlin had some files out. I don't want to tear through the man's desk, you know? If you see them, could you send them down?"

"What did he have?"

"Bunch of files on Cambodia."

Cambodia? Eddie took the ledger. Most of the entries were printed in soft pencil, in Durkin's heavy block letters. The Cambodia files were signed out in ink, in Nowlin's light, slanted handwriting. He had taken them out four weeks before he died, according to the date he had entered in the ledger.

"Did he check these out when you weren't here?" Eddie asked.

"Must have. I don't like it, but I realize this is a twenty-four-hour business."

"How'd he ever find them?" Eddie asked. "Where were they filed?"

"Under C."

"C? For Cambodia? That makes sense."

"No. C for country," Durkin said. "They're supposed to be under A, subcategory S. That's for Asia, Southeast, where we keep most of the Cambodia files. The ones he took wouldn't fit there, so they got parked in C while I was looking to vacate some space."

Nowlin had taken every Cambodia file he could find. And then a breathtaking woman of Cambodian descent stole a lock of his hair at his wake. "Gimme the rest of those files," Eddie said. "This could be important."

Durkin nodded. "Affirmative. They're in row five." He pointed. "Thataway."

Eddie was confused. He pointed in the other direction. "Weren't we just in row five, over that way?"

"This is the other row five."

"Why," Eddie pleaded, "is this place organized like a Mensa exam?"

The big man smiled. Light twinkled off his diamond earring. "Job security, son," he said. "Job security."

◇ ◇ ◇

Eddie spent the rest of the afternoon at his desk, the Cambodia files in his lap and a vending machine coffee in his hand. The concussion had left him with a vague headache, a heavy feeling in his head. His neck was getting sore, too. He filled a plastic sandwich bag with ice from the lunchroom freezer and taped it to the back of his neck.

Nowlin had taken the entries about Cambodian immigration, which had peaked in Lowell a few years after the Khmer Rouge regime fell from power. Eddie's quick search of Nowlin's desk didn't turn up those files.

Danny had missed the folders on Cambodian businesses, festivals and culture. Why hadn't he just asked Durkin for them? The question troubled him.

Most of the files were flimsy, just like the newspaper's half-assed coverage of the Cambodian community. The Empire had been slow to recognize the flood of Cambodian immigrants to Lowell. Most came straight from refugee camps in Thailand to the triple-deckers of the Acre.

One file was fatter than the telephone book. It was a collection of stories on Sawouth "Samuel" Sok, a reclusive Lowell philanthropist who had immigrated to the Acre with two sons soon after the Vietnamese army drove the Khmer Rouge from power. Though he never talked about it for the record, Sok had somehow survived the four-year Khmer

Rouge genocide, which killed some two million Cambodians, including most of the country's educated people.

Samuel Sok converted to Catholicism in America, made a fortune in historic home renovation and tried to give away his money as fast as he could make it, it seemed. Ten years ago, he had retired to an estate deep in Lowell's most affluent neighborhood.

Eddie found a clip from Sok's last public appearance, five years ago at the annual St. Patrick's Day breakfast. He had not been seen in public since, but his charitable contributions continued. According to another clip in the file, Sok had given more than a million dollars to local causes in the last year. The most recent clip was four months old. Melissa had written it. It quoted Sok's public relations spokesman announcing a thousand-dollar donation to fly a local chess club to a tournament.

Melissa had a good line in the story: *Businessman Samuel Sok's two passions are God and chess, which he devoutly maintains in that order.*

The Gospels first, Bobby Fischer second. Made sense, even if Luke had never beaten Boris Spassky. Eddie's mind wandered to a mental image of the apostles playing a round-robin chess tournament in DaVinci's Last Supper. Half of the guys would have to move to the other side of the table. A line near the end of Melissa's story perked him from the daydream: *Sok is pondering plans to expand his sizeable influence—which he wields from Tyngsboro to Ayer, spanning the depth of the Merrimack River Valley—to promote Cambodian causes in business and politics.*

Reading past Melissa's overwriting, Eddie's eye stuck on the word "politics." He dug the notebook from his overcoat and found the name of the political action committee he had jotted down: the GLCI PAC.

He called the state Office of Campaign and Political Finance in Boston and confirmed a hunch. The PAC was registered as the Greater Lowell Cambodian Interest Political Action Committee. Its co-treasurers were Sarom and Pen Sok, the sons of Samuel Sok, known in Lowell by their Christian names: Peter and Matthew.

Through his PAC, Sok had spread money to the City Council incumbents. It made no sense. The challengers' platform had more to offer the immigrant population, much of which was still poor and struggling to fit in. Plus, the PAC had given money to every candidate likely to support Councilman Eccleston's plan to tear down the old church, and to redevelop the Acre immigrant neighborhood.

It was nearly six o'clock. The rally to save the old church would be starting in a few minutes. Might be worth his while, he decided, to see why Vaughn, or anybody else, would want to save the old building. Eddie rubbed his neck. Icing had not helped. Still, he found himself looking forward to meeting with Hippo. If there had been a cover-up of Danny's death, Eddie Bourque wanted to know what was worth covering up.

Chapter 13

St. Francis de Sales Church at the edge of the Acre neighborhood was completed about 1850 in gothic revival style. It's a wedge-shaped behemoth of gray Chelmsford granite, fat on the bottom and stepping up to a sharp blade at the top, decorated by a spine of jagged spires. Stone buttresses, guarded by gargoyles that spit in the rain, jut out into overgrown shrubs along the long sides of the building. The huge stained glass windows between the buttresses are dark and meaningless from the outside.

Twenty stone steps lead to a main church entrance of three oaken double-doors, recessed within gothic archways. Twin spire towers are the building's most imposing feature. Soaring a hundred fifty feet, the towers are festooned from the ground to their needle-like tips with ornamental arches and columns, mini-spires and spikes.

The church had been closed about seventeen years. Momentum had been building among Lowell's inner circle of politicians to take the land for redevelopment. Grass-roots opposition, organized under the name SAVIOR, had hastily assembled to save the church, with Congressman Vaughn's blessing.

The opposition had yet to get any ink in the paper. Franklin Keyes had low regard for political amateurs, especially neighborhood groups, and had ruled that the issue lacked the critical mass to make a full-blown story. He had not bothered to assign a reporter to the save-the-church rally.

The Empire was missing a good story. Volunteers from SAVIOR passed out candles to a crowd of about a hundred people, most of them old enough to have baptized their children in St. Francis de Sales before it closed. SAVIOR was an acronym for Save All Valuable Interests for Our Re-use. The neighborhood group was a little GOOFY (Gone Overboard On Finding an acronYm), but their motives seemed pure.

Congressman Hippo Vaughn's aide, Tabby, was toward the back of the crowd, cradling a stack of white folders. Tabby commuted from Boston to run Vaughn's district office in Lowell. Her smooth, dark skin came from her Lebanese parents. Her smoldering beauty, unspoiled with not a dab of makeup, came straight from Allah.

Whenever Eddie and Tabby spoke in person, she would tilt her head a little, curve her lips into a tiny smile, and touch Eddie's arm. Was she flirting with him? Or was he just wishful? She maintained an interminable, live-in relationship with a boyfriend who taught oboe in Central Square in Cambridge. That was all Eddie cared to know about him.

Tabby handed a radio reporter a press folder from the top of the stack. She handed Eddie the one on the bottom. "It's some history on the church and a copy of the congressman's remarks to open the rally," she explained.

"Is Hippo around?" Eddie asked.

The whites of her eyes were big and flawless behind the dark pupils. She said, "He made his comments and excused himself for another appointment."

Eddie flipped through the paperwork. "So, does Hippo really support these SAVIOR people?"

She put her hand on his and closed his folder. "The congressman's remarks are clear. You won't need his staff around to explain them." She smiled and walked off.

Eddie watched the rally for twenty minutes. Speakers addressed the crowd with a bullhorn from the front steps.

The speeches were all the same. How many ways can you say "save our heritage"? Boring.

Seated on the church steps, Eddie looked through the folder. There was Vaughn's two-page speech, which called for the church to "stay as safe as a two-run lead with The Monster on the mound," a reference to 1960s Red Sox reliever Dick Radatz. There was an old church photograph from the Historical Society, a timeline of church history, a list of well-known church members, and a copy of a twenty-year-old letter from the last pastor of St. Francis de Sales, imploring the Diocese to keep the church open to serve the Acre and its new wave of immigrants from Southeast Asia.

Eddie scanned the list of prominent church members, recognizing a handful of former mayors, a former U.S. senator and others who seemed familiar only because of the streets named after them.

One name stuck out: Sawouth "Samuel" Sok, the reclusive philanthropist whom Eddie had spent the afternoon researching.

The folder also contained a sealed white envelope. Eddie tore it open and dumped a stubby silver key into his hand. It was shiny and sharp, apparently just cut.

That was it? No instructions? Hippo Vaughn occasionally tested Eddie's patience with his bizarre sense of humor.

Eddie gathered his paperwork and looked for a conspicuous lock. He walked both blocks next to the church, spying every door and delivery truck for a padlock. No luck. The church itself, maybe? The giant double doors were shut with chains and locks, but Eddie couldn't test them with all these people around.

He walked around the church. If there were any other doors, they were hidden by thickets. Eddie checked the black and white photograph in his packet. It was taken in the 1930s, when they used to trim the shrubs. The picture showed a small door on the west side of the church, one of the long sides with the buttresses and stained glass.

He hustled around the building and battled through an overgrowth of ornamental bushes. Panting, and with fresh scratches on his hands, he reached the stone foundation. There he found a wooden door, gray and needing paint, shut by a silver padlock.

The key popped the lock. The door resisted at first. Eddie put a foot against the wall for leverage and yanked it open with one violent jerk. A steep wooden staircase, practically a ladder, rose out of sight.

"Hippo?" he called out.

Nothing.

Eddie climbed the steps. They led to the church vestibule, behind the three great oaken double-doors.

"Hippo?" he called again.

He started into the main church sanctuary, unconsciously reaching his right hand to dip a finger in the holy water at the door. The dish held naught but dust. He blessed himself anyway with the sign of the cross, and felt sheepish doing so in the long-abandoned house of worship.

The impressive outside architecture of St. Francis de Sales could not compare to the inside, which seemed even more immense than Eddie had imagined. He gaped at its beauty. Two rows of white columns, linked by sharp gothic arches, divided the main body of the church into three sections, each filled with rows of cherry wood pews separated by narrow aisles. The ceiling chamber above the center aisle, rising higher than on the sides, peaked in a web of arches and vaults adorned with scenes from the Old Testament. Moses on the mountain. An angel staying the hand of Abraham. The serpent coiled in the tree. These characters played their parts on a background painting of a starry night sky.

The setting sun lit the stained glass into the Stations of the Cross, in a pale blend of blue and red light. The figures seemed to leap from the glass. The talent of the artist—of all the artists who had made this place—was plain to Eddie.

So was seventeen years of neglect. Hunks of plaster had plunged like meteors from the ceiling and exploded into fragments on the floor. The church smelled like mildew and wet cement.

No splendor or decay could stop his eyes from lingering upon the eight-foot church crucifix, like none he'd ever seen. It dangled two stories above the church altar on wires running from the tips of the crossbeam to a black chain, which disappeared into a hole in the ceiling.

The Christ figure on the cross wore dust like snowflakes, and seemed too real for art. The head slumped forward, the eyes bulged and pleaded for help, the lips parted in a gasp. This Jesus would have spoken, "Why hast thou forsaken me?" Only its hugeness showed any artist's license. Real iron spikes through the wrists and feet pinned the plaster Christ to a cross of round timbers lashed together with rope. The lean body tensed against the nails, stretching its plaster muscles. The nude figure was positioned in a twist on the traditional crucifixion pose; the statue's legs were bent at the knees and swung to the figure's left side. A single spike piercing both feet entered through the right ankle. The twist made the figure seem even more pained and real, though it may have been designed that way just to hide its private parts.

Eddie shook off a shiver and called again for Vaughn. "Hippo? Are you here?"

The church's granite walls dampened the city noise outside. The bullhorn at the rally sounded far off. This was no place to trespass. Eddie turned to leave, but the thought of finally getting some answers about Nowlin rooted him. He had already trespassed. Might as well see it through.

The building's vastness swallowed his footsteps up the center aisle. Eddie imagined the empty pews full of nineteenth-century working-class folks on their knees, hands clasped and knuckles white. Mill workers, most of them— the carders who combed out the rough cotton fibers, the spinners who twisted the fibers into yarn, and the weavers who interwove yarn into cloth on the looms. They would have been thankful for the blessing of a job in the mills. Yet they begged for a better life. A teenaged girl who left the family farm to spin yarn made fourteen dollars a month, minus a fiver for a bunk in the company boardinghouse. Bells controlled their lives. The mill bells told them when to start work in the morning, and when to quit fourteen hours later. The bells told them when to eat and when to stop eating. The church bell called them here on Sunday.

The church's main aisle finally ended at a low wooden railing. The altar table beyond the railing was a square marble slab on granite pillars.

Eddie turned left, walking along the front row of pews, and under a high arch between two stone columns. Ahead, three confessional booths stood, along the west wall of the church. Their oaken doors had a patchwork design, and looked heavy. Tarnish blackened the brass doorknobs. The largest booth, in the middle, was where the priest would sit to hear confessions. A decorative iron bracket on the door held a glass lantern. Back when the church was active, the priest would light a candle under the lantern as a sign he was inside, ready to hear sins and dispense absolution.

The lantern was lit.

Dusk seemed to fall suddenly, robbing light from the windows and dulling the colors of the church. The candle put Eddie's shadow in a pew. And Fear nibbled his ear.

He walked in silence to the door. Hot white wax rolled down the candle. The brass doorknob was almost too big to grip. It would not turn, wouldn't even click. Could a priest be working here now?

The door on the right, where parishioners entered to confess, was unlocked. A light tug swung it open without a sound on three massive hinges. At first, there looked to be nothing in the darkness inside. Then, as Eddie's eyes adjusted, fabric drapery appeared on the walls, and a padded kneeler came into view beneath the screen that separated the parishioner from the priest. The booth smelled like a top-rate consignment shop. He stepped in. The door clicked shut behind him and the place was black. *See it through.* His heart hammered against his ribcage, wanting out through the bars of bone. Fear draped herself over him.

Eddie dropped to his knees, wincing at the pain in his hip. His right hand traced the sign of the cross. And then, in the confessional whisper he had learned in catechism, Eddie said, "Bless me father, for I have sinned."

The barrier behind the screen slid open with a bang. Fear raked her nails across his back.

"Oh, do tell, Edward, and make it juicy."

Vaughn! "You old bastard!" Eddie said, still whispering. "You nearly gave me a heart attack."

The congressman giggled. "Come now, unburden your soul, young man. And just the action, don't bore me with tales of coveting—I do plenty of that myself." Vaughn continued to giggle until Eddie couldn't help himself, and laughed along with him.

"You have always had the weirdest sense of humor," Eddie said. "When the Red Sox win the Series, I will piss on your tombstone, you crazy S.O.B."

Vaughn laughed even louder and applauded himself. "When the Sox win the Series, I'll be sitting behind home plate in a seat worth five figures. But I'll raise my cup to my old friend Eddie, who'll be watching at home on a portable TV, with a coat hanger for an antenna."

They both laughed. There's a little truth in every joke.

"I thought it important we meet this way for several reasons," Vaughn said. "The first is obvious—it was funny." He giggled some more. "Also, I want to stress to you the importance of keeping the secrets I intend to share today. Nothing is more secret than the sanctity of the confessional. Even a second-string Catholic such as yourself knows that."

"I may have lapsed, but I still know the church rules," Eddie said. "I'll protect you." He'd go to jail to protect a source. So would most of the people he knew in the business. It almost never happened, but reporters ached for the opportunity to prove their gallantry to a judge, and to each other.

Vaughn continued, "Finally, this odd arrangement offers me a wee bit of protection, should someone deduce from your future inquiries that you have inside information."

"How so?"

"I never lie, but in sensitive times I may not offer the whole truth. Should someone ask me if I proffered inside information to you, I would take umbrage, and swear, my right hand to God, that I have not seen Eddie Bourque for weeks. That is true. I did not see you come in, and we cannot see each other through the screen. *Capiscono?*"

"Yeah, I understand."

"The autopsy report is done," he said. "I was able to get the executive summary. The facts are scant, but they'll have to do." He sucked a deep breath and eased it out. "The medical examiner concluded that Daniel was viciously beaten. He was murdered."

Of that, Eddie was already sure, despite what that lying Frank Keyes had said. Still, it stung to hear the news confirmed, like when a relative on a deathbed finally passes; it was a shock, though not a surprise.

A penlight clicked on behind the screen. Vaughn crinkled some papers.

"He had orbital fractures around both eyes, and the zygomatic bones—the bones that lift the cheeks—were beat to shards with a blunt weapon. Terrible injuries, all of them, but probably survivable."

"That's survivable?"

"Most likely, though he'd need a plastic surgeon to repair the face, like reassembling a mirror that fell off the wall." He shuffled more papers. "They estimate Danny was struck between six and eight times. The worst of the blows left a depressed skull fracture over his right ear. The epidural bleeding that followed is an awful thing. The expanding clot and the skull work like the jaws of a vice, squeezing the brain as it bleeds. Even with medical attention this is often fatal."

Vaughn coughed and cleared his throat. "But that's not what killed him."

"You said it was fatal."

"In a matter of hours it would have been. But something else got him first." He shuffled still more papers. "The medical examiner has determined that Daniel P. Nowlin died of diacetylmorphine poisoning."

"In English," Eddie demanded.

"Heroin, Eddie. Danny died of a heroin overdose."

Vaughn let Eddie digest the concept in silence for a full minute. Eddie's brain recalled the image of Leo under the bridge, melting heroin in a tin. Except that the image had Nowlin's face on Leo's malnourished body. Eddie willed the image away and felt the prickle that comes before nausea. Could Leo and Gabrielle have lied about finding Nowlin's body? Could they have attacked him?

Vaughn continued, "The drugs entered through a vein in his upper left thigh and overwhelmed his system. The best guess is a dose of approximately six hundred fifty milligrams." His voice was flat, like he was dictating scientific notes about an interaction in a test tube.

"Is that a lot of heroin?"

"Depends who you are. That's probably not lethal for a daily user who might inject fifteen hundred milligrams or more, due to a tolerance built up over a long time. But five hundred is plenty to kill a casual user, or someone new to it."

"I wouldn't have noticed needle marks if Danny shot up into his leg," Eddie said. "But I can't believe Nowlin was a regular user."

"Neither does the examiner. She found no other recent needle marks on the body—I mean, on Danny." Hippo's voice seemed human again. "One more thing, the left elbow was dislocated. But there was no bleeding from a damaged artery.

That means no blood pressure, and the elbow was probably a post-mortem injury caused by something jarring."

Like being dumped in a canal.

"So Danny died of an overdose," Eddie said. "He certainly didn't smash his own melon."

"True. The blow that injured his brain came from behind. There were no defensive wounds on his hands, so it's logical Danny didn't fight back. Once a skull is crushed like that, there'd be no fight left in any man."

"Do the cops have leads?"

"Just that his computer notes were utterly destroyed by a virus, a complex one, apparently. And with nothing else to go on, here's the political reality—there's heavy pressure on the mayor to keep the investigation low-key, to minimize publicity. They assigned the case to Lucy Orr, the least experienced detective on the force. And I imagine the political pressure will make it tempting to write this off as drug-related violence, practically unsolvable."

Something about Detective Orr—her subtle intensity, maybe?—made it hard to believe she'd ever give up on anything. A detective didn't need experience to be a bulldog.

"Who's applying all this pressure?" Eddie asked.

Vaughn smacked his lips. "I'm hearing lots of things, and some point to your office."

"To The Empire? But Danny was our employee. We should be pushing the other way, for an ass-kicking investigation. Round up everybody Danny ever talked to and give 'em a polygraph."

"That would stir controversy," Vaughn said. "I've noticed the paper has been rather vanilla lately—nothing controversial at all."

Vaughn was right. "They rewrote a shooting story I did this week," he said. "Edited out the sexy parts. I heard the order came from Templeton. And Keyes lied to get me to drop Danny's story."

"Sounds like Templeton and his minions want to keep things calm before the election."

"That's no way to sell newspapers," Eddie said. "Alfred Templeton hired me to pump up the political coverage."

"He did a good thing there, bringing you back. And I'll bet that Dracula was nice to his cocker spaniel, but he still was a goddam vampire." Hippo chuckled. "I'm still not sure how Templeton ended up in charge of the paper all those years ago."

"I heard he just showed up at a board meeting in control of a majority of the shares and appointed himself publisher."

"But how he bought those shares on a journalist's salary has always mystified me," Hippo said. He fidgeted behind the screen. "His bagman called my office to offer an editorial supporting one of my pet environmental projects—if I got on board with this church redevelopment, and some other crazy project to fix this neighborhood. I'm tempted to have a press conference to expose the whole rotten deal. You know, call all the statewide media, offer them free beer and good story. Except that once I do that, The Empire brass will be out to get me forever."

"You turned down the editorial?"

"I told them to take their carrot and fuck off," Vaughn said with a chuckle. "So I got an eye out for the stick. I like this old church. The last priest they had before it closed was a real wordsmith, gave a good sermon."

"And how would a Methodist know that?"

"Your formerly fine newspaper used to print 'em every week, back in my younger days."

Eddie laughed. "Back in your younger days the Apostles would autograph your Bible. Find that priest's new church. There's nothing stopping you from hearing his sermons in person."

"Except that he ain't around—ran off to California, or something." He sighed. "People have been abandoning this church for years. Not me, though."

Eddie thanked Hippo for his help, and then got up to leave.

"Don't forget your penance," Vaughn said. "You should pay in advance for the trouble you're going to cause. Gimme a thousand Hail Marys."

Chapter 14

The advertising department at The Empire was more corporate-looking than the newsroom. Green fabric cubicles in a maze-like grid accounted for most of the floor space. The desks were neat, the ceiling tiles snowy white, and the computers new. Customers sometimes walked in off the street to do business with the advertising department, so the employees there couldn't curse like the newsroom staff. Poor pent-up bastards.

A night's sleep in his bed, rather than under a bridge, had soothed Eddie's stiff muscles, though his bruised hipbone still ached and his hands had scabbed over. He tried not to dwell on the memory of being thrown in the canal, but the experience had left him jumpy and scatterbrained.

It was just after eight in the morning, an hour before the advertising office opened. The lights were off, the place still empty. Eddie snaked through the cubicles and headed for a former walk-in closet tucked in a back corner. The hand-lettered door read "Intellectual Consultation and Technical Services Department—Stan Popko, Director."

Eddie knocked and went in. The room was long and narrow, more like a hallway that didn't go anywhere than a room. It smelled like dust and smoldering wire insulation, an odor recycled by tiny fans whirling inside a dozen humming metal boxes. The machines were spaced across steel shelves and connected by a rainbow of tangled wires draped like bunting. A police scanner was relaying the details of a traffic stop.

The computer room was smaller than two cubicles in advertising, yet contained the electronic brains for the entire news department. The shelves and wires ended at a chubby guy seated at a desk, his back to the door. He was playing a video game on a computer screen set between a microwave oven and a chrome toaster. The guy was in his late twenties, and had skin so pale it approached translucent. He thumped his keyboard and guns blazed. Monsters on the screen died in pools of their own pixilated blood.

"Excuse me, Stan?" Eddie said. "How's it goin' man?"

The chubby guy kept his eyes on the game. "I got shingles," he offered. "And you?"

Eddie needed a favor; he ignored Stan's bad bedside manner and tried for common ground. "So, is that Doom you're playing?"

Stan rolled his eyes. "It's Doom II, a classic, one of the most important games in history, and it came out long after the original Doom." He shook his head at Eddie's ignorance.

Eddie watched for a minute. "Wow, you're really slaughtering them. Computer monsters everywhere shall come to fear you."

Stan made a sour face. "Real funny," he said without smiling. "Who writes your material? Does he still have a job?"

So this is why they call him The Bitter Comic. Eddie stood by as Stan continued his game. Maybe he'd be more receptive once the universe was safe.

A robotic spider gunned Stan to death. He slammed a fist on the keyboard. "Damn!"

"Stan?" Eddie said.

He looked at the guest in his office. "You're still here?"

"I have to talk to you about computers, and I guess I need a favor."

Stan swirled a finger in his ear. He withdrew the digit and inspected the results. No wax. He frowned at the finger that had failed him. "Of course you need a favor," he said. "You want to ram some dumb computer project down my throat."

Eddie forced a chuckle to make another try at common ground. "Good one," he said.

"Huh?"

"Ram it down your throat. Computer memory is called RAM. I get the joke."

Stan perked in his chair. "You do?"

"Though it's more of a pun than a joke, right? I'm no expert."

Stan's eyeballs parked for a moment in the left corner of their sockets as his cranial circuits computed what had just happened.

"You're Bourque," he said.

Eddie nodded.

"I thought so." There was cockiness in the way he said it, as if the name was something Stan was not supposed to know. "People say you're funny, Bourque."

"People say lots of things," Eddie replied. The conversation began to feel like the stare down across the saloon before they drew their six-shooters.

Stan blurted, "I'm socially awkward."

"Really?"

"But I want to be funny."

"Well, we all do, I guess."

"No, Bourque," Stan said. "I want to do comedy on stage. I want to do it as a job."

"You do computers for a job. I hear you're a genius."

Stan sneered. "I hate computers. I hate people who need help using computers even more."

"That's a bad quality in the field of tech support, isn't it?"

Stan ignored him. "I've studied the great comedic minds, from Bennett Cerf to Bill Cosby. I've written gigabytes of original material, and polished my delivery, night after night, in a mirror." Stan looked down to his canvas sneakers. "All while trying to ignore the obvious."

"Which is?"

"Everybody is funnier than me."

"I'm sure you're funnier than you think," Eddie said, convinced that the glummest guy in the leper colony was probably a laugh riot compared to Stan.

"Make me funny, Bourque."

"What?"

"Make me funny and I'll grant your favor."

Stan could have asked Eddie to topple the Cross-Point office towers with his bare hands. At least then there'd be some hope.

"Uh, I don't think I'm qualified—"

"Then I don't think I'm qualified to help you with whatever computer problem you have." He crossed his arms over his chest. The window of opportunity was closing.

"But that's your job," Eddie protested.

"No. If it was my job, it wouldn't be a favor."

"All right," Eddie said with a sigh. "I'll try. But I can't make you funny. I can only try to unlock your—er, natural inner funniness. And no guarantees."

Stan considered the offer, and then stuck out a pudgy hand. They shook on it.

"Let's get started," Stan said.

"First, you tell me everything you know about computer viruses."

Stan took to the task with genuine enthusiasm. He lectured Eddie on what viruses can be programmed to do, and how they hide. He described how they replicate, and what may trigger them to execute their commands.

Eddie told him what had happened when Detective Orr checked Nowlin's computer.

"Sounds like a logic bomb," Stan said.

"What's that?"

"A virus set to trigger by an event, or series of events. It can sit dormant on the hard drive, or in the RAM, for days or months before it's triggered. You could open your email fifty times without a problem, for example. But the virus is keeping track. And on the fifty-first time—bam!—it drops its payload and reformats your hard drive, or sends a thousand filthy emails to every person in your address book."

Dabs of pink pooled in Stan's white cheeks. "These are often Trojan Horse programs—technically not viruses because they don't replicate. But they can be just as destructive. The Trojan Horse appears to be a benign application, until the trigger event."

"So why did it garble the text? Why not just erase it?"

"Because your saboteur is smart, that's why," Stan said. "Standard deletion doesn't actually destroy files, at least not immediately. It just tells the computer not to list that file anymore, and gives it permission to reuse that storage space on the hard drive. The computer doesn't actually write over the spot until it needs the space for something else. It could be months, depending on your use, before the file is completely written over."

Stan's breathing grew heavier. He forehead was shiny. "By garbling the files—presumably with a randomized algorithm to prevent any pattern that could be decoded later—the Trojan Horse has eliminated any chance they could be recovered."

Eddie digested the explanation, and then asked, "How did it get on Danny's computer?"

"That's the tricky part." Stan pointed to a metal box impaled with fat gray wires. "That's our firewall. All data coming into the building from the Internet must pass through it, and it's programmed to destroy any whiff of a virus."

"So the virus couldn't have come from the Web?"

The flush in his cheeks spread, as if by osmosis, over his face. "I can't guarantee the network is always clean—nobody can—but our firewall is strict," he said. "And the anti-virus software on every computer in the building is set to execute local disinfections at three o'clock every morning. I probably could write a virus to defeat our defenses. But even with my knowledge of the network, it might take weeks."

"Then how would the virus get to the newsroom?"

"I'd say it took the elevator."

"Is that a computer term?"

"Somebody walked into the newsroom and infected Nowlin's computer directly," Stan said. "Either knowingly or by accident."

"Who would know how?"

"It wouldn't take a master hacker to load a virus," he said. "Anyone with access and opportunity could do it if they knew our system. It would have to be somebody who knew Nowlin's password—either because he told them, or because they saw him type it. Or maybe it's somebody who knew him well enough to guess it."

Eddie admitted, "Nowlin told me his password on the phone a few months ago. He was home, and needed some numbers from his electronic address book. I don't know if he ever told anybody else."

"Reporters work odd hours sometimes, with few people around," Stan said. "So you could have delivered the bomb." It was an observation on his part, not an accusation. "And, since I maintain password lists for everyone, so could I."

"Could somebody have lifted Danny's password from your lists?"

Stan shook his head hard enough to disturb his blond wisps. "No way. I store them off-network. They're hidden under false names and encrypted with code I wrote myself. A hacker would need days of uninterrupted time in this room to even find them. And I assure you, nobody but me spends much time here."

Something in Stan's tone acknowledged that he was generally a bastard. Eddie listened for a hint of regret, but didn't hear any.

"If you and I didn't do it, then who?"

Stan wrenched back his fingers and cracked his knuckles one by one. The last pinkie needed three good yanks before it gave up the pop. "There's one person besides us who had both access and opportunity," Stan said. "That's Daniel Nowlin himself."

Eddie had thought the same thing. But why would Danny destroy his own notes? Maybe he knew he was in danger, and left the virus to sanitize his files in case something happened to him. Was he protecting someone? Or protecting his own reputation?

The conversation had reached its natural end and Stan was eager to change the subject. "Now for your part of this bargain," he said. "Make me funny."

"Fair enough." Eddie paused to consider where one begins when tunneling to China with a spoon. A radio test crackled over the police scanner. "Turn that damn scanner off," Eddie ordered. "And then let's start with your smile, the cornerstone of humor."

"The smile's important?"

"Are you kidding? You can't tell a decent joke with that vinegar puss. You look like a guy getting the hernia test from his elderly mother."

Eddie's logic computed, and Stan nodded. He turned down the police scanner—down, not off, but it was a start and Eddie let it slide. "Let me see you smile," Eddie said.

Stan formed a bug-eyed, jaw-clenched grin. Creepy.

"You look like a serial killer with constipation," Eddie said.

"What's wrong?"

"Goddam, man—everything." Eddie polished Stan's toaster with his sleeve. "Watch your reflection. Keep it natural. We can't go any further until we get this right."

Stan smiled into the chrome. With coaching, his grin grew a little less scary. You wouldn't run screaming from him, though you'd still want a restraining order.

"A little better," Eddie said. "Make sure you practice in your spare time."

Eddie turned to leave. Stan jumped up. "Bourque! How much should I practice?"

"Oh, try five sets of twenty smiles, three times a day."

"Three hundred a day?"

"We gotta overcome years of facial inactivity and build muscle strength. Stick to the program. I'll be in touch."

Back in the newsroom, Eddie found it nearly impossible to work with the dull ache behind his eyes. He distracted himself by checking his voicemail.

The message chilled him, like a recording from Fear herself—it was the chant he had recorded in the old triple-decker, minutes before he had fallen through the floor.

Who were those people? What did they want with Nowlin's hair? Eddie wondered if the police had found them. He called the station and spoke to the detective's bureau—no new information on who might have attacked him and thrown him in the canal.

Eddie hung up and listened to the chant again. This had to mean *something*. He transferred the message to a microcassette. Then he searched the Internet for college courses in the Khmer language, and picked one in California, near Long Beach, which had a sizable Cambodian population. The professor's office number was in the on-line campus directory. A teaching assistant answered. She was happy to help. Experts loved to help journalists; it proved they were experts. She listened to the chant three times, left the phone for a full five minutes to look something up, and then offered a translation:

Temples of stone wear to dust in the wind, and so too this body gives out. But the lessons of goodness stand forever against time.

"What the heck does it mean?" Eddie asked.

"Just what it says," she said. "It sounds like a Buddhist death chant. A monk would repeat the verse to comfort someone near death."

"And if they're already dead?"

"Then the chant could continue to help free the dead one's energies while the body is prepared for the funeral fire."

He double-checked the spelling of her name, thanked her and hung up.

The mystery woman with the red mittens had her own funeral for Nowlin? Eddie wondered if there could be an innocent explanation to account for how Danny knew that woman so well.

Who is she?

Chapter 15

General VonKatz met Eddie at the door. The cat's snout flexed as he sampled a scent in the air. He had detected the pastrami Eddie had picked up on the way home, in a bag with two bulky rolls. Eddie scooped up the cat and rubbed his head. The General's eyes closed and his purr sounded like it came from deep inside. Eddie could win a Pulitzer or lose his job; it wouldn't matter—the General purred when Eddie rubbed his head.

Eddie reviewed the battle frozen on the chessboard. He had been playing this game against himself for a month, but it had seemed trivial since his canal ride on the ice gondola with a frozen rat. He forced himself to see the game through. He advanced a pawn one square into territory thick with the enemy. It was a suicide mission, with high reward. A knight and a rook from the opposing army were trapped. Either piece could escape, but the pawn would claim the soldier left behind. Eddie spun the board around, leaving Sophie's Choice for tomorrow.

His Aunt Therese's voice was on the answering machine. He pictured her lips, caked in pink lipstick, and the way her mouth seemed to roam all over her face when she talked, like she had been painted by Picasso.

"Edwaaaard?" She stretched his name. "I have a ham planned for Sunday. Would that be all right? If you come before eleven, we won't be here. We'll be at Mass. You could come before ten, if you want, but from ten to eleven your Aunt Victoria and I will be fulfilling our Sunday obligation."

Real subtle. His aunts were always after him to get back to church.

There had been no life-defining incident that drove Eddie away from religion, no anger at God over a cosmic injustice. Eddie still believed, not in all the rituals, but he *believed*. He had simply come to think that the man in the collar—who was twice his age, never had a date and didn't pay rent—was no longer speaking to him. It seemed too convenient, anyway, to go running back to church right after somebody had tried to drown him.

Eddie realized that he had not prayed in the old triple-decker, or in the canal. He had been inches from slipping off the ice to drown, and probably minutes from freezing to death, and he did not pray. Was there something wrong with him? Or had living three decades in comfort and safety clouded his perception, making life seem stouter and more lasting than it can ever be?

General VonKatz squirmed out of his hands. Enough affection—it was time to eat. The pastrami boiled up tough. Eddie's head throbbed when he bent to put the General's share on a paper plate on the floor. Eddie slathered his portion with mustard and ate it on a roll.

Dinner ended abruptly when the lost moth fluttered into the kitchen on powdery brown wings. The General's pupils swelled. He sprang at the beast, smacking it in midair with one paw. The moth flapped backwards to the living room, staggered like a prizefighter who had walked into a left hook. General VonKatz peeled out on the linoleum, and a reckless chase ensued in the living room. It sounded like somebody bouncing turnips off the walls.

Eddie cringed and yelled, "Watch the chessboard!" The chase ended with a thump, a pause, another thump, and a hiss of frustration. The moth was back on the ceiling, pumping its wings as if exercising with an itty-bitty Thigh-master. The General crouched below, tail twitching.

"You got closer today, General," Eddie said, scratching the cat's ear. "But you just can't seem to get your paws around it, can you?" The cat assumed a sentry position on the back of the recliner, facing the evil Mothra. He licked his paw and pretended he wasn't interested anymore.

Eddie got the lone can of Guinness from the fridge. The beer flowed dark and creamy into a mug, with a head thick enough to pitch a tent on.

The General followed Eddie into the bathroom. The cat perched on the vanity to monitor water dripping from the faucet, while Eddie ran a shower. Thundering water pressure was the one perk of Eddie's rickety living quarters. He sipped Guinness and leaned backwards into a spray just shy of scalding hot.

He wiped fog from the shower door and watched General VonKatz through the glass. The cat's eyes had narrowed to diagonal slits. Eddie envied the General, who could sleep anywhere, anytime. A single untamed thought about a news story would give Eddie insomnia. Not tonight, though. Not with a belly full of fatty meat, a mug of stout in his veins, and a hot shower.

Suddenly the General perked. His ears rotated like radar cups. Eddie chuckled. "You sure hate that moth," he said.

But, no, that wasn't right. The moth was making noise?

Eddie set down his mug and shut off the water. The General hopped off the vanity without a sound and clawed at the edge of the bathroom door. It opened six inches and he stalked out to the living room.

Eddie's front door squeaked shut.

Fear rubbed cold hands over the slick of soap bubbles on his chest. He sensed movement in the next room and strained to hear. Stiff carpet fibers in the living room inhaled under the weight of a shoe, and exhaled when it lifted away.

Eddie grabbed a threadbare towel from the vanity and wrapped it twice around his right hand. He could swing as hard as he could without breaking his fist, if he got the chance.

The footsteps went past the bathroom door. Eddie got out of the tub. He tensed, hands shaking, and reached for the door. Naked and armed with a towel, he could only hope to land a clean punch and get away. He yanked open the door and stormed into the living room.

Jesse Nowlin was there, snooping in the old newspapers that Eddie kept in the piano bench.

She wore a tight sleeveless dress, maroon, with a slit up the side, black tights and heels. Her hair was teased up. Her lips matched the dress. Eddie had never seen her so dressed up, so stunning.

Jesse let the bench-top slap down, and looked Eddie over as well. He made no effort to cover up. He would not be sent scurrying in his own house. And he did not want to turn his back to her.

She grinned and winked at him. "What were you going to do to me with that thing?"

Eddie unwrapped his fist. "Nothing," he said. "Just drying off."

"I wasn't talking about the towel." She laughed and turned away. "Do you have anything to drink?"

"Beer."

"Got anything stronger?"

"Look around."

She rummaged through Eddie's kitchen cabinets. He toweled off and slicked back his wet hair with his hands. He put on jeans, an old sweatshirt and sneakers. Ugly clothes. An outfit a man wears when he's not interested in impressing a woman.

"Is this the General VonKatz you talk about?" she called out. "He's so cute."

"Yeah, that's the General." He realized Jesse had never been to his place before. Why was she there now? Danny was barely in the ground.

She spoke baby talk to the General. "Are you a cute boy? Yes you are. You're sooo cute."

Eddie had never seen Jesse without Danny, except at the wake. And even then she had been at his side. She had never flirted with Eddie, not even in his imagination.

He joined her in the kitchen. Jesse poured vodka over shrunken ice cubes in two short glasses. "You had this bottle of Absolut in the cabinet under the sink," she said. She handed him a glass and took the other for herself. Eddie followed her to the living room, where she sat in the recliner. Her coat was on the floor. The slit in her dress slid up her thigh. She did nothing to fix it.

Jesse swirled the vodka in the glass, downed a gulp, and winced.

Eddie's few experiences with hard alcohol were hard to remember. He sipped the drink. The ice had tainted the liquor with freezer burn. He leaned against the wall and watched her. Jesse was in no rush to get to the point and Eddie resolved to wait her out. Her finger traced the rim of the glass. She gulped more vodka and raised her eyebrows at the spirit's bite. Eddie studied her arms. They were well defined, yet still feminine. Most likely the work of a personal trainer, two sessions a week on the biceps machine. Were those arms powerful enough to crack her husband's skull? Maybe, if she were mad enough.

She made Eddie uneasy, just sitting there silently, fingering the glass. At the wake, she had been the ice widow. And now? He didn't know what she was. Her presence stirred his most primitive instincts. Danny's widow, the ultimate forbidden fruit, lazing in his chair with a drink and paying no mind to the rising hem of her dress.

But she repulsed him, too, for the same reasons. And it had been a long time since his carnal side called the shots. She would not see his bed tonight.

Finally, she spoke. "Have you ever lost something?"

"Not like you did," he answered.

"Loss is loss. Whether you lose out to a cemetery, or to an English teacher."

Pam's husband-to-be taught journalism in Vermont, not English, but Eddie got the point. He shrugged. "When Pam and I split, we both lost something."

"Did Pam lose you? Or leave you behind? There's a difference."

Eddie didn't like where Jesse was going with this, but he wasn't afraid, and he sought to prove it. "Pam left me, met a male model with a master's degree, and moved to a mansion with a view of the Green Mountains," he said. "Her Doberman's doghouse is bigger than my place, and I bet a little nicer, too."

Jesse threw her head back and laughed. "Always the wordsmith," she said. "Danny dreamed about writing like you do."

"He was getting there."

Her voice grew bitter. "Be honest, Eddie. Danny dug the dirt better than anyone but he never made it sing. He was a hacker and a technocrat, full of facts without any spirit." She slugged more vodka. Her voice softened, all the way to sultry. "Tell me which was worse," she said. "Losing Pam, or realizing you had trusted the wrong person?" She eyed him.

Eddie considered the question. Jesse had assumed too much. "Wasn't about trust," he said. "It was about success. I wanted it and was willing to put in the hours to get it."

"And she was jealous of the time you devoted to work."

Close, but not quite. "Pam couldn't appreciate what success means to me."

"What she couldn't appreciate," Jesse said, "is not being the most important part of your life. It sounds like you were two-timing her, not with another woman, with your job."

"That's ridiculous," Eddie said. She had irritated him. He took care to edit his tone, to keep it flat.

Her eyes narrowed. "Oh really?" Jesse was smiling, but the ice widow was back. "Look at you, still lying to yourself about it. I can imagine how you must have had to lie to her."

"Why are you here?"

She studied him, saw his harsh body language, and frowned. She put down the glass and casually pulled her dress to cover her leg, a silent acknowledgement that the widowed vixen act wasn't working. Her fidgeting attracted General VonKatz. He sniffed around her shoes.

"I'm curious about what you know about Danny's death," she said, businesslike. "The police have told me very little."

Eddie had no way to verify what she said. He could not decide if he could trust Jesse, so he chose not to.

He shrugged. "I know what's been in the paper."

Jesse scrutinized his poker face. He'd never had a great one. She said, "It's not in your nature to let sleeping dogs lie, Eddie. You and Danny had that in common. It's why you worked well together. It's one reason you could have been close friends."

Could have been? So Jesse had noticed the distance between them. Maybe that's why she thought the vixen routine would work. But work for what? To get Eddie to talk? What did she think he knew?

He had no comeback. Jesse was right, of course—Eddie poked every sleeping dog in his path. General VonKatz picked that moment to hop into Jesse's lap. She stroked him.

"He likes you," Eddie said. "He's usually skittish around people he doesn't know."

"Aren't we all?" she said. Her tone had changed again, to soft and mournful. She sighed, looked into her empty glass and said, "My husband had no personal items on him when…when he died. Did Danny ever mention to you where he might keep things like that?"

Is this what she had come for? Eddie drank some vodka. "Like what?" he asked.

"You know, family photos, the little poems I wrote him, his keys?"

Just his wallet, under a bridge in a heroin den. "Let me check around," he said. "I bet I can find something like that, for you to remember him by."

She stood up with the General and nuzzled her face into his fur. She thanked Eddie, and set the cat down. Eddie picked her coat from the floor, helped her slip it on and then walked her to the door.

"One more thing," she said. "I think you're much better off without Pam."

He humored her. "Yeah, sure."

She looked him in the eye. "Relationships without honesty don't deserve a place in our lives," she said. Her heels clicked down the cement steps.

Eddie shut the door and wondered which of Jesse's personalities was the true one, if any. And then he locked the deadbolt for the first time he could remember.

Chapter 16

In the morning, Eddie spent fifteen bucks on the way downtown for six coffees and a dozen doughnuts. He drove south past the Empire building toward the train depot. He veered onto Chelmsford Street and passed over the railroad bridge under which he had spent the night before last. He then turned right, down a steep hill, and inched through a cramped residential area clogged with apartment houses and parked cars. He left the Mighty Chevette near a neighborhood pub, and carried the coffee and doughnuts in a box to the railroad tracks.

He watched his feet along the catwalk, balancing the food in his left arm. His right hand felt for handholds along the retaining wall.

Gabrielle saw him coming.

"Hey reporter man," she yelled. "You here to tell the story of our little underworld?"

"I'm here with breakfast," Eddie answered, offering half the truth.

Leo was away. Four other men were under the bridge. Three lay swaddled in blankets and old clothes. One sat overlooking the tracks, his legs dangling over the ledge. He sucked hard on a cigarette stub and mumbled to himself between drags.

The campfire crackled; smoke lingered between the I-beams. Leo's candle, unlit, stuck up from the cement, ready for the day's cooking.

Eddie handed Gabrielle the box of food. She took a coffee and a powdered-jelly doughnut for herself, and then passed the box around. It didn't come back. Eddie wished he had taken a java for himself first. A caffeine withdrawal headache stirred behind his eyes. He dismissed it as psychosomatic.

"Where's your husband?" Eddie asked.

"He's out buying," she told him. Her honesty about their crimes and addiction was hard to get used to. "Do you want to interview him?"

Warmer weather had put a dab of pink in her cheeks. Squinting just enough to blur her ravaged features, Eddie saw a face with pretty angles.

"I can't do the story," he said. "At least not yet."

She shrugged.

Eddie explained, "It's my editor. He won't let me, the prick."

"It's all right," she said. Disappointment had long since lost any effect on Gabrielle.

"I'll get it done somehow," Eddie pledged. "Maybe as a freelance magazine piece."

She shrugged again. Big promises had also lost any effect.

Eddie watched with envy as she blew the steam off her coffee and sipped it. He took out his notebook. "I wanted to talk about the man you found in the canal, the man I knew," he said. *I want to believe you, but I have to be sure.*

"We told you everything," she said.

"Tell me again. I have the time if you do."

She laughed. It was a hoarse, honking laugh, like a goose with a sore throat, and it led to a wet cough. She cleared her throat and spat over the ledge. "I can squeeze you in between appointments," she said.

She told Eddie again how they had found Nowlin's body hung up on branches at the edge of the Worthen Canal while they were walking to meet their heroin supplier. They took his wallet, and sent the body adrift so somebody would inevitably find it and call the police. Not one detail had changed from when she had first told him the story. Continuity was as close to confirmation as Eddie was going to get.

He asked her, "Had you ever seen that man—Danny Nowlin, that was his name—before that night? Did you ever see him alive?"

Gabrielle shook her head. "I don't remember him. I could have passed him on the street—who knows? I don't remember people unless I meet them. And it's hard to meet people who think I'm invisible."

None of the men under the bridge remembered Danny, either. Eddie wondered if any of them remembered last July.

"Was your friend a user?" Gabrielle asked.

Surprised, Eddie said, "He tried heroin at least once—how did you know?"

She smiled. "Why else might we know him down here on the Island of Misfit Toys?"

Eddie knew the Island of Misfit Toys from an animated Christmas special he watched as a kid. It was easy to forget that Gabrielle had a childhood. "Is there any way to find out if he shot up often?" he asked.

"Lots of chippers buy in the city," she said. "White collar guys like you. Recreational users, you'd call them. But we don't shop at the same stores."

"Let's assume he wasn't a regular user. Where would he shop?"

Gabrielle bit the doughnut and chewed the bite down. "To buy one hit?" she said.

"One hit."

She wiped powered sugar from her lips with her sleeve. "Most of them chippers snort, or smoke the black tar," she said. "They don't use the spike."

"Suppose he did."

Gabrielle considered the possibilities. "A one-time user looking for a taste might just walk the Acre to see who's open," she said. "Would he need a rig too?"

"A needle?"

She nodded.

"I don't know," he said. "But he hadn't used for a long time, if ever, before last week. So let's say, yeah, he buys a needle, too."

She thought some more, and then said, "Young, handsome, middle-class guy with no history, looking for a bag and a clean rig within the past week—somebody might remember him. We'll ask around."

Eddie gave her his business card and a handful of pocket change for the pay phone. "Call me if you get anything," he said. "It's real important."

She looked at the coins in her hand, and then at Eddie. She laughed. "Been a while," she said, "since I had a job."

Chapter 17

The advantage of an afternoon paper was never getting scooped. If the morning rags had a story The Empire did not, then the editors assigned the reporter on the morning "fireman shift" to chase it down by deadline, with help from additional reporters, as needed, as they filtered in. The disadvantage was deadline crunch for breakfast every day. Rules of polite society peeled away, and the level of profanity rose with the stress. The newsroom at deadline was like a pan of water approaching a boil. The trick was to put the paper together before the pan boiled over and the paper was late.

Any day's deadline was actually many incremental deadlines. If a reporter was late with a story, the copy editors might sacrifice part of their editing time to make up the difference, or they might pass the delay along to the paginators who map out the pages on computer. The buck stopped at the press. If it rolled late, The Empire missed deadline. And the union truck drivers started pulling overtime for standing around, chain-smoking Kents.

Eddie got to the newsroom by ten o'clock, smack in the middle of the morning deadline. Boyce Billips had pulled the six-o'clock fireman's slot this morning. He waved Eddie over.

"What do you think of this top?" Boyce asked, pointing to the first ten lines of a story on his screen.

Boyce made no mention of the fat yellow dog nibbling its own belly on the floor next to his desk. The dog's leash was tied to Boyce's chair.

Eddie read over his shoulder. Two people had been hurt in an accident on the Lowell Connector, a short stretch of highway linking the city with Route 495. It was known for wrong-way crashes and roadside shrines for the victims.

"Christ," Eddie said. "The Connector is about one fatality short of a nickname. Something like Suicide Alley, or Murderer's Row. That'll be great for tourism." He advised Boyce to move up a line about the number of past accidents on the highway. "The pols won't fix the road until the readers threaten to throw them out," Eddie said. "And the readers won't do it unless we whack them over the head every chance we get."

Eddie also nit-picked a few wording changes to tighten the language. "But overall, it's strong," he said. "Good job."

Boyce didn't have the condition reports for the victims. He kept typing from his notebook while Eddie called the hospital's patient information number. As long as he had the victims' names, their condition should be available. The cops had been quick to provide Boyce the names after the crash, usually a sign that the injuries were not life threatening. One victim was listed in "serious" condition, and the other in "satisfactory." That's jargon for "somewhat mangled," and "not so badly mangled." Both should live.

Eddie dictated the information to Boyce, who tapped it into the story.

Phife hollered over the deadline bustle. "Boyce, I need that accident brief."

"Two minutes," Boyce yelled back.

"No, Boyce. Right now! Hit the goddam button!"

Boyce finished typing a final sentence and then filed the story. "I didn't have time to run the spell-checker," he shouted to Phife, who was already reading the story, and ignored him.

"I hope he's not mad," Boyce said. "Do you think he's mad at me? What if he's mad at me?"

Eddie ignored him, too. The yellow mutt on the floor stuck its snout up Eddie's pant leg and sniffed his ankle. Eddie's socks were on their second wear since their last wash, though they had aerated a full week on the floor before he had put them back on. The dog took thirty seconds to catalogue the sock's potpourri of flavors.

With Boyce's deadline crisis over, Eddie dryly asked him, "Is this Take a Fat Dog to Work Day?"

"He's my mental health dog," Boyce said. He looked the mutt over. "Do you think he's too fat?"

"A mental health dog?"

"Like a Seeing-Eye dog, except he helps keep me mentally balanced."

"I don't think Keyes allows dogs in the newsroom," Eddie said.

"He has to allow Superdog," Boyce insisted. "He's certified. My psychiatrist signed for him. Mental-health companion animals are allowed anyplace a Seeing-Eye dog can go—stores, restaurants, airplanes, and places of business. It's all right here in the law." He offered Eddie a stack of photocopies, which Eddie waved off.

The mutt snorted and flopped its head on the rug with a thump.

"Superdog, eh?" Eddie said. "He looks slower than erosion."

"He was more active when he was young," Boyce explained. "He's seven. That's forty-nine to you and me."

Eddie groaned. "If I'm like that at forty-nine, just cover me with compost. Is he trained for this?"

"No. His calming effect on my mental state is the product of our relationship." He scratched the dog's belly. "Any more questions?"

"Why is he so fat?"

"Do you really think he's too fat?"

Eddie left Boyce to contemplate his dog's weight problem, and settled in at his own desk.

Detective Orr, her voice lacking its usual patronizing politeness, was on his voicemail. "I need to ask you some questions of an immediate nature, Mr. Bourque, relative to your relationship with certain known and alleged dealers of narcotics."

Detective Orr might be new to the force, but she spoke fluent Cop. Did they talk that way at home? *Take me, my lover, in a horizontal-type manner. Commence intercoursal activities and do not cease until 0600 hours.*

She had obviously spoken to Keyes, who had told her about Eddie's pitch for a story about Leo and Gabrielle. Keyes had it wrong again, naturally. They weren't dealers, but Orr wouldn't know that. Of course, she had the autopsy report, and knew that Nowlin died of a heroin overdose.

Eddie called her back and left a message.

Phife had just cleared deadline. His eyes were closed. He pinched the bridge of his nose with a thumb and forefinger. Eddie walked over to him. "Tough morning?" he asked.

"The worst," Phife said. "Getting the stringer copy into shape was a heavy lift."

The newspaper used stringers, part-time writers, to cover municipal meetings in the smaller suburban towns. Most were not professional reporters, and the paper relied on Phife, the editing maestro, to whip the copy into form. Phife was in charge of hiring stringers, too. He favored nubile, grad school co-eds.

"We gotta stop paying these people by the word," Phife said. "They're using six inches to tell me what the Conservation Commission chairman wears to the meeting."

"You got too many good-looking stringers who can't write," Eddie pointed out.

Phife grinned. "I thought you endorsed the quality of my hires."

"I just ogle. You have to edit them."

Phife leaned back, his feet on his desk. "I don't mind a reasonable amount of trouble," he said.

That had to be a movie quote, but Eddie couldn't place it.

"You disappoint me, man," Phife said. "That's Bogie, in *The Maltese Falcon.*"

Eddie eyed his friend with suspicion. "Your new girl ain't on the payroll, is she?"

Phife laughed. "I don't mind a *reasonable* amount of trouble. I know better than to fish off the company pier."

"Driving range tonight?" Eddie said.

"Usual time?"

"Just ring my phone. And the beer's on you."

"Damn," he said. "My turn already?"

"And do me a favor," Eddie said. "Tell Boyce he did all right on that accident."

"I will," Phife promised. "Once in a great while, Ed, you actually seem like a nice guy."

"We all go a little mad sometimes."

Phife snorted. He said, "You're trying to slip that quote past me? A line from *Psycho*?" He shooed Eddie away. "Take your grade-school film trivia and get out of my face."

Back at his own desk, Eddie examined Nowlin's wallet. He wondered if Jesse would want a memento that was water-stained, given that her husband was found dead in a canal. He'd find a tactful way to ask her, he thought.

Eddie slid out Danny's license. Pretty good picture for a Registry of Motor Vehicles shot. It was a wonder they didn't reshoot it, maybe with a cup of caterpillars down his pants to get his expression just right. That was how Eddie looked on his own license.

He turned the card over. There was a white sticker on the laminate with an address written on it. The Registry gave out those stickers to record any change of address. The front of the card listed Danny's home address in Chelmsford, the upscale town to the south. The house was a white Cape with a pebble driveway.

The address penned on the back was in Dracut, Eddie's blue-collar hometown. North of Lowell on the New Hampshire border; a typical Merrimack Valley mill town, too crowded in the developed parts, growing too fast in the rustic parts. The address was in rural north Dracut. Eddie didn't know that area well; it had been just woods and farms when he was growing up.

If Danny had moved, his new address would be on file at the Registry. Any police officer could get that information with a telephone call. But what if nobody checked? Eddie had told the police where Danny lived when the cops found the body. They'd have no reason to verify the address with the RMV.

From the Empire Building, the address in Dracut was about a nine-mile drive.

Chapter 18

People enjoy the Merrimack Valley because you can point your car toward New Hampshire and find forest ten minutes outside of downtown Lowell. Narrow country roads wound Eddie past stone walls, evergreens and sprawling fields in which black earth pushed into piles showed where new subdivisions would be built. This was the way in all the rural towns within The Empire's circulation area.

The road eventually led to an old farmhouse with a dirt driveway and two mailboxes out front. The house was a lime-sherbet color, with dark green trim. Several gables added character to the building; an iron weathervane on the roof supplied charm. Thick hemlock encircled the building and a large yard strewn with wind-blown leaves.

Eddie left the Mighty Chevette on the street and marched up the driveway toward the screened porch. Three chubby kittens at play sped across his path.

This place hadn't seen a paintbrush in a generation. Cracks sliced through several windowpanes. Holes in the screens were big enough for bumblebees. Inside the porch, the door to the main house had two police crime-watch stickers on the window. Seemed unnecessary way out here, but the daily headlines in any city newspaper can sell a lot of locks.

Eddie knocked.

He was about to knock again when the inside door scraped open and Frank Sinatra's "Luck Be a Lady" flowed out. The music was warm and scratchy, probably a vinyl record. A moment later, a woman of perhaps eighty, in a flannel housecoat and a wool cardigan, eased onto the porch. Fragile-looking, she moved in slow motion, as if considering the risk before every step. Her head trembled gently, like she was forever saying no.

Eddie decided to play it open-ended and let her fill in the blanks.

"Hello, ma'am," he said. "I hope I have the right address. I'm looking for Danny's place."

She looked him over for twenty seconds. Her wrinkles bent into a smirk. She said, "He told me he goes by Daniel now. He lives 'round the back. In the carriage house. Moved in six weeks ago."

Lives? She didn't know he was dead.

Eddie smiled and softened his voice, careful not to sound like he was addressing a small child. "At least I found the right address. Even if I knocked on the wrong door. My apologies."

"I'm afraid you have traveled for nothing," she said. "Daniel hasn't been here for the past few days. Haven't seen him at all."

Eddie wrinkled his brow. "Do you know when he left?"

"Sometime between my bedtime Friday night and my breakfast last Saturday morning. Can't be any more specific. I got no use for the clock anymore."

The crime-watch stickers were bad. If he leveled with her, she'd want the police here. Eddie doubted Detective Orr would let him see what was inside that carriage house. And the landlady had offered no hint that she'd let a stranger into Danny's place. Eddie had to become more than a stranger. He sighed. "I've come such a long way," he said, not sure where he was going with this. "He said he'd be back from… from Toledo by now. Maybe his flight was delayed."

She stepped closer and squinted up at him. "Back from where, you say?"

Poor eyesight, eh? Eddie suddenly knew where he was going with this.

"Ohio. It's where our parents live."

She clapped her hands, barely making a sound. "Are you Daniel's brother? How marvelous. He never mentioned his family."

Eddie figured there was a special room in Hell for people who would con information from a half-blind old lady. His moral compass was spinning like a roulette wheel, and spraying shame. He told himself that this would not be the worst neighborhood in Hell—he'd be rooming with the lightweights of the eternally damned—the ticket scalpers, people who stole cable TV, and Catholics who ate meat on Fridays before Easter.

"Dan's always been kinda private. It's not personal, I'm sure," he said.

She leaned closer still. "Forgive me for not seeing the resemblance," she said. "I don't have my glasses. Let me find them." She headed back inside.

Eddie said, "Don't bother on my account."

"No trouble," she said. "Come in, come in."

Eddie followed her inside and closed the door. They were in a drab kitchen with butterscotch wallpaper and fake wood paneling. A few dozen pictures of family gatherings, photographed in bad light, were displayed in stand-up frames around the counters.

She hobbled around the room. "I had those spectacles a minute ago."

A pair of tortoise shell glasses lay in plain sight on the counter. Eddie grabbed a picture near them and said, "You have a lovely family."

"Those are my youngest boy's twin sons. Walter and William. They're in high school now. Well, William is."

Eddie put the photo down in front of the glasses, upgrading his reservation in Hell. For hiding the old lady's specs, he'd be bunking with Stalin and sharing work detail with Vlad the Impaler.

"Is that Sinatra I hear?" Eddie asked.

"Oh yes. Do you like it?"

"Sure do." At least that was the truth.

She gave up the search for her glasses and sat down. Her name was Mrs. Evans, but Eddie could call her Ruby, she said. They chatted about the music. Eddie knew enough about Sinatra to hold a five-minute conversation with a true fan. When he ran out of material, he changed the subject.

"Do you know Danny well?" he asked.

"Nice boy," she said. "He cleaned my gutters. I don't see much of him. He's always working at that computer of his. Frightful things, aren't they? I don't even own a television, and I've given up on the radio. Nothing *good* on anymore. Where are the old shows?"

Eddie frowned and agreed with her. Talk radio had been awful for years. He asked her, "Does Danny get many visitors? I worry he doesn't meet enough people."

She sniffed lightly, drew a white handkerchief from her sweater pocket and dabbed her nose. "Can't say I've seen any visitors over there."

"Have you seen a blonde woman here? About this big?" Eddie held his hand at Jesse's height, five feet off the floor.

"No, I would have remembered her."

It was suddenly obvious that Jesse would not be satisfied with Danny's wallet as a "memento." Not after she specifically mentioned his keys. That was what she had been playing Eddie for—the keys to Danny's secret apartment. Jesse never mentioned that her husband had moved out. What else hadn't she mentioned?

"Alone all the time? Danny must be sad," Eddie said, more to himself than to Mrs. Evans.

She grinned. "Not that boy," she insisted. "There's a joy about him. Take my word. I got a sixth sense about people."

Eddie smiled. *I hope not. Because here comes my pitch.* His hand covered a yawn. He said, "Ruby, I'm a bit tired. Would it be too much trouble for you to let me into my brother's place so I can nap until he's back?"

She pursed her lips and pressed the pink from them. She took what seemed a long time to decide, and then said, "Let's walk over together."

The carriage house was a one-story wooden cube, painted the same two-tone green as Ruby's house. It had a few small windows and an angled, Victorian-style roof that showed off the real slate shingles. Three steep cement steps led to a white door with an iron horseshoe knocker.

She turned a key in the door and swung it open. "I hope it satisfies your needs," she said. "I'll be back in the house. See me before you leave."

Eddie thanked her and went inside. The heat was on and the apartment was warm. The front door opened to a small living room that held a couch and a television. Both looked second-hand. The walls were plain white, and Danny hadn't bothered with curtains.

The bathroom was immaculate, not a speck of grime. Typical for Nowlin, that goddam neat freak. The bathroom cabinet held cough drops and aspirin. No unmarked bottles, no syringes.

A tube he almost mistook for toothpaste caught his eye. There was too much fine print on the side: it was a contraceptive cream.

Eddie stood there with the tube and tried to reconcile the family man he knew with the evidence in his hand. Danny and Jesse had known for years that Jesse could not conceive; they were trying to adopt. Yet this tube was half empty.

There was another woman. That's why Nowlin had moved here alone and didn't tell anybody.

Danny, what the hell were you doing?

He put the tube back and checked the kitchen. Two raw steaks, six Guinness, and some fruit were in the fridge. The freezer held coffee beans, cheap vodka, and a dozen frozen dinners. Danny had regressed quickly to bachelorhood, except for the fruit.

The bedroom was tidy. The full-sized bed was made with a down comforter. Danny's laundered work shirts hung in the closet. Five pairs of shoes lined up in formation on the closet floor. Danny's tennis racquet and baseball glove hung on hooks, his golf bag stood at attention in the corner. Eddie realized he could never have been Danny's roommate; it would have been like living at West Point.

Nowlin had made a cubbyhole off the living room into an office. An unfinished pine table supported his computer and its keyboard and mouse, a telephone, and a microphone on a ten-inch stand bent like a dental instrument. The missing Cambodia files from The Empire's library were on the floor. It seemed as close to disheveled here as Nowlin could get.

Eddie sat behind the desk and turned on the computer. It beeped alive, and then called for a password. How many computer passwords would Nowlin have cared to remember? One, probably. Eddie punched in Danny's Empire key code. The machine agreed and let him in.

Eddie ransacked Danny's files. His folder of audio files was full of easy-listening songs—awful, just awful. A folder marked "video" had one ten-second baseball clip—Bucky Dent's home run against the Red Sox in Fenway in 1978. It plunged Eddie into a sour mood. Why in the name of Smokey Joe Wood would a New Englander have that clip on his computer? Sox fans should be eradicating all evidence of that home run, the way doctors went after smallpox.

He opened Nowlin's Internet browser and nosed through a list of sites Danny had bookmarked. They included the Poynter Institute page for journalists, and the electronic editions of the New York Times and the Wall Street Journal. There was a porn site, the "Erotic College Sluts of Suburbia," and the on-line version of the King James Bible. A final bookmark took Eddie's breath. The home page of the New York Yankees baseball team. Eddie couldn't deny it any longer. Nowlin had been a closet Yankees fan!

Eddie dug a little deeper, snooping for a record of the Web pages Danny had recently visited. Nothing. All his off-line content had been cleaned out.

Danny's email program was set to remember his password, which saved Eddie the trouble of guessing it. The computer dialed into the email server and the two machines engaged in a mating call of beeps and hisses until they settled on a connection. Eddie downloaded Danny's email, and then hung up the modem.

Danny had two new messages.

An on-line bookstore had confirmed Danny's order of *The Elements of Style*, the most important book for writers ever written. Eddie's ragged copy was held together by packing tape.

The second message had come today from Boyce Billips, who had not removed Nowlin's email address from his master list. Boyce's latest paranoia was a list of symptoms for the Ebola virus, which he had forwarded to every person in his on-line address book, including Eddie.

Eddie clicked "reply" and sent Boyce a message that would carry Nowlin's return address:

> Dear Boyce,
>   Either I rest in peace without spam email, or YOU WILL.
>   Got it?
>   Wear a yellow necktie tomorrow if you promise to stop spamming people.
>   Now delete this message immediately, and never speak of it to anyone.
>
> Sincerely from the grave,
> You Know Who

Cruel? Absolutely. But that Bucky Dent video had really bothered Eddie. Boyce was lucky it wasn't the Bill Buckner clip from the World Series. Or Eddie would have ordered Boyce to wear a yellow *skirt*.

A message box popped up when Eddie opened the word processor. It asked him to choose either the keyboard or voice-recognition software.

Nowlin had finally licked carpal tunnel syndrome—he didn't type. The document folder was empty. Not one file. The computer's recycling bin, where junked files went before they were flushed, was also empty. Eddie cancelled the word processor and wondered why Danny, a writer trying to improve his work, would have no writing on his computer. Especially after he installed word processing software that recognized his voice.

This computer mystery was above his head. It was time to call tech-support. He dialed The Empire from Nowlin's telephone and punched an extension he had recently committed to memory.

The phone rang a dozen times, but Eddie persisted.

"Yeah?" Stan answered, finally.

"It's Bourque. How's the funny training?"

"My face is sore," he moaned. "I can't do any more smiles."

"Comedy ain't for quitters. What if Larry Fine quit the first time Moe poked his eyes?"

"Larry was the Stooges' straight man, a buffer," Stan said in a robotic monotone. "Moe's physical retaliations were generally directed at Curly or Shemp."

Eddie was indignant, "Are you saying Larry Fine couldn't take a poke in the eye?"

"No, just that—oh, never mind." Stan sighed into the phone. "All right. I'll do my exercises."

"Larry would be proud. In the meantime, I need some computer help."

"A deal's a deal," Stan said. He sounded glum.

"You told me before that information deleted from a computer is not actually destroyed right away, and can be recovered, right?"

"Sometimes."

"How do I get it back?"

"Did you lose a file?"

"Yes—well, maybe," Eddie said. "I really don't know." He had no choice but to be straight with Stan. "I'm someplace I shouldn't be right now, breaking into a computer I shouldn't be messing with."

"Is that so?" Curiosity put life into Stan's voice. "Does this have to do with Nowlin?"

"Yeah. And I'm not sure how legal this is, but I'm gonna guess 'not very.' So you'd be smart not to ask me too many details."

"Right, right," he said, disappointed. "What are you looking for?"

"Maybe nothing. But I want to see what's been deleted off this machine recently."

"I have a program that can help you," Stan said. "A little utility I wrote myself. Can you come here and get it?"

"This may be my only chance at this computer."

"Okay, okay, let me think—can you get on the Internet?"

"No problem."

Stan told him to hang on. Eddie could hear him fumbling through his desk. And then his plump little fingers rapped his keyboard for a minute.

"Still there?" Stan asked.

"Still here. What's the plan?"

"I put my recovery utility on the paper's Internet server, and created a link from my private area of The Empire's Web page."

"You have a private area on the paper's Web page? For what?"

"For whatever I want. And the newspaper picks up the tab—not that they know it."

Eddie was beginning to like Stan. And to trust him.

Stan instructed Eddie to log into The Empire's Web site under the name "Bob Newhart." The password to Stan's private page was "Mrs. Webb."

"Who's Mrs. Webb?" Eddie asked.

Stan's voice flat-lined again. "She was a character in a Newhart comedy monologue," he stated. "In that act, Newhart was the driving instructor and Mrs. Webb was a student unskilled in the safe and legal operation of a motor vehicle. Their resulting mishaps and adventures, relayed by Newhart with understated dry wit, are quite comedic."

With the way Stan droned, he could have been lecturing on kelp, or the life cycle of the stink beetle. But he was explaining humor, and that was *funny*. Okay, maybe closer to amusing than sidesplitting, but hearing a comedy routine analyzed in Stan's lifeless monotone broke Eddie into a smile.

Eddie interrupted, "Tell me, Stan, when you tried doing stand-up, what were your routines about?"

"I stayed faithful to the staples of contemporary comedic material—poor service by the airlines, the follies of big government, and the curious differences between men and woman."

There it was again—funny. Eddie was onto something.

"Stan," he said, "the Edward Bourque School of Funny needs some homework from you. Write me a two thousand-word essay on great comedy. The Marx Brothers, Abbott and Costello—whatever. Break down a classic routine and explain why it gets laughs."

"How about the Three Stooges?"

"Fine. Whatever. It doesn't matter."

"You want me to email this to you?"

"Nope," Eddie said. "You're going to read it to me. And then we're gonna talk about the comedic properties of irony."

"Huh?"

"Forget it," Eddie said. "We'll cover this later in funny class. How do I work your utility program?"

Stan explained a few simple functions.

Eddie thanked him and said goodbye.

"Bourque! Wait!" Stan yelled.

"What is it?"

"This report isn't just busy work, is it? This is going to make me funnier, right?"

"Write it well and you'll be a goddam riot—if you develop a smile that won't put your audience into cardiac arrest. I'll check with you later."

They hung up.

The computer dialed the Internet. Eddie followed Stan's directions. As Stan had promised, the program soon offered him a list of two dozen deleted files. Most had been thrown out within the past few weeks.

A few had been deleted late Monday night.

When Nowlin was already in the morgue.

Somebody had beaten Eddie to Nowlin's computer, to make sure nobody would ever see these documents. They snuck past nearsighted Mrs. Evans, and they got past Nowlin's password, but they didn't consider the computer prowess of Stan Popko, The Bitter Comic. *You beat me here, whoever you are, but I got the better geek.* Winning his first round against his unknown adversary warmed Eddie like a caffeine buzz, but without the jitters.

Two of the most recently deleted files were Nowlin's resumé, and a letter dated two weeks ago to the talent recruiter at the Boston Globe:

> *Dear Ms. Dannon,*
>
> *Thank you for the pleasant interview last week. You folks certainly asked the tough questions and brought the best out of me. I'm looking forward to my tryout next month. Please let me know what would be a convenient date to come in, and I'll schedule the time off at The Empire....*

Buzz kill. Eddie slouched. Danny had never mentioned an interview at the Globe. And this wasn't just a pity chat;

they were bringing him back for a tryout. The room grew hot. Eddie slipped off his jacket.

They wanted Nowlin? *The guy couldn't write for shit.*

Eddie had long considered Danny a competitor for newspaper jobs. But the race was over, and Danny had died in the lead. An interview is no guarantee of a job. Once the Globe editors saw his raw copy, they probably would have passed on Danny for somebody more polished. But Nowlin had broken through the membrane enveloping all great newspapers. His turn inevitably would come.

Eddie thought about how much of the newspaper business is luck and timing. A reporter can labor for years building sources and developing a beat. After a while, even the most lunkheaded pols learn there's a watchdog on their asses, and that they can't get away with anything. So they feather their own nests the hard way—by providing good government. Services get better, taxes stay low; it's the only way to stay in office if you're clean.

What does a reporter have to show for all this good government? Lots of copy about economic development and land preservation. It's what makes good neighborhoods, but doctors prescribe those clips at insomnia clinics.

And then there's the dimwitted scribe on his way to the bar. He happens upon a hostage taking. The material is so compelling, nobody could screw it up. It's like winning the news lottery. Awards pile up, and job offers follow.

What was it about Nowlin's political coverage that got him noticed? Eddie couldn't say for sure. But Danny never wrote just to fill the paper, and if that meant Keyes bitched at him for a low byline count, so be it. Nowlin didn't waste time shoveling coal. Eddie shoveled lots of coal, writing too many boring stories to satisfy the pressure to fill the white space. It was journalistic origami, the art of making copy from nearly nothing. Start with a single fresh fact. Fold some background in here, tuck some irrelevant quotes there—poof, it was a swan.

Another document caught Eddie's attention.

It was labeled Story Draft, and Stan's program could recover only a few lines, in two fragments:

> *of the communist guerrilla group, the Khmer Rouge, which swept into Phnom Penh in April 1975 and cleared Cambodia's capital city of its inhabitants with lies about American bomber planes on the way.*

> *The citizens were marched out into the country and forced into a slave-like existence as subsistence farmers. Many were worked to death. Within the ranks of commoners, the Khmer Rouge hunted down educated people whom they perceived to be a threat and took them away in the night for execution.*

The second fragment made even less sense out of context:

> *showing amazing instincts, he mated each of them in March and was crowned their King*

Eddie copied the lines into his notebook. He tore out the page and stuffed it in his wallet.

The last file of interest looked like a love poem in the making. The top wasn't bad, but where was Danny heading with the ending? The poem trailed into nonsensical free-form verse:

> *Color my world, my artist, and melt tubes of cherry butter paint*

> *Onto my Irish pale cheeks.*

> *Color my world with a secret dance we share in the night*

> *Your brush swipes at the canvas like a conductor's wand.*

> *Hello. Who else would it be. What time. Yeah I'll be right there. I got plenty to tell you and it's going to blow your mind. That's right the jackpot. I found it*

*in the microfilm. The homilies. It was right there all
along. No. Chanthay doesn't have a phone. But you
could page her.*

The poem ended with numbers spelled out in words. Eddie
wrote them as digits in his notebook. Together, they formed
a number in the millions—seven digits.

A seven-digit number? Eddie looked from the computer
screen to the telephone, and then to the microphone on the
table. Danny had answered the phone while writing this
poem. His voice-recognition software had dutifully typed his
half of the conversation. The program's auto-save feature had
preserved it. And then somebody had erased it. Eddie checked
the file's creation date. Friday night, eleven-forty-five. Poetry
was usually slow going, and Nowlin was a slow writer anyway.
Figure half an hour to write the first four lines. That would
time the call at around twelve-fifteen on Saturday morning.

Yeah I'll be right there, Danny had said. So he didn't go
far, and he never came back. It was Danny's last phone call—
he may have been talking to his killer.

Eddie weighed a calculated risk, and then decided to see
it through. He dialed the seven digits on the telephone. There
were three high beeps from a paging service. He punched in the
number written on Nowlin's desk phone and then hung up.

For four minutes he sat mesmerized by the hum of the
computer.

He jumped when the phone rang.

"This is Eddie Bourque," he said upon answering. "I think
we should meet."

There was silence for a moment, and then a woman's voice
replied, "Yes, Mr. Bourque. I think we should meet."

Mrs. Evans caught Eddie in the driveway. She wore a ski
parka and a knitted watch cap. In her mittens she held a wire
rake. She trembled over a meager pile of leaves.

"Um—Danny called," Eddie tried to explain. "I need to get him at the airport."

She frowned. "Stow that crap." Her voice was sharp. "Did you find what you came for, *Mr. Edward Bourque?*"

Eddie's mouth fell open. "You knew? How could you know?"

She chuckled. "I gave up on TV and radio, but I read three papers every day. You get my drift, son? One of them is the typo-infested Lowell Empire. Why can't you people catch the little mistakes? They go right to your credibility, they do.

"I saw your picture in the paper after Daniel died, the poor man. So you thought he might someday win a Pulitzer?" She laughed, showing her teeth. It was nearly a cackle.

"If you knew, why did you let me in?"

She shrugged. "The police were here yesterday and they didn't find anything, so what's the harm? And it's like I said, I got a sixth sense about people. I think you're all right, Mr. Bourque. Even if you did hide my glasses. So what did you do with them? I can't read my crossword."

Eddie assumed this meant he was not going to Hell. At least not for this.

Chapter 19

Traffic bunched at the Merrimack River bridges on Eddie's way back into Lowell. The city's Mile of Mills stretched along the river's far bank. It was hard to see where the river ended and the mills began; they seemed to float on the water like a fleet of great red barges. The afternoon sun yellowed their sterns from the west. Their brick smokestacks pricked the sky.

Massachusetts Mills led the armada down the river, followed by the Boott Mills, the Merrimack Mills, and the remnants of Lawrence Mills. An unexplained inferno had cremated the complex in the 1980s. Run-down Billings Mill sailed rear guard.

The brick hulks could be depressing on gray days. Not today. Eddie sensed an aura around the mills left by the ghosts of the people who built them and worked them. Those immigrant mill workers spun southern slave cotton, and only the mill owners got rich, but it was on their backs that industrial America was built. And Lowell's mills were where the little guy learned to stand up to The Man. The "mill girls" staged the first labor walkouts to protest pay cuts. In these mills, French-Canadian, Polish, and Portuguese textile workers learned to strike together, in three languages. The legacy of their labor was a city so mule-headed it thought it could recover from any economic disaster, and so it had. Lowell's wage earners survived the mill closings of the 1920s and '30s, and their grandchildren persevered when the city's savior, Wang Laboratories, crashed in the '80s.

Eddie drove west past the steel-beam University Bridge that carries traffic over the dry rocks beneath the Pawtucket Dam, and then onto Pawtucket Boulevard, which runs along the river. He pulled his car into the parking lot for the city's paved riverwalk. The Mighty Chevette was alone in the lot. In summer, the lot was often jammed. Every year, on the first spring day over fifty degrees, pale-legged Lowell yawned awake, pulled on shorts, stepped into running shoes or Rollerblades, and headed to the riverwalk.

The asphalt walk runs through the swath of lawn between the river's northern bank and Pawtucket Boulevard. It's lined with old-fashioned lampposts and park benches. The path is shaded by oak, maple, and poplar, and short pine twisted like giant bonsai trees.

Eddie traded his sports coat for the lined leather jacket he kept in his car, and then strolled upstream on the riverwalk. A bum under a blanket of newspaper dozed on a park bench. A runner in pink tights sped past him and kept going.

Eddie stuck his hands in his pockets and walked toward the gray lattice Rourke Bridge, about a mile west. The steel bridge rose gradually from the river's northern bank, stretched a quarter mile across the river on seven pillars, and landed on a high point on the southern bank. Through bare trees on the far bank, he could see the backside of industrial buildings, and a freight train crawling west on tracks that parallel the river.

Chunks of ice flowed downstream. They reminded him of his trip down the canal. He still had the physical scars, but the event seemed like long ago, like a bad memory from childhood. He thought about the people who had dropped him in the canal. What did evil look like? He had covered court trials, seen murderers convicted and sentenced. But he had never seen a killer outside captivity, as far as he knew, and that included his brother, whom Eddie had never seen in his life.

Would I recognize a killer? Danny didn't, it would seem by his final telephone call.

The river was high, flooding swampy areas along its bank, lapping against patches of ice. Swamp plants dampened the current, trapping black logs, tires, liquor bottles, and foam cups. Ducks bobbed with the trash, waiting for a handout of bread or crackers from Eddie.

Eddie thought about what he and Danny had in common. Same job, same beat, same insatiable drive to get the story. He remembered the last time he had seen Danny alive, last week in the elevator, just the two of them. Eddie pictured that moment. They had talked about Manny Eccleston, the interview that Danny wanted to dump. Their conversation had been all business.

Eddie felt a surge of regret. Would they have been so businesslike had they known one of them would be dead in three days?

He reached the bridge and looked around a flat, grassy area behind it. He waited there a few minutes. *Where is she?* The steel bridge clattered under its traffic like a shoddy amusement park ride. Eddie marched back down river, the breeze at his back. Two kids on bikes whizzed by. A big black dog plodded against its leash, pulling a man in the black satin jacket of the Pawtucketville Social Club.

Back at the parking lot, the bum on the bench rolled over. That was it. There was nobody else around.

Eddie cut across the lawn toward his car, muttering under his breath. He didn't like to be stiffed.

"You give up too easily," someone called out.

Eddie spun around.

The bum sat up and swept the blanket of newspapers to the ground. The wind lifted her long black hair. She wore tight black leggings tucked into black boots, a gray turtleneck, black ski vest, and red mittens.

"Let's walk," she said, pulling off the mittens. She had no accent, like a network newscaster.

"I've *been* walking."

"I thought they followed me here," she said. "I had to hide to be sure they were gone."

"Who might have followed you?"

She stuffed the mittens in her vest pockets. "It's my problem, not yours," she said. "We can walk the other way if you're bored."

They did, strolling along the boulevard. They passed the Sampas Pavilion bandstand, and headed toward the riverfront mills and the university buildings. The riverwalk ended and they continued along the sidewalk. Eddie felt exposed walking along the street.

"Your name is Chanthay?" he said.

"That is the name I'm using right now, so that is what you may call me." Her tone carried authority. This was a woman accustomed to giving orders.

Eddie asked her, "Were you born here? Or Cambodia?" It sounded like an interview question. He instantly regretted asking it so soon.

She was unfazed. "Cambodia. And I intend to go back when I'm finished here."

Finished? That was an invitation to another question. He asked her, "What is it you need to do?"

"Kill somebody."

It was a statement of fact, lacking any moral undertones. The words hung there a minute, and rolled along with them as they walked toward the mills. She broke the silence. "Don't worry, it's not you. And it wasn't Danny Nowlin, either."

"I know," Eddie said. "Danny was your lover."

She flinched. He had surprised her.

Eddie let the silence linger a while, and then broke it. "Who are you here to kill?"

Her lips pressed together in a sign that this was none of his concern and she would not be giving up the answer. Her tone was dismissive. "Those of us involved swore an oath of silence to protect each other, which I do not intend to break for a newspaper reporter."

"Then why meet with me at all?"

"Our paths have crossed several times this week, Mr. Bourque—"

"It's Eddie, please."

"Yes—Eddie. Our paths have crossed and I want to know why."

"I want to know who killed Danny—same as you," he told her. "And I want to know who threw me in the canal after I fell through the floor."

She was quiet for a while, and then said with resignation, "There are casualties in every war." Eddie heard sadness in her voice, but didn't trust it, not yet. She continued, "They tried to burn us to death. We barely escaped. I thought you had led them to us."

Eddie knew better than to ask who had attacked her. That would have to wait. He said, "And you no longer think I led them to you?"

"No. I believe they followed me from Danny's wake, just as you did," she said.

"Why did they throw me in the canal?"

She shrugged. "Who can say why madmen do anything?"

Eddie pried for more about her past. It was a reporter's trick. Get the subject to talk about herself, to share harmless details until she got comfortable. Comfort led to trust, which led to information. "You were under the Khmer Rouge when you were little, weren't you?" he asked.

"You guess that by my age?"

"And by the figures you painted inside that old triple-decker." It was an educated guess. Danny, in his love poem, had called her "my artist." And the pain in those paintings was worthy of a holocaust.

She flinched again with surprise. Her tone was not so dismissive this time. "My mother died when I was an infant. My father taught music—piano—in Phnom Penh. When the Khmer Rouge soldiers came to our neighborhood, at first we were happy. Anything had to be better than the war.

"They told us we were in great danger in the city, from American bombs. And everyone had to leave. We took what we could carry and marched at the end of a gun for two weeks, to the countryside. The Khmer Rouge made surnames illegal, so families were mixed and confused. They banned money and tore up the calendar, so time could start over."

"They enslaved you."

She nodded. "We dug irrigation canals. I was thin—I could not lift the pick above my head. They fed us watery rice and we ate weeds or bugs we could pick."

Eddie knew the history. The Khmer Rouge came at night for the educated people they perceived to be threats, and shot them. They starved countless others, or worked them to death.

"At night my father would put my hand on his, and his fingers would pretend to play the piano, maybe Bach or Claude Debussy, while he sang the notes," she said. "One day my father caught a fish and cooked it for my brother and me. But a soldier discovered it. He said my father was greedy because he kept the fish as his personal property, and personal property was not allowed. This soldier walked him to the ditch I had dug. He brought my brother and me to watch. And he stood on my father's back until he drowned."

She told the story in a cold narrative, as if detached from it. Or was she simply so strong she could tell it without tears? Eddie could not tell, but he was beginning to see why Nowlin had fallen for her.

"I watched my father's hand under the water," she said. "His fingers played Debussy."

Eddie wondered about his chances of getting a tale like this into print. Not from her, of course, she'd never speak for the record. And probably not in The Empire, the way the brass was spiking his stuff. But there were thousands of Cambodian immigrants in Lowell, and every one who survived the genocide had a story like Chanthay's. And there were other papers in the world.

Part of him felt like a ghoul for obsessing over a news story, with Danny dead and his killers on the loose. But Eddie's point in life was telling stories like this, no matter how cold-blooded it made him feel for the moment.

They passed Pawtucket Dam and crossed the river over University Bridge. The bridge surface is an unpaved metal grate. Eddie could see the river below. Car tires moaned over the grate like the wail of the undead. Eddie and Chanthay walked through the university campus, between dorms built of chocolate brick. They left the street and stuck close to the river as they approached Billings Mill. Eddie thought about Chanthay's story. It clicked, and he realized his reporter's trick had worked.

"You're still fighting the Khmer Rouge, here in America," he declared.

She scowled at him.

"Revenge," Eddie said. "You're here for revenge."

Her face went to stone. That was all the confirmation Eddie needed. "But why was Nowlin killed?" he said, as much to himself as to her. "And why was he shooting heroin? Still too many questions."

"What are you saying? Danny didn't use heroin."

"The autopsy says—"

Squealing tires cut Eddie off. He whirled. Two men climbed from a blue sedan. They were both short and dumpy-looking, in matching tan overcoats. Thick clothing beneath their coats gave them a top-heavy look.

"It is them," Chanthay said. "Keep moving."

They walked quickly toward Billings Mill, a brick monstrosity, five stories high. Arched windows run along each floor of the long sides of the rectangular building. A grassy slope from the riverbank climbs gently to the mill's ground-floor windows. Every window was dark.

The two men marched toward them at a brisk pace. One pulled a pistol from his belt. It was black and long. The barrel grew fat near the end.

Chanthay grabbed Eddie's sleeve and steered him at the building. "This way," she yelled. "To the window." They sprinted toward the wall of red brick. She sputtered, "Hired muscle…thirty-two caliber semi-automatics…sound suppressors…not accurate if you're on the move."

Eddie screeched, "They can't shoot us out here!"

"They can…they will."

Eddie slowed as they approached the wall. *There's no way in.* His voice cracked, "Where do we go?"

"You're wearing leather," she answered. "Cover your head."

She grabbed Eddie's left arm with two hands and slung him forward with a grunt. She used his own momentum to heave Eddie towards a window, clinging to his arm just long enough to spin him around. Eddie staggered backwards four steps before his backside burst through the glass. Wooden panes hollowed by dry rot shredded to fibers. The window blew inward with a muffled pop. The sill tripped Eddie at the knees, and he toppled like a Ponderosa pine. His hands drew over his face. A shower of glass tinkled around him.

He looked up from a pine floor soaked by machine oil. The ceiling twelve feet above was a grid of retrofitted pipes beneath heavy crossbeams. Plasterboard partitions divided the space around him into crude offices, one of the many failed reuse plans for Billings Mill.

Chanthay hurdled through the window and helped Eddie off the floor. A one-inch cut on the pad beneath Eddie's left thumb was white for a moment, before it oozed red. The lump on his head throbbed again.

There was a noise from outside, like a car door slamming. Red dust burst from a brick in the window arch. A bullet had knocked out a chunk.

A black pistol appeared in Chanthay's hand. She ducked behind a partition.

"Go!" she yelled. "Run!"

Chapter 20

Eddie raced deeper into the old factory, which grew ever darker the farther he ran from the outside light. He gauged the vastness of the place by the distant glow of windows along the far wall. The mill looked as big as a city block. It was like running through a giant department store with no lights. As he entered the shadows, he realized he was running alone. Skidding to a stop on the greasy floor, Eddie looked back. The two men outside held their guns inside their overcoats and marched toward the broken window. They walked with purpose, but didn't seem rushed.

Chanthay held her ground behind an office partition.

She balanced on her toes, her knees slightly bent, poised to spring like a cat. She held the gun by her ear, pointing straight up. She was waiting for her shot, unable to chance a peek at her targets, content to let their footsteps be her guide.

A fool's courage, Eddie thought. In a moment she would be dead.

No, he would not watch that happen. Loping strides brought him back to her.

She grimaced at his presence and shooed him away with the gun. Eddie grabbed a handful of her ski vest and pulled her to the darkness.

A bullet thumped the plywood partition like a kick from a steel-toed boot.

They ran together. Behind them, wingtips crunched on broken glass. Chanthay followed Eddie through alleys, between wooden crates stacked high on pallets, past dark mounds of machinery and oil drums rising into pyramids. The alleys were dark, but the obstacles were darker, and Eddie steered a competent path between them.

Billings Mill was not a modern-day success among the behemoths of the Merrimack. When the Lowell textile industry abandoned its cradle, entrepreneurs invested in the Mile of Mills, with varying degrees of success. Part of Massachusetts Mills was converted to luxury apartments. The old Boott Mill became a museum of culture and history. Lawrence Mills was to be a college campus, before the fire.

In the 1970s, a plan to develop Billings Mill into office space flopped. The next owners tried a warehouse. The pols frowned at the idea, and the business community yawned— no job creation. Billings employed two thousand men and women in 1875, and about nine muscleheads on the loading dock a hundred years later. Warehouse rents offered a low margin, and the place closed within a few years. Much of the crap stored there in the '70s was abandoned, or offered to the owners in lieu of past due rent. It was an indoor junkyard under a pall of dust, a maze in the dark.

The paths through the junk turned and split at random, like the streets in the Acre. Eddie chose a zigzag course toward the center of the warehouse. There, the alley emptied into a straight avenue, the width of a driveway, running lengthwise down the middle of the building.

They slowed to a walk, choosing silence over speed. The pounding of leather shoes, still deep in the maze, stopped moments later. Their hunters had chosen silence as well.

Eddie caught his breath, and then whispered, "If they shoot us here we'll be skeletons before anybody finds us."

"I could have killed them both at the window," she answered.

"Don't think so," he said. "Did you see their puffy shirts? Body armor. Fibrous layers—light but impenetrable. I wrote a story on it when the cops got new vests last year."

"Then I'd have shot their faces."

So sure, so confident. Maybe she would have. She was in the shadows; they were in the light. She had the element of surprise—even if they had assumed she was armed, would they have expected her to set an ambush? Then bang, bang. Two head shots from behind the wall, two dead hitmen.

It was possible, Eddie supposed. But he was unwilling to let her risk herself on lousy odds. Not for him, not while he skulked off into the darkness. She radiated an old-world dedication to a purpose at any cost, a quality Eddie had never sensed in such abundance. She was not to be wasted on a long shot.

The bank of windows opposite from where they had entered glowed like sunrise beyond a horizon of junk. Eddie's hand bled and the blood slimed his fingers. "We can head for those windows and smash back out," he whispered.

"If you think you can take it," she said.

He smiled. *A sense of humor, too.* "We'll find a crowbar or something this time." It seemed she had forgiven him for ruining her ambush. Only their escape could have made him happier.

"Can you fight?" she asked.

"I won my first four fistfights," he said, "but the last one was in fifth grade."

"I will remember that if those men send children to find us."

They crept along the center aisle. Eddie scanned to his right for a promising passageway toward the windows. Chanthay was a silhouette against a wall of crates. Her hands were folded before her, as if in prayer. In them she held her gun. Eddie could feel what her tiny weapon meant. *Those men must risk their lives to take ours.* The odds favored the pursuers—they had two guns—but the fight was fair, the stakes equally lethal.

Another pistol wouldn't have done much to level the odds. Not in Eddie's hands. He had never fired anything more potent than a BB gun. The kids in his neighborhood used to take turns shooting squirrels in the Dracut State Forest. Oh, how those rodents ran, ricocheting like rubber balls from a cannon. Eddie shot and shot, never could hit one. After a while he started to miss on purpose, and wondered later if he had done so all along.

Could he kill a man? Chanthay could, and with just one gun that was all that mattered. But could he? If he had to? He could shoot back, perhaps, into the darkness at an unseen foe. What the bullet found in the shadows would be its own business.

Eddie inched along on his toes, breathing silently through his mouth. He kept watch to the rear and looked for passageways. There was no fear, just hair-trigger alertness. Where was Fear? He had felt her presence when the first bullet struck blindly at the brick. But in the rush through the maze, he had run right past her. She was lost out there, too, somewhere in the junk.

Few passageways led toward the windows. One aisle started in the right direction, but soon veered off. Another path dead-ended after thirty feet. *What about a direct route? Straight over the junk.* The crates along the aisle were stacked about nine feet high. It was hard to tell if there was an easy way up there.

Something hit Eddie's chest and crashed him to the floor.

He yelped in surprise. *Am I shot?* Chanthay clamped a hand over his mouth. She had shoved him down in mid-stride. He nodded that he was all right and she took away her hand.

Somewhere in the junk the footsteps pounded again. The men were running.

Chanthay pointed at Eddie's left leg. It had vanished beneath the knee. He flexed the leg and it returned. His eyes trained on a square on the floor, twelve feet across, darker than the space around it.

"A hole," Chanthay whispered.

Eddie yanked a button from his shirt and dropped it in. Several seconds passed before it rattled off something metallic. This was not an option for escape. Straight above, in the ceiling, was another hole of the same size.

Eddie leaned to her. "Probably an elevator," he said. "Retrofitted into the building, and then torn out."

The footsteps seemed louder than before. Echoes made it hard to tell from which direction they came. Eddie and Chanthay stepped around the hole and hurried down the corridor.

They passed an aisle to their left and someone yelled, "There!"

There was a white flash. Even with a sound suppressor, the noise shook the air. The slug popped against a crate above their heads. The shot sent Eddie running like a starter's pistol for the hundred-meter dash. He had not trained much since college track-and-field, but muscles have amazing memories; his thighs pumped to top speed in three steps.

Another man yelled, "Kill her, grab him!"

Or was it, "Kill him, grab her?" Eddie did not wait to find out.

The end of the corridor came quickly. One staircase went up, another went down. Eddie bounded up the stairs three at a time. At the first landing, he looked back. Chanthay had just reached the bottom.

"Split up!" she yelled. And she vanished down the stairs.

Eddie kept going. Heavy footsteps banged up the stairs behind him. Just one set, he thought. They sounded clumsy. *This guy's in worse shape than me.* Eddie flew up two more flights and ran out to the fourth floor. Its layout was similar to the first level below—a main corridor straight through the junk, with side paths snaking off. He ran down random paths—left, right, left, left, right. He threw himself behind a pallet stacked with wooden crates, and panted for breath. His left hand, still bleeding, was in a glove of blood and dust.

He pressed his right palm on the cut, and held his hands over his head to help stop the flow.

Climbing the stairs had lengthened his lead on his pursuer, but now Eddie was too high up to jump from a window.

The stomping on the staircase stopped on the fourth floor landing.

Funny, Eddie thought. Before his ice ride down the canal, nobody had ever tried to kill him. And now, days after being left to drown, he was hiding from a professional murderer. The backbeat of his heart pounded in his inner ear. Sweat ran down his face. He thought about Nowlin, and wondered if Danny knew he was about to be murdered. Did he have flashbacks about what he had done in his life? Or visions of what he would never do?

Eddie shook those thoughts from his head—it was too soon to give up. But he needed a plan. *Stay alive until Chanthay gets here with that gun.* A fine concept, but a few details short of a plan. He had options. Assuming the building was symmetrical, he could negotiate the junkscape and find stairs back down on the other side. That would bring him closer to Chanthay. But the stairs down also headed toward the other gunman. And if the one already on his tail were to follow, Eddie would be in a sandwich. He would be meat.

Or he could head for the windows. Yes, it was too high to jump, but he could attract attention somehow. He could heave crates out the window. *Real subtle. He'd be on me in a minute.*

That left hiding. Yeah, hiding sounded good. Eddie crept around, looking for a crate to slip into.

The man with the gun yelled out, "This don't gotta be so hard!"

The words soared over the junk and died to silence in the far reaches of the room. The sweat on Eddie's face ran cold. The low voice with a New York City accent was raw and phlegmy. It sounded so close. Eddie had run at least a hundred feet through the twisting passages before he stopped to rest, but the hitman wasn't half that far away in a straight line.

The man yelled again, "What's your name?"

Eddie was silent.

The man waited a few seconds, and then shouted, "You won't say, so I gotta give you one. I'm gonna call you Carl, 'cause you ran like Carl Lewis up them stairs." The man laughed as if this was the funniest thing he'd heard in a month. Eddie heard the flick, flick of a cigarette lighter.

"You a smoker, Carl?" the man yelled. He let the words die out, and then added, "Don't ever start—these fucking things will kill you." He chuckled again.

Then the man began to walk. His footsteps progressed down the center aisle.

"Lemme tell you how this works, okay?" He spoke in a polite, unhurried manner. "You listening Carl?" Silence, then, "We could say that I'm on the clock right now, except I don't get paid by the hour, see? I get paid by the job." He coughed and cleared his throat. "Don't ever work salary if you can help it, Carl."

Career advice? From a hitman?

"People take advantage of you—they don't care, they just screw ya. Christ—what I wouldn't give for a half-decent union." The man chuckled some more. "Hey! Do they let Republicans join a union? I've been Republican since Ford. I like a guy who knows how to grant a pardon." He laughed again. "Nixon fucked it up for Ford, the poor bastard shoulda beat Carter."

The voice drew closer. The man with the gun had started down the same left turn Eddie had chosen. He got back to the subject at hand. "Now, your girlfriend downstairs—she gotta be whacked, and that's that. And we're all real sorry because she's a great piece of ass, but we got no options with that broad. I guarantee that Mick ain't even talking to her down there, the way I'm talking to you right now."

Eddie caught a whiff of tobacco. He didn't know the brand, but it was foul.

"But you're another story, Carl. We ain't getting paid to do you, and we don't usually do stuff for free. But you can't blame us for being curious. Right? We wanna know who you are, who you're working for—that kinda shit."

The man with the gun hacked a wet cough. Then he stepped slowly down the same right turn Eddie had taken. *He guessed right again!*

"Now lemme remind you that I'm being paid by the job here. The longer it takes, the less it works out per hour. Get my drift? What I'm hinting at, Carl, is I don't want to blow my afternoon in this pisshole, because that's not smart business."

The man with the gun came to another intersection, and again chose the path Eddie had taken.

"So what I'm saying is, you can come out. And then we can sit down together and have a chat. You tell me what you're doing with the foreign chick, and if you're truthful to me, we both can put this behind us. You hear me, Carl?"

Eddie never considered his offer. Not for one second. The man was curious—that part Eddie believed. But he would never let him go, not while Eddie could identify him. Put this behind us? *Yeah, put a slug behind my ear, you mean.*

The man's voice grew closer.

"The problem we have here, Carl, is that after a finite period of time, I'm gonna get pissed. I got this temper, all right? The wife nagged me to get some pills for it. But they make me sleepy—ask Mick. He gets bitchy 'cause he has to drive all the time when I'm too sleepy. So I don't take them sometimes. And you know what? I don't think I took them today."

At the next intersection, the man with the gun again chose the correct path.

"I gotta warn you, Carl. Once I get pissed, it's no longer business for me. I don't think I'll be in the mood to hear your story. It ain't a threat—not really—it's just how it is. So why don't you save us both a lot of trouble and come out?"

Eddie trembled as the voice got louder. He battled the urge to run. One more turn and the man would be on him. Eddie peeked around a crate in the man's direction. The footsteps stopped in the middle of an intersection and the man bent over. In the yellow light of his cigarette lighter, Eddie's tracks through the dust were plain to see. The man turned right.

Eddie shoved over a crate and bolted.

There were two shots, the second so soon after the first it seemed like an echo. The bullets rang against a steel barrel twelve inches to Eddie's left. A white-hot spark seared his wrist and he gasped. The barrel hummed.

Eddie dashed recklessly through the darkened paths.

The man with the gun waded through the debris Eddie had dumped and charged after him. He was quick and just as reckless over the short haul, but Eddie, running for his life, out-raced him deep into the junk. The man gave up in a coughing fit.

"Carl," he howled, "you're beginning to piss me off!"

Eddie ran to the windows before he stopped. There was freedom, just fifty feet away. But it was fifty feet straight down. He had little time to rest. The man would be tracking him again, and Eddie was an easy mark in the light of the windows. He looked for a weapon, something to cover his tracks—anything. He tore through nearby crates. He found garden hose nozzles in one, ceramic lawn elves in another. The labels on the boxes were from a defunct hardware chain. Yes, tools! Eddie rifled through more boxes of the same label. He took a curved claw hammer and a screwdriver, a long brown smock and a roll of electrician's tape. He found three dozen cans of silver spray paint in a cardboard box.

Eddie thought for a moment, and then scooped up the box and slipped into the darkness.

His pursuer was quiet now. Eddie didn't like that. At least when he was talking Eddie knew where he was. Eddie wound through the passageways at a quick clip. He made no effort to conceal his footprints, but he needed to build up time, lots of it, if he was going to stop the hitman from tracking him.

When the case of paint became too heavy to lug any longer, Eddie set it down in a narrow four-way intersection, between high stacks of wooden pallets. Working mostly by feel in the shadows, Eddie used the screwdriver to pry the caps from the spray cans. He gathered the cans into a bunch and wrapped them together with five winds of tape. Then he flipped the cluster over and carefully set it down so the cans stood on their nozzles in the center of the intersection.

He pulled apart the top of a nearby wooden crate and crisscrossed the slats over the cans. Then he muscled pallets onto the floor as quietly as he could. Sweat beaded again on his face. He layered the pallets two deep—approximately the height of the cans.

To pass through Eddie's redesigned intersection, one had to walk over his handiwork. He snuck down a corridor to watch and to wait.

He wondered how Chanthay was faring. Better than he, he hoped. He had heard no gunshots from the basement, but would he in this place?

What if she had escaped? What if she was outside right now, getting away and leaving him, as she did in the old triple-decker? No, he had to have faith. He had risked his own life to go back for her at the window. She would come back for him. *Just stay alive until she gets here.*

Eddie smelled tobacco again. He rose onto his toes and readied to run.

Footsteps approached the intersection from the direction Eddie had come. The red end of a cigarette floated in space. It stopped at the edge of the pallets Eddie had placed on the floor. It waited there. *Come find me, you stupid bastard.* Finally, the pallets creaked under the weight of the man with the gun.

Flick, flick, flick went the lighter. The flame illuminated the man's face. He had a thick brow, lumpy features. And yup—he looked *pissed*.

The man stepped into the intersection and bent over with the flame. The spray cans hissed beneath his foot, and the propellant gases ignited in a whoosh.

A fireball roared to the ceiling. The man cried out, flung the lighter, and dove aside. Spiraling orange flames devoured the gasses and quickly burned out, leaving a ghostly green spot before Eddie's eyes.

A puddle of plastic that was the man's lighter burned on the floor a few seconds more, and then went out for good.

Eddie slipped deeper into the shadows.

The man screamed himself hoarse. "You think you're cute Carl? I'll beat you dead with my bare fucking hands. That's a promise! You hear me? My bare fucking hands!"

Eddie took the man at his word and hustled away. He would not be tracked anymore, but his enemy still had his gun, and he would never give up. With no lighter, the hitman wouldn't be smoking anymore, either. *I can forget about hiding until he dies of lung cancer.*

Eddie trotted on his toes toward the middle of the sprawling junkyard. The man stomped blindly after him, heading a quarter-turn in the wrong direction and crashing crates to the floor.

How long could Eddie survive? The man would need an hour to search the whole floor in semi-darkness. If Eddie kept on the move and stayed lucky, he might survive until nightfall. At night the place would be black and neither of them would be able to move. Dawn would break the stalemate in favor of the man with the gun. And if bitchy old Mick ever came up from the basement, Eddie's life expectancy would be halved. A torch or a flashlight in the wrong hands would halve it again. Eddie decided to get out of there before dark.

The man with the gun was stalking him quietly again. Twisting passageways led Eddie to the main corridor, down the center of the warehouse. He trotted along the aisle, measuring the weight of the hammer in his right hand. Surely one blow to the skull would knock a man unconscious—or worse. Eddie didn't want to kill him. Just hurt him bad enough to get away. Knock him down, take his gun. Then inform the man that Ford lost because Carter out-debated him, and run away. Real fast.

Eddie stopped to wrap the hammer's slick hickory handle in tape. It improved his grip, but not his chances against the man with the gun. How the hell would Eddie ever get close enough to use it?

He took a practice swing, and jostled the roll of tape from his jacket. He reached down for the roll, saw it bounce once on the floor and then disappear without a sound. Eddie froze. He withstood the prickly heat wave of another close call. He had stopped two feet in front of another dark square on the floor, twelve feet across—the elevator shaft.

Eddie looked up. There was a similar hole in the ceiling. He looked from one to the other, and then had an idea, a terrible thought he could not believe was his own. His chest tightened.

There's got to be another way.

But was there?

Eddie reluctantly put the hammer down, crawled around the hole and felt for its edge. Standing with his heels inches from the shaft, he filled his chest with a deep breath of dusty air and let it out slowly. He inhaled again, even more deeply, and held the breath for a second before he eased it out. He did this until he could no longer hear his heart thumping inside his ear.

Then Eddie exploded into a sprint down the aisle.

He pumped his arms and concentrated on a hard, even pace, pounding down the pathway like a sprinter in a dash.

He counted each time his right foot struck the floor. *One— two—three....*

When he reached eight, a crate crashed to the floor over his left shoulder. At twelve, the man cried out, "You're dead Carl! Dead!"

Footsteps came after him.

At twenty-one, his right foot struck upon the sill between the mill floor and the stairwell.

Twenty-one.

Eddie scrambled up the stairs to the fifth floor, and stopped. The boxes were piled higher on this level; the corridor was black.

His body wanted to run—run away from the man plodding up the stairs. *Not yet.* Eddie faced down the long, dark center corridor and placed his feet on the sill between the mill floor and the stairwell. He bent over, grabbed his pants at the knees and fought for his breath. The footsteps were almost on him. The man with the gun was growling.

Eddie's last thought before he ran was of Congressman Hippo Vaughn, in his silly white suit, gazing up at the last out of the World Series. It was a lazy fly ball that hung in the air so long, the fans had already started to celebrate the Red Sox championship. Vaughn was cheering in slow motion. There was no audio in this daydream. Next to Vaughn was an empty seat.

Uhhh! Eddie grunted and tore down the center of the aisle. Knees high, arms driving, his toes barely tapping the floor. The high walls of stacked junk on either side formed a canyon of pure shadow, through which Eddie hurled himself blind.

The man roared, "You're mine!" He stormed after Eddie.

A gunshot rang out.

Eddie counted his steps. *Six—seven—eight.* Even pace, even pace. Together, they raced, stride for stride, down the darkened warehouse floor. *Fourteen—fifteen—sixteen.*

Another shot echoed.

The bottom of Eddie's right ear sizzled and then went numb. Hot blood drizzled down his neck.

In Eddie's mind, Hippo's beaming smile twisted to slow-motion horror. The ball was coming down and there was nobody underneath to catch it. But it was too late now.

Twenty-one. Eddie slammed down his right foot, threw up his hands and leaped. Twelve feet was not a far jump—not if his stride was perfect and his takeoff accurate. But what if he had left too early? His feet churned. At his apex, he stretched his legs forward and reached, reached for every inch of distance. Time seemed to stop as he moved through the air, as if he wasn't moving at all but was suspended, weightless, in dark space.

Where the hell is the floor?

Bang! Eddie hit it and rolled.

From deep below, the man with the gun screamed once.

Eddie lay panting for a minute. His fingers felt where the bullet had taken a chunk, half-moon shaped, from his earlobe. The tip of his thumb fit in the hole. Blood streamed from the wound. Eddie gathered himself at the edge of the shaft. There was nothing visible in it. His mind's eye saw the man splayed face down across a mound of strange machinery that was sharp and irregular like a coral reef.

He felt a mix of joy and detached terror.

Eddie was safe.

And Eddie was a killer. Self-defense or not, he was a killer, now and for the rest of his life.

He spat down the hole and then spoke into it, "Carl Lewis was a long-jumper, too, you son-of-a-bitch."

Chapter 21

Eddie flexed his right hand around the hammer, which he had retrieved from beside the hole on the fourth floor. The tan smock he had found among the tools was tied around his waist. He had crudely patched his ear with some of the tape he had wound around the hammer.

He had decoded the weird logic of the passageways. It was something of a honeycomb pattern. Eddie silently negotiated back to the first floor and returned to the stairs that Chanthay had run down.

He listened from the top of the stairwell. Nothing.

Eddie stepped down to the first stair. His foot skidded on something slick, and he lunged at the railing to keep his balance. He reached a hand down. The stair was spattered with blood.

Chanthay and the gunman had come back up.

He couldn't know whose blood it was, but Eddie could not shake the sick feeling he was too late.

Suddenly, from deep across the mill came a tremendous crash, like an avalanche of debris falling and bouncing and tumbling on the floor. Eddie whirled, stepped in the direction of the crash and heard a muffled gunshot. Two sets of footsteps carried across the junk.

She was alive.

He trotted toward the sound.

Eddie needed several minutes to reach the scene of the crash. A stack of crates had been purposely toppled into a pyramid of metal drums, judging by the vast debris field and the crude lever and fulcrum left where the crates had stood. A few of the barrels leaked fluid that burned Eddie's sinuses with a stench similar to model airplane glue. The mess seemed like Chanthay's doing. Eddie couldn't imagine a New York City hitman going through all the trouble. They didn't get paid by the hour.

Eddie needed to find Chanthay before he ran into the gunman. This part of his evolving plan relied on chance. Fifty-fifty. Better odds than blackjack, and Eddie liked blackjack. He proceeded quietly through the aisles, stopping every few steps to listen for clues.

His mind wandered. He pictured Chanthay with Danny Nowlin.

She was an urban warrior bent on homicidal revenge; he was an anal-retentive political reporter still learning to write. The irony police would have collared that odd couple. What had brought them together? Danny couldn't tell him, and Chanthay probably wouldn't, so the best Eddie could do was wonder. Did they have plans together? Hard to imagine Danny would move out on Jesse for a fling, unless it wasn't by his choice. Had Jesse found out about Chanthay? Or had she just heard Danny's cheating heart beat when the lights went out?

Eddie stopped beside a wall built from bags of cement mix. Each was the size of a thin pillow from a cheap hotel. They were piled eight feet high, like sandbags around a bomb shelter. He listened. Nothing. Or was that something? The scuff of a shoe in the distance?

He was about to move on when something tickled his ear. Fine particles of cement dust leaked from a bag on the pile. Eddie stood back and looked up.

Chanthay squatted on top of the stack, wrapped in a dark oily cloth.

She had fared worse than he, by the look of her. Her ski vest was missing and her turtleneck was ripped from her right armpit to her navel. Her sleeve was blood-soaked; she had tried to bandage her upper arm with a rag. Her face was bruised. She pushed dark drool over her swollen bottom lip, and then wiped her chin on her sleeve.

They stared at each other for a minute, neither moving.

Chanthay clutched a knife in her right hand. It was a little thing, just a pocketknife, but it was proof that the fight carried on. Beaten up but not beaten, too noble for her own good. Eddie's instinct to maintain journalistic distance buckled under her allure. He realized that his competition to wring information from Chanthay was over; he couldn't compete against her again. *I would trade my life to save this person.* He would kill to protect her, too. That fact awed him.

Eddie untied the smock from his waist. He cleared his throat and rolled the goo to the back of his tongue. He put a rasp in his voice, and mustered a New York accent. "Hey Mick," he called out. "She's over here."

There was a pause, and then a voice came across the field of flotsam.

"Is that you, er—Chester?"

Would a chain-smoking New York City hitman go by *Chester*? Probably not. This was an old reporter's trick. Eddie yelled, "No, dickhead, it's Gerry freakin' Ford."

There was a laugh. The man yelled back, "Right—your hero. Sorry, Ray, you don't sound so good."

"I been running all over this pisshole chasing that skinny fucker."

The voice sounded closer. "You get him?"

"What do you think?"

Another laugh. "You get anything out of him?"

"Naw, he pissed me off."

There was a loud sigh. "You're a goddam animal with that temper and it's going to get you into trouble." The voice was closer still. "Where's the girl?"

"Here. She's dead. Looks like she bled out."

"Yeah, I cut her good. Where are you?"

"Over *here*."

The gunman suggested, businesslike, "Give her two slugs in the hat to be sure. And let's get the hell outta here."

"You do it. I'm taking a piss."

Eddie lowered himself to the floor and slipped beneath the smock.

The gunman shouted in a festive tone, "Lemme tell ya, that was one tough bitch. It's no wonder they're paying what they're paying, making us rich—not that those guys don't have the money."

He yawned loudly, getting closer. "Chick wore me out. I thought the hot little whore would want one last ride before reincarnation. Didn't want her dead right away, just to hold still for half-a-fuckin' minute, you know? Where the hell are you, Ray? Anywhere near the stack of cement bags? Ray? Oh, never mind, I see her."

His footsteps drew near. "She could have had ecstasy, but she had a beating instead," he said. "Some women got too much pride, no matter how bad they want it." He laughed a silly laugh, more suited to a little girl.

The gunman had arrived. "Hey baby," he said in a low silky voice. "Are you still warm?"

He pulled the smock away.

Eddie winked at him.

The gunman gasped. His face twisted into a horror mask. "Over here, Ray!" he screamed. He grabbed furiously for the gun in his waistband, but the bag of cement was already in the air. It thumped off his shoulder and the side of his head. He grunted and stumbled to one knee. Eddie swung the hammer. The man was unconscious before his jaw hit the floor.

Chanthay dropped from her perch and took the man's pistol.

"Where's your gun?" Eddie asked, but she wasn't listening.

"Mick?" she said in disbelief. "You knew his name?"

Eddie shrugged. "That's what the other guy said."

"Did you two sit around upstairs talking sports?"

"Politics, actually—he's Republican."

"Yeah? Where is he?"

Eddie stared at her. He said flatly, "That guy dropped out of the race." Chanthay looked him up and down, at his ear and the blood down his neck, and nodded.

"You're hurt," Eddie said. He raised a hand toward her face.

She stepped backwards out of his reach and shook her head.

Eddie lightly bit his bottom lip. He should have known better. He gestured to the man on the floor. "What about this asshole? Can we get him to the hospital?"

Chanthay straddled the man and shot him through the back of his head.

When the bang had died away, she said, "It's too late for him."

Chapter 22

Chanthay sat at attention on a corner of Eddie's piano bench. She did not flinch when Eddie reached kitchen shears to her arm. His hands trembled as he snipped away her sleeve and the bloody rag wrapped under her armpit and around her shoulder. The sopping cloth fell onto a newspaper spread over the floor. There was so much blood that Eddie couldn't see the cut. He pressed a twice-folded hand towel to the wound and held it there.

The numbness had drained from Eddie's ear, replaced by a burning sensation. The makeshift bandage of electrical tape seemed to be holding, so he left it there for the moment. The fresh gauze he had taped over the cut on his left hand was still white. That wound had stopped bleeding.

Eddie peeled the towel back and peeked beneath it.

Oh, Jesus. It was a straight four-inch slash, deep, diagonal across her shoulder and more than a quarter-inch wide. He put the towel back. "It's soaking through," he said. He grabbed another towel from the stack he had brought from the bathroom and pressed it over the first one.

General VonKatz sniffed the stranger's boots, and then sat on the coffee table to monitor Eddie's work in case it suddenly turned into some kind of chasing game.

Chanthay sipped water from a paper cup. She paid no attention to Eddie's effort at first aid. She looked like a woman waiting for a bus.

"Is that an act?" Eddie said. "The stoic soldier?"

She looked at him. "Would it be easier to treat me if I was hysterical?"

There was no good comeback to that. Eddie clamped his lips shut. He counted the towels on hand—four more. If he ran out of towels, he could use T-shirts.

If I run out of towels, she'll be dead.

Chanthay noticed the chessboard. "Whom were you playing?" she asked.

"Myself."

She shook her head. "You compete against yourself?"

Yeah, Eddie thought, he competed against everybody. "I started competing before I was born," he said.

"That makes no sense."

"Against my brother, not that I knew him."

Eddie held the towel. "My parents married young, and had my brother Henry right away," he explained. "Hank was a genius, I guess, and a top athlete. They thought that kid would run the world someday. He was nineteen when he got tangled in some idiotic robbery scheme—I don't know much about it except that an armored car driver was shot dead. The cops never found the money, but they found Henry. He's doing life in a federal pen in New York.

"My folks were devastated, of course. And even though they were both pushing forty, they decided to start the family over."

"And you were born?" she said.

"Yup. They thought they'd have another Hank, except I wasn't quite as good in school, not quite as natural an athlete. I had to work harder to keep pace with what he had done in class and on the field."

Eddie looked over the captured pieces alongside the chessboard. He was the pawn that had outrun two hitmen, the pawn who had saved the queen. He felt a whoosh of dread. *What if I can't stop the bleeding?*

"Such a family cannot survive," she said.

Eddie nodded. "My folks split when I was a kid, my father moved out west. My mom worked a lot. She had two sisters, both young widows, who roomed together. They'd baby-sit me. Sometimes I'd spend the night with them and my mother would pick me up the next day. After a while, I started living with my aunts, and they started raising me. There was never anything official about it—my mom just stopped picking me up."

Eddie turned to the chessboard and considered his next move. Two soldiers were in peril. A chess master would keep the knight, whose ability to leap other pieces added a third dimension to the game. Eddie's game was still linear; to him the rook was more valuable. He moved it to safety and spun the board around.

"You'll lose your knight," Chanthay said.

"Soldiers die—you ought to know," Eddie replied. He did not look her in the eye.

She paused a moment and then asked him, "Did it bother you, in the mill, my shooting that man?"

Eddie's mouth went dry. "That guy was no threat to us—not at the time."

"He tried to rape me on the stairs."

Eddie stared at the towel he held to her arm. "I know," he said. "I know."

"He would have killed us both and then stopped for a sandwich."

"*I know.*"

Eddie muttered a curse. He wiped his brow with the back of his hand. Chanthay's brutality in the mill had shocked him. When the gunshot echoed, he had braced himself against a wave of horror and remorse over the execution. The wave crashed over him, and Eddie had discovered that he was the same person, standing in the same spot, with a dead gunman at his feet. It had bothered him, and now he knew why. *Shouldn't I be different somehow?*

"I was taught, you know, in church, to respect human life," Eddie said, frowning at the bloody towel.

"By whom?" she said. "A cleric who learned to wear a robe in school? Do you think he ever saw evil like those two men? Be glad that humanity is rid of them."

No remorse.

The towels were growing heavy with her blood. "The bleeding's not going to stop," Eddie said. "You need a doctor."

"We discussed this," she reminded him. "Pinch the pressure point—here." She put his free hand on her shoulder, his thumb in the hollow behind her collarbone. He pinched.

She nodded and gave him a sleepy little smile.

He craved to forgive her.

Chanthay had slain the gunman without hesitation, the way Eddie would swat a mosquito on his arm. He wondered how many people Chanthay had killed in her war, and how many more she had to go. "How will you know when you're done," he blurted.

"Done with what?"

"With your assassinations, with hitmen chasing you through old mills, with the secret cabal that got Nowlin killed and nearly me, too. How much revenge is enough for you?"

She was silent for a while. Eddie's hand cramped from pinching her shoulder. He refused to ease his grip.

Finally, she said, "My father used to dream of revenge when we were working the fields. These fantasies brought him joy, the idea of his enemy's heart on a stick. He said that civilized people have mistreated revenge, and locked it from its rightful place in our hearts. Revenge, he would say, is the bastard child of happiness." She looked at Eddie. "You can never have too much happiness."

The General interrupted with an angry gurgle. The moth had flapped in from the kitchen. It bobbed a few times and disappeared into the bathroom. The General dropped to the floor, flattened himself against the carpet, and scurried in pursuit.

Eddie encouraged him, "Good idea, General. Go sneaky."

"You could just swat it with a newspaper," Chanthay offered.

"I don't like to interfere with the General's business."

"No," she said. "Just mine." She smiled at him.

Eddie's distress over the death in the mill slipped away. *Careful, careful.* Too late—for once, Eddie could not force himself back behind his reporter's skepticism.

The second towel had not soaked through; the bleeding had slowed. "Hold the towel—I think I have some butterfly bandages," Eddie said. "Maybe I can close the cut."

The bandages and an antiseptic were in the first aid kit in his closet. Eddie got a clean T-shirt and ripped it to strips. He balled a strip and soaked it with antiseptic. "This is alcohol-based," he told her. "Gonna hurt like hell."

She nodded.

Eddie peeled the towel back. It released a thick metallic stench. Blood seeped slowly from the cut. "It's better," he said. Chanthay's arm jerked slightly when the antiseptic touched it. Her eyes squeezed shut. Eddie cleaned the gash and the area around it.

He fanned the alcohol dry with his hand, and then closed the cut with eight butterfly bandages. Then he wrapped her arm in gauze and sealed it with athletic tape.

Eddie patted her shoulder. "No bowling for a week," he said.

She inspected the bandage. "Not bad. Were you a Boy Scout?"

"Only until I realized there was no merit badge for chasing cheerleaders."

She snickered. "Did you catch any?"

Eddie rubbed his neck. He asked her, "Who killed Danny?"

Her smile fell. "I don't know."

"Those goons from the mill?"

"Those two were nobodies, just cheap labor. There are probably two more on the way as we speak."

"Why was Danny shooting heroin?"

"He wasn't," she said. "Drugs were not his weakness."

"So who shot him up with dope?"

She sighed, exasperated. "I don't *know*. I've been searching for those answers since Danny disappeared." She turned the conversation around. "What have *you* been doing? I have been looking for clues in the paper, and have found nothing. Where are the stories about Danny?"

Eddie looked at the bloody cloth on the floor. "I'm not allowed to write them."

"Then what were you doing following me from the wake?"

"Danny was my friend. Or, he should have been. I owe him answers, and I'm not going to stop until I have them. Same as you, I would say."

Chanthay ignored him. She swung her leg over the bench and faced the piano. Her right hand played one chord. She frowned. "A little sharp," she said. "Is it yours?"

"Yeah. You want it?"

She smiled devilishly, and began to play, one-handed. Her right hand roamed up and down in a melody. The sound was modern and experimental, both beautiful and off-putting. As she played, she seemed to stare at a spot past the piano, through the wall, and into the other room. She finished with her hand hard on the keys.

Eddie clapped. "What was that?" he asked.

"Claude Debussy. A favorite composer of my father. You know him?"

"Never heard of him," Eddie admitted. "He sounds French. Is he dead?"

"He is both French and dead."

Eddie reasoned, "That's why I never heard of him."

She groaned at his lack of culture. "American men are a lost cause." She yawned, got up unsteadily and sat on Eddie's recliner.

"Danny liked easy-listening tunes," Eddie said. "Must have made you nuts." His ear throbbed and felt gigantic on his head. "We can help each other, maybe, if we put together what we know."

"Maybe," she said.

Eddie rolled his eyes. "Fine. Me first." He told her about the autopsy report, about the heroin in Danny's veins, and about the dent in his skull. How Leo and Gabrielle found the body. And he told her of the story Nowlin was writing, which seemed to concern the Khmer Rouge.

Chanthay nodded at the end, acknowledging that it was her turn. "Danny was working with us," she said.

"Who's *us*? You and Danny and who else?"

"Two others—don't ask for names." Eddie didn't ask, and she continued. "I met Danny at the library about three months ago. He was studying Cambodian history, and he knew a few words of Khmer, from his time in my country as an editor. We struck up a conversation."

From the bathroom came the crash of shampoo bottles into the tub. The General hissed. "Ignore him," Eddie said. "He's obsessed."

"Inform your cat that obsession is a full-time job." She combed her fingers through her hair. "I was also at the library for research. I realized from the material Danny had collected that our areas of interest overlapped. He seemed to have integrity, and I thought he could help us."

Chanthay shifted in the chair and grimaced in pain. She leaned back. Her eyes fluttered. "Danny was a good investigator," she continued. "He knew how to get records we couldn't get. He confirmed rumors that would have taken us months to track down. And he brought on someone to help us, whom he said we could trust."

"Help you how?"

"To confirm the identity of the one we have come here to kill," she said. She frowned at him. "There would be jeopardy if you knew any more."

"Look at my goddam ear," Eddie yelled, pointing at the wad of electrical tape on his head. "I'm already in jeopardy."

Her eyes narrowed. "Not jeopardy for you, for our mission."

Eddie slumped against a wall and slid to the floor, impatient and irritated. She was like a bomb falling from the sky, wired only for destruction, in her own way just as driven and competitive as Eddie. "That's all goddam well," he said. "But what did Danny get from this arrangement?" Eddie looked her over. "Besides you, of course?"

She shot him a sharp look. "His news story," she said. "Danny called it his ticket to the major leagues. Does this makes sense to you?"

Eddie suddenly noticed his headache, like his eyeballs were being squeezed from behind. "Perfect sense," he admitted.

"I spoke with Danny on Friday by telephone," she said. "He was upset. Livid. It was something about his story. He didn't say what. We planned to meet Saturday night at the house in the Acre. But Danny never showed up. After they found him in the canal, I went to his home and destroyed his notes to cover our tracks."

"How did you get the virus on his computer at The Empire?"

Her eyebrows lowered. "I know nothing about that."

Eddie believed her. She might not tell him everything, but he had saved her life, and she would not tell him lies. He weighed his next question for a long while. "Tell me this," he said, "did you bed Danny to keep him loyal, or was there more to it than that?"

Chanthay pushed back in the recliner and closed her eyes. She waved her hand over herself and said, "This body is just a container for the mind."

"Just a tool to get what you want?"

"Your words," she said.

What the hell did that mean? Eddie was curious, but she was tired. He let it go.

Her breathing grew louder as she began to drift off. Eddie got a blanket and covered her. She seemed to shrink under it, to become a little girl, a half-starved slave digging a ditch, too weak to lift the pick over her head. He watched her for a long time. Funny, he thought, they had spent the day together in a bloody fight for their lives, and his first glimpse of her humanity had come in something so ordinary as sleep.

◇ ◇ ◇

Eddie lunged for the phone before it could ring a second time.

"Yeah?" he answered, looking out into the living room. He could see Chanthay on the recliner by the light of a streetlamp.

"We still on for later tonight?" Gordon Phife asked. "I got a sure-fire tip to cure your slice."

"Gordie, this ain't a good time," Eddie whispered.

"You can't cancel tonight!"

"Take it easy—it's just golf. We'll talk at work tomorrow."

"No, Ed, we gotta talk tonight."

Eddie watched Chanthay stir under the blanket. The thought of leaving her in the middle of the night nearly made him retch. "This isn't about my slice, is it?"

"This is serious."

"Tell me now."

"I won't talk about Keyes or Danny over the phone," Phife insisted. "Later tonight."

Eddie said nothing.

"Are you in or not?"

Eddie mouthed a curse word. Then he said, "Yeah, I'm in."

At five minutes to three, the telephone rang three times. Eddie woke feeling grouchy. He dressed and grabbed his keys. Chanthay was on her right side on the recliner. The General snoozed beside her, on the arm of the chair, guarding the injured woman from the moth. Eddie tried to slip out without waking them.

"Where are you going?" she mumbled.

"To meet a friend. I'll be back soon."

She reached a hand to him. "Keep me as your secret," she said. "Please."

The "please" struck him. It was an admission that she needed him, or at least needed something from him, and that was close enough to the same thing for Eddie. Her eyes were closed beneath wisps of hair across her face. An angry shiner glowered beneath her eye. Eddie winced at the sight of it, and was glad the hitmen were dead in the warehouse.

He took Chanthay's hand. They both squeezed. "You're my secret," he promised.

This night was warmer than the last time Gordon Phife had worked on Eddie's swing. It was in the forties on The Empire's rooftop, almost balmy, but Phife had bundled up in gloves, a hat, and winter coat, precisely as he had before.

Eddie complained about the lesson plan. "You want to practice with a one iron?" he said. "I never take mine out of the bag."

"That's why we need to practice," Phife insisted. "And when I say we, I mean you." He handed Eddie a Rolling Rock. The green bottle looked rusty brown in the red light of The Empire's giant neon E.

"What's with the Band-Aid on your ear?" Phife asked. He looked Eddie over. "And the tape on your hand? Jesus, Ed, if you got run over, I hope you got the license number."

"Yeah, they had New York plates," he said.

Gordon shrugged. "Major, right now you have me as confused as I ever hope to be."

"I saw that movie—*Where Eagles Dare*." Eddie tried to grip the club without angering the cut on his left hand.

Phife laughed. "You are on your game tonight. But can you hit?"

Eddie didn't care enough about his shot to wreck it by overthinking. He wanted to hear what was too important to wait until tomorrow. He whacked a line drive down the street, and his body ached.

Phife admired the shot. "See what good backswing tempo can do."

Eddie said, "Lesson over." He leaned on the club. "What have you heard?"

Phife seemed unbothered by Eddie's harshness. He looked at the dozen golf balls on the roof, and then to Eddie. "It's something Keyes said to me," he said, softly. "But it's more than that. Lemme back up." He drank beer. "Keyes has been on me about the political coverage—what events should be staffed with reporters, which get photogs and which get blown off."

"Keyes is a micromanager and a prick," Eddie said. "We knew this."

Phife waved his hand in excitement. "Not like this, we didn't. In the past week, Keyes has scratched the news coverage for a dozen political events I had scheduled to cover. I couldn't figure it out. Some were even early-morning press conferences tailored to Empire deadlines. It wasn't until I went back over my calendar that I realized what those events had in common—all were for City Council *challengers*."

"Every one?"

Phife nodded. "So I did a little more checking. Keyes made sure that we covered every event scheduled by the incumbents, no matter how inconvenient, or how minuscule the news value."

Eddie sipped his beer and considered what Gordon was saying. "He's using the paper to manage the election."

Phife shrugged. "I couldn't think of any other explanation, so I went to Keyes and that's what I told him."

"In those words? That's he's managing the election?"

Phife smiled. "Well, maybe I softened it a little. But it didn't matter. He started raging that I shouldn't be questioning him." Phife glanced around the rooftop, as if looking for eavesdroppers, and then said in a low voice, "Keyes told me, 'You saw what happened to the last guy who questioned my authority at this newspaper.'"

"Did he mean Danny?"

"Who else? I didn't stick around to ask."

Eddie thought about the dozens of times Danny had defied Keyes. "Danny never argued with him," Eddie said. "He just nodded whenever Keyes told him what to do, and then Danny went out and did whatever he wanted. He usually produced a better story on his own, so it was hard to fault him."

"Maybe Keyes decided he had enough of that."

"You fire a guy like that, you don't kill him," Eddie said. What Gordon was saying didn't make any sense.

"What have you found out?" Phife asked.

Eddie told him about the autopsy report. He described how he had broken into Danny's home computer and found the fragment of a news story, which Danny had called his "ticket to the major leagues."

Phife whistled at the magnitude of the information. "Sounds like the cops are getting nowhere," he said.

Eddie had information about that, too. "I hear there's a lot of pressure to make this case go away, including from the brass here at the newspaper," he said.

"From Templeton? Well, he's got a lot of yank in this town."

"I wouldn't count on Detective Orr easing up on the investigation," Eddie said. "I don't think that woman will ever give up."

"You got good sources. I'm impressed," Phife said. "I'm sure whatever you're doing, it's against the law."

Eddie knew that quote, too. "*Close Encounters.*"

"Right again."

"And here's one more for you," Eddie said. "If Keyes wanted Danny out of the newsroom, all he had to do was wait. Danny was interviewing at the Globe."

"You're joking!" Phife said. He slapped his knee. "The Globe?" He thought about it over two slugs of beer and then concluded, "Danny wasn't ready. He was a great reporter, but his writing left me too much reconstruction work. Not like you, Eddie."

Eddie shrugged, saying, "I can't get any love from the big metro dailies."

Phife seemed not to hear him. "I had to come in early when Nowlin had a story to file." He suddenly grew bitter. "No, check that—I didn't *have* to come in early, I did it because I'm a professional, and my job is to make the reporters look good." He gulped down more beer. "I carried Danny's ass—nearly carried it all the way to the Globe, apparently. But I never heard him acknowledge to anyone what I did for him."

Eddie smiled. Copy editors have sung this lament since they corrected Homer's spelling in The Iliad.

"You need an eye opener to get noticed," Phife offered. "A page-one splash to put on top of your resumé. Something that leaves the statewide press clawing over each other in your dust." He drank some more. "What about the story you say Danny was working when he died, his ticket to the big leagues?"

"What about it?"

"What's to stop you from following the same leads and getting it into print?"

Eddie swung the club gently with one hand. He said, "I don't have much to go on. The story was about the Cambodian Khmer Rouge. That's about all I could lift from Danny's computer, that and something about church homilies."

"Homilies?" Phife asked. "That reminds me of something Danny said a couple weeks ago. He asked me why the paper no longer runs religious sermons from local pastors. I didn't even know The Empire used to run them."

"Long time ago," Eddie said.

"Danny mentioned that he was going through old homilies in some back issues. He thought they were pretty good, and might boost circulation in the Monday paper." Phife rubbed his chin, as the details seemed to come back to him. "I asked why he was studying old homilies, and I never did get an answer. He distracted me somehow—with a movie quote, I think. Something from *A Fish Called Wanda*...."

Phife went on, but Eddie wasn't listening. He thought back to his B&E on Nowlin's computer. What had Danny said?

The homilies. It was right there all along.

Eddie interrupted, "Gordo, my friend, if you weren't my immediate supervisor, I'd kiss you full on the mouth, and I wouldn't spare the tongue." He tossed the one iron back to Phife, who caught it mid-shaft.

"I gotta go," Eddie said.

"We got four beers left."

"Save them for the back nine. I need to get to bed—too much research to do tomorrow."

Phife nodded, and warned in a solemn tone, "Don't pull a Nowlin on me. Promise you'll call me when you hit trouble."

Eddie yelled from around the giant E, "I swear it. You're a good friend, Gordo."

The Mighty Chevette putt-putted through empty streets. If Danny had found a clue in old issues of The Empire, Eddie could find it, too.

The car stopped outside his house with the metal-on-metal grind of worn-out brake pads. *That sounds expensive*, Eddie thought.

He slipped into the house and leaned into the door. It creaked shut.

The General was on the piano. The recliner was empty, the blanket Eddie had given Chanthay folded over the arm.

"Chanthay?" Eddie called out. "Hello? Hey General, is she in the bathroom? Chanthay?"

She was gone.

Eddie's chessboard had been turned around. A king was on its side. She had made his next move for him, charging the queen across the battlefield, into checkmate.

Chapter 23

An Ethiopian Sidamo coffee grind, thick with cream, provided the caffeine that defibrillated Eddie's brain in the morning. The coffee's glorious aftertaste was still on his breath when he stepped off the elevator and over a dog's leash.

Boyce Billips and Superdog were waiting to go downstairs. Boyce was unusually pale and twitchy, even for him. He seemed too young for the dark circles beneath his eyes. He wore a yellow-patterned necktie with pink swooshes and white squares. It looked like three ugly ties had been stitched into one supremely ugly tie.

"Nice noose," Eddie said.

Boyce laughed nervously. "The tie? I got it yesterday. Would you say this tie is yellow?"

"I suppose."

Boyce spoke too fast to make much sense. "It has some other colors in it, too. But they didn't have any ties that were just yellow. I checked everywhere. But this one is mostly yellow, so wouldn't you say, if you were looking for a yellow tie, that this tie was—yes!—yellow?"

"Boyce, have you slept recently?"

"Not recently." Superdog shook his head hard and flogged himself with his own ears, and then snorted like a steam shovel.

"It's yellow," Eddie confirmed, feeling a mixture of remorse and morbid curiosity at having incited Boyce's paranoia with the email from Nowlin's computer. Eddie spoke slowly, careful to pronounce every syllable in full, as he might speak to a jumper on a ledge, "I'm going to my desk now. Okay Boyce?"

Boyce grabbed Eddie's elbow. "I sent you an email yesterday," he confessed. "Don't open it! Just delete it. I didn't mean to send it. It's stupid. I realize that now."

"I'll delete it."

"Thank you, Eddie. And you're sure this is yellow?"

"Your fingernails are digging into my arm."

Boyce let go and led Superdog into the elevator. "I'm doing a feature on the cat that lives at the Dracut library," he said. He smiled weakly and yelled as the elevator doors were closing, "I hope he likes yellow ties!"

And yellow dogs. Eddie made a mental note to speak to Boyce about ghosts.

The morning quickly got worse—Detective Orr and Franklin Keyes were at Eddie's desk. Orr was in plain clothes again: black slacks, bomber jacket, purple scarf. Keyes wore a business suit worth more than the Mighty Chevette.

"Bourque? You still work here?" Keyes said. "I haven't seen your byline for so long, I forgot."

Eddie mentally welded his eyes in place before they rolled. "I'm filing my election analysis this morning," he said. "And I got another idea to pitch after that."

"More dope fiends?" Keyes said. He sneered, and then glanced at Orr. "Reporters need to produce around here, Bourque. But I think Detective Orr needs a word with you before you start, ah…producing."

"Fine with me," Eddie said.

They stood there.

Orr shifted her weight from foot to foot. Eddie checked the clock. Keyes scratched his nose. Orr finally suggested, "Maybe you could offer us your office, Mr. Keyes?"

Keyes snapped to attention. "Of course." He led the way, opened the office door and stood aside to let them in; first Orr, then Eddie.

"Thanks, Frank," Eddie said, shutting the door before Keyes could enter. Keyes froze a moment, unsure, and then abruptly spun and marched away.

Eddie headed for the editor's chair behind the desk, but Orr stopped him. "I would prefer to sit in Mr. Keyes' chair," she said.

So she did. Eddie took a chair in front of the desk. "Is that a police thing?" he asked. "You sit in the seat that projects the most authority?"

"No," said Orr, unbothered by his smart-ass analysis. "I prefer not to be between you and the door, so as not to imply a physical barrier. You are not in custody, and therefore free to leave any time." She smiled, all teeth and phony. "Makes it more difficult for lawyers to argue that incriminating statements were coerced. It's just policy."

Eddie shook his head and shrugged.

Detective Orr took an index card from her shirt pocket and slid it across the desk. "Read this, please," she said. "Then print your name in the space, sign the bottom and date it. In ink, please." She gestured to a pen on the desk, as if there was some question about what she meant by ink. "Speak up if there's anything you don't understand."

On the card was printed a short paragraph. Eddie got one line into it:

> I _____ understand that I have the right to remain silent....

He looked up. "What the hell is this?"

"Your Miranda warnings. These are rights determined by the Supreme Court—"

"Yeah—I've seen *Dragnet*," he said, cutting her off. An image of the hitman plunging down the elevator shaft flashed into his mind. His voice inched higher. "Why are you giving this to me? Am I under arrest?"

"No, Mr. Bourque." As Eddie grew excited, she became proportionally more calm. "I said you were free to go any time. We can make an appointment to meet at headquarters, if you'd like, and you may bring your attorney. But please finish reading the card."

Eddie understood the damn card. It meant she would use whatever he said to nail his ass, if at all possible. And if he could not afford a lawyer, the state would provide a public defender two years out of night school, who was already juggling thirty cases.

What the hell does she want from me? I leveled with her last time.

He signed, in ink.

With the little card back safe in her pocket, Detective Orr took out her notebook, a spiral flip-top model like Eddie used, except smaller. She wasted no time. "What were you doing at Mr. Nowlin's apartment?"

"Um...." *How could she know that?*

As if reading his thoughts, Orr explained, "I followed up yesterday with Mr. Nowlin's landlady. She mentioned that you had been by. I didn't know you liked Sinatra, Mr. Bourque."

Okay, at least the landlady hadn't ratted about Eddie's con job. "I was fishing for clues," he admitted.

"Doing *my* job again."

"Not that I doubt the way you—"

"How did you know Mr. Nowlin's address?"

"Huh?" She had trapped him. He looked at his feet. "I found Danny's wallet the night those people saved me from the canal," he said.

"Found it where?"

"Under a bridge." He ran his hand through his hair. "These people, they're drug addicts, okay? They had found Danny's wallet. But he was already dead—I'm sure of that."

"Fine," she said. "Let's talk some more about your connection to certain known users and possible traffickers of narcotics, namely heroin."

"I've been talking to these people, these heroin addicts, under the bridge, for a news story. That's my job."

Orr flipped the page in her notebook. "Uh-huh. Let's start at the beginning, Mr. Bourque. Who are these people under the bridge?"

Eddie told her about his night with the addicts.

Orr scribbled it all down. She looked him over and frowned. "Every time I see you, Mr. Bourque, you look a little worse. Mind explaining where you were yesterday?"

Eddie got a mental picture of the other hitman, face-down in Billings Mill, like he was peeking through a hole in the floor.

For a moment, Eddie considered leveling with her. Detective Orr seemed like an honest, effective cop, who was pressing on with her investigation despite political pressure to make the case go away. Eddie had information that might help. But there was no way to help Detective Orr without breaking his promise to keep Chanthay's secret. And no way to help her without explaining the two dead men in the mill, one impaled on God-knew-what at the bottom of an elevator shaft and the other with a cracked skull and a bullet in his brain.

So much for leveling with her.

Eddie squirmed through the interview, evading questions when he could, offering the truth whenever possible and flat-out lying when he had to. He did not fool her—that much was obvious. But with no hard evidence with which to challenge his story, Detective Orr was stuck with what he gave her.

She closed the notebook and rose in one motion. "I have taken a good deal of your time, Mr. Bourque, but investigations such as this depend greatly on the recollections of the people who knew the deceased," she said.

"I know that." *Just leave.*

"That's why the statements I collect are so important," she said, waving the little notebook. "And why it's a crime if anything false gets in here."

Eddie eyed her. "You think that notebook is sharp enough to cut the politics in this town?"

She hesitated—just a split-second, but Eddie saw it. "I'll be in touch," she said, and walked out smiling. Good God, how Eddie hated that phony smile. But her hesitation had confirmed for him that someone was applying pressure to ease off the investigation. Not that Orr would, and Eddie felt sick that he could not level with her. He sat in Keyes' office, clutching his head and counting the ways she could puncture his tale. They seemed endless.

Melissa poked in her head. "I'm braving the elements and brutalizing my body for the sake of stimulating the mind," she said. "Care to come on a coffee run?"

"She thinks I'm obstructing the investigation," Eddie said, still clutching his head.

"Who? That police lady with the fabulous Ann Taylor scarf? I love that color, not quite violet, more like a plum—"

"Did you hear me? She thinks I *don't* want her to find out who murdered my beat partner. Remember him? The chipper redheaded guy who sat next to me and would have scooped my ass all over town if he were my competitor instead of my partner? Or at least that's what the Globe thinks—do you ever listen to what I'm saying?"

Eddie didn't realize until he finished that he had been yelling.

Melissa recoiled one step back. Her hand drew over her heart.

"Maybe it's time you switch to decaf," she said softly.

She left him there.

Eddie started after her. But Melissa sped away on her long getaway sticks. Eddie couldn't catch her without running, and that would just draw attention to a bad scene. This was becoming the worst day of the week—and he had already been thrown in a canal and chased by two New York hitmen. Both, Eddie suddenly realized, probably had been Yankees fans.

Chapter 24

Back at Eddie's desk—more bad news.

There waited City Councilman Manny "The Mangler" Eccleston, dressed in a wrinkled gray suit and a black knit necktie so far out of style its age would have to be carbon dated. With a fedora in hand he looked like a Depression-era panhandler.

The Mangler looked around the newsroom, which had started to simmer in anticipation of deadline. "It's always a pleasure to visit the ninth estate," he said. "I wanted to be a reporter when I was a boy. But to do this day after day, you need paper in your veins."

"What's the good word today, Councilman?" Eddie asked.

"The word today is building report," Eccleston said, pointing to a large brown envelope on the desk. It was addressed to Eddie. "The report on the old church I promised you the other day. Let nobody ever say that Manny Eccleston can't make a promise."

"I'll correct anybody who tries to say that," Eddie pledged, reaching for the envelope.

Manny squirmed. "Ah, ah, ah—can you wait until I go? Wouldn't want anyone to know where you got the packet."

Eddie looked again at the address printed in black marker on the envelope:

TO: Edward Bourque, Lowell Empire reporter.

FROM: Lowell City Councilman Manuel G. Eccleston Jr.

RE: Church Structural Analysis Report.

Eddie sighed. "Sure thing, Manny."

Eccleston leaned close. His breath smelled like Greek salad dressing and orange Tic-Tacs. "But I don't mind telling you," he said, "that this report is going to knock a hole in your socks."

"Oh really?" Eddie's attention was on the envelope. He wanted to ditch the councilman so he could read the report, but The Mangler sat on Eddie's desk and sank roots.

"There's all kinds of structural deficiencies," he said.

Eddie did a doubletake. Did Manny just say *structural deficiencies*? "This report says that?" he asked.

"Oh yeah," Eccleston assured him. "To recalibrate this place would be improbable. The cost would be prohibited. The Diocese doesn't need the building anymore, but they want to spare parishioners the heartache of a property auction. I hear they'd settle for the assessed value if the city takes it eminently by domain."

Eddie pictured a wrecking ball thudding against the belfry, and the gargoyles hobbling away, dragging their knuckles. "That's a beautiful old building," he said. "Isn't the past worth saving? You guys saved the old mills."

Manny shook his head. He said, "I appreciate you playing devil's surrogate, but the old mills have business value."

"What about historic value?"

"History doesn't feed the piper."

Eddie said, "This ain't a gimme. That save-the-church group had good numbers at their rally, and they got Hippo Vaughn. This will be a fight."

"They won't win. Vaughn's a lone dog on this. We got five votes on the Council."

"If the election goes right for you incumbents," Eddie noted.

"Let's presume it does," Manny said. "Vaughn can beat the rug all he wants on this, he's not bigger than the whole political inner circle."

"Can't fault your logic."

Eccleston nodded at winning the argument.

"But what's the plan for the land?" Eddie asked.

The councilman grinned. "You and I have a deal about that—not until after we win the election," he said. Suddenly Manny's wristwatch was in his face. "Gotta go. Meeting with your publisher about an editorial. So where do I find his office?"

"Take the elevator all the way up," Eddie said. "And go through the glass door that says Alfred T. Templeton. Take your time, Templeton is always up there."

"A work addict, eh?"

"Either that, or he's afraid of sunlight."

"Enjoy the report," Manny said. "Write it up good." He tried to salute but gave up half way, settled for a wave and walked off.

Eddie settled into his chair with the contents of the envelope. It was a fifty-page consultant's report, commissioned by the Diocese to assess the physical condition of St. Francis de Sales. The report was dated two days ago and still marked "draft." Eccleston had good sources if he got the draft before the final report was even finished.

Like most consultant reports, this one left room for interpretation and was not a slam-dunk for either side. The consultants had found problems, but Manny had overstated their conclusions, which were overstated in the report's one-page introduction. The building needed substantial work to stabilize the outer stone face and one tower, but its basic structure was sound.

It was a decent news story. Eddie called the Diocese and reached a pleasant spokesperson who, after checking with various clergy, refused to comment because the report was a draft, but was very interested in where Eddie got his copy.

Eddie offered his stock answer, "Things just seem to appear here." The call had mined no further information, but the hubbub confirmed that the report was authentic.

Eddie called the head of SAVIOR, the save-the-church group, who was also very interested in where Eddie got the report. Same pat answer. Eddie typed as they talked. He gathered a few usable quotes on the general dispute over saving the building.

He phoned Gordon Phife across the room and negotiated for thirteen inches of space in the local section of the last edition.

In just over an hour, Eddie had a story that began this way:

> LOWELL—*St. Francis de Sales Church, whose twin granite spires have towered over the Acre neighborhood for more than a century, would need extensive work and a sizable investment before the building could be redeveloped, according to a Cambridge consulting firm hired to study the building.*
>
> *But the basic structure of the granite church is solid, like the faith of the saint for whom it was named.*

Eddie had taken some artistic license in the second paragraph. He didn't know Francis de Sales, the man. But saints are faithful. Everybody knew that.

Bang. He hit the send key.

Phife read through the text while Eddie watched over his shoulder. With a few dozen keystrokes he trimmed the fat and tuned the sound of Eddie's words. Phife had a great ear for language. Gordon knew which words made music together and which combinations were sharp or flat. Some editors butchered news copy so that every story, no matter who wrote it, sounded the same. Not Phife. His line editing was gentle. He brought out the best in every author's voice.

At the bottom of the story, Phife nodded and said, "This is good." He scrolled to the top and typed from memory a long string of characters that could have been nuclear launch codes. The coding told the typesetting computer which font to use for the byline and body of the story. Another line editor would give the story a second read, and write a headline.

"Do I see the white smoke?" Eddie asked.

"You are dismissed," Phife said.

"Can you keep Keyes away from this story?"

"Don't worry, Ed, it's a good read. Now get away from here before I open the correspondent copy. The stench can be overpowering if you're not used to it."

"One pass through the Phife-O-Matic ought to fix it," Eddie said. He clapped Phife on the shoulder and left him to his dirty work.

Back at his desk, Eddie called Durkin in the library and asked if he had old church homilies on file.

"Do I?" Durkin howled. "What do you want with those old things? Nobody has touched those files in years."

"Can you find them, old man? Or must I do it myself?"

"You couldn't find them in a month down here, but if we printed it, I can put my hands on it. What era?"

"The old days," Eddie said. "Back when they chipped the paper out of stone every morning. You were probably my age at the time."

Durkin's laugh sounded like a nine-hundred-pound grizzly enjoying the Goldilocks story—the part when the bears gave that little thief what she deserved. "I got what you need," he said. "What church?"

"Shoot, I dunno," Eddie said. His eyes fell to the consultant's report on his desk. He remembered there was no such thing as coincidence. "Let's start with St. Francis de Sales. And don't send the file up. I'll come down."

Chapter 25

The musty, unlabeled file on Durkin's desk was an inch thick with typewritten sheets. The papers contained the wisdom of a hundred Sundays with Father Zygmunt O. Wojick, former pastor of St. Francis de Sales Church. Each homily was two pages, fastened by a staple.

Eddie started with the earliest entry, about the dangers of judging people by their looks. He thought about Leo and Gabrielle. Had they once been invisible to him? Right up until they saved his life?

He pictured the clergyman hunched over an old Underwood typewriter, nearly twenty years ago, banging out his message to the flock and then performing the piece from the pulpit. He read one about gambling:

> *There exists in some men a yearning, not of God but of man, to dream a dream of luxury by which he arrives not by the sweat of his brow, the strength of his back nor the cut of his wit, but by way of a much easier path. A path along which honest labor has no place, where reward is not earned. Those who walk this road surrender the choice of whom they shall become, and instead trust their future to chance. This path of ease, and of sorrow, is called gambling—*

Eddie liked the piece. It was more like an op-ed essay than a sermon—uncompromising and well argued, yet eloquent and gentle.

He dove deeper into the file. Father Wojick's words steered a consistent, conservative course through the social problems of the nation and of the Acre: poverty, failing schools, domestic abuse, the disintegration of the family, racism, unwanted pregnancy, drugs, violence. Eddie searched for keywords or patterns in the essays. Nowlin had made his revelation seem obvious. *It was right there in the homilies.* Maybe it was obvious if you knew what you were looking for. *Where is it, Danny?* Halfway through the stack, Eddie rubbed his eyes.

Durkin was clip clopping around on his crutches, adding stories cut from the paper to files throughout his library. The odor of coffee tugged Eddie to his feet.

"Hey Durk," Eddie yelled. "You making coffee over there?"

"You won't want any of this. This brew ain't for topsiders." Topsiders—what Durkin called the collar-and-tie types who worked above ground.

"Try me," Eddie said.

"I'm warning you, pencil neck."

"Try me, before I bounce your crippled ass from A to Z."

Durkin, thrilled by the combat, laughed and relented. He brought Eddie a cup. The brew was endlessly black, like the moment before Creation. A metallic aftertaste lingered past the bitterness, and the caffeine rush was instant. Three gulps switched Eddie's internal organs from "play" to "fast-forward."

"My God, this stuff is wonderful. What is it?" Eddie asked.

"Supermarket coffee, mixed double strength," he explained. "But to give it kick I use caffeinated mineral water from the vitamin store. Have a few cups, then enjoy the cardiac arrest." He laughed some more and went back to his work.

Eddie breezed through the rest of the homilies. The pages quivered in his hands. Alert? He felt alert enough to solve cold fusion equations in his head.

The last of Wojick's homilies was shorter than the rest, just a few lines. It had more typos fixed with correction paper than any ten other homilies together. Eddie read it over again, slowly this time:

> *April 16*
>
> *God's love knows no bounds, my brothers and sisters, but with His miracle of forgiveness comes responsibility.*
> *Confessing is not enough. Do we expect God to forgive the hurts we do not seek to mend?*
> *If one among us is responsible for pain and death beyond most mortal imagination, can he expect to simply confess in the dark and find God's forgiveness, while he hides from the laws of man?*
> *No, I say.*
> *Turn yourself in and pay for your crimes!*
> *I now must beg you, my brothers and sisters, for forgiveness, for I have today broken a vow of my robe. I am sorry.*

Durkin asked, "Find what you're looking for?"

"Maybe. Got any more sermons from this guy, Wojick?"

"Naw. He took off at the end, just before the church closed. Abandoned the whole congregation. Nobody ever saw him again."

"Oh right, I've heard something about him running off."

"He even apologized before he split, although nobody knew what he was apologizing for until he left. The whole thing was hushed up. I went to St. Joseph's—the priest was quicker there—so I don't really remember the details."

"You better get me the staff-written Wojick clips," Eddie said.

Durkin snorted. He needed more action. "The last time I followed orders from a college boy my leg got blown into a tree," he said.

Eddie smacked his fist into his palm and said, "If you want to keep the leg you've got, you'll get me the goddam clips."

A tremor of laughter shook Durkin's mountainous shoulders. "All right Bourque," he said, struggling to get the words out. "No need to get rough."

Eddie refilled his cup with Durkin's racing fuel and dug through the files. The yellowed clips sported bylines from Empire reporters long gone. Several stories about dwindling attendance at St. Francis de Sales foretold of the church closing. One report questioned the wisdom of buying a new church crucifix.

There was just one story on Father Wojick's disappearance. It had no byline, and had run on page five.

LOCAL PRIEST LEAVES PARISH, ALSO TO LEAVE THE CLOTH

LOWELL—*Father Zygmunt O. Wojick, pastor of St. Francis de Sales Church, is retiring from the church and leaving the priesthood, according to sources close to the pastor.*

Wojick celebrated his last Mass on Sunday, which was also the occasion of a first-communion ceremony for twenty-two second-graders and one adult.

Sources say Wojick is leaving for California, and intends to give up the priesthood in order to wed a woman he knows there....

The story ran three days after Father Wojick delivered his final odd little homily, in which he had begged for forgiveness.

The church closed immediately, citing difficulties in finding another pastor among the thinning ranks of clergy, according to another clip. At first, there was hope it would reopen. The paper ran a two-column picture of the new crucifix being delivered, the one that still hung over the church altar. Stories over the next several months were less and less hopeful about the parish's fate. A few recent pieces speculated on redevelopment plans.

The last item was filed out-of-order—a three-column picture of the church's final First Communion class, gathered in rows on the church steps like pupils in a school photo. The girls were in white dresses, the boys in tiny clip-on neckties. The barrel-chested man with a crew cut, white collar and stern face was Father Wojick. Eddie stared at Wojick's image. It still amazed him that dots of ink, gray and black, could combine with white space to replicate something as complex as a human face. The children would be in their twenties now; Eddie recognized none of the names.

But he knew the adult who had made a First Communion that day, though he had not seen the man in years—nobody had. It was Sawouth "Samuel" Sok—refugee, Catholic convert and Lowell's reclusive civic benefactor.

He called out, "Durk, you're a devout Catholic, right?"

The answer came from behind a row of cabinets. "Converts are always devout. I converted from atheism on the transport to Vietnam. The Good Lord got me out of there—well, most of me."

"What must Catholics do before their First Communion?"

Durkin heaved himself to Eddie on his crutches in a few graceful strides. "I had to study prayers, learn what the sacrament is all about." Durkin said. He thought for a moment. "And make my first confession."

Eddie held up the newspaper picture. "So all these people would have made their first confession to Father Wojick, right before he disappeared."

"I guess."

"And the priest is never to divulge what is said in confession."

"Neither by word nor deed," Durkin said. "You're Catholic, you know all this."

"What if somebody in this First Communion class told Father Wojick about a sin so horrible, the priest couldn't help but divulge what he heard—by hinting at it in his last homily."

"That's serious—that would be breaking a vow."

Eddie held up Wojick's final homily. "He admitted breaking a vow right here. After he disappeared, everybody assumed he was talking about his vow of celibacy. But what if he was apologizing for hinting at something he had heard in confession?"

Durkin read Father Wojick's tattered last homily. He grunted and said, "I see what you mean, but it's ludicrous. These kids were in second grade. What could any of them confess that was so terrible?"

"They weren't all in second grade," Eddie said. He tapped his finger on the picture, at the image of Samuel Sok. "This dude was in his forties."

"I suppose," Durkin said. "But there again, Sok's a philanthropist. What terrible thing could *he* have done?"

Eddie looked over the papers spread before him. *Whatever it was, could it have brought Chanthay here for revenge?*

Chapter 26

"So what you're telling me," Keyes said, trying for the second time to repeat what Eddie was telling him, "is that you want to do a story on Cambodia?" He crunched his lollipop, an amber one. "This is the Lowell Empire. This isn't the Cambodian, uh, well, whatever they call their papers over there, if they even have any."

Eddie laughed, a cheery little laugh that hid the homicide in his heart. He had to play this encounter just right—he needed Keyes to get to Sok.

He explained again, "What I mean to say—and believe me, Frank, I can imagine how annoying it must be that I keep saying it wrong—" He laughed again. "—I mean to say I want to write about the Cambodian community here in the city. There's a large population, and other than covering the Cambodian water festival, I don't think we've made an effort—and I'm really talking about myself here, not you or the paper—*I've* not made the effort to shake more stories from that important community."

Keyes tapped a pencil against his desk a dozen times.

Was he thinking? Or just tapping a pencil? Was he thinking about tapping a pencil?

Eddie thought about the threat Keyes had made to Phife. Was it just bravado? Or could somebody as obtuse as Frank Keyes really have had something to do with Danny's death?

The threat clashed with what Keyes had already told Eddie—that he didn't believe Danny had been murdered.

"I don't see it, Bourque," Keyes said. "Let's be honest. The immigrants, they don't buy the paper and they don't advertise. Why should we waste the resources on them?"

Eddie nodded earnestly, buying time to edit the sarcasm from his gut response. He said, "Maybe we should break new ground in newspapers and cover the community first, so then they'll start reading the paper and buying some ads." He didn't edit *all* the sarcasm, but he nipped enough to get it over Keyes' head.

The boss was not convinced. "Those people are not our readers. We'll cover their water festival and nice stuff like that. But we can't be missing a story in Wilmington to cover a Cambodian story in Lowell."

Keyes meant, of course, that The Empire couldn't miss a story about middle-class white people in suburban Wilmington to cover a Cambodian story in Lowell.

"I think I'm getting your meaning," Eddie said. Faking reverence to Keyes was hard enough, but Eddie had to sound like he respected his opinion, too. "You're saying we need to concentrate on the real political players who affect life around here."

Keyes brightened. "That's right," he said. "Tell me what the players are doing. They make everything go."

Eddie grabbed his chin and looked thoughtful. "Wouldn't it be great if the Cambodian community had a player." He let the suggestion sink in a moment. "Then we could do both."

Keyes shrugged. "They don't have players, except Sok, and he's been out of touch for years."

"Hmm," Eddie said. "That's a great idea, Frank. I'll touch base with Sok."

Eddie had shown a little too much enthusiasm. Keyes eyed him with suspicion, but quickly let it fade in the aura of his great new idea. "Nobody's talked to Sok directly in a while,"

Keyes said. "But I don't think we've tried too hard. You know how lazy reporters are."

"We're slugs," Eddie agreed. "Could you call Sok's office and set it up?" Keyes grimaced. Eddie quickly added, "Sometimes it takes one political player to get to another."

It was true. Lowly Eddie Bourque could not get an audience at the Sok estate without a ticket from a real player in city politics. Keyes was such a player because of his job at the paper. Should he ever lose his post, he'd be out, and then not even directory assistance would take his calls. That would be one fine day.

"I'll handle Sok," Keyes said. He leaned back and plunked his feet on the desk the way important men are supposed to. He stared vacantly at Eddie, who had not left his office. Eddie looked at the phone. Keyes got the idea. "Right now?"

"Why not set your plan in motion?"

Keyes took his feet from the desk and reached in slow motion for the telephone. *Just make the goddam call, Frank.* He picked up the receiver and dialed the in-house switchboard. He spoke into the phone, "Joanne? It's Frank. Could you look up the number for Samuel Sok? No, not the publicist. Yes, call me back." He hung up.

And so began an eternity of uncomfortable silence as they waited for the number. The red second hand on the clock above Keyes' head scraped past twelve and hit the brakes. Keyes tapped the pencil some more. Eddie looked for a similar toy within reach and found none. No books to inspect, no newspapers to read. He looked out the window into the newsroom. Phife had left; Melissa was hidden behind her computer monitor. Nobody else dared make eye contact with him. There was nothing to do but sit and wait with the editor who probably wanted to fire Eddie as much as Eddie wanted to throttle the editor. The second hand passed six and struggled to climb against gravity. The pencil went tap, tap, tap. Eddie couldn't stand it anymore. "How's business?" he blurted.

"Business? Like ad revenue?"

"I suppose. Anything."

"Ad revenue is stable," Keyes said. "The problem is all these expenses. This high tech newsroom was supposed to save money. High tech, my ass." He backhanded a messy pile of papers on his desk. "Invoices, all of them. I'm paying correspondents to write what the staff doesn't want to cover, and freelance photographers to shoot what the photo room can't get to."

"That's a shame," Eddie said. And Joanne was taking forever to find that goddam number. Did she know the phone book was *alphabetical*?

Keyes swirled the pencil in the air like a conductor's baton. "I'm paying consultants out my asshole. I got consultants telling me how to lay out a news page. I got them telling me what people want to read. I'm paying an outside computer expert, I'm paying an engineer who plans our truck routes on a big map, and I'm paying for the big damn map." He fanned the pencil back and forth until it blurred. "Don't get me started."

But Eddie had already gotten him started, and the expenses that were cutting into the manager's profit-sharing plan were in for a tongue-lashing. "The truck drivers—there's a greedy bunch. Not one goes a week without filing for overtime. Overtime? Why should it take longer to drive the route one day out of five? Every one of them sons-of-bitches has the Labor Relations Board on speed dial. I'm juggling a dozen complaints at a time."

The telephone rang. Sweet mercy.

Keyes frowned at the interruption, and then answered it. "Yeah? Uh-huh." He wrote down a number and hung up. "What really burns me is the newsprint prices. Through the roof. Canadian paper mills are screwing me. They're too lazy to make the paper any faster. Goddam Frenchies need to turn off the hockey game and get to work. You French, Bourque?"

Eddie nodded, his gazed fixed on the seven digits Keyes had written. "French Canadian," he said.

"Well get on the horn and tell your cousins that Gretzky needs a new hockey stick, so start chopping some trees."

"I'll see what I can do," Eddie said. "It's getting late. Maybe we should—"

"Mandatory recycling is a white elephant if I ever saw one," Keyes continued. "Some dumb state legislator wants to force me to take back old newspaper. This guy should be shot. He'd have me save trees by opening a recycling center down there in the lobby. Have you ever heard of anything so stupid? Canada is nothing *but* trees—"

And on he went.

Eddie tried to interrupt with body language. He slouched. He rested his chin on his fist. He rubbed his eyes, even yawned. Nothing could offend Keyes into stopping. The red second hand had staggered fifteen laps before Keyes talked himself out.

When Eddie could finally speak, he said, "It's amazing that with all you have to do, you still have time to call Samuel Sok for me." He glanced at the telephone.

"Didn't I call him already?"

"No sir."

Keyes was paralyzed for a moment, and then he dialed the number. His voice dropped an octave, "This is Franklin Keyes from The Empire—the editor. Give me Samuel.... What? He's not? Then give me one of the boys." He put his hand over the mouthpiece and said to Eddie, "The secretary is getting one of the sons." He barked into the telephone, "It's Keyes. Which one is this? Matthew? Okay, Peter—whatever. Look, I got a reporter here who needs a word with the old man.... No, not the publicist."

Keyes listened to a lengthy explanation, occasionally nodding and making listening noises, "Right...right...uh-huh."

Finally, Keyes said, "Then how about you and your brother talk to him? Well, you just said you're handling things right now. Fine, eight o'clock tomorrow morning." He hung up without saying goodbye and warned Eddie, "They got some religious thing happening at nine-thirty, so don't be late."

Eddie left before Keyes could trap him with another diatribe.

Back in the newsroom, Boyce Billips shouted into his telephone, voice wavering, "You're going to sue me? Ha— I'll sue you first." He raised the receiver above his head to smack it down, but wimped out half way and returned it gently to place.

Eddie tapped his shoulder. "You all right?"

Boyce shrieked. He whirled around. "Eddie—it's you."

Eddie nearly shrieked himself at the puffy red scratches on Boyce's cheeks and the soot smear on his forehead. His yellow tie was shredded.

"What the hell happened?" Eddie asked. "You dance with the burning bush?"

Boyce quivered and took a deep breath. He explained, "I went to do a story on Milton, the library cat." His voice squeaked. He paused to collect himself.

"Where's Superdog?" Eddie interrupted.

"Animal Control took him away." Tears welled in Boyce's eyes. "It was a horrible scene, Eddie—the blood, just horrible. I tried to break it up, but I was afraid he might try to kill me too. It took three officers to pry open his jaws."

"Oh no, don't tell me—Superdog killed Milton the library cat? Now Animal Control will think he's vicious. They'll put the fat old mutt to sleep!"

Boyce gave Eddie a funny look, like he was deciding if he had forgotten to unplug the iron. "No Eddie, Animal Control took Superdog to the vet," he said. "They took Milton into custody."

"They arrested the cat?"

"He pounced on Superdog from a stack of science books— astronomy and space, I think. I remember trying to fight him off with Yuri Gagarin's biography." Boyce paused and gave a far-off look. His voice dropped to a husky whisper, "The cat was ferocious. Like a little lion, nothing but claws and fangs and little-bitty rippling muscles."

Eddie cautioned, "Take it easy, Boyce."

But Boyce would not take it easy. "He sprang like a ninja," he said. "Right on Superdog's head, and he wouldn't let go. The noises they made—the growls and these high-pitched screams." Boyce shuddered. "Superdog ran around the library with Milton on his head. They knocked down books and bowled over the children. And those little claws just *raked*." Boyce scrunched up his face and made little raking motions with his hand. "I never knew they had razors on their feet.

"When I tried to save Superdog, he knocked me into a stack of paperback fiction—L through M, by author—but he was just trying to get away from Milton, you gotta believe me! The bookcase fell over on a computer. It made some sparks. We think that's when the fire started."

"There was a fire?"

"They lost everything from Clancy to Updike, but the firefighters saved Vonnegut. They were so brave."

Keyes bellowed from his office, "Boooooyce!" The newsroom fell silent. "The librarian is on the phone. Get in here!"

Boyce swallowed and slowly stood. "Dead man walking," he whispered.

That reminded Eddie. "Speaking of dead men, Boyce, I wanted to talk to you about ghosts and email—that sort of thing."

"The least of my problems right now," he said. "The very least."

Chapter 27

The subconscious is an amazing instrument. It runs dreams, and works all the time at the job, collecting ideas while we're awake. At night it bounces those ideas off a funhouse mirror and onto the movie screen inside our eyelids. Sometimes, during the day, the subconscious notices things we'd otherwise miss. If it's not A-plus material for dreams, and if the subconscious is so inclined, it may whisper what it knows to the conscious side, though the messages are never tidy.

As Eddie wrestled the Mighty Chevette to the curb outside his house, his subconscious passed along a tip: *Something here is wrong.*

Eddie slammed the car door and looked around. The street was quiet. Windows around the neighborhood glowed yellow. His mail was safe in the mailbox—a credit card offer and three pieces of campaign literature, which City Council candidates were spreading throughout the city like pollen.

His shoes scraped slowly up the cement steps.

The door to his home was six inches ajar. Its frame had splintered around the spot where the deadbolt had been kicked in. Eddie pushed open the door, reached in and flipped on the light.

Like the door, the apartment had taken a beating; it had been ransacked by somebody in a hurry to find something, or maybe just trashed by people interested in sending a message. Eddie's recliner was on its side, slit open and hemorrhaging foam stuffing. The coffee table had been flipped over, the television screen smashed. Eddie bent and picked a chess piece off the floor. The black king.

The General!

Eddie rushed inside, shouting, "General VonKatz? General?" He tore through the debris in his living room. The General was not there. Into the kitchen. The silverware drawers had been yanked out and emptied onto the floor. The cabinet doors were open. Cereal boxes and canned food were tossed about. The refrigerator hummed, its freezer door wide open. Eddie checked the ice cubes. Wet, but still mostly ice. This hadn't happened long ago.

He raced to the bathroom. Somebody had pried the medicine cabinet off the wall, shaken the contents over the floor and smashed the box through the shower door. No sign of the General.

To the bedroom. His blankets were balled on the floor, his mattress slashed, the guts yanked out. Books were scattered everywhere. Four dresser drawers had been pulled out, emptied, and discarded into a stack like firewood. He yelled desperately, "General? Are you here?"

Okay—try to be positive. The General was a shifty individual. And he could read minds. When Eddie even *thought* about a veterinary appointment, General VonKatz disappeared. And just try to catch the General for a flea bath. He'd lead you through a household obstacle course that would make your shins purple. If he made it outside he'd probably still be in the neighborhood. Eddie would walk the streets, knock on doors and get some kids to help him crisscross Pawtucketville. He would put posters on telephone poles. He could get a lost-and-found ad in The Empire, and offer a reward. *Somebody will find the General.*

His closet door was closed. Closed? That door was never closed. Eddie ran across the bed and ripped open the door.

On the closet floor, beneath trousers still on their hangers, behind golf clubs still in their bag, two greenish-yellow eyes blinked in the light.

◇ ◇ ◇

It was the first thing the two cops wanted to know. Was anything taken?

These cops were from the same embryo, big-shouldered types, with crew cuts and all sorts of fancy equipment dangling from their Batman belts. They were in their late twenties, still young enough to be forced under the seniority system to ride the four-to-midnight shift, but old enough that a tossed Pawtucketville apartment didn't inspire the adrenaline erection that had pointed them to the Police Academy in the first place.

"Hard to say what's missing," Eddie said. "Nothing seems to be, but everything's such a wreck."

The cops walked around together, pointing out broken stuff and making little notes in their little cop notebooks. Then they wanted to know if Eddie knew who might have done this.

"No idea."

"Had any threats lately?"

"Other than two guys throwing me in a canal the other day, no."

"Got any enemies?"

"Obviously I do now."

The cops didn't like that. Humor had no place in police work, at least not until they were back in the car and Eddie couldn't hear what they were saying about his crappy three-room shack.

"Frankly, Mr. Bourque," one of the clones said. "If nothing was taken, this simply looks like a random prank, or like somebody's pissed off at you." Case closed. He shut his little cop notebook and slid it into his shirt pocket.

"That's it?" Eddie asked.

"We'll talk to the neighbors before we make a report, but nobody ever sees anything in these cases. They would have called us if they did."

"Shouldn't you be taking fingerprints, or something?"

"Wouldn't find anything," the other clone said, frowning deeply. "You said you searched through the place looking for your cat."

"But I didn't touch everything," Eddie argued. "How about the medicine cabinet in the tub? Didn't touch that."

The cop sighed, annoyed by the necessity for the truth. "The BCI unit is all tied up." For the benefit of the civilian in the room, he added, "That stands for the Bureau of Criminal Investigations. They do the fingerprinting."

"I know what it stands for."

"And they can't come to every housebreak in the city."

Eddie was about to begin an argument he absolutely could not win when a knock at the door cut him off. "It's open," Eddie yelled. To nobody in particular he mumbled, "Not that I could lock the damn thing if I wanted to."

A familiar voice said, "When I heard at the station what had happened here, I came right over."

Detective Lucy Orr, in uniform this time, cleared a path through the rubble with the end of her baton. The clones greeted her with deference, and relayed in cop-speak the details and particulars of this criminal-type incident, essentially that the place was wrecked. She nodded and sent them on their way.

"I'd get this door fixed," one clone suggested on his way out.

Eddie grabbed a handful of his own hair and tugged until it hurt.

The General sniffed around Detective Orr's black high-tops. He pronounced her worthy by sideswiping her ankles.

"Lovely cat," she said. "He was shut in the closet during all of this?"

"That's where I found him."

Orr looked around. "I'm beginning to wonder about the type of persons you have been associating with, Mr. Bourque."

"Could you call me Eddie?" he said. "Mr. Bourque makes me sound like a defendant."

She smiled over a delicious punchline she would keep to herself. "Okay, Eddie," she said. "Don't you think it's time to come clean with me?"

"About what?" he protested, without much enthusiasm.

"Come on, Eddie. You've deputized yourself in the Danny Nowlin case, and you haven't told me everything you've found out."

Eddie didn't bother to pretend otherwise. "Look at this place," he said. "Somebody's scared. That means I'm getting close."

"If you mean close to a cemetery plot, I'd agree. And the one who should be scared is you."

Eddie frowned. *He* was supposed to be the wiseass around here. "Don't you have a little card for me to sign before the interrogation?"

"We're off the record," Detective Orr said. "You're a reporter. You know what that means. Whatever trouble you've stirred up is only going to get worse. Next time they bust up this place, they might do it when you're home. I can help you get out of this, whatever it is."

Eddie wavered. Maybe she had a point? He could give her what he knew and let her take over.

No, he decided, not yet.

Detective Orr was a blunt instrument. If Eddie told her he suspected that Nowlin was mixed up in Chanthay's plot to take revenge, and his belief that Sok was involved, Orr would march onto the Sok estate and interview him, face to face, with a dozen lawyers in the room, and no trickery allowed. Eddie was convinced he could learn more from Sok his way—he could take shortcuts around the law that Detective Orr could not.

"Soon, Lucy. I'll call you real soon," he promised.

She bounced the baton lightly on her shoulder and took thirty seconds to study his eyes, which stared back at her, unblinking. She concluded, "You're either guilty of *something*, or you're in way over your head."

Eddie nodded. "You got that right." He looked over the destruction and said, "Any chance you can pull some strings and get the fingerprinting crew over here?"

She nodded. "Maybe early tomorrow morning."

"I'll leave it open."

She smiled and retreated through the mess to the broken door. On her way out, she said, "We'll send you a copy of the report when it's done, assuming you're still around to receive it. In the meantime, I'd get this door fixed."

After she'd gone, Eddie gathered the contents of his toolbox from the kitchen floor and nailed the front door shut.

Chapter 28

The intercom crackled, "Who is it?"

"It's Eddie. Buzz me in."

"Eddie? It's—six in the morning. Go away." Click.

Eddie did not go away. He waited by the intercom outside the apartment building.

Tiny snowflakes from a morning squall swirled around him, and the cold air felt good in his lungs. The General whined from inside his plastic pet carrier. Eddie carried a coffee can with a plastic lid. The can was heavy. A similar can bulged in his coat pocket. That one was light.

Two minutes passed before Melissa asked over the intercom, "Are you still there?"

Eddie leaned to the speaker box. "Yes."

"I figured."

The door buzzed.

Melissa met him at her apartment door in a long white nightshirt. Her hair was tousled, her cheek creased from the pillowcase. She kept one hand on the door, ready to close it if she didn't like what she heard. Then she saw General VonKatz. Surprised, she asked Eddie, "Whatever is this?"

"Could the General crash here?" he asked. "My house has some, um, security issues." His hands were full so he gestured with his head in the general direction of his house.

Melissa beckoned Eddie inside and closed the door. Her apartment was bright, modern, and antiseptic: beige carpet, bone white walls and recessed lights in a vaulted ceiling. Her three-piece living room set, done in matching fabric, was clustered into a little conversation area. The magazines on the coffee table were highbrow reading on politics and theater. The television, nasty thing, was hidden away in a cabinet.

"What's wrong with your place?" she asked him. Eddie assumed she meant what *new* was wrong with his place. Melissa often chided him about living like a castaway.

He put down the pet carrier and told her about the break-in and the destruction of nearly everything he owned.

"Good thing your stuff was so dreadfully awful," she said. But her voice was too tender for the dig to really dig. "Who would do such a ghastly thing?"

"Who would do a lot of stuff we report in the paper every day? Who would kill Danny?"

She wrinkled her nose at his comment, as she bent to the pet carrier. "Of course the General can stay here," she assured Eddie. She glanced up at him and smiled wickedly. "You, on the other hand, cannot."

She opened the carrier's wire gate. General VonKatz rushed out, riding low to the ground. There were many, many things to be sniffed in this strange place, and he set right to work.

Eddie showed her the heavy coffee can. "Clean cat litter," he explained. "Just pour it in a plastic tub or something." He put the can down and pulled a bag of dry cat food from the carrier, which he gave to her. "Dump some of this in a bowl. He'll eat when he wants it."

"How long do you think it will be?" she asked.

"No more than a day or two—I hope."

Melissa finally noticed Eddie was dressed for work. "You're heading in early."

"I have an interview at eight," he said. "Look Melissa, the General likes you. If anything were to happen to me—you know, things can happen to people—I'd want you to adopt the little guy."

She laughed nervously. "What do you mean?" And then she gave him a hard stare. Fright stirred in her big wet eyes.

Eddie lowered his voice. "I'm sorry about yelling at you, at the office."

"I know."

"You're nobody I should be mad at."

"Forget it, Eddie," she said, softly. "Just be careful." She reached her hand to his. He touched her fingers and felt forgiveness in them. She let the touch linger for a moment. And then, as if forcing herself to break the spell, she asked brightly, "Want a coffee for the road? I can put some on."

"Sure, I got a minute," Eddie said. His eyes narrowed. "This won't be decaf, will it?"

She smiled. "Would I put kryptonite in Superman's mug? You need your caffeine."

"You're right. Coffee without caffeine is like," Eddie searched for the right metaphor, "like a night with a prostitute—it's warm in your hands, but where's the love?"

Melissa giggled and slapped his shoulder. Her forgiveness was complete. She headed for the kitchen, calling out, "Cream? Sugar? How do you want it?"

"Black is fine, thanks."

As soon as she turned the corner, Eddie took out the other coffee can, the one in his pocket. He peeled off the lid and shook the General's brown moth into the air. He fanned at it, and encouraged, "Go, go." The beast flapped up, bounced off a wall and made a fluttering nuisance of itself along the peak of Melissa's vaulted ceiling.

Chapter 29

The newsroom had the sizzle of a big story in the making. Gordon Phife had called in three extra reporters to help on the morning fireman shift. They had telephones welded to their heads. Line editors with no lines yet to edit yapped amongst themselves in excited low voices. The police scanner was cranked to maximum volume. It broadcast snippets of conversation across the newsroom, none of which made much sense out of context.

Phife spotted Eddie and waved him over. "I've been calling you," he said in his no-nonsense, hard news tone. "Your number just rang and rang. Is your answering machine broken?"

It was. The harmless plastic thing had been squashed under a boot or a baseball bat or whatever. "I gotta get a new one," he said. "I'm leaving for an interview in half an hour. What can I do until then?"

Phife groaned. "I need more reporters, not reporters with appointments," he said. "You probably can't do anything. Unless you can find out in thirty minutes why two dozen cops taped off Billings Mill and brought in the body-sniffing dogs."

Eddie stared at him, wide-eyed. "I may have a source on that," he said. He abruptly spun and marched off.

At his desk, Eddie put on a show to waste some time. He dialed his home number and pretended to have a conversation. The phone rang for real when he put it down.

"Bourque," he answered.

"Is this Eddie?"

Eddie recognized the woman's sandpaper voice. "Gabrielle? Nice to hear from you. You just caught me before I had to run out."

"I tried you a few times this morning," she said. "I didn't leave a message because there's no way you can get back to me. The phone company is slow to put service under the Chelmsford Street Bridge." She honked, laughing.

"You're up early," Eddie said. "Everything all right?"

"Leo and I couldn't sleep last night because of what we know. We wanted to tell you right away, because you asked us to help you investigate, and we did."

How long had it been since somebody trusted Leo and Gabrielle? How long since somebody from the world outside the bridge had thought they had something to offer? She raced through the story:

"Leo and me checked with our paperboy first to see if he remembers selling horse and a spike to your friend. He hadn't sold a spike for weeks. We tried some other dealers we know, and they didn't remember anybody like that, either. So Leo and me split up and started talking to friends. And they told us about some other dealers we didn't even know about, which is both good and bad for us, you know what I mean, Eddie?"

"Yeah, I know."

She continued, "So this one girl tells me about this guy, name's Swindale or Swindle or something—that's a funny name if you're selling, ain't it?" She honked again. "And we go talk to him. He remembers selling one bag last week to this guy in a fancy raincoat, who he figured was just some chipper who works downtown and chased the dragon on weekends. And this guy wants a needle too. So Swindle— yeah, that's his name—names a price. He starts out real high so when he comes down, the price is right. But the guy doesn't blink. He takes out his wallet. Swindle charges him triple and the guy doesn't blink.

"So Swindle thinks he's a first-timer looking to get his wings. He offers his pager number, you know, to start a relationship. But the guy says no, he won't need any more horse—ever. Does this sound like your friend?"

"I'm afraid it might," Eddie said.

"One more thing," she said. "Swindle said your friend asked about a piece."

"A gun? Did he sell him one?"

"No. But he gave him some names. Ain't hard to get one."

He thanked her and they hung up. Nowlin wanted heroin and a gun? The gun made sense if he was fighting Chanthay's war with her, or if he wanted to protect her—Eddie knew that feeling. But the heroin? A one-time hit? There was still a lot about Danny he didn't know.

Eddie wasted another ten minutes on the phone with the cinema's automated movie line. Then he ran to Phife.

"My source says the cops have two bodies in Billings Mill," Eddie told him.

Phife jotted this down and then peppered him with editor's questions. "Junkies? Suicides? Men? Women? Do you know?"

"Two men. One homicide for sure—bullet in the hat, execution style."

"And the other?"

"Fell down an elevator shaft."

Phife wrote this down. "You got names?" he demanded.

Sure—Mick and Ray. Not that Eddie could share anything the cops hadn't yet discovered. "Gordon! Gimme a break," Eddie pleaded. "I had half an hour."

Phife put up his hands, surrendering. "I know, I'm sorry. Great work. How solid is this stuff? Can we run it?"

"It's a rock."

He nodded, impressed. "We'll try to get the cops to confirm it on the record. If not, I'll lobby Keyes to run it as exclusive material from unnamed sources. How should we characterize it? An unnamed police source? Or simply a source close to the investigation?"

Eddie considered the question. He had never permitted something false to get into print. "Let's not get specific about the identity, okay?" he said. "My source would be screwed to the roof if he's uncovered." Which was absolutely true.

Chapter 30

The Mighty Chevette whirred east down a concrete boulevard. Harsh weather had battered away the last stubborn brown leaves from the sugar maples that reached huge limbs over the street. The homes along the road were all pleasant, a few even grand, if you were impressed by size, ornamental pillars and gardens. The early morning snow squall was over, not a trace remained on the ground. Clouds and sun split the sky evenly, and the air had warmed near forty.

Eddie steadied the steering wheel with a knee and studied a street map. The side streets meandered, in no hurry to get Eddie where he was going. The homes grew farther apart, backyards got bigger and stone walls reached higher. The Mighty Chevette coughed up a hill, on another boulevard divided down the middle by granite curbing, a strip of lawn and crab apple trees.

The fences along this street were taller than Eddie. Pointy iron crosses topped the stone walls around the Sok estate. They praised God, and discouraged thieves.

A gap in the wall appeared, and Eddie slammed the brakes. The Chevette made that metal-on-metal grinding again. He pulled the car into the gap and stopped at a black iron gate made of interlocking swirls. The swirls along the top curled toward the street and were tipped in serrated barbs, like fishing hooks for a Great White shark.

Beyond the gate, a pebble driveway curved right and vanished behind hemlock. Facing the drive on both sides, like pedestrians watching a parade, were about twenty-five large-as-life statues. Probably meant to depict the anonymous minor characters in the Bible—fishermen and shepherds, prostitutes and tax collectors—the figures looked like beatnik hitchhikers, dressed in robes and sandals. They had been painted lifelike colors, which the New England weather had faded unevenly.

There was no gate attendant or intercom box. Eddie rolled down the window and called out, "Hello?"

The reply, a woman's voice, was as clear as a local telephone call, "Mr. Edward Bourque?"

The words seemed to come from the center of the wall beside the car, so that's where Eddie directed his response. "Yes. I have an appointment with Matthew and Peter Sok."

The gate parted at its middle and swung inward.

The Chevette's tires crunched on the stone driveway. The car crept through the columns of figurines. One of the statues held a shotgun. No, Eddie realized, that was a man, an armed guard, who eyed the car as it passed. Eddie noticed another guard, and then a third, patrolling the grounds.

The driveway curved four times, left and right, before ending at a gravel parking area and a four-car garage. The parking lot was half-moon shaped, the garage castle-like, with battlements along the roof and two small stone turrets. A miniature of the garage would have been perfect at the bottom of a fish tank.

Two other vehicles were in the parking lot, a silver BMW sedan, and an ambulance, its back doors open. A man and a woman, both thirtyish and dressed in matching blue uniform jackets, were sitting on the back bumper, chatting in the sun. They held magazines, *Sports Illustrated* for him, *The New Yorker* for her. Eddie parked beside them.

They nodded hello when he stepped from the car.

"Everything all right?" Eddie asked.

"We're on call," the man said. He had a deep voice, like the overnight disc jockey on a blues station. "Finally got a nice day, too. They say it might hit fifty this afternoon."

"That'll be nice," Eddie agreed.

The woman added, "Better than freezing our butts off, crammed all day in the front seat."

"You stay here all day? Every day?"

"Not just us," the woman said. "Second shift gets here at three-o'clock." She winked. "Nice to have money, huh?"

"The Soks hire you?"

"They hire our company," she said. "Round-the-clock. Ted and I pull this detail a few days a month. Not much action, but it's a nice break."

Eddie pointed down a stone walkway. "The house down this way?"

"Past those trees," the man said. "Across the chessboard. You'll see."

The path took Eddie along a knoll landscaped with bark mulch, and then through a grove of Douglas fir, each a little too big to be an indoor Christmas tree. It climbed the knoll, leading to a sculpture garden on a forty-foot checkerboard of red and white squares. Cement chess pieces as big as people—one side white, the other reddish like clay pottery, were positioned on the board and the sidelines, like during a game between giants.

More fir trees crowded the edges of the board, like spectators leaning in for a good view. Eddie strolled across the sculpture. From a strategic standpoint, the red pieces held the advantage; the white side had lost more players and was on its heels. A copper plaque bolted to a boulder made sense of the scene:

Final Positions before Checkmate
Merrimack Valley Chess Masters Club Championship
Sawouth "Samuel" Sok Defeated the Field and Named "King"
March 25

There was no year listed. Tarnish, the color of month-old bread, speckled the plaque.

Eddie laughed out loud at Sok's personal monument to a third-rate amateur chess club championship. The wealthy were simply another species.

He was still laughing when a line on the plaque echoed in his head.

Defeated the Field and Named "King"

Had he read that before? He had skimmed scores of clips on Samuel Sok from The Empire's library; several had mentioned Sok's love of the game, but Eddie couldn't recall reading about Sok's club championship.

Danny's story!

Eddie yanked from his wallet the notes from Nowlin's home computer, the fragment from Nowlin's story draft: *...showing amazing instincts, he mated each of them in March and was crowned their King.*

Danny's secret story had been a profile of Samuel Sok. The scent of Danny's trail was suddenly overpowering. Eddie hurried along the path.

The estate house was surprisingly modest. More charming than stunning, it could have been a bed and breakfast on Nantucket. It was three stories, mostly clapboard, pale yellow, and cluttered with windows, round, square and oval, and no two alike in size. The trim was white, as were the carved wooden pillars supporting the portico. The building's peaks and gables complemented two small cupolas and a circular widow's walk with a white railing.

Cold weather had blunted the front yard's summer glory. It was landscaped with shrubs and fruit trees. Concord grape vines swarmed a wooden gazebo. There were cement benches in a rock garden and a dozen more Biblical sculptures, all men in robes. The Apostles, maybe?

Eddie walked under the portico, and up two stone steps to an imposing wooden door. Fixed to it at eye-level was an iron bell shaped like an army helmet, and a metal hammer dangling on a chain. There seemed to be no conventional doorbell. Eddie clanged the bell twice with the hammer. The tone was low and sweet. The two chimes reminded him of a movie, *The Postman Always Rings Twice*. Not one of his favorites. He rang a third time.

The lock mechanism clattered from the inside, and then the massive door jerked inward an inch, before momentum took hold and it swung open. A housekeeper, a woman of about fifty, no bigger than the average sixth-grader, greeted Eddie in a thin voice and led him down a hall to a sitting room.

The inside of the Sok house looked like a monastery run by monks who had discovered a loophole in the vow of poverty. The walls of the sitting room were angel-white, decorated with a chair rail and intricate moldings along the nine-foot ceiling. An Oriental rug was on the parquet floor in front of a fireplace. Religious figurines on pedestals prayed and wept and raised their swords. Seven paintings of the Madonna with child were hung around the room. There were three fabric sofas, each with an entourage of end tables, reading lamps and overstuffed pillows.

Eddie gasped.

On the wall above the fireplace hung a three-foot statuette of a bloody Christ figure, struggling from the cross. It was identical, except for size, to the crucifix hanging over the altar in abandoned St. Francis de Sales Church.

The housekeeper caught Eddie gaping at the cross. "Beautiful, isn't it?" she said.

"Fascinating," he answered, trying to be diplomatic.

"Mr. Sok is very talented."

Eddie pointed. "Samuel Sok made this?"

"Mr. Sok made everything in this home, and on the grounds. These figures were his business."

"I thought his business had to do with historic homes?"

She nodded. "He made custom molding for historic replication." She gestured to the molding around the room until Eddie got the point and nodded. "But as you can see, a higher power asked him to expand his enterprise."

She excused herself and promised to alert Peter and Matthew that he had arrived.

Eddie draped his coat over a sofa. Sok's sons joined him in two minutes. One built like a jockey. He wore brown suit trousers, a formal white shirt, and a buttoned, olive-colored vest. He camouflaged his receding hairline by shaving his head.

The other man was tall and bear-like, with sloping shoulders and a mess of black hair on a big oblong head. He wore a white T-shirt and a sports coat with jeans. Black chest hair curled over the shirt collar.

The bald one offered a hand with silver rings on each finger. "Welcome, Mr. Bourque," he said. "I am Peter Sok. And this rather large gentleman—"

And then he just stopped.

Eddie gripped the outstretched hand and pumped it twice. Peter Sok held his smile, but the emotion behind it had drained away, leaving a corpse's face. Then he recovered as suddenly as he had frozen. "—And this gentleman is my brother, Matthew. We're pleased to be your hosts for our conversation this morning."

Eddie thanked him and nodded. He shook Matthew's hand. The big guy's grip was powerful, but his hand too soft to make much of an impression. Matthew bit his bottom lip and squinted at Eddie. He asked, "Do I know you?"

"Of course not!" Peter scolded his brother. "Mr. Bourque is a writer for the newspaper. He is not a person we would have met before today."

Matthew looked unconvinced, but dropped the matter. They sat down, each man on his own sofa.

Eddie declined their offer of tea. They chatted for fifteen minutes about the house and the grounds and the hope for a warm afternoon. Peter spoke for the brothers.

When they seemed loosened up, Eddie said, "Nobody has seen your father at city functions in several years. Such an influential man is easily missed. How has he been?"

Matthew looked at his brother, who looked at Eddie and assured him, "He is very well."

"Would it be possible, when we're done here, for me to get a word with him?" Eddie asked.

No, it would not.

Peter gently explained, "Our father has come to treasure his privacy." He pronounced the word priv-a-cee, with a short *i* sound. "He prefers to see no one. My brother and I are his spokespersons."

That brought Peter to the point. "How may we help you today, Mr. Bourque?"

Eddie took out a note pad for the sake of maintaining a sense of authenticity, and then lied, "I'm researching a story on your father's recent step into city politics with the formation of his own political action committee."

"You know about that?" Matthew asked, alarmed.

Peter seemed comfortable, even relieved, by Eddie's inquiry. He said to his brother, "Mr. Bourque is obviously skilled in the review of obscure public documents." To Eddie, he said, "We had intended to remain anonymous on our first foray into politics, in case we were not successful. But you have found us out."

Peter continued, offering long, corny quotes about the importance of being part of the democracy and contributing to the government of the people, blah, blah. Eddie had no need for his comments, but he jotted them down.

Matthew found his confidence and added his own platitudes. He seemed to enjoy participating on the same level as Peter, who was clearly the brains behind the Sok operation. Matthew was well spoken, but his thoughts came from shallow waters. He struck Eddie as a lunkhead with a million-dollar education.

Eddie asked, "But why give donations only to the incumbents?"

"They support our interests," Peter said.

Added Matthew, "They're behind our project."

Eddie perked at that.

Peter hissed at his brother, "That's enough!"

What project? Eddie could imagine only one, the redevelopment project for the Acre neighborhood that Councilman Eccleston had tipped him to. It was not much to go on. Even when he bluffed, Eddie preferred a better hand. After half-a-beat to steel his nerves, Eddie said with confidence, "The Acre redevelopment proposal—I'm aware of it. An undertaking that huge needs a majority of the council behind it. You're right to think the incumbents would be with you."

Matthew blanched. "Templeton said his reporters would not know until after the election!"

Peter popped up. "Enough!" He bowed to Eddie. "Pardon us one moment." Then he took his brother by the arm and led him toward the door. He whispered to the big man, "If you tried all day, could you *be* any more stupid?"

Eddie dropped his notebook. His pen slipped from his fingers.

He recognized Peter's words, spoken in his whisper. He had heard them in the Worthen Canal, as he lay half-conscious on the ice.

These men had thrown Eddie off the bridge.

No wonder Peter's brain had short-circuited when he met Eddie that morning. He was seeing a ghost. And Matthew, big as an ox and just as smart, had recognized him too, but he couldn't place the face of the man he had tried to drown.

A foul rage stirred inside Eddie. His hands trembled. He closed them into fists.

And Eddie suddenly realized why he hadn't felt *different* after Chanthay had shot the hitman on the floor—the change had already taken place. Eddie had lost his boyhood nemesis, Fear, in Billings Mill. Her breath would never raise the chill it once did.

He grew angrier for all the times she had haunted him.

Peter ushered his brother from the room and snicked the door shut. He returned to his seat, explaining, "My brother is unaccustomed to forums such as this. He will tend to some business matters while we continue."

Eddie willed his fury behind a calm façade, picked up his pen and notebook and concentrated on the task before him. He said, "Off the record—it's obvious to me who's really in charge here."

Peter smirked and straightened his vest. "You have no idea," he said, laughing and showing perfect teeth. "Those business matters I just sent him to attend? Unloading a truckload of paint."

They shared a good laugh. And then Eddie pushed a little harder. "So how's he supposed to help with the Acre project?"

Peter throttled back. "You can imagine my dilemma, if you know the scope of the project."

He was testing Eddie's knowledge. Eddie had to be straight; he didn't know enough to fake it. "All I know is it's big," he said. "Tell me—how big?"

"I cannot discuss it until after the election."

"Then you must expect controversy."

"We can proceed through controversy," Peter insisted. "God in Heaven created this entire world from chaos."

"God didn't need five votes on the council."

"Precisely why I cannot speak of this now."

"Then tell me off the record," Eddie suggested. "I'll be covering this story when it breaks. Having the background now will help me later."

Peter frowned. He seemed about to turn him down, when Eddie added, "I can't put this in the paper until Templeton, my publisher, says it's okay. If I wrote it today, he'd just hold it until after the election." He set the pad and pen on the couch.

Peter seemed to recognize the truth in Eddie's argument. Maybe he even liked the reporter he had thrown from a bridge without learning his identity, and who now sat there like Irony himself, asking questions and going about his job. Peter relented, and told the tale:

Samuel Sok had proposed a total reconstruction of the Acre neighborhood. The city would use eminent domain powers to take ownership of blocks of tenement buildings. It would evict the occupants and sell the homes at cost to Sok, who would demolish them. Then Sok would solicit bids for the land from private developers, who would agree to build single-family homes and luxury condos.

What was in it for everyone?

The city would get rid of its most troublesome neighborhood. The lower density and the higher rental rates of new housing would attract the middle class, which would soon spread out and gentrify what was left of the older housing in the Acre. The developers would repay the city's investment, so the taxpayers wouldn't take a bath, and no politician could be criticized—God forbid—over the tax rate.

The plan depended on the incumbents holding their majority on the council through the election; the challengers would never approve such a radical destruction of low-income housing. For pushing the incumbents to victory with slanted news coverage, the brass at The Empire would get a new neighborhood of coveted middle-class readers. Boosting circulation would allow them to charge higher advertising rates, and that was good for the manager's profit-sharing plan.

What was in it for Sok? He would profit as the middleman in the land transfers to private developers. And Sok got something else, too:

"The city will condemn St. Francis de Sales Church as unsafe, settle with the diocese, and sell the building to us for demolition and redevelopment," Peter said.

It suddenly made sense why Councilman Eccleston had fed Eddie the structural report on the church. They needed to undercut that save-the-church group before it posed real opposition.

"What good is the church to you?" Eddie asked. "Is the land under it so valuable?"

Peter shrugged. "No more than any other. It's my father's old church. My brother and I were baptized there. Someone will tear it down eventually. We prefer to be the ones."

"Just sentimental, are you?" Eddie asked, the doubt thick in his voice.

Peter raised an eyebrow at Eddie's tone. "For family reasons," he said.

"It might not work if that church group pitches a decent redevelopment plan."

Peter scowled and smacked a tiny fist on his thigh. He insisted, "It shall work."

The tone of the interview suddenly lurched toward adversarial. Eddie badgered Peter, "What about the neighborhood? Do you really want to destroy the Acre?"

"The neighborhood will be reborn."

"The buildings, maybe. But not the people. They're getting the boot."

"Persons displaced by the demolition shall have first choice of the new housing," Peter said, sounding exasperated. "That will be in the plan."

"Please," Eddie said. "The folks in those tenements can't afford better housing—that's why they're in those tenements. Your project will price them right out of town."

"We are improving the quality of the city," Peter insisted. "Where are social problems more concentrated than in the Acre? The crime? The drugs? Violence? That will all be gone. Let the suburbs offer some affordable housing. The city has done its fair share."

"For a hundred and fifty years Lowell's been a landing pad for new immigrants. Why screw with that kind of history?"

"History is for books," Peter declared. He fidgeted and checked his wristwatch. "I believe our time is short, Mr. Bourque."

"For books? You don't believe that, Peter." Eddie tapped into his anger and let it flow over him. "The people in the Acre are first and second-generation Americans, immigrants just like you and your father."

"Bah!" Peter rose and jabbed a finger at Eddie. "They're nothing like my family."

Eddie stood and slapped the finger away.

Peter stepped back. The child of privilege was wide-eyed at the sting of physical contact. He backed away as Eddie advanced on him. Eddie spit his words. "I suppose they're not like your family. They don't have a warrior from the old country stalking the family patriarch, *looking for revenge.*"

"No!" Peter cried. He covered his ears to protect them from the truth. He backed into a wall and shrank against it.

Eddie grabbed two handfuls of the smaller man's vest and hauled him upright. Peter struggled meekly; he was frail and quaking with fear.

Eddie spoke low and hoarse, and the words came out wet. "Goddam right, Peter. Your old man confessed something to Father Wojick, didn't he?" Eddie got no answer. He shook Peter and shouted, "And Wojick freaked out."

Still no answer.

He pulled Peter close, and then slammed him back into the wall.

Peter moaned and squeezed his eyes shut.

Eddie warned him, "I've had a bad week, and I'm done getting jerked around." He held Peter against the wall. "Wojick freaked out and wrote a sermon just short of calling your father the criminal he is. What is he? A rapist? Some kind of killer? Your old man thought Wojick would tell the world that Lowell's famous civic benefactor is scum. So he got rid of him. He got Wojick to go to California and disappear. How'd he do it, Peter? How'd he get Wojick to go?"

Peter hung limp in Eddie's hands and wept.

Eddie pressed Peter to the wall. He whispered at him, "Wojick stayed away and everything went great for years.

But then Chanthay came to Lowell looking for revenge. And everything went to hell. That's why you got all the security here, the guys with guns walking the grounds."

Between sobs, Peter blurted, "I did not know her name."

At last, confirmation. "You and your brother set fire to the old house in the Acre with her in it, but she managed to escape," Eddie said.

Peter nodded and shook tears onto Eddie's hands.

"And your hired New York hitmen couldn't take her out, either."

"We never heard from them again."

"And when you found Nowlin with her, you beat his brains and dumped him in the canal."

Peter's eyes opened, full of tears and terror. He shook his head. "No, please," he begged. "Not us. That's wrong."

Eddie shook him again. "You dumped my beat partner in the canal, just like you dumped me, you stupid son-of-a-bitch."

Peter gasped. "No—you fell through the ceiling right at our feet. We saw your notebook, with The Empire emblem. We realized you were one of Templeton's reporters. We dragged you out, to save you."

Eddie's hand slid around Peter's throat. "You save people by throwing them off a bridge?"

"We thought you were dead," Peter insisted, tears running into his mouth. "Matthew checked you. He had a year of med school." Anger flashed across his face. "Matt is an *idiot*. I should have checked you myself."

Eddie eased his grip. "Then how'd I end up in the canal?"

"We read about that other reporter in the paper, the one they found in Worthen Canal. It made sense—dump the body in the same place. We thought you were *dead*."

What Peter claimed was possible. There were a hundred fine spots along the Worthen Canal to dump a body; it was why so many bodies ended up there, and everything dumped in the canal flowed to the same place.

Eddie demanded, "Why did you trash my apartment? What were you looking for?"

Peter gasped for breath. "Not us. We didn't know who you were until you came here this morning."

That figured to be true, too, judging by Peter's reaction when they had met. But if Peter and Matthew didn't wreck Eddie's house, who did?

"One thing you haven't answered," Eddie said, tightening his grip on Peter's vest. "How did your old man get Father Wojick to go to California?"

Peter said nothing. His eyes were bloodshot. They looked back into Eddie's eyes. Neither man blinked. Eddie pressed Peter against the wall and snorted, like a bull. "I can have a hundred cops, armed with a hundred warrants, tear this place apart," he said. "You're an arsonist, at the very least. Do you trust your brother not to crack under interrogation?" Eddie glared at him. He asked slowly, "What happened to Wojick?"

Peter glanced over Eddie's shoulder.

Eddie turned to look. There, on the wall, was the horrid, twisted crucifix, like the one in the old stone church.

And the truth fell hard upon Eddie Bourque. Father Wojick had never left St. Francis de Sales. He was entombed there, seventeen years, in the crucifix.

He glowered at Peter. "Your old man is a murderer. He *killed* Wojick."

Peter's mouth moved to speak, but nothing came out.

Eddie held him against the wall and thought about Wojick's last homily, about Danny's secret profile, and Chanthay's plot for revenge.

Peter was like a cadaver in Eddie's hands; the family secret had sapped his strength to stand.

Eddie felt his own knees weaken beneath the weight of another revelation—Chanthay was hunting a criminal of the Khmer Rouge genocide.

Chapter 31

The veranda on the back of the Sok estate house overlooked a man-made pond, frozen white, that reflected the sun with such glare it was impossible to look at without squinting.

"So the story about Father Wojick leaving for some woman was fake?" Eddie said.

Peter swirled whiskey in a glass and gulped it. "That's right," he said. He leaned on the veranda's polished railing and looked past the pond, to the gardens that rolled two hundred yards to the wall. "My brother and I are the only ones who know what happened to Wojick. And, I suppose, my father." He took another sip. "And now you."

Peter's eyes were still puffy from crying. He had wept a long time, curled on the floor of the sitting room, after Eddie had let him go. Eddie had spent that time staring at the scale model of the crucifix of St. Francis de Sales Church.

When Peter had recovered, he got drinks and brought Eddie to the veranda. The truth seemed to relax him. Seventeen years ago, Peter explained, as Samuel Sok prepared to make First Communion, he had offered to create a new crucifix for St. Francis de Sales. Sok wanted his donation to be anonymous, so Father Wojick never told anyone from whom he had ordered the figure. Sok had already finished the scale model when he made his first confession, in which he told Wojick about his part in genocide.

Peter did not know what had happened in the confessional. But Wojick's last homily had unnerved Sok, who feared he would be exposed. When his sons were away, Sok lured Wojick to the estate and knifed him through the heart. He had to hide the body. By chance, the mold for the full-scale crucifix was ready.

Sok routed the finished piece through several artists and trucking companies to conceal its origin. The Diocese installed it, but, given the shrinking number of communicants and the structural concerns about the church, never assigned another priest to St. Francis de Sales. No wine ever turned to blood under the murdered form of Father Zygmunt O. Wojick.

Eddie drank beer and organized the facts. "That's why you can't let the church be redeveloped," he said. "You're afraid the secret might be discovered, and your father would be exposed."

Peter sighed. "Not really," he said. "The records of the statue were so thoroughly confused, I doubt anyone could trace it here." He tipped the drink to his lips and emptied it. "My brother and I were just children during the Khmer Rouge. Only later did we come to understand our father's connection to them, and to their tactics. We had believed that St. Francis de Sales Church broke that connection. Our father's conversion to Christianity was genuine. He believed in his heart he would be saved. He became a generous man. You have seen his gifts to strangers."

Peter examined his thick-bottomed cocktail glass a moment, and then hurled it onto the ice. It bounced with a clink and skidded fifty feet to the far shore. "What happened to Wojick...." That thought trailed off and another began. "The crucifix must be buried. It can't hang in a house of God, mocking my father's chance for redemption. And then, we pray, our Heavenly Father may begin to forgive our earthly one."

Eddie finished his beer and left the bottle on the railing. "When I asked who knew about Wojick, you said you *suppose* your father knows. Wouldn't he know better than anyone?"

Tears flooded Peter's eyes again. He pressed his palms over them and gritted his teeth. He staggered back into the railing and knocked the beer bottle over the side. It fell to a walkway and smashed to bits.

"Do you wish to see?" he asked.

The guard outside the second-floor bedroom sat stiffly on an antique wooden chair with a pink velvet cushion. He nodded at Peter trotting up the stairs, and then stared at Eddie, who trotted two steps behind. Peter pointed to the bedroom door. The guard nodded again, rose without a word and unlocked the door with a key on a chain.

Peter grabbed the guard's elbow. "Anything today?" he asked.

The man frowned. "Not a peep, sir. I'm sorry."

To Eddie, Peter said, "This is our cross."

He pushed open the door and they went inside. The bedroom was white and sunny, with a view through an oval window of a grove of poplar. It was warmer than the rest of the house, too warm. It smelled mostly like household cleaners, though Eddie caught a whiff of urine.

Six odd machines arranged in a ring beeped and buzzed, like bystanders bustling over somebody having a heart attack on the sidewalk. The machines reached tentacles of wire and plastic hose to the victim. They seemed to be arguing in different languages over what to do.

In the center of the argument was a withered man on a twin-sized bed. He was covered to his chest by a purple blanket. His cheeks and throat looked caved, as if somebody had sucked the air out of him. A plastic tube brought oxygen to his nostrils. His hands were outside the blanket, palms up. Intravenous bags dripped clear liquid to needles in each wrist. Someone had crossed two long-stem red roses on the pillow above his head. They bloomed big in the heat.

Peter approached the bed and stroked the man's white hair. He whispered, "Papa? Please speak to me."

Only the machines answered.

"How long?" Eddie asked.

"Five years," Peter said. He continued to touch the man's hair. "He could do nothing for himself after the stroke. We have a nurse on staff here, and you probably saw the ambulance outside. We tend to his body. We've given up on his mind."

"He can't understand?"

Peter shrugged. "No one can say. I doubt it. He speaks, but we never make sense of it."

Eddie shuddered at the magnitude of this news story. He said, "Nobody in the city knows this. Everyone thinks Samuel Sok is a millionaire recluse. Why is this such a secret?"

Peter adjusted the blanket around his father's chest. "Because a millionaire recluse is more powerful than a man dead in every important way," he said. "Dead, but does not know it."

"You admit that, but yet you'd kill to protect him?"

Peter stepped back from the bed. He washed his hands under an invisible faucet. "It's almost funny," he said. "We are at war with this woman and her organization, and I did not know her name until you spoke it in the sitting room."

Eddie cringed. He tried to atone for his loose lips. "That's not her real name."

"It matters nothing."

"Do you know why she wants to kill him? What did he do during the genocide?"

"I could only imagine," Peter said, looking down to his shoes.

"Explain this to her," Eddie said. "Show her he's no threat. Christ, Peter, this is barely the same guy. Maybe I could convince her."

Peter folded his arms and turned away. He concluded, "It is too late now. She will not stop until he is dead. A Cambodian-born priest from Paris is in Lowell, visiting family. His timing is very good. We persuaded him to come here this morning in secret to perform my father's last rites."

"I'm going to talk to her for you," Eddie pledged.

"Do as you wish."

A voice croaked out. Peter and Eddie glanced at each other, and then to Sok. Peter rubbed his father's chest. The old man repeated himself in his first language.

"What did he say?" Eddie asked.

Peter frowned. "He said, 'Look at all the stars.' "

They stood there a while, beside the bed, two more bystanders crowding in for a good look at the guy on the sidewalk.

◇ ◇ ◇

Peter walked Eddie down the path that crossed the grounds. "You come here with knowledge dangerous to my family," Peter told him. "I want you to understand our position, so I have hidden nothing from you.

"I can speak to Alfred Templeton and stop The Empire from publishing what you have seen here. But I cannot stop you from repeating what I have shared. Whatever you say will become rumor. Rumors are very damaging. The true ones are the hardest to kill."

Peter took a deep breath, and then delivered his pitch. "My father will pay God for what he has done. Must his reputation pay as well? What of his generosity? His family name? And our ability to be benefactors in his place? Must it all pay?"

Eddie walked in silence. He thought about the sins in his own family, the fifty-year-old brother he'd never met. "What I don't get," Eddie said, ignoring Peter's larger point, "is what is your leverage with Templeton?"

"What does that—?"

"You said you could get my story spiked, and I believe you," Eddie said, interrupting. "But I want to know how."

Peter rubbed his little hand over his naked scalp. "Mr. Templeton and my father have an old friendship."

"It's more than that."

Peter nodded. "When Father Wojick, uh, disappeared, my father was worried—he didn't want any manhunt. So he asked Alfred Templeton, just an editor at the time, to plant the story in The Empire saying Wojick had fled to California. This is true. I have a note Templeton wrote my father."

Eddie recoiled, offended. "Why would any journalist agree to print a lie?"

"My father gave Templeton the money he needed."

It made sense. "The money Templeton needed," Eddie said slowly, "to buy enough Empire stock to appoint himself publisher."

"That is what Templeton wanted."

"And your father got what he wanted—Wojick's name was so smeared, the church membership considered it bad form to even mention him."

Peter kicked at the stone path. "Father Wojick soon fled from memory." He washed his hands in the air again. "So, Mr. Bourque, what of my request? Can my father keep his good name?"

Eddie gazed across the grounds, to the far stone wall. What to do? Samuel Sok was a philanthropist, and he was a killer. Which legacy did Sok deserve? And who was Eddie to rule on such a question?

There were no *good* answers. So he picked the one he could live with—a compromise. "I can keep my mouth shut," he said. "But I need you to trust me, and play a few things my way."

Peter's eyes narrowed.

Eddie said, "You can't make amends for all your father's crimes, but you can undo one of them. He stole a good man's reputation with that bullshit story about Wojick abandoning his church. Let both men have their good names."

"But how—?"

"Leave that to me. You said yourself there's no way to trace that crucifix."

Peter held his palms out. "The police might suspect," he said.

"Let them. There's no proof if you destroy the miniature cross in your sitting room. I'll cover your tracks."

Peter clenched his fists and pledged, "I will crush the small statue to dust."

"Wojick will get his proper burial," Eddie promised, "so you won't need the old church. Leave it alone. And there are plenty of triple-deckers in the Acre that could use your money for rehabilitation. Pull your cash out of the demolition project. Kill the deal—it can't happen without you."

"You would have me disappoint my friends in the community? Your boss, even?"

"He's going to have bigger problems."

Peter nodded. "Agreed. What else?"

"My last request," Eddie said, "is material in nature."

Peter inhaled and held his breath. He squeaked, "What is your price?"

Within minutes, Eddie had what he wanted in an envelope in his shirt pocket. He retraced his steps along the path, back through the sculpture garden.

He believed what Peter had told him. The Sok brothers hadn't bashed Nowlin's skull. Peter had supplied a lot of answers, but not to the big question.

Another set of footsteps crunched up the path toward Eddie, the priest here to deliver last rites to Samuel Sok, just in case Chanthay ever snuck past security. He was about Eddie's age and height, broad in the shoulders and handsome. He carried a black leather bag on a shoulder strap and whistled an odd, familiar tune.

Eddie nodded hello.

The priest smiled and bowed his head as the two men passed.

Back in the parking lot, Eddie chatted with the ambulance crew for a few minutes about the weather and the giant chessboard, and then he eased the Mighty Chevette down the driveway, back through the gauntlet of plaster pedestrians. The gate opened automatically to let him out.

He steered down the hill. There were no pay phones in this neighborhood; he would have to wait to place a call. Goddam Frank Keyes was too cheap to issue Eddie another cell phone....

That melody!

Eddie slammed the brakes. The Chevette squealed and bucked and skidded toward the granite curb. The right front tire hit with a whump. Metal scraped on stone. Eddie slammed forward against the shoulder belt. The car rocked twice, complained with a rattle, and stalled dead.

The priest had been whistling Claude Debussy, the melody Chanthay had played on Eddie's piano—her father's favorite. He remembered what Chanthay had told him:

One day my father caught a fish and cooked it for my brother and me.

Chanthay's brother. He had been the man chanting out of view in the old triple-decker. And he was the assassin pretending to be a priest.

Eddie turned the key. The starter coughed. He pumped the gas, he pounded the steering wheel, he shouted encouragement at the Mighty Chevette, and then he shouted filth. The car refused to be abused any longer. He jumped out and sprinted toward the Sok estate. He ran until his lungs were full of lava and his legs of lead. It was no use; there was still a mile to go, and then the gate. He moaned and staggered to a stop.

Eddie walked back to the Chevette, panting.

If the brother was anything like Chanthay, Samuel Sok was already dead.

Chapter 32

Eddie rubbed earwax off the receiver and pumped two quarters into the gas station pay phone. The Mighty Chevette idled nearby. Having finally coaxed it to life, Eddie was afraid to shut it off. He dialed The Empire, and then punched in a familiar extension.

Stan Popko picked up on the ninth ring, a marked improvement in response time.

"It's Bourque," Eddie said.

"Eddie! I'm nearly through researching my essay on the Stooges."

"Stan? What's wrong with your voice? You sound strange."

"It's my mood," Stan answered. "I think it's good."

"And the blind man learns to see. Good for you, but don't overdo it."

"I'll be careful," Stan assured him, with no hint that he was kidding.

Eddie counted the coins in his hand and got to the point. "Listen, Stan, does the paper hire outside computer consultants to give you a hand, or take jobs you can't get to?"

"Not that I know," Stan said. "I'm overpaid and hardly worked."

"Your candor still stuns me, man. I'm gonna ask you to do something beyond our original deal. You'll probably get fired if you're caught. And the legality of it is kind of gray."

"This isn't dangerous, is it?" Stan's good mood teetered over a cliff.

"Sort of."

Stan gasped, and then stammered, "I'm non-violent. I abhor violence, Eddie, whenever it's done to me—"

"Wait, wait!" Eddie interrupted. "Not that kind of dangerous. I want you to hack into The Empire's accounting department and search their records."

"Oh." Stan paused. "I do that all the time."

"I should have guessed."

Eddie heard keys clicking. Stan rambled as he typed, "The accounting department is supposed to be a completely self-contained local area network—the bean counters don't need to surf the Internet. But, naturally, I have developed my own back door."

The clicking continued for thirty seconds. Eddie dropped another quarter into the phone.

"Ah-ha!" Stan was in. "What are we looking for?"

"Keyes said something off the cuff yesterday that bothered me," Eddie said. "He was on a rant, you know—reporters are lazy, blah, blah, blah—and it slipped out that he was paying an outside computer consultant. I want to find that invoice, but I bet they tried to camouflage it."

"Could be listed under anything. Any more information?"

"Check within the past week."

Clicking, clicking, lots of clicking, and then Stan said, "The company has paid seventy invoices this week, from a high of nine thousand dollars—looks like for ink—to a low of fifty-four, for cable TV."

"Seventy invoices—that's more than I figured," Eddie said. "If my hunch is right, this would be a one-time payment. Does that help?"

"Yes—it—does," Stan said slowly over a barrage of keystrokes. "I'm issuing an exclusion command against the payee database. This should eliminate accounts the paper pays regularly." There was one final click, and then silence.

"Peculiar," Stan said. "There are two first-time accounts. One is for wallpaper."

"Keyes is redoing his office. What else?"

"The other is for exactly five thousand dollars, for data consultation."

"That's the one. Who'd they cut the check to?"

More clicking, and then a pause. "I know this name," Stan said. "Mary Chi. She's a doctor of computer science at the university."

"That's right," Eddie said. "And you were right about the virus that destroyed Nowlin's computer notes—it came up the elevator, and Dr. Chi carried it."

"Huh?"

Eddie pumped his fist in the air. He shouted, "Goddam, Stan, it was perfect! She got me to punch in Nowlin's password, and I was standing *right there* when she put in the disk. She was supposed to be copying his files, but that's when she uploaded the virus."

Stan was new to these cloak and dagger concepts; it took him a minute. "And this accounting record—you think the paper paid her to do it?"

"Five thousand bucks for a ten-minute job. Nice work if you can get it."

Stan got excited, like a little kid. "What are we going to do?"

"Let's break 'we' into its basic elements—you and I. You are going to keep this quiet. I am going to find out why The Empire's brass paid five grand to torch Nowlin's notes. I have a plan to flush out the truth." *Though the guy I need to help me hates my guts.*

"Oh—the brass," Stan said, "they're looking for you, but I guess so is everybody."

"For me? Like who?"

"Well, Ed, the police. I've heard your name on the scanner a few times. Sounded serious."

The police? Eddie switched the phone to his other ear. "You're telling me this *now*?"

"Now's when I'm thinking of it."

"Christ, Stan, did the cops say what they wanted?"

"I can't say—been working on my essay and playing games, so it's hard to hear. Keyes has been paging you over the intercom, too."

"And what the hell does *he* want?"

"Could have to do with the cop car outside the building. Been there all morning."

"This is weird," Eddie said. "Do me a favor and don't tell anybody you talked to me today."

"Who's to tell?"

"Right." Eddie hung up. He drummed his fingers on the telephone. What were the police so anxious to talk about?

Forget it, they'll have to wait.

Eddie got a number from directory assistance and dialed it. A receptionist answered on the first ring and spewed in one breath, "Thank you for calling Channel Eight, Boston's number-one, twenty-four-hour news leader, to whom may I direct your call?"

"Newsroom."

The line transferred and rang four times. Another receptionist answered.

Eddie said, "Chuck Boden, please."

"Yessir. Mr. Boden is in a news meeting. Whom may I say is calling?"

"Tell Boden it's Eddie Bourque, and he's got no balls if he doesn't come to the phone."

After a moment of stunned silence, Eddie heard a click, and then two minutes of numbing banter between the anchors on Channel Eight's wakeup show, taped that morning. Then Boden got on the line. "Nice manners, Bourque," he growled. He snapped his gum in Eddie's ear. "The receptionist doesn't get paid to deal with assholes."

"Then give her half your clothing stipend and let her retire to the Vineyard."

Boden snorted. "Still the funny man. Did you call to share your wit, or just to wreck my day?"

"This ain't fun for me either," Eddie said. "But I got a gift for you."

"Any gift from you," Boden swore, "I will turn over to the bomb squad."

"It's a story, and it's in your size—big."

"Yeah? What?"

"You have to come out here to find out."

Boden said nothing for a moment, and then, "Not interested, Bourque. You have nothing I'd want." But he stayed on the line, and he chewed the gum faster.

"I have every station's lead story for a week, and I'm offering it to you."

"Why aren't you writing it?" Boden demanded. "You could win a big prize and get your ass out of that two-bit rag."

"I got my reasons. Don't tell me that you suddenly care about what I write."

"I don't," Boden said. He chewed his gum for a few seconds. "Why me, Bourque?" He added with suspicion, "Is this about those story tips from when we were interns?"

"Not a chance, Chuck. I'm over that."

Eddie meant it. All it took was a near-death experience with a warrior goddess in an abandoned warehouse. Should have done it years ago. "Don't get me wrong," Eddie explained. "I still think you're a prick. But my opinion is now based solely on your wretched personality. Unfortunately for me, you're also a big name in TV news, and that'll give the story more weight. I need a big punch."

"You're setting me up," Boden accused. But he didn't sound convinced.

"As much as we hate each other, Chuck, we both respect the news," Eddie reasoned. "You sensationalize the hell out of it, like every TV clown, but you're a reporter, not a script reader. And I'm sure we agree you're the best in Boston." He paused. "Now that I've said that, I need to go puke."

Boden chuckled. "So touching. By leaking this to me, I assume you hope to screw somebody."

"With a flagpole. Till his distant cousins are sore."

Boden thought for a moment. "Nothing leads at Channel Eight without video."

"You'll get film," Eddie promised.

Boden spit out the gum and mumbled something under his breath. He warned, "So help me, Bourque, if you're wasting my time..."

Chapter 33

Eddie could not shake the feeling that he should avoid the police until he had what he wanted.

Twice on the way downtown he had spotted cruisers on patrol, and had jerked his car into the nearest driveway, out of sight. He wasn't sure why he was hiding. The cops might want to talk to him, but they wouldn't be prowling the city looking for him. *Would they?* He had misled Detective Orr on a couple points, but the police wouldn't send out an APB for that.

Still, he needed a few more hours. It was time to dump the Mighty Chevette; the car was too old, ugly and conspicuous to drive when he was trying not to be noticed.

Eddie motored slowly down side streets spiraling through a thickly settled neighborhood of concrete apartment buildings and boxy duplexes, about a mile from downtown. Every street in the neighborhood was jammed, both sides, with cars parked bumper to bumper: SUVs and minivans, older-model German convertibles and Japanese econo-boxes of every make. There might have been two thousand cars crammed in this cramped maze of two dozen streets, a perfect place to hide one little Chevette, if he could find a parking spot.

He drove around muttering about how frustrating it must have been to live in that neighborhood, until—success!—he spied a patch of blacktop between two massive, battered sedans. The space at first looked too small to be called a parking spot, but Eddie was a determined driver in an old junker, and he bumper-knocked the car in there, tight to the curb. For drivers traveling in either direction, the Chevette would have been nearly invisible.

Eddie put on his leather coat and black sunglasses. He popped his Red Sox cap on his head and pulled it down low.

The sun was bright above a few high clouds. He strolled sidewalks piled with trash bags and plastic recycling bins. He saw two dog walkers, some kids racing on their bicycles, a few joggers, and an old man picking returnable cans from the junk.

Eddie turned a corner onto a commercial stretch of street-level storefronts built into the first floor of triple-decker apartment homes.

A police car was coming toward him on the street.

Eddie ducked into a doorway of some kind of bookstore. He faced away from the street and pretended to tie his shoe. The cruiser's reflection passed in the storefront's milky white windows.

The door opened and a man came out dressed like Eddie: dark glasses, baseball cap low on his head. He cradled a brown paper bag in his arm. He mumbled to Eddie, "Lithuanian erotica, fifty percent off."

"What?"

"Nice selection, too."

Eddie stepped back and read the sign above the door. "Oh," he said. He had heard of "The Licker Store," an adult book outlet, but never knew where it was. Eddie got indignant. "Lithuania, you say? I was told all of Eastern Europe would be on sale. I'm never shopping here again."

He spun and marched on toward downtown, keeping watch for police patrols. From a distance he saw the police car, two cops inside, stationed outside The Empire.

Still there? Waiting for me?

Eddie turned up his collar and hustled across an intersection to a neighborhood pub with clean views of both the Empire Building and police headquarters.

◇ ◇ ◇

Chuck Boden did as Eddie had asked, and parked the Channel Eight van in front of the police station. Any Empire editor glancing out the newsroom window would see the truck. The editor might call the police to make sure nothing big was brewing. But if the cops had no murders, political corruption or quirky crimes—a holdup at a bowling alley or an assault with a weed whacker—the van would blend, chameleon-like, into the downtown streetscape.

A dumpy man in jeans and yellow work boots got out on the driver's side. He would be the guy paid to run the camera. The newsman paid ten times more got out on the passenger's side, looking like a Wall Street mogul in a gray suit and black overcoat. His hair defied wind.

Boden waited while the cameraman collected his equipment. A car horn beeped. Boden grinned and waved to the driver. They crossed the street and met Eddie in the bar. Boden let the dumpy guy lug the camera, the tripod and a gym bag stuffed with wires and microphones and other TV junk.

Boden slid across the booth from Eddie. The cameraman took a chair nearby and busied himself with testing batteries.

Boden started to offer his right hand to Eddie, but changed his mind and pulled away the moment Eddie reached for it. Then Eddie pulled back, just as Boden reached for *his* hand. Then they repeated the whole awkward scene, moving like lumberjacks working a two-handed saw, until they both gave up and Boden asked, "Are we in a rush?"

"No."

The TV man checked his reflection in the window. He said, "What a picture, huh? You and me—at the same table. I know a few people who'd bust a vein if they saw this." He called to the cameraman, "Hey, Rusty, get some film of me and my new best friend."

The cameraman gave a dismissive wave and set at untangling a gob of black wires.

Eddie said, "Thanks for coming, Chuck. I know it couldn't have been easy because, well, you know, our history."

Boden flashed perfect teeth in an angry wolf's smile, a wolf with caps. "You don't get it, Bourque," he snarled.

"Why don't you explain it to me?"

Boden leaned over the table, close enough for Eddie to see his eyeliner. "You think I hate your guts because you accused me of stealing story tips off your computer all those years ago, and nearly got me fired?" He jabbed a finger at Eddie. "Get over yourself."

Boden leaned back and gazed out the window at traffic. The anger lines smoothed from his face. "We were both working the cop beat. Did it ever occur to you that I might have heard on my own that three councilmen were about to be indicted for kickbacks? It's not my fault you sat on the story in secret, trying to nail down every little detail. When I got it, I ran with it.

"You're a hyper-competitive, needling little bastard," Boden said. "By calling me a thief, you nearly ended my career before it started." He laughed, spitefully. "But the funny thing is—when we were interns together, I actually looked up to you. You had Pam, who's terrific, and you obviously had talent in this business. You were going places.

"When you left for the full-time gig in Vermont, I thought you'd be in Boston in a year, and in New York in two."

Boden gently waved off a waiter who had come to take his order.

"But you wasted your time in Vermont," he continued. "You had to prove to everybody that you were the baddest guppy in the fishbowl, and you couldn't leave until you did. *That's* what I can't respect. And I've heard you let Pam drift away because she was in competition for your time, and you'd rather talk to your sources than to her. You're an idiot for losing her, by the way."

The TV man shrugged. "And then you come slinking back to The Empire? You come back to the small time for *what*? To be close enough to the big papers to see what you're missing? Sorry, but when a man lies down like a doormat, Chuck Boden wipes his shoes on him."

Boden clasped his hands behind his head, smiled and said breezily, "So fuck you, Ed, and your story tips from seven years ago. That little dust-up taught me to take command of where I was going, and not let other people control my career. I've been moving up ever since. Which is more than I can say for you."

The lashing burned the tops of Eddie's ears. He nodded, shrugged and said, "You're right."

"Hold on! Should we roll tape on this? You agree?"

"This has been an enlightening week," Eddie explained. "For my whole career I've been demanding the truth from politicians. Now I'm demanding it from myself."

The cameraman had stopped what he was doing and was intently eavesdropping. Eddie zapped him with a dirty look.

Boden said, "Rusty, can you *pretend* to be minding your own business?"

Eddie lowered his voice. "In Vermont, there was always another little secret to expose, always another story that I had to get in search of the perfect resumé. I got into a competition with myself, trying to outdo all my past work. I recognized after a couple years that Pam and I were growing apart, and I did nothing to stop it. It pissed me off that she was ready to settle down in some small town and start *living*, while I still thought of Vermont as a temp job on my way to the big time. The more she tried to make life comfortable there, the harder I worked...." He let the thought trail off.

"I was stupid to think that just getting my work back into this market would bring the big dailies to my doorstep," Eddie admitted. "A guy stepping backward in the business to his old paper must trigger all sorts of red flags."

"After seven years at a mid-sized daily in Vermont, yeah, I'd say so," Boden said. "No matter how good the writer."

That sounded like a compliment, but Eddie was unsure it was intentional. "I envy the chances you've taken in your career, Chuck," he said. "I thought you were a fool when you gave up newspapers for a shot at TV."

"So did a lot of people, even me at first."

"But you saw it through," Eddie said. "I've played it safe my whole career." He felt the tone of the conversation sliding toward morose and clapped his hands. "But no more. I've learned this week that nothing extraordinary comes without risk."

Boden nodded, pleased and intrigued. "Now *this* I should get on tape."

"Maybe not. If my scheme doesn't work you'll see my career in the obituaries." *And maybe me, too.*

"What's your game plan?"

"It starts with you leading tonight's six-o'clock broadcast with the story of the year."

"Yeah, about that—where the hell's my scoop?" he asked. "I got political capital with the boss riding on this."

Eddie slid him a photocopy of a seventeen-year-old Empire story.

Boden pulled reading glasses from his coat pocket and set them near the end of his nose. He nodded when he had reached the end of the clip. "I remember the Father Wojick scandal," he said. "He falls in love and goes to California to get laid. People gossip, he's never heard from again. The end. What's the new hook? And where's my video?"

Eddie slid out of the booth. "Let's take a walk."

Boden frowned. "You're not going to tell me until the last second, are you? See what I mean—you're a needling little bastard."

They strolled into the Acre. Their slow pace stirred no interest, not even from folks out on their front steps, bored speechless by being poor and waiting for entertainment to happen by. Boden let old Rusty carry all their equipment. He seemed impervious to the cameraman's huffing and puffing. Eddie led them through the brush to the side door at St. Francis de Sales Church, and opened the padlock with the key Hippo Vaughn had given him.

"Please," Boden said as they entered, "let there be a sex cult in here."

Rusty staggered up the stairs behind them. At the top Boden looked to Eddie and rolled his eyes to apologize for his cameraman's whimpering.

"So this was Wojick's church," Boden said. "Impressive. A shame they don't use it anymore. This bright enough in here, Rusty?"

The cameraman wiped a sleeve over his shiny forehead. "I got lights. It'll be fine."

"Look around," Eddie said. "Take some film of the sanctuary, but don't go near the altar until I get back. This could take a while."

Eddie hustled down the main aisle. His heavy footsteps echoed through the vast church like distant cannon fire. He skirted the altar and slipped through an arched doorway to a stripped-down room, painted white from the hardwood floor to the twelve-foot ceiling. A tall wardrobe cabinet, two sagging cafeteria-style tables and a few mismatched chairs were scattered around.

The room had two doors. The first led down to a dark basement. Wrong way. Eddie needed a passage leading up.

The second door led to a narrow corridor, just wide enough to walk through, which passed behind the altar to a similar room on the other side, probably at one time a dressing room for the altar boys. This room contained a dozen old folding chairs—wooden and missing slats—and two empty wardrobe cabinets.

No passage up.

Eddie peeked behind the cabinets, and then searched the rest of the walls, pushing and tapping, for a panel or utility door. Nothing. He searched back along the narrow corridor, found nothing and performed a similar hunt in the first room. He sat in a dusty chair, defeated. *There has to be a way up there.*

He looked up. In the ceiling was the square outline of a trap door. Eddie smacked his forehead with the heel of his hand.

The wardrobe, he decided, would make an excellent base for a makeshift ladder; it was sturdy and tall, with a top big enough to support a chair. But it must have been made from the same wood as Eddie's mysteriously heavy piano, because the damn thing would not budge.

Instead, Eddie dragged a cafeteria table under the trap door. On the table he placed an armless wooden chair with a spindle-rod backing. On that chair, he placed the sturdiest of a rickety bunch of folding chairs from the other room. And on that chair, Eddie placed his feet.

His fingertips clung to the back of the chair until the whole tower stopped quivering. The trap door wasn't hinged; it was just a piece of plywood painted white to match the ceiling. He pushed it in, and then over to the side. With much scuffling and grunting, he pulled himself up.

He entered a utility room, the same size as the room below, but unfinished. Three of its walls were just planks nailed to wooden beams. The fourth was stone, the granite outer wall of the church. A minimal steel ladder, something like a fire escape, was bolted to the outer wall, leading up into darkness.

Eddie was prepared for the dark. He took a penlight from his pocket, clicked it on, held it in his teeth and started up the ladder. Twenty rungs later, he was still climbing. The exercise, combined with the height, produced a sweat Eddie could smell. It was the odor of parachuting or rock climbing, activities that combine sports with the chance of death. He stopped to wipe his hands, one at a time, on his pants.

The ladder finally reached a roof of heavy timber. Eddie stepped to a triangular platform. It creaked under its first load in decades, but seemed up to the task. He wormed his shoulders into a cubbyhole through an inner wall of the church, and emerged in a crawl space between the ceiling of the sanctuary and the roof of St. Francis de Sales.

The space was about four feet high, cluttered with a crisscross of wooden beams and a web of support wires. Fingers of dust hung from everything, swaying like undersea plants in the dead air Eddie had disturbed. He crouched on parallel wooden timbers, loose insulation between them. What was beneath the insulation? Maybe just thin plaster, like in the old triple-decker in the Acre. He would stay on the timbers, and off the Channel Eight news.

He kept the flashlight in his teeth and crept under support beams and over the wires. Above the altar, right where it should be, he found a metal winch bolted across three timbers. It was the size and shape of an overturned wheelbarrow. Brass gears interlocked on the outside of the winch. A crank handle screwed into an axle.

Eddie gripped the handle. "Okay, Father Wojick," he whispered, "time to come home from California."

He pulled.

And nothing happened. The crank didn't budge. He pushed. Still nothing.

"Don't piss me off, crank," Eddie warned. He pushed it with his feet, and then tried again from the other side. The crank refused to listen. He looked closer.

A steel claw, the size of a finger, was wedged into a gear, locking it in place. The lock was on a pivot, but the stubborn thing would not move. Eddie pulled at it, and then kicked it with his heel. He was *so close*, and this foolish metal claw was thwarting him. He needed something to pry it open. He tugged at a support wire. It might have been possible to loop wire around the claw and pull it free, but he'd need a wrench to loosen a wire. And if he had a wrench, he wouldn't need wire.

Eddie unscrewed the crank handle, which, once removed from the machine, resembled a crowbar. He tried wedging it against the claw to pry it loose, but the end of the tool was too fat. Furious at this nagging little detail for which he had failed to plan, Eddie whacked the claw with the handle. A spark shot into the darkness. The clanking noise vibrated through the crawlspace.

He hit it again, and then again.

And the machine gave up its ghost.

Gears whirled. The giant crucifix plummeted on its chain like a battleship's anchor. Eddie shut his eyes and squeezed the penlight in his teeth. The chain whipped back an instant after the crash and rang the winch like a church bell. Plaster chunks scattered below.

By the time Eddie got back down, old Rusty had the tripod and a portable light set up. He panned the camera back and forth.

A vaguely human form was splayed face-up on the altar, arms and head bent limp over the edge of the sacramental table. Chunks of plaster clung to the form. There was no odor. The moisture in the body had long since evaporated through pores in the plaster. What remained was the husk.

Boden held a piece of white plaster embedded with a tuft of hair. The newsman's complexion had faded, and Eddie could see the spots touched up by makeup. Boden's bottom lip quivered. He glanced to the news clip Eddie had given him, and then said, "Is this—"

"Father Wojick," Eddie confirmed. "That old news story is all wrong. He never ran away for a woman in California. And he never abandoned his flock. You'll set the record straight."

Boden nodded. He swallowed, and then said, "Who did this to him, Ed?"

"That's the new mystery you'll offer your viewers tonight at six."

Boden plopped into a dusty pew, showing no concern for his suit. He pulled out a cell phone and had a hushed, five-minute conversation. He raised his voice one time: "I am *not* drunk!"

He hung up and told Eddie, "I'm leading the broadcast tonight." His eyes lingered on the form on the altar. "My boss will need smelling salts when she sees this video."

Eddie asked, "What time you go on?"

"The news is at six."

"No, what time do you go on—exactly what time."

Boden studied his wristwatch. "The show's intro is ninety seconds. Then Jill and Willy introduce me and set the scene. Figure another thirty seconds. I'll be live by six-oh-two, the latest."

"This needs to be exact, not a minute either way."

"My watch is synchronized with the station clock," Boden assured him.

"Great. Gimme your watch."

"Why?"

"Because Rusty has one and I need yours tonight."

Boden handed over his Rolex without protest.

The cameraman declared he was finished. Eddie sat next to Boden while Rusty packed. "Do me a favor," Eddie said. "Cover my tracks, and don't call the cops or the diocese until the video is on the air. I don't want this story getting around before you break it."

"Not a problem," Boden said. "I'm sure they'll be calling me when they see it."

They left the church with old Rusty bringing up the rear again. Eddie locked the door. Boden sent the cameraman away for video of the church exterior, and of the neighborhood. He offered his hand and left it there until Eddie shook it.

"Thanks," Boden said. "For picking me."

"Pull no punches tonight," Eddie said, knowing that Boden never did. The Rolex read four-thirty. Plenty of time for a coffee before he barged into the office of Empire publisher Alfred T. Templeton.

"Gotta go," Eddie said. "I need to quit my job."

Chapter 34

Eddie slouched on the red vinyl bench and peered over a four-year-old edition of *Field & Stream*. Another police car slowly passed outside. That made three patrols in the twenty minutes since he had ducked into the barbershop on the outskirts of downtown.

"They're looking to take you in," the barber said. He was stooped, and spotted with age and spoke in a thick Cuban accent.

Eddie spun around, startled. "What's that?" he said.

The barber looked oddly at Eddie. "I was joking to my friend here," he said. He pointed a comb at his customer, a balding middle-aged man with a black beard that brushed his potbelly.

"Oh. Sorry."

The barber grinned. "You got a guilty conscience, eh?" He went back to snipping his customer's black horseshoe of hair. "S'okay. S'okay. I give you a prison cut."

Eddie laughed. "Are there normally so many cops around here?"

The barber shrugged. "What's normal? Seems like a lot today."

Yeah, it seemed like a lot for the late afternoon shift. This was strange. The closer Eddie got to the Empire Building, the thicker the police patrols had become. They were looking for somebody. "Is there a phone around here?" he asked.

The barber pointed with scissors. "Pay phone outside, around the corner."

Eddie went to the phone. He pried purple chewing gum off the coin slot with a discarded Popsicle stick and then jammed in fifty cents. Whom could he call? Whom did he trust? Eddie dialed an extension at The Empire.

"Newsroom," answered Boyce Billips.

"Hey, it's Bourque."

The intern shrieked in Eddie's ear and hung up.

"Boyce? Boyce? Hey!" Eddie said into the dead telephone. *What the hell is his problem?*

Eddie dug another fifty cents from his pocket and dialed back.

A tiny voice answered after six rings, "Hello?"

"What's the matter with you?"

Boyce whispered, "Whatever happened, I just want to say I have nothing but respect for you and all the help you've given me the past year, and I'll say that under oath."

Eddie checked Boden's Rolex—five minutes to five. "Goddammit, Boyce, I don't have time for riddles. Tell me what you're talking about."

"*You don't know?* Please, Eddie, don't shoot the messenger—oh God, I didn't mean it like that! I mean it's just an expression...."

Eddie hollered, "Boyce!"

Eddie heard Boyce's telephone crash off his desk. After some fumbling noises, Boyce got back on the line. "Sorry," he said with a nervous laugh, "dropped the phone." He quickly added, "Not that I'm afraid or anything, it's just startling. I mean, you're startling, not the phone. Not you, personally, it's just...."

"Please," Eddie interrupted. He turned his back to an approaching car, a late-model rust-colored sedan. He let it pass, and then gave a little sigh. "Tell me what's going on."

"The cops, Eddie, the cops found the weapon, so just turn yourself in."

"Again with the riddles? What weapon?"

He could hardly hear Boyce whisper, "The murder weapon."

"You mean from Danny's murder? Jesus, Boyce, this is *good* news. Finally a breakthrough. Where'd they find it?"

There was a pause. Boyce creaked, "In your house."

My house? Eddie stood stunned, a man of marble with a telephone to his head.

"I guess some investigators went there early this morning," Boyce continued.

Eddie wasn't sure he could speak. He was surprised to hear himself say, "Yeah, I had convinced the cops to follow up on a break-in at my place."

"Like I said, whatever happened...."

"Shut up, Boyce," Eddie hissed. "I didn't kill Danny." He noted a rust-colored Buick slowly coming toward him. *Is that the same car from a minute ago?* "How do they know it's the murder weapon?"

"They found blood and fingerprints on it," Boyce said. "The word leaked from the police lab a little while ago. It's Danny's blood. And *your* fingerprints—they match your media I.D. application."

Eddie got stern. "Boyce, listen to me. This is a setup."

"Uh-huh...."

The Buick stopped about forty yards from Eddie. Two people were inside. "Boyce, I'm in some trouble here, and I need you to believe me."

"Whatever you say."

"No, Boyce!" Eddie shouted. He caught himself and said calmly, "You have to believe me for real. Think about all we've gone through together."

"Like what?"

Like what, indeed? Eddie tried another line of reasoning, "Think about all those emails about hepatitis you sent me last month. And remember the time you called at five in the morning when you thought you got V.D. from a picnic blanket?"

"There was something crusty on it."

"Whatever," Eddie said. "Boyce, think about all the annoying things you've done in the past year."

Two men in black slacks and matching blue windbreakers got out of the Buick.

Eddie gently said into the phone, "If I was really a killer, wouldn't you be dead by now?"

The phone was silent.

The two men started walking toward Eddie. They had matching crew cuts and badges on their belts. Eddie recognized one of them from when he worked the night shift on the police beat.

"Think fast, man," Eddie said. "I really gotta run."

"Yes, I guess so. I'm sorry."

"Forget it. Stick by the phone. I may need help."

Eddie hung up and ran.

One cop raced back to the car.

The other raced after Eddie. He ran heavy, arms across his body, more like a football halfback than a track sprinter. Eddie tore across a parking lot, vaulted a low chain fence, cut through a playground and zigzagged down side streets into a neighborhood of low-rent apartments, mini-malls, and light manufacturing plants.

Fleeing on foot through back yards and back alleys kept Eddie's mind off what the police had found in his house. He thought only about getting away, and getting to the publisher's office in time for the six-o'clock news. He had one shot to squeeze Templeton for some answers about Danny, and he didn't care about the risk.

Up ahead, a police cruiser screeched to a stop, its nose diving at the ground. Eddie fled into an alley between two brick buildings. A big blue Dumpster blocked the way. He turned sideways and scraped past it, just as his pursuer on foot came into view.

"In the alley," the cop huffed into his radio. "Seal the other end."

The other end was thirty yards away. Eddie dashed for it. The rust-colored Buick beat him there; the car skidded on the concrete sidewalk and stopped across the narrow exit. Eddie hurdled the front fender in stride, slid over the hood and ran blindly across the street. Car horns blared. Brakes screamed. Somebody shouted, "Asshole!"

The driver gunned the Buick's engine. Tires spun on sand and the car roared after Eddie down a side street lined with interconnected faux-brick condominiums.

Eddie gasped for air. The Buick growled louder. Ahead on the left, a roll-down garage door was closing. Eddie dove under it and rolled. The door closed behind him. Outside, the Buick squealed to a stop.

Eddie rested on an oil-spotted cement floor, allowing himself a few deep breaths. He was in a one-car garage with a low-end Toyota and a scattering of dirt-caked garden tools. Three wooden stairs led to a doorway.

A doorbell chimed. A cop pounded the front door. "Police! Police!"

Eddie got up and made for the doorway. It led to a hall covered with pictures of an aged couple surrounded by what probably were grandchildren. A weather report blared at maximum volume from a television ahead. Eddie tiptoed down the hall. The doorbell rang again; he could barely hear it over the TV.

The condo had a spacious, open floor plan. To Eddie's left, their backs to him, an elderly couple sat hand in hand on a sofa, learning, at earsplitting volume, about a coming cold front. To Eddie's right was a dining room. Straight across—a back door.

There was no sense startling these people into heart attacks. Eddie crept behind them, and then let himself out the back. He was in a common courtyard with a parking lot, a few scattered hardwoods and picnic tables, enclosed by an iron fence.

Immediately, a police cruiser screamed around the building into the parking lot and stopped.

Now that's not fair. Eddie broke into a sprint. No wonder criminals were so bad-tempered in court—the cops ganged up on them by radio. He headed for a gate in the fence. A uniformed officer jumped from the cruiser and raced after him. This guy was jar-headed and beefy, not a long-distance runner. But he was fresh and Eddie was near-exhausted and the chase stayed close through an urban industrial block of grimy brick buildings, loading docks and rusted tractor-trailer hulks.

A train whistled ahead. *The five-fifteen.* Gravity grabbed harder at Eddie's tired legs. The cop closed in behind him.

Eddie turned toward the whistle, onto the cement pad of a demolished warehouse. Kids had drawn a baseball diamond in blue chalk. Beyond the pad was a trash-strewn outfield of patchy grass, and beyond that, the railroad tracks.

The silver freight train, coming from Eddie's far right, clanged along at maybe fifteen or twenty miles per hour. He spied another police car on his far left. Both front doors opened and two more uniformed guys got out.

Eddie ran for the tracks, angling ahead of the train.

The two new cops yelled, "Stop! Police!"

Eddie would never stop, not before he learned what happened to Danny, and who had set him up.

The train hammered down the tracks, growing ever louder. Eddie pumped his burning thighs. His lungs sizzled like steaks on the grill. The cops yelled something he couldn't make out over the rumbling train. He focused on the tracks, at the spot he would cross ahead of the engine. The whistle was deafening.

He stretched one last stride across the tracks in the shadow of the locomotive. The engine nicked his right heel. His shoe flew off. The blow spun Eddie in a pirouette and deposited him, face down, in a crushed granite embankment on the far side of the tracks.

The trained clattered by. Three cops on the other side watched Eddie between the cars. He had maybe three minutes. He retrieved his shoe, some thirty feet down the tracks, and staggered away, down a concrete hill, under a highway overpass, and into the warehouse district. The cops no doubt had already radioed his position to other units. More officers, fresh and ready to run, were on their way. He had to hide, but where? *There's no time.*

An older-model Mercedes, a light lilac color, peeled around the corner and slammed to a stop. Eddie whirled and started back toward the hill.

"Bourque!" a voice yelled.

Eddie turned around. "Stan?"

Stan Popko leaned over and popped the front door. "Get in!"

Eddie dove into the front seat. Stan pounded the gas. The car jerked forward as Eddie was slamming the door.

"On the floor," Stan ordered.

Eddie knelt in the foot space, panting, his head and chest on the seat. Stan drove off.

"Hello officers," Stan said calmly to himself.

"More cops?"

"Going right past us. Just stay down."

"How…how did you know?"

The dashboard police scanner crackled with excited voices, barking commands and relaying positions. Stan turned it off. "The police have been quite explicit in their description of the chase," he said in his pitch-perfect monotone.

"You'll go to jail for helping me."

Stan frowned. "Only if I'm caught." He turned the car onto a residential boulevard. "Which seems highly improbable at this point."

Eddie lay quiet for a minute. His strength came back. Who could have planted the weapon at his house? What kind of monster would allow Eddie to decompose inside maximum security for forty years to life? It struck him as bizarre that even the hitmen in the old mill had more compassion than whoever had set him up. The hitmen would have shot Eddie through the heart, but they wouldn't have murdered him little by little, for forty years.

"I didn't kill Danny," Eddie told him.

Stan said, "You are a thorough and cunning investigator. I find a low probability that you would leave incriminating evidence in your dwelling. And though I have knowledge of several unlawful activities you have perpetrated during your investigation, those crimes were consistently committed toward a uniform higher moral purpose."

"You believe me?"

"Didn't I just say so?"

Chuck Boden's wristwatch said the time was nearly five-thirty. "Barely half an hour," Eddie said. "I need a phone."

Stan handed him his minuscule cell.

"Start heading toward The Empire," Eddie directed, while dialing. "And pay attention to this call. We gotta work together." Into the phone, he said, "Boyce, here's what I need you to do...."

Chapter 35

"Are the cops still parked there?" Eddie asked from a crouch on the floor of Stan's Mercedes.

"Right across the street from the front door."

"Anybody around?"

"Sidewalk is clear."

"Okay, let's do it. Get as close to the curb as you can."

Stan pulled up outside the Empire Building's main entrance, the only way inside that wasn't locked. The car's tires scraped the cement curb.

"Not *that* close," Eddie said.

Stan frowned. "Mom's not going to like that."

"Buff the rubber with olive oil. She'll never know."

Stan stopped directly in front of the door, shifted the transmission to park and let the car idle.

"Are the cops watching?" Eddie asked.

Stan looked to his left. "Mm-hmm."

"Do you see Boyce?"

He looked the other way. "Mm-hmm." From the side of his mouth, Stan said, "He's coming out now with two bundles of newspaper."

Boyce shuffled to the car and set the bundles on the roof. Then he opened the front passenger's door. "Hi Stan," he said. "Are two bundles enough?" He did not look at Eddie.

Stan nodded. "Nice improvisation," he said in a low voice. "Load them in."

Boyce took a wide stance and reached for a bundle on the roof. Eddie dove between Boyce's feet and crawled on knees and elbows across the sidewalk to The Empire's glass door. He looked over his shoulder. Boyce loaded the second bundle into Stan's car. The Mercedes completely blocked the view of the policemen across the street.

Stan and Boyce thanked each other, and then Boyce nonchalantly stepped over Eddie and pulled open the door. At that instant, Stan got out on the driver's side and yelled over the car, "Hey, one more thing!"

Boyce turned around, still holding the door. "What's that?" he yelled back.

Eddie crawled inside, under a picture of publisher Alfred Templeton posing on a putting green with a U.S. senator, and headed for the stairwell.

"Oh, never mind," Stan said. "I'll catch you later. Thanks again for the scrap paper."

"Anytime," Boyce said with a wave. He went inside. Stan drove off.

Eddie pounded up ten flights of stairs. At the top landing, he bent over to catch his breath. The time was 5:54.20 p.m., according to the borrowed wristwatch that was worth more than Eddie's car. He wouldn't mind giving it back. Eddie didn't care for pricey timepieces, or for anything that cost a lot of money for the sole purpose of being expensive.

Eddie pushed through the glass door on which was stenciled: *Alfred T. Templeton, publisher*.

Templeton's decorators had dressed up his outer office like a fine hotel lobby—maple paneling, dwarf trees in big clay flowerpots, and a small stone fountain—into which people had actually thrown spare change. The secretary's desk was empty. The door to Templeton's office was cracked open. The office was dark.

Eddie fought off a rush of doom. *Templeton always stays late*. How could he have picked that evening, of all evenings, to leave before six?

But then music lumbered from the publisher's office— cello music, too thick to be a recording. The notes were long and slow. Gloomy. Like the end of a tragic opera, when the wounded hero crawls around stage looking for a place to die.

Eddie pushed open the door. The lights were off, the shades drawn. His eyes took a moment to adjust. He could make out the desk, two chairs, some bookshelves cluttered with golfing memorabilia, and a computer on a table. Templeton's high-back leather chair faced away from the door. A television, dark at the moment, was suspended from the ceiling like at a sports bar.

Eddie knocked twice.

The music stopped but there was no other sound.

He knocked again.

"Who is there, please?" Templeton asked tenderly from behind the tall chair. His voice was so warm, so comforting— like a hypnotist's voice, telling you to relax, just relax—

"It's Eddie Bourque."

The cello complained with a tiny hum when Templeton leaned it against the wall. The chair slowly spun around. The publisher of The Empire was tall and lean. His white eyebrows bent into points, like upside-down Vs, and his short white beard was trimmed to a triangle beneath his chin. He offered Eddie a chair with a gentle wave of his hand.

Eddie descended into the chair, an uncomfortable squishy thing. He sunk in it, and had to look up to make eye contact. The chair's message was clear—not even the furniture would support you in the presence of Alfred T. Templeton.

Templeton reached across the desk in slow motion and tugged a little chain dangling from a desk lamp. The bulb, no more powerful than a flashlight, cast its light straight down, putting both men in shadows. Templeton nodded, satisfied with the light, and folded his hands on the blotter.

He looked Eddie over, and then said, "Everybody in the city is looking for you." He nodded to his desk phone. "I touch a button and the police are here."

"We both know I had nothing to do with Danny's death," Eddie said. "And you would have called the cops already if you weren't interested in why I'm here."

Templeton was expressionless a moment, and then a smirk creased his lips. The publisher was amused—a servant had outgrown his station.

Eddie said, "What was it about Danny's story that frightened you?"

The publisher tugged his beard. "Mr. Nowlin wrote many fine stories before his terrible end." That voice, so smooth, reminded Eddie of a lion in a fable, persuading the hare to *come closer, just a little closer.* "Do you have any story in mind?"

"The story about Samuel Sok."

"I don't recall Mr. Nowlin publishing anything on that topic." He was playing with Eddie. No problem, they had a few minutes to kill.

"Not from a lack of trying," Eddie said. "He came to you with the story shortly before he died—I'd wager a couple days before. Then, last Friday, you spiked his piece." Eddie was guessing, but felt good about his chances. Chanthay had said that Danny was upset about his story on Friday. It was obvious Frank Keyes didn't know about the piece…the editor wouldn't have sent Eddie to see Sok if he did. So that left Templeton.

The publisher was inscrutable behind his smirk. "Why would I do such a thing?"

"Political power and money," Eddie said. "Why does anybody do anything around here? Bad press before the election would kill Sok's renewal project for the Acre."

Templeton sat back in the chair, still smirking but clearly surprised. He played with Eddie some more. "Meddle in politics? Me? Why, I'm just a paperboy with a nice office."

"I've done my homework," Eddie said, with cockiness that comes from knowing you can't be fired if you've already decided to quit. "You paid Dr. Chi to destroy Danny's notes. And you're behind the paper's aggressive management of the news before the City Council election. Nothing gets in the paper that could undermine public confidence in the incumbents. You gotta protect those incumbents. You own them, and you need their votes to ram the Acre redevelopment deal through."

The publisher's smirk fell. One of his servants was getting uppity.

Eddie ranted on, enjoying himself, "And this stupid renewal project is your dream come true. Yeah, what a great idea—we'll cure poverty in Lowell. Fuck the poor, tear down their houses. They don't advertise anyway."

He stopped short of telling Templeton that Peter Sok was pulling his family money out of the deal. Let him enjoy that surprise later.

Templeton folded his hands into a little pyramid on the desk. His voice took a sinister edge, like a sorcerer casting a spell. "Mr. Nowlin did not get it, and neither do you." He swiveled back and forth in the chair, but his eyes locked on Eddie. "Have you bothered to check the crime statistics for your precious Acre? The drug use? The illiteracy rate? Abominable. It is a blight to be stamped out. This newspaper shall always support what's good for the city."

Eddie squirmed out of the quicksand chair and paced the room. He grabbed the TV remote control from a bookshelf. "You mean what's good for the city as *you* see it," he argued. "Why should you decide what's good for the city? Why should your voice be so much louder than the rest?"

The publisher was losing his patience. "When you were a child, your mother told you what to do because you did not yet understand."

Eddie laughed bitterly. "You've sacrificed this newspaper's neutrality and its role as the people's watchdog—the things that gave it integrity. You'd rather have a great city than run a great newspaper, and you don't understand that you can't have one without the other."

"I've given my life to this city," Templeton growled. "I know what makes a city great."

"Great for whom? Rich old white men?" Eddie pointed out the window. "Have you walked around out there recently? This ain't your city anymore. It left you behind."

"It has done no such thing," Templeton shouted. He banged a fist on the desk, bouncing his pen off the blotter. "And you, Mr. Bourque, have taken enough of my time."

The Rolex said six o'clock and ten seconds. "Not yet I haven't," Eddie said. "I wanna know how Danny ended up dead the day after you spiked his story."

"I know nothing about that, except that the police suspect *you*. And you—you no longer work here."

Eddie ignored him. He paced the darkened office. "Danny was pissed off, right? Maybe worse than pissed off. Maybe he threatened to take the story someplace else. The Globe, maybe—he had contacts there. So you saw the Acre project falling apart. And it's easy to imagine the political fallout when the public learned that the local paper refused to print the story. Why, it might be enough to take down an empire."

"Did you hear me?" Templeton bellowed. "You're fired!" His face twisted in horror, as if his words were bullets that had failed to drop his foe.

Eddie shouted over him, "You couldn't take the chance Danny would get the story published someplace else, so you picked up your phone and dialed some hood and *you had Danny whacked*. It was your good fortune he was stoned on heroin at the time, and it looked like he died in a drug dispute."

Templeton grabbed his telephone. "I'm calling the police."

Six-oh-two, exactly.

"Don't bother," Eddie said. "The cops will be busy with this—" He clicked the television to Channel Eight.

"—*We warn viewers that the scenes you're about to see could be disturbing, and we advise parents of young children to send them out of the room. We go now live to Lowell, where Channel Eight's Chuck Boden is in the field with this exclusive story.*"

Boden, somber-looking, walked down the steps of St. Francis de Sales, toward the camera. Templeton's eyes narrowed against the television's light. He froze with the phone in his hand.

"Thank you, Jill," Boden began. "It has been seventeen years since the church bells sounded the start of Sunday services here at St. Francis de Sales Church. This place of worship was closed after its pastor, Father Zygmunt Wojick, suddenly disappeared. The Lowell Empire reported at the time that Father Wojick ran off with a woman to California. But an exclusive Channel Eight source has shown that to be—" he paused one beat for drama—"nowhere near the truth."

Cut to film from inside the church, showing the murals, the stained glass and the giant crucifix, still on its chain.

"These exclusive pictures taken earlier today show the final resting place of Father Wojick. And I remind viewers these scenes may be disturbing." Close-up of the cross. "For nearly twenty years…Father Wojick has been entombed inside this statue."

Cut to film of the body draped over the altar. "Lowered by a Channel Eight source, this statue broke apart to reveal Father Wojick's horrifying end." He was silent for a moment, to let viewers soak in the video.

"Jill and Willy, it is not known yet where this cross came from, or who may have placed Father Wojick inside. But you can be sure police are going to be on this case, and we hope to have a word with them later in the broadcast. From Lowell, as one mystery ends and another begins, I'm Chuck Boden, Channel Eight news."

Eddie clicked off the television. Templeton stared slack-jawed at the black screen. Then he noticed the telephone receiver still in his hand and set it down. It rang immediately. Templeton jerked his hand away as if the phone had fangs. Then he answered it.

"Yes?"

Eddie recognized Keyes' panicked squeaking.

"Yes, Frank, I saw it," Templeton said. "Well, get a reporter on it." He hung up. To Eddie, he said, "You've been busy."

Eddie sat again in the soft chair, which seemed more comfortable than before. He slid Templeton the old news clip about Father Wojick running off to California. Templeton glanced at the headline and read no further.

"You knew this story was a lie when you wrote it," Eddie said.

Templeton smirked again, but this one looked forced; the eyes weren't involved. "There's no byline—no way to tell who wrote this piece," he said.

"I figured you'd say that." Eddie took from his pocket the envelope Peter Sok had given him and flipped it onto the desk. Templeton looked at it a long time. He seemed to be deciding what was inside. When he could not, he opened it and took out a handwritten note, dated the same day The Empire published Templeton's bogus story about Father Wojick.

"It's a photocopy," Eddie said. "And I made enough copies for every news crew in New England—who are no doubt speeding here right now for a piece of this story."

Eddie watched with delight as Templeton's eyes passed three times over the words:

> Samuel, I hope today's story is what you were looking for. Now we're even.
>
> A.T.T.

"It's signed A.T.T.," Eddie said. "I don't think that's the phone company, and I'll wager that's your handwriting. I know that Sok lent you the dough to buy control of this newspaper. That was quite a favor. Of course, so was printing that bogus story, so I guess you were right, you were even. I can't prove you knew that Sok killed Wojick, but you must have suspected."

The publisher looked up from the letter. His gray eyes darted around the room, and then landed on Eddie. Reflected in those eyes, Eddie saw a familiar tramp in a leather mini skirt. She had haunted Eddie since he had been a little boy trapped in a well. But this time, she was flirting with Templeton.

Eddie stood over the desk.

Templeton glanced at his phone. Eddie slammed his hand over it and demanded, "What did you do to Danny?" His finger hit the blotter in time with the words.

Templeton's lips puckered sour. He opened his desk drawer and dug out a computer printout, about ten sheets, fastened with a paper clip. He dropped it on the desk. "That is my property and I trust it will not leave this office," he said. Templeton was still the boss, even in defeat.

Eddie tilted the papers toward the light. The cover sheet had two lines:

Samuel Sok Profile
By Daniel Nowlin

Templeton explained, "Danny sandbagged me with that bit of ugliness last week. I had no idea he was working on it, and neither did Franklin—though he's so useless, he never knows what his people are doing. The story was nearly done. All that remained was a response from Sok." Templeton spun the chair a quarter turn and faced away. "Obviously, I couldn't let something like this run. Do you realize what these revelations would do to our project, and to me, if anyone discovered my link to Sok?" He sighed, and answered his own question, "Yes, I suppose you do."

"You sat on this story a few days?" Eddie said.

"And I talked with our lawyers about ways to keep Danny from taking it elsewhere."

"But Danny didn't cooperate."

Templeton shook his head. "Danny didn't make it any easier," he said. "He was in here every day last week, demanding I set a publication date. And he wanted me to get him an audience with Sok. I told him on Friday that the story would not be published—there were just too many, well, considerations. He quit on the spot and swore he'd get the Globe to run it."

He spun the chair toward Eddie. "We would have crushed Nowlin," he insisted, holding up a fist. "My lawyers were going through Danny's tax returns, his credit report, the movie titles he rented from the Video Depot. We would have found something to hang over his head, to keep that story quiet. Everybody has something they don't want out—everybody." He shook his seventeen-year-old note to Samuel Sok. "Even me."

"You're saying you didn't kill him?"

There was no gentleness left in the publisher's manner. "I'm saying Danny Nowlin was a fly speck, and I didn't have to kill him to shut him up. After he died, I figured he had confronted Sok somehow, and Sok, that maniac, beat him to death."

"And Dr. Chi? Destroying Danny's notes?"

Templeton fumed under a scowl. "Chi was an insurance policy to obliterate any trace of the story."

"And then you applied political pressure to phase out the investigation."

To that, he shrugged. "Imagine the irony if the publicity over Nowlin's death turned the focus of the campaign to crime and public safety, and then cost the election for my incumbents. That would jeopardize the whole Acre project. I don't think Mr. Nowlin would want that responsibility on his soul."

Eddie flipped the page and read the beginning of Danny's story:

LOWELL—*The city's honored philanthropist, Sawouth "Samuel" Sok, whose name graces a wing at the County Hospital, two branches of the Public Library and a veteran's hall, was a Khmer Rouge officer in Cambodia charged with overseeing the execution of hundreds of civilians, including women and children.*

He stashed ill-gotten wealth in Swiss banks and fled with his two sons to Thailand upon the Vietnamese invasion of Cambodia. There, he blended with the refugees of the Khmer Rouge regime and took on a new identity. Under a false name, on the pretense of a false life, he painted himself a victim of the movement he helped lead—

Eddie was stunned. In his shortsighted zeal to tear down the Acre, Templeton had spiked a potential Pulitzer Prize. He read on.

Danny had assembled exquisite details—a paper trail, stretching from Lowell to Phnom Penh, supported the facts. He had interviewed Cambodian officers, immigration officials, and the merchant marine who captained the ship that carried Sok and his sons to America. He quoted men and women who survived the killing fields; he had interviewed foreign correspondents and authors who studied Pol Pot's Khmer Rouge regime, and the reconstruction of the country that followed it. The story was logically structured and the writing was wonderful, so smooth.

Eddie tossed the paperwork on the desk. He had been sure that Templeton had plotted to kill Danny. And now? The publisher had prostituted the paper, the greatest sin in journalism, but that wasn't even a crime under the law....

He rubbed his eyes.

Wait a minute....

Eddie snatched up the paperwork and skimmed it again. The story gave Eddie a dizzying new insight; a revelation he didn't like. He slapped the papers down.

"I gotta go check something out," Eddie said. "Stay off the phone until I'm gone."

"The police need no help from me to catch you, Mr. Bourque." The publisher's smooth voice had returned. "And when you stand before a judge, be assured that this newspaper's coverage of the blessed event will rightfully reflect your discretion with certain information."

"Is this the way you extorted Danny to shut him up?"

Templeton leaned forward. His chair squeaked. "Every reader is a potential juror," he said, spitting words hammered from iron. "You got the drop on me this evening, Mr. Bourque. But not for long. This newspaper will hang you from its masthead, if need be. By the time I get done covering your legal case, your *best friend* would convict you of every unsolved murder since Jack the Ripper."

Not if I expose Danny's true killer.

Eddie gave the publisher a sarcastic little salute. "Thanks for firing me," he said. "Saves me the trouble of typing a resignation."

Chapter 36

Eddie didn't trust the publisher.

He waited for the elevator doors to close, and then pushed every button on the panel. The elevator stopped first at the ninth-floor photo production office, where Eddie got off. The photo department was a sprawling space cluttered with large-screen computer terminals for electronic editing. It reeked of the darkroom chemicals still used by the paper's old-timers, who refused to shoot digital pictures. Eddie peeked out a darkened window—as he had figured, the police were running across the street to The Empire.

Eddie tiptoed down the stairs.

Three flights later, he heard boots stomping up. One set. That meant the other cop was downstairs in the lobby, waiting for the elevator to make its stop-and-go descent from Templeton's office. Eddie ducked onto the sixth floor, the back-issues office. The department was closed, and nobody was working the counter. Eddie ran behind it.

He let the police officer pass, and then darted across the room to the west side of the building. He tore an insulating plastic sheet off a window frame and knocked open the window with the heel of his hand. Cold air rushed in. Darkness had fallen and a few faint stars were visible.

Eddie stepped out onto the fire escape, a terraced system of iron grates and ladders under many sloppy layers of black paint. The fire escape was probably as old as the building, and it trembled under his weight. The bolts fixing it to the wall squeaked as Eddie pattered down to the second floor, where the last ladder ended. The drop looked a lot higher from above than it ever had from below. Eddie pulled off his belt, looped it around the bottom rung, and climbed down it. He hung as low as he could, but his feet were still nearly ten feet above the sidewalk. Eddie wished he were fatter. *I'd have a longer belt.* He waited until he stopped swaying, and then let go.

The ground rose to meet him. His teeth clacked together at impact. He rolled over a sidewalk speckled with pigeon droppings and popped up. The balls of his feet stung as he dashed away.

The neighborhood where he had left the Chevette was confusing by day; it was a maddening labyrinth by night. Eddie paced through it, afraid to run and attract attention. After half an hour, it seemed that he had walked every street twice. Had the Mighty Chevette been stolen? That would defy logic. Who would bother?

He found it a few minutes later, wedged in a dark space between a minivan and a full-size pickup. Eddie got in, muttering to himself. He slammed the door, inserted the key, and then smelled hot coffee.

"Did you forget where you parked?"

A dark figure sat in the front passenger's seat. *Detective Orr!*

"I was tempted to hit the horn the second time I saw you go by," Orr said. She was in uniform, sipping coffee from a plastic Thermos cup.

Eddie threw his head back and stared through the roof, at a mental picture of the inside of the police station. "How'd you find me?"

"It's terribly hard to park in this neighborhood," Orr explained. "All these spots are restricted, and the residents are rabid about calling the authorities when somebody parks here without a residency sticker."

Eddie shook his head. How stupid to not have thought of that. "Have you been waiting long?"

"Since you dove in front of the train," Orr said. "Very dangerous. Do you mind telling me how you got away?"

"I'll plead the Fifth on that one." For a moment he considered fleeing from the car, but decided against it. "Do you mind pouring me some coffee?" he asked. "I feel a caffeine withdrawal headache coming on."

Orr handed him her plaid Thermos. "You'll have to drink from the bottle."

"Fine, anything." The coffee was a medium roast, black, very smooth, and the perfect temperature, cool enough to sip, but still too hot to guzzle.

"I didn't kill Danny," he said.

She clicked her tongue. "Wouldn't be an impossible case for the district attorney," she said. "I'd even say the odds would be on her side to win a conviction."

Eddie considered that in silence.

Orr continued, "You and Danny were competing for the same jobs in Boston."

Eddie looked at her, surprised. "You know that?" He sighed. "You probably checked the applicant pool at every major newspaper in the country."

"Most of them," she confirmed. "So there's a possible motive, albeit a pretty weak one."

"Very weak," Eddie agreed.

"You don't always have to prove motive to win a conviction," she said. "There are no witnesses, so the case would come down to physical evidence. The BCI team found the weapon in your house, with your fingerprints and Danny's blood on it."

"I know—the smoking gun."

"So to speak."

Eddie considered fleeing again, but decided he couldn't outrun Detective Lucy Orr. Oh, he'd probably beat her in a footrace, but she'd turn up uninvited eventually. It seemed to be a habit for her. "Are you at least going to tell me where they found the weapon?" he asked.

She nodded. "In your bedroom closet."

Eddie thought for a moment, and then clutched his head. *Jesus, no....*Much became clear. He pictured Danny collapsing, the side of his head caved in. He said slowly, "They found it in my golf bag."

"Hmm. That's right."

Eddie rapped his knuckles against his skull. "I know who killed Danny," he said. He met her eye. "But I need your help to prove it."

◇ ◇ ◇

Eddie dialed Chanthay's pager service from his home telephone. She wouldn't recognize his number, but maybe she'd be curious enough to look up Eddie in the telephone book, to see that the numbers matched, and call back.

He waited. There was no answer.

He paged her again.

Eddie looked out his window. Detective Orr's unmarked black police SUV was parked behind the Mighty Chevette. She was speaking to four other cops who had arrived in an unmarked white van.

C'mon, Chanthay, call back. I'm up the river if you don't call back!

◇ ◇ ◇

The phone rang seven times before Gordon Phife answered with a confused, "Hello?"

"It's me," Eddie said. "Wake up. I need help. The cops— I'm in trouble."

"What?" Phife said, still confused. "What time is it?"

"Three-forty-five in the morning, according to Chuck Boden's wristwatch."

"Do you always talk like a Chinese fortune cookie?"

Eddie recognized the line from *Remo Williams: The Adventure Begins*, a movie that assumed sequels that never happened. "For Christ's sake, Gordon. Can you be serious? This is no time for quotes."

"I'm awake now. What the hell happened?"

"A gorgeous Cambodian war crimes hunter set me up for Danny's murder."

"Huh? I take a day off from work and the world goes crazy. Where are you?"

"That's not important," Eddie said. "Just listen—I tried to make a deal with the cops to lead them to the woman who framed me. They gave me the rest of the night to make this happen. The district attorney is bringing my case to the grand jury after breakfast, and I'll probably be indicted by lunch."

"Jesus, Ed, do you have a lawyer?"

"To hell with a lawyer, Gordon. I'm dead if I can't find this woman, and I need help! You told me to call if I hit trouble, and, well, I got in deep."

"Sure sounds like you slammed your dick in the door," Phife said. His voice quivered. "Okay. Okay. Okay. Let's think this through."

"Not on the phone," Eddie said. "I don't know who could be listening."

Eddie could hear Gordon opening and slamming drawers. "I'm getting dressed," he said. "Where can we meet?"

"How about the driving range?"

"Sure. There's some leftover beer from last time."

"Half an hour?"

"Uh-huh." Phife took a fatherly tone. "This is just a monumental screw-up, Ed. We'll get you through this."

They hung up.

Eddie stepped from his bedroom to the living room.

"Well, that was it—the last call," he said. He dropped hard onto the piano bench.

Detective Orr dangled a little metal box, about the size of a pager, on a thin black wire. "Take the shirt off," she said.

Eddie, suddenly self-conscious, reluctantly complied.

"I still don't like the idea of bringing a third party into the mix tonight," Orr said. She pressed the metal box to Eddie's lower back. It was cold. "Hold the battery pack for a sec."

Eddie reached back and held it. He said, "I can see how you might be uncomfortable, but this is someone I trust with my life."

Orr made a tiny grimace. "You may be doing exactly that." She tore sixteen inches of cloth tape from a roll, ripped it with her teeth and affixed the batteries to Eddie's skin. Then she pressed what seemed like the world's thinnest micro-cassette recorder to Eddie's chest. He held it for her.

"This is purely a local recording setup, not a transmitter," she warned. "I won't be able to listen in and decide when you're in trouble."

"Where's the good equipment?" Eddie cracked.

"The good equipment is for *authorized* investigations," she said. "Be thankful I scrounged up two sets of this old stuff."

Eddie grabbed her arm. "I am thankful, Lucy."

Orr nodded. "I can give you a panic button to press. We won't be far."

She tore another long length of tape.

Eddie cringed. "That's gonna hurt coming off. Do you need so much tape on my chest?"

Detective Orr stuck her hand on her hip and looked over the few dozen lonely hairs on Eddie's torso. "Is it really going to matter?"

Chapter 37

Eddie reclined in The Empire's satellite dish and looked over the city. It had never looked more magnificent to him. When he had worked for The Empire, he had seen Lowell as a reporter. He hadn't been able to see past the politics and dirty deals, drug busts and broken hearts. But to an unemployed writer, Lowell at night was special. The neighborhoods along the river were clusters of yellow specks, like candlelights. He imagined that each speck was a life, and that he was watching an entire city sleep. He thought about his investigation into Danny's death, and how he could finally see how the pieces fit together, like he was looking down on it from high above.

The trap door flopped open behind the giant neon E. Gordon Phife had left his warm house in the middle of the night to help his friend in trouble, just as he had promised. He had dressed in jeans, a leather jacket, and his black racing gloves. The light from the giant E stained his face red.

Phife frowned at Eddie. "I'm speechless," he said. "Either that or I should be screaming at you. What pile of shit have you been digging in? You're up for *indictment* tomorrow?" He looked at Eddie, apparently waiting for an answer, and then clucked in disgust and threw up his hands. "I was right the first time. I'm speechless." He dug around at the base of the E and came up with a beer.

Eddie hadn't expected Phife to berate him so aggressively. "Mr. Diamond, there's a bullet hole in your jacket," he said, quoting from a movie.

"Now?"

"You're the quote master. What's the quote?"

Phife looked to the heavens. "Can you believe this guy?" he said to nobody.

"It's a modern-era film."

"Who gives a shit, Ed? You're in big trouble, and I could be too for just meeting with you."

Eddie rolled his eyes. "C'mon, Gordon—a blip in the career of Peter Falk."

Phife sighed, exasperated. "Don't you even appreciate I'm putting myself at risk?"

"Mid-seventies."

"I can't think right now."

"Two-star film, maybe two and a half."

Phife gave an exaggerated shrug. "Congratulations," he said, incredulous. "You finally stumped me. Now let's get to work finding this woman."

"Don't you want to know the film?"

"Fine!" he shouted. "What's the film?"

"*Murder by Death.*"

Phife blinked a few times. He twisted the cap off his beer and flicked it across the roof. He sipped from the bottle. Suddenly aloof, he said, "You can't really care about movies with what you're facing right now, Ed. I sure can't." There was no place for him to sit, so he stuck one hand in his jacket pocket, and slouched against an imaginary wall. He looked out over the city, and said, "We really need to get to business. Tell me about this Cambodian woman. And how do you expect to find her?"

Eddie was in no hurry. He noticed a star moving across the sky, and watched it for a minute. A jet? Perhaps a satellite, now beaming Eddie's ass on this metal dish to newspapers around the world. He swung his feet out of the dish and sat upright. "You will never guess what crazy thing I did today."

"I'm sure you're going to tell me."

"I stormed into Templeton's office—"

He perked up. "You barged in?"

"Well, I knocked first, but I would've barged if he hadn't invited me. You wanna hear this or not? So I walked in at his invitation, sat down and accused the publisher, right to his face, of having Danny whacked."

"What!" The news spun Phife around like a weathervane. "You're insane. I can't believe he didn't fire you on the spot."

"He did. But I had already quit—at least in my mind I had. Small matter when you're a murder suspect, wouldn't you say?"

Phife smacked his lips a few times. "I suppose," he said. "So you've left The Empire. That's probably good, considering everything that's happened. Assuming you get this thing with the cops cleared up, you'll land someplace better." He drank three long slugs. "None of that matters now, not one damn bit. What's important is finding this woman. Tell me what you know about her."

"I was wrong of course—about Templeton," Eddie said. "He didn't kill Danny. He was right, he didn't have to. He wanted to shut Nowlin up. To do that, all he needed was proof Danny was having an affair. That's the blackmailer's trump card."

"I swear that we're having two different conversations," Phife said, annoyed. He finished his beer and heaved the bottle off the roof. It spun end over end ten stories down and exploded to dust. "Forget *Danny*." He spit the name like a mouthful of gasoline. "He pissed off some drug dealer and got his head bashed in. He never should've fooled around with that element, and he paid the price. You've got real problems because of him. Now, how can we find this woman?"

Eddie leaned back in the dish and hunted for the satellite in the sky. There it was, pretending to be a star. There was no turning back now. He eyed Gordon Phife. "Must have been frustrating for you," he said, "when Chanthay stopped answering your calls."

Phife's mouth twitched. "What are you saying? Is that her name?"

"Cut the bullshit, Gordon, you were involved with them—with Danny and Chanthay and her brother. Why not just admit it?"

Phife squinted at Eddie. His lip curled. "Where do you get off accusing me?" he said in a hard voice. "You're the one with the murder weapon in his house."

Eddie put his hands under his head and studied the stars. The white pinprick he had been following was the only one in motion. He wondered if it was a spy satellite. It could be watching him, too. He winked at it.

"I made an ass of myself accusing Templeton," Eddie said. "Hey, it wasn't the first time—I had already accused somebody else of attacking Danny, but that's a long and ugly tale and I don't want to get into that right now. Templeton let me see Danny's secret story. You know the one." Eddie held up his hands as if the story was in them. "And once I read it, I knew you were involved."

Phife cleared his throat. "You can't be serious," he croaked. "I came here as your *friend*."

"The story was beautifully written, Gordon," he said, cutting across Phife's confusion. "It sang like the Ode to Joy. We both know Danny couldn't write like that—not without help from the best editor in the business."

Phife pressed his lips tightly together.

"Nothing to say?" Eddie said.

"I offered to help because I thought you were innocent, but now you're freaking me out," Phife said. "I'm outta here. You're on your own."

Phife took one step and stopped.

Chanthay was leaning against the giant E, arms folded over her chest. She had dressed in all black, except for a long white scarf wrapped once around her neck.

Phife's mouth slowly dropped open.

Eddie said, "I invited our mutual friend. Care to say something now, Gordon?"

A breeze lifted wisps of Chanthay's hair. The Empire E made a loud pop and stuttered like a strobe for a few seconds, before recovering its steady red glow. Eddie's pulse quickened at the sight of Chanthay awash in ruby light, scattered stars above the horizon behind her.

Phife squinted hard at Chanthay. He rubbed the back of his neck, frowned and then giggled. Then he froze, lips parted, like he was about to say something, but couldn't remember what.

Chanthay held a finger to her lips, signaling Phife to stay quiet. She walked purposefully to Eddie, grabbed his jacket and dragged him out of the dish.

"Hey!" Eddie yelled. "What the…?" He tripped over a leg she had angled in front of him, and her weight on his back drove him to the roof. He landed face-down with an *oof!*

Before he could move, she reached inside his jacket and ripped out the wire connecting the recorder and its batteries. "He was taping you," she said, flipping the wire to Phife's feet.

Phife looked around the roof. He huffed like a marathoner on Heartbreak Hill.

"It's just us," Chanthay said. "I made sure." A gun appeared in her hand. She pointed it straight down, but there was no mistaking the threat in her tone. "I want answers." She glanced at Eddie. "From both of you."

Phife stomped on the wire and ground it into the pebble roof. "I should have known you were up to something, Ed."

Eddie wiped grit off his lips. He looked up at Chanthay, "He's the one you should be throwing in the dirt."

"That's not true," Phife growled through clenched teeth. He looked at Chanthay and his harshness softened. He held out his hands. "Where have you been?" He sounded mournful.

"She's been with me," Eddie said, hauling himself up.

Phife's face wrinkled. "You're a liar," he said. "And a killer." He told Chanthay, "You have to understand, the police found the murder weapon in *his* house." He jabbed a finger at Eddie. "He killed Danny. He's the one you want. He's a murderer, just like his brother."

"How long did she keep you on a string?" Eddie asked him.

Phife answered with a glare.

"Not that I blame you for thinking her interest in you was genuine—it's what she wanted you to think."

Chanthay looked at Eddie, expressionless.

Eddie raised an eyebrow to Phife. "Can't hear me all of a sudden? I'm asking *how long* before you learned of her affair with Nowlin?"

"You shut up," Phife said. His eyes were big.

"Must have hurt to discover that whatever she did with you was merely to keep you loyal."

"You don't know her," Phife said, his wet eyes turning to Chanthay. "He doesn't know anything."

"You told me yourself that people will do crazy things for love," Eddie said. "Killing a rival is pretty crazy. But Danny had Jesse. You thought it wasn't fair that he had Chanthay, too."

Phife shook his head at her. "No," he sputtered. "We were all working together, for one cause—like you said."

Eddie went in harder. "Danny had the right idea bringing you into the faction. Your whole existence is the movies—all fantasy and larger-than-life drama. It's like you've been training all your life for an international murder and revenge plot."

Phife's face was slick with sweat, gleaming in the red light. "He knows about Sok!"

She nodded. "I did not tell him. He deduced it somehow."

"He's dangerous to us," Phife insisted. He set his jaw, and told Chanthay in a steely voice, "We could avenge Danny together, right here." He cleared his throat. "Then we can *go!* Let's get the hell out of here, travel the world together.

Hunt the criminals *together*." He closed his lips tightly and shook his head with grave determination. "You opened the world to me. I can't come sulking back to this miserable building every day, cleaning up the shit other people write, day after day, with no glory, not even a fucking pat on the head."

Eddie tried to swallow the dryness in his throat. "You're almost right about me," he said, his voice a half-octave higher than normal. "What I *know* is dangerous. Friends of mine told me about a middle-class guy buying his first hit of heroin and a needle in the Acre not long ago. I thought they were describing Danny. Now I know they were talking about you."

"He's all wrong," Phife said to Chanthay.

Eddie wagged a finger at him. "My sources say you got ripped off," he scolded. "Street dealers are like ticket scalpers, they expect you to *negotiate*. You called Nowlin on Friday night and lured him to the old house. You gave him a couple whacks, and then shot dope in his leg to make him look like a victim of the streets."

"Don't listen to him," Phife begged Chanthay. "He's twisting everything around. He's been acting all crazy, chasing after Jesse, bitching about Danny getting job interviews that he couldn't get, breaking into Danny's house." He pointed at Eddie. "His fingerprints were on the weapon! It had Danny's blood on it."

Her gun swung from one man to the other.

Eddie said, "The Worthen Canal was the logical place to dump the body—you'd know that from working in the news."

"He knows that he's about to be indicted for murder," Phife told her. His eyes flickered to the edge of the roof. "He's humiliated by the accusation, tortured by guilt. It would look like suicide if he…fell. Then we can get out of here—no loose ends, nobody left who ever saw us together."

"The frame-up was absofuckinlutely brilliant," Eddie said. He laughed. "Hell, even I started to wonder if I had done it." He sat again on the edge of the satellite dish. *What the hell?* he thought. *Get comfortable!* He reclined and put his feet up.

Eddie explained to Chanthay. "Gordon needed a Plan B, in case you or the cops ever started to suspect he had done Danny's murder—"

"He's lying!"

"—But it wasn't enough to just plant the murder weapon in my house, not without fingerprints. A good lawyer could get me off—I had no motive."

Chanthay nodded. "Go on."

"So Gordon brought me up here in the middle of the night with some lie about our boss, Frank Keyes, making a crack about Danny's death."

Phife growled, "Tell her you're lying." He put his hands out like claws and stumbled at Eddie.

"Let him finish," Chanthay ordered. She swung the gun toward Phife. He recoiled from it.

Eddie sat up and flashed Phife an ironic smile. "And then Gordon insisted I swing his golf club, to put my fingerprints on the murder weapon."

Chanthay glared at Phife. He seemed to shrink.

"Gordon knows he and I play the identical brand of club," Eddie said. "And in the light of this ridiculous Empire E, there was no way I could see the blood stains. I took one swing that night, but one was enough. Wasn't that a one-iron, Gord?"

Phife wiped his nose on his sleeve. He looked feverish and shocked. He seethed, panting hard and growling as he exhaled.

"The one problem was my front door," Eddie continued, staring at Phife yet speaking to Chanthay. "He must have been shocked to find it locked when he went to switch clubs. In my carefree days of, oh, a couple weeks ago, I was famous for never locking it. Gordon had no choice but to break it down. Then he had to trash the place to cover for the busted lock. The only spot he didn't wreck was my closet. He took my one-iron and left the murder weapon in my golf bag, like a bomb that he controlled. If he ever felt any heat, one anonymous tip to the cops and I would be cooked."

A truck rumbled far below. Eddie squirmed on the dish. The cold had seeped from the metal to his skin.

Chanthay turned to Phife and shredded him with her eyes. "You killed him," she said. "He was *important* to me."

Phife took one step backward and lowered himself to his knees. He put his hands up. "I invited Danny to talk, that's all," he whispered.

Her fingers flexed around the gun. She said, "We all swore an oath to each other."

"All I wanted to do was talk," Phife insisted. His face tightened for a moment and he looked like he was about to sob, but then he shook it off. "Danny shouldn't have been doing what he was doing, behind Jesse's back, behind *my* back. I had to tell him that."

"You must have followed Danny and me to his apartment," she said.

"You got so distant," Phife said. He trembled, his eyes flooded. Were they tears of sorrow? Or of fright? "Danny was distracting you—from the mission, from why we were all together." He pressed his hands over his eyes and seemed to be wrestling with himself on the inside. "All Danny ever did was *take* from me. I *made* him as a reporter, and he never shared an ounce of credit. He had to have it all. He was the worst kind of *glutton*."

Chanthay closed her eyes for a moment, breathed deep and then said softly, "Why did you do it, Gordie? I need to know why."

"Danny wouldn't listen," he told her, breathlessly. "He wouldn't promise to leave you alone." He squeezed his eyes shut and tears streamed out. When he opened his eyes, Eddie felt a stab of pity for him. Phife stammered and said, "I had to get rid of Danny, *for us*." He collapsed on the roof and wept.

Eddie looked up to the stars, then turned to Chanthay. "Did you get it?"

She reached up her sweater, pulled out a microcassette recorder and tossed it to Eddie. He caught it and shut it off. "You better put your gun away," he said. "I'm calling Detective Orr."

"No," Chanthay said. "You're not."

She leveled the gun to Eddie's face. He looked down the barrel, into the peephole to infinity.

"Put your hands on your head," she ordered.

Eddie stared at her and did as she said. He bit his lip, furious with himself. "I trusted you," he said.

She glanced to Phife, who was curled on the roof, and then asked Eddie, "Which pocket?"

"Find it yourself."

Chanthay pressed the gun to his temple and patted his jacket pockets. He said nothing more, because he knew nothing he said to her would matter. She reached into his jacket and took the police call button, which looked like a TV remote control with one big button. She hurled it off the roof.

Eddie fought to keep calm. He put his hands down and listened for the call button to smash. "I'm going to have to pay for that," he said.

"Bill me."

Phife was a quivering mass, his face buried in his jacket. Chanthay pointed her gun at him. "He murdered Danny."

Eddie saw revenge smoldering in her eye and fought off a shiver. He eased off the satellite dish. "Whoa—this is not what we planned."

She did not look at Eddie. "You have the tape," she said. "You're cleared. Go away and leave us alone."

"You can't shoot him in cold blood," Eddie said.

"That's the first time you've been wrong all night."

Dive for the gun? Or try to talk her out of it? Neither option seemed like it would stop her. Eddie chose to talk. He stepped toward her; the gun swung around at him. He said, "Let the cops take him."

She said nothing.

"He'll never hurt anybody again, I promise you," Eddie said.

The muscles in her face tensed. "It's not about that."

"Then what is it? Is this a lifelong contest between you and the people who've hurt you? Is there a scoreboard hanging somewhere?"

She studied Eddie with a puzzled face.

Phife gave a low throaty snarl. Over her shoulder, Eddie saw Phife reach a hand toward them. Red light glinted off a silver gun.

Eddie drove his shoulder into Chanthay.

Phife fired. The bullet ricocheted off the satellite dish. Eddie rolled over Chanthay and pulled her behind the Empire E. Phife fired again. Glass shattered. Half the E went dark.

Chanthay pushed Eddie aside, scrambled to her feet and reached her gun around the giant E. She fired three blind shots.

Commotion stirred on the floor below. Footsteps clomped up the ladder. "Shots fired! Shots fired!"

Phife dashed across the roof. Chanthay and Eddie gave chase.

At the roof's west edge, Phife vaulted the safety wall and disappeared over the side.

"No!" Eddie screamed.

There was a metal clang, and then footsteps. Eddie and Chanthay glanced at each other in surprise, then rushed across the roof. Eddie leaned over the parapet and saw Phife pounding down the fire escape.

From the trap door on the other side of the E, someone yelled, "Police! Hold it there!"

Chanthay sprang over the safety wall. She dropped the twelve feet to the fire escape and landed with a grunt. The platform squealed and trembled. She popped up and ran down the stairs, gun drawn.

Police officers poured onto the roof.

Eddie traced the sign of the cross as he went over the side. The fire escape's tenth-floor landing wobbled when he hit. The blow yanked rusted bolts from the wall with a sharp screech, and the platform wailed like an iron beast as its welded metal joints bent under the strain. Eddie threw himself headfirst down the steep stairs toward the next iron landing. The welds gave out; the top platform lurched from place. It rushed past Eddie and plummeted toward the river of asphalt ten stories below. Eddie turned a somersault down the stairs and felt them give way beneath him, ripped down by the falling metal. He grabbed for the next platform, catching three fingers in the grate. Momentum swung him under the landing, shearing skin off his fingers. He snapped back and dangled in space, nine stories above the street. His other hand clawed for a hold.

The tenth-floor platform, its railing and stairs, a quarter-ton of iron, slammed into the ground.

Eddie grabbed at the metal grate and scraped his hands raw pulling himself up. There was no time to catch his breath. He stormed down the stairs. The belt he had left earlier on the last rung was still there. It slipped through his bloody fingers. Eddie dropped hard on the sidewalk. He groaned, slowly hauled himself up and caught sight of Chanthay sprinting down the street.

A shot flashed from the darkness ahead of her. She dove to the ground, rolled and fired back.

Phife screamed. He staggered under a streetlight and into an alley, clutching his hip.

Chanthay ran after him; Eddie ran after her. He was hurt and tired, but adrenaline overpowered the part of him that wanted to quit. He didn't want another murder on Chanthay's soul; didn't want another on his own. But something even greater pushed him on. There was an invisible web that connected him to everyone he knew, and then to everyone *they* knew, and so on, forever. How many holes had been punched through that web? Father Wojick. Danny Nowlin. Samuel Sok. Sok's faceless victims. Even the two hitmen in the mill. Back alley revenge might work in her world, but this was Eddie's turf.

This is where it stops.

Eddie clenched his teeth as he whipped every muscle fiber to run, run faster. He barreled into the alley.

Phife was on the ground, propped up on a discarded truck tire. His head was down. Blood pooled under him. His gun was under Chanthay's foot.

She raised her gun to his ear.

Eddie shouted, "Enough!"

She turned to him and scowled. "You have no business here," she hissed. "He has to pay."

Eddie wheezed. "He'll pay. Murder one, no parole."

"I will take revenge for Danny."

Eddie spat on the ground. "Liar," he cried. "This isn't for Danny. This is for you."

She glowered at him.

"You're so used to taking revenge, you don't know why you do it anymore," he said. He stood over Phife to block her line of fire.

"I'll shoot through you," she threatened.

Eddie sighed and said gently, "You told me how you like revenge, the feeling it gives you, and I don't doubt it's good. This one time, for me—see how justice feels."

They stared at each other, as they had done in the old house a few days before. Eddie imagined his finger tracing the bulge of her cheekbone. A police siren wailed in the distance. Chanthay backed away, deeper into the alley. They held their gaze until darkness swallowed her, and she vanished.

Chapter 38

The predawn horizon smoldered pink.

The giant neon E was dark, its glass tubes silent and dead white. Eddie sat in the satellite dish, sipping a beer left over from the night Gordon Phife had tricked him into touching the murder weapon. Seemed like ages ago. The paramedics who had taken Phife away had wrapped Eddie's fingers in gauze. The police who had taken his statements had gone.

Eddie was brittle but wide awake. He had come back to the roof to watch the sunrise.

And he wondered, *What next?*

His only plan was to pick up the General in a few hours. He couldn't see any further into the future. The crash of emotions after the night's events had blown out his pilot light.

The trap door slapped open. Shoes crunched on the pebble roof.

Detective Orr came around the E. She admired the sunrise for a moment and then plopped down next to Eddie. "Beautiful view," she said.

He nodded. "I think there's another beer left."

"A wee bit early for me," she said. "I'll take my wire, though."

Eddie reached under his shirt, yanked the recorder off his chest—she had been right, it didn't hurt that much to take it off—and handed the contraption to Orr.

"How's the other tape?" he asked.

"It'll hold up in court, but we're assuming he'll plead out."

"You remember our deal?" Eddie said.

"The tape gets fuzzy when you talk about a story Mr. Nowlin had done. Static, you know."

Eddie nodded. "Thanks."

They watched the sunrise for a few minutes. The light gathering at the horizon finally ignited into sunfire. Eddie was glad the night was over.

"Thanks for believing me," he said.

Her face glowed yellow in the new light. "The bloody golf club did have your fingerprints all over it, but your story was too weird to be made up. You guys really hit golf balls off this building?" She grinned. "I'll tell the chief I solved that rash of broken windows."

Eddie tried not to smile, but couldn't help himself. He sipped some beer.

"Will you be writing this story?" she asked.

"Don't work here anymore." He slouched on the dish.

She frowned. "I'm going to have to talk to somebody. Who can I trust to be fair?"

Eddie thought a moment. "Do me a favor," he said. "When The Empire calls for this story, insist on giving the scoop to Boyce Billips."

Detective Orr promised she would. She put her hand on his and squeezed gently. "You did the right thing, and you played your part perfectly, first on the phone with him, and then here on the roof."

Eddie sighed and poured out the rest of his beer. A puddle of white foam burrowed into the gravel.

"Enough angst," Orr declared. She playfully punched Eddie's shoulder. "Tell me what you know about this body in St. Francis de Sales."

"Oh Christ," Eddie muttered. "You don't want to know."

He thought about the church and had an idea. He straightened up. "Do you have a phone?"

Orr squinted at him, smiling. She unclipped her telephone from her belt and handed it to him. "Is this the appropriate time of day to be making a call?"

Eddie dialed a townhouse in Washington D.C. "It'll be fine," he assured Orr. The phone rang five times before someone answered with a gravel-throated, "Dammit all to hell! *What?*"

"Hey Hippo, it's Bourque," Eddie said. "You gotta catch the early flight to Logan. It's time to have that press conference you talked about, to spill the secrets about the plot to destroy the Acre. I can fill you in on how Templeton and The Empire were in on it."

Eddie jerked the phone away from his head. The little device ranted.

He shrugged at Orr and said, "I thought guys his age got up early."

Chapter 39

The woman waited for Eddie at a little round table reserved for Bourque, party of two, right in front of the stage. Eddie looked her over from across the club. He had not seen her for weeks. He recalled an image of her in his recliner. She looked so different now, dressed modestly in a blue knit top with a neckline that hugged her Adam's apple. She had done nothing to accentuate her good looks, and she wasn't turning heads. But she held your eye, once she had it.

She waited patiently, nursing a syrupy-looking drink, bright red, in a dainty stemmed glass. She smiled and stood as Eddie wound through the mushroom patch of little tables.

They embraced. She kissed his cheek.

"Good to see you, Eddie."

"You too, Jesse."

They sat. A waitress hustled over, balancing a pint of stout beer on a tray. She placed the drink in front of Eddie and said, "Somebody's been waiting all night to buy you a beer."

"Is he nervous?" Eddie asked.

The waitress held her hand flat and tipped it back and forth. "A little, not bad." She bustled off.

Jesse tapped Eddie's arm affectionately. "I saw the piece you freelanced to The Globe's Sunday magazine on those heroin addicts under the bridge," she said. "What a wonderful story. Frightening, but I couldn't put it down."

Eddie sipped his stout and then wiped away his beer moustache. "Thanks. I got a lot of feedback on that story. This treatment center in Connecticut has offered two free beds for them, if they commit to the in-house program. Leo and Gabrielle are thinking it over. I hope they do it."

"You sound good for a guy with no job."

"I have two more freelance pieces in the works. I'm starting to think I don't need a job."

"Good for you!" she said. "Looks like you quit The Empire just in time."

Eddie smiled. "Congressman Vaughn's press conference sure rattled that place. There's nothing a newspaper hates more than becoming part of the story. Some neighborhood groups in the Acre are organizing a circulation boycott. It won't be long before the advertisers buckle and Templeton is forced out."

"He's not the only one with problems."

"Yeah, Vaughn nearly torpedoed the whole incumbent City Council, too. That wasn't an election, it was a turkey shoot." He sipped. "And how are you?"

Jesse frowned and looked into her drink. "It's been harder lately than it was at first. The key is staying busy. My girl-friends have been taking me to the symphony a lot." She looked up and smiled. "You should tag along sometime."

Eddie clinked his glass to hers. "Maybe I will," he said. "You tell me when they're playing Claude Debussy."

The houselights dimmed and a spotlight beamed to the stage. An emcee introduced the first act. "Fresh from his mother's basement, puh-leeeeeeeze welcome—comedian Stan Popko!"

The audience clapped politely and welcomed Stan to the microphone.

Stan shuffled on stage in a wrinkled gray suit and a polka-dot bow tie. He sighed, fidgeted with the microphone, and gazed over the group as if barely interested in the crowd. Then, in the leaden monotone only Stan could command, he droned, "Welcome students—to the first day of comedy class. I am your professor of hilarity—Mr. Popko."

Perfect. Giggles passed over the audience.

"Today's lesson is entitled, The Three Stooges: Why a Finger in Curly's Eye—Puts a Stitch in My Side."

The crowd didn't love him, that would have been asking too much, but they *liked* him. Laughter simmered throughout Stan's lecture, and the warm applause at the end was sincere.

Jesse leaned to Eddie and spoke over the applause, "You're absolutely beaming! Is that fatherly pride?"

Eddie nodded. "Look at him—he's smiling."

COMING SEPTEMBER 2004

FROSTLINE

by Justin Scott
ISBN: 0-7434-8704-4

In quaint Newbury, Connecticut, real estate broker Ben Abbott gets caught in a nasty land battle between two neighbors: cantankerous Vietnam vet Richard Butler—whose troubled, violent son, Dicky, has just been released from jail—and Harry King, a high-powered former diplomat and owner of Fox Trot estate. King wants Abbott to act as mediator in buying a sliver of Butler's property that just into Fox Trot.

But when a dam used to create an artificial lake for the estate is blown up, and a body turns up among the debris, Abbott takes it upon himself to investigate. He may not like the answers he finds....

To receive a catalog of other Poisoned Pen Press titles,
please contact us in one of the following ways:

Phone: 1-800-421-3976
Facsimile: 1-480-949-1707
Email: info@poisonedpenpress.com
Website: www.poisonedpenpress.com

Poisoned Pen Press
6962 E. First Ave. Ste. 103
Scottsdale, AZ 85251